David Peace is the author of *The Red Riding Quartet* and was chosen as one of Granta's Best of Young British Novelists in 2003. In 2004 he won the James Tait Black Memorial Prize for his novel *GB84*. *Tokyo Year Zero*, the first book of his *Tokyo Trilogy*, will be published in Autumn 2007. He lives in Tokyo with his wife and two children.

Further Praise for *The Damned United*:

'The strangest, most compelling football novel ever written.' Nick Rennison, *Sunday Times*

'An extraordinarily gripping portrait of Brian Clough at his peak, it is surely the best football book ever written.' Dominic Sandbrook, Books of the Year, *Evening Standard*

'Incomparable ... a brilliant novel ... Peace's work might be fiction, but its reading of the paranoia, incompetence and venality at large in football's corridors of power is almost painful in its accuracy.' Jim White, Books of the Year, *Daily Telegraph*

'The most compelling football book of 2006 ... Shakespearean in its scale, ambition, depth and elements of tragedy, farce and betrayal.' Phil Shaw, Books of the Year, *Independent*

'Now this, young man, is what you call an exceptional football book, as bold, brilliant and unconventional as Brian Clough himself, whose voice is vividly brought back to life ... It is a great story grippingly revived.' Matt Dickinson, Books of the Year, *The Times*

'This was an exceptional year in that it produced the best football novel. Ever. David Peace's meticulous recreation of Brian Clough's 44 days at Leeds United has power, authenticity and drama.' Hugh MacDonald, Sports Books of the Year, *The Herald*

The Damned Utd

DAVID PEACE

faber and faber

First published in 2006
by Faber and Faber Limited
Bloomsbury House
74-77 Great Russell Street
London WC1B 3DA

This paperback edition published in 2007

Typeset by Faber and Faber Limited
Printed in England by CPI Bookmarque, Croydon

A CIP record for this book
is available from the British Library

ISBN 978-0-571-22433-3
ISBN 0-571-22433-4

For Jon Riley, with love and thanks

I have forsaken mine house, I have left mine heritage;
I have given the dearly beloved of my soul into the hand of her enemies.
Mine heritage is unto me as a lion in the forest;
It crieth out against me, therefore have I hated it.
Mine heritage is unto me as a speckled bird, the birds round about are against her;
Come ye, assemble all the beasts of the field, come to devour.

Jeremiah, Chapter 12, Verses 7–9

The Argument II

Repetition. Repetition –
 Fields of loss and fields of hate, fields of blood and fields of war –
 Their sport upon the walls, their sport upon the floor.
 Milton! Thou shouldst be living at this hour: England hath need of thee . . .
 In her shadow time.
 On our terraces, in our cages, from Purgatorio, we watch,
 With our wings that cannot fly, our tongues that cannot speak:
 'Destroy her politics! Destroy her culture! Destroy her!'
 But our wings are thick with tar, tongues heavy with her coin,
 On our broken backs, our broken hearts, she'll dine again tonight.
 In her shadow place –
 We are selfish men: Oh, Blake! Orwell! Raise us up, return to us again.
 These civil wars of uncivil hearts, divided and now damned –
 The old is dying and the new cannot be born –
 By Elland Road, I sat down and wept; D.U.F.C.

THE DAMNED UTD

An English Fairy Story

Wednesday 31 July – Thursday 12 September 1974

THE FIRST RECKONING

First Division Final Positions, 1973–74

| | | P | Home | | | | | Away | | | | | Total | | |
			W	D	L	F	A	W	D	L	F	A	F	A	Pts
1	**Leeds United**	42	12	8	1	38	18	12	6	3	28	13	66	31	62
2	Liverpool	42	18	2	1	34	11	4	11	6	18	20	52	31	57
3	Derby County	42	13	7	1	40	16	4	7	10	12	26	52	42	48
4	Ipswich Town	42	10	7	4	38	21	8	4	9	29	37	67	58	47
5	Stoke City	42	13	6	2	39	15	2	10	9	15	27	54	42	46
6	Burnley	42	10	9	2	29	16	6	5	10	27	37	56	53	46
7	Everton	42	12	7	2	29	14	4	5	12	21	34	50	48	44
8	QPR	42	8	10	3	30	17	5	7	9	26	35	56	52	43
9	Leicester City	42	10	7	4	35	17	3	9	9	16	24	51	41	42
10	Arsenal	42	9	7	5	23	16	5	7	9	26	35	49	51	42
11	Tottenham H	42	9	4	8	26	27	5	10	6	19	23	45	50	42
12	Wolves	42	11	6	4	30	18	2	9	10	19	31	49	49	41
13	Sheffield Utd	42	7	7	7	25	22	7	5	9	19	27	44	49	40
14	Man. City	42	10	7	4	25	17	4	5	12	14	29	39	46	40
15	Newcastle Utd	42	9	6	6	28	21	4	6	11	21	27	49	48	38
16	Coventry City	42	10	5	6	25	18	4	5	12	18	36	43	54	38
17	Chelsea	42	9	4	8	36	29	3	9	9	20	31	56	60	37
18	West Ham Utd	42	7	7	7	36	32	4	8	9	19	28	55	60	37
19	Birmingham C	42	10	7	4	30	21	2	6	13	22	43	52	64	37
20	Southampton	42	8	10	3	30	20	3	4	14	17	48	47	68	36
21	Man. Utd	42	7	7	7	23	20	3	5	13	15	28	38	48	32
22	Norwich City	42	6	9	6	25	27	1	6	14	12	35	37	62	29

Bottom 3 clubs relegated.

I am a Yorkshire Man and I am a Cunning Man –
And I curse you!
First with gift, then with loss –
I curse you!
Loss and then gift, gift and then loss –
Until you lose. Until you leave –
I will curse you!

Day One

I see it from the motorway. Through the windscreen. The kids in the back. Fallen off the top of Beeston Hill. *Are we nearly there yet*, they're saying. *Are we nearly there, Dad?* In a heap up against the railway and the motorway banking. Asking me about Billy Bremner and Johnny Giles. The floodlights and the stands, all fingers and fists up from the sticks and the stones, the flesh and the bones. *There it is*, my eldest is telling my youngest. *There it is*. From the motorway. Through the windscreen –

Hateful, hateful place; spiteful, spiteful place . . .

Elland Road, *Leeds, Leeds, Leeds.*

I've seen it before. Been here before. Played and managed here, six or seven times in six or seven years. Always a visitor, always away –

Hateful, spiteful place, flecked in their phlegm . . .

But not today; Wednesday 31 July 1974 –

Arthur Seaton. Colin Smith. Arthur Machin and Joe Lampton . . .

Today I'm no longer a visitor. No longer away –

No more zombies, they whisper. *No more bloody zombies, Brian . . .*

Today I'm on my way to work there.

* * *

The worst winter of the twentieth century begins on Boxing Day 1962. The Big Freeze. Postponements. The birth of the Pools Panel. The Cup Final put back three weeks. People will die in this weather today. But not at Roker Park, Sunderland. Not versus Bury. The referee walks the pitch at half past one. Middlesbrough have called their game off. But not your referee. Your referee decides your game can go ahead –

'Well done, ref,' you tell him. 'That lot down the road call off anything.'

Half an hour before kick-off, you stand in the mouth of the tunnel in your short-sleeved red-and-white vertical-striped shirt, your white shorts and your red and white stockings and watch a ten-minute torrent of hailstones bounce off the pitch. You can't wait to get out there. Can't bloody wait –

Sleet in your face, ice under foot and the cold in your bones. A stray pass into their penalty area and a sprint across the mud, your eye on the ball and your mind on a goal; twenty-eight this season already. Twenty-eight. Their keeper is coming, their keeper is coming, your eye on the ball, your mind on that goal, the twenty-ninth –

Their keeper is here, your mind still on that goal, his shoulder to your knee –

Cruuuuuuuuuuuuuuuuuuuuuuuuuuuuuuuuuuunch . . .

The roar and the whistle. The silence and the lights out –

You are on the ground, in the mud, your eyes open and the ball loose. Twenty-nine. You try to stand, but you can't. Twenty-nine. So you crawl –

'Get up, Clough!' someone shouts. 'Get up!'

Through the mud, on your hands and on your knees –

'Come on, ref,' laughs Bob Stokoe, the Bury centre-half. 'He's fucking codding is Clough.'

On your hands and on your knees, through the heavy, heavy mud –

'Not this lad,' says the referee. 'This lad doesn't cod.'

You stop crawling. You turn over. Your mouth is open. Your eyes wide. You see the face of the physio, Johnny Watters, a worried moon in a frightening sky. There is blood running down your cheek, with the sweat and with the tears, your right knee hurting, hurting, hurting, and you are biting, biting, biting the inside of your mouth to stifle the screams, to fight the fear –

The first taste of metal on your tongue, that first taste of fear –

One by one the 30,000 will leave. Rubbish will blow in circles across the pitch. Snow and night will fall, the ground harden and the world forget –

Leave you lying on your back in the penalty area, a zombie –

Johnny Watters bends down, sponge in his hand, tongue in your ear, he whispers, 'How shall we live, Brian? How shall we live?'

You are lifted onto a stretcher. You are carried off on the stretcher –

'Don't take his bloody boots off,' says the Boss. 'He might get back on.'

Down the tunnel to the dressing room –

You are lifted onto a plinth and a white sheet. There is blood everywhere, through the sheet onto the plinth, down the plinth onto the floor –

The smell of blood. The smell of sweat. The smell of tears. The smell of Algipan. You want to smell these smells for the rest of your life.

'He needs the hospital,' says Johnny Watters. 'Needs it quick and all.'

'But don't you take his fucking boots off,' says the Boss again.

You are lifted off the plinth. Off the bloodstained sheet. Onto another stretcher. Down another tunnel –

Into the ambulance. To the hospital. To the knife.

There is an operation and your leg is set in plaster from your ankle to your groin. Stitches in your head. No visitors. No family or friends –

Just doctors and nurses. Johnny Watters and the Boss –

But no one tells you anything, anything you don't already know –

That this is bloody bad. This is very fucking bad –

The worst day of your life.

* * *

Off the motorway; the South West Urban Motorway. Round the bends. The corners. To the junction with Lowfields Road. Onto Elland Road. Sharp right and through the gates. Into the ground. The West Stand car park. The kids hopping up and down on the back seat. No place to park. No place reserved. The press. The cameras and the lights. The fans. The autograph books and the pens. I open the door. I do up my cuffs. The rain in our hair. I get my jacket out of the back. I put it on. My eldest and my youngest hiding behind me. The rain in our faces. The hills behind us. The houses and the flats. The ground in front of us. The stands and the lights. Across the car park. The potholes and the puddles. This one big bloke pushing his way through the press. The cameras and the lights. The fans –

The black hair and the white skin. The red eyes and the sharpened teeth . . .

'You're bloody late,' he shouts. Finger in my face.

I look at the press. The cameras and the lights. The fans. The autograph books and the pens. My boys behind me. The rain in our hair. In all our faces –

Our faces sunned and tanned, their faces pallid and wan . . .

I look this one big bloke in his eye. I move his finger out of my face and tell him, 'It's got nowt to do with you whether I'm bloody late or not.'

They love me for what I'm not. They hate me for what I am.

Up the steps and through the doors. Out of the rain and out of the press. The cameras and the lights. The fans. Their books and their pens. Into the foyer and the club. The receptionists and the secretaries. The photographs on the walls. The trophies in the cabinets. The ghosts of Elland Road. Down the corridor and round the corner. Syd Owen, chief coach here for the last fifteen years, leading out the apprentices –

I put out my hand. I give him a wink. 'Morning, Syd.'

'Good afternoon, Mr Clough,' he replies, without shaking my hand.

I put my hands on the heads of my sons. I ask him, 'You think you could spare one of your young lads here to watch these two of mine while I make myself known?'

'You're already known,' says Syd Owen. 'And these apprentices are here to develop their capabilities as professional footballers. Not to entertain your children.'

I take my hands off the heads of my sons. I put them on their shoulders. My youngest flinches, my grip too tight –

'I won't keep you any longer then,' I tell this loyal servant, left behind.

Syd Owen nods. Syd says again, 'Not here to entertain your children.'

There's a clock ticking somewhere, laughter from another room. Down the corridor, round the corner. The sound of studs stomping off, marching on together.

My eldest looks up at me. He smiles. He says, 'Who was that, Dad?'

I ruffle his hair. I smile back. I tell him, 'Your wicked Uncle Syd.'

Down the corridor. Past the photographs. Round the corner. Past the plaques. Into the dressing room. The home dressing room. *Keep on fighting* above the door. They have left out an away kit for me; yellow shirt, yellow shorts and yellow socks. The kids watch me change. I pull on my own blue tracksuit top. They follow me down the corridor. Round the corner. Through reception and out into the rain. The car park. The cameras and the lights. The autograph books and the pens. I jog through the potholes and the puddles. Past the huts on stilts. Up the banking. Onto the training ground –

The press shout. The fans cheer. The camera lights flash and my own kids duck.

'Morning, lads,' I shout over at them –

Them stood in their groups. In their purple tracksuits. There are stains on their knees, stains on their arses. *Dirty Leeds*. Their hair long, their names on their backs –

Bastards. Bastards. Bastards . . .

Hunter. The Gray brothers. Lorimer. Giles. Bates. Clarke. Bremner. McQueen. Jordan. Reaney. Cooper. Madeley. Cherry. Yorath. Harvey and Stewart –

All his sons, his bastard sons. Their daddy dead, their daddy gone . . .

In their groups and their tracksuits. In their stains with their names on their backs. Their eyes on mine –

Screw them. Bugger them. Fuck the bloody lot of them.

I do the rounds for the press. For the cameras and the lights. For the fans. For the autograph books and the pens. A handshake here and an introduction there. Nothing more. *Hold your tongue, Brian. Hold your tongue.* Watch and learn. Watch and wait –

Don't let the bastards grind you down, they whisper.

The rounds done, I stand apart. The sun comes out but the rain stays put. No rainbows today. Not here. Hands on my hips. Rain in my face. Sun on my neck. The clouds move fast round here. I look away. My eldest in the car park. A ball on his foot. His knee. His head. In the potholes and the puddles, the rain and the sun, there he is –

A boy with a ball. A boy with a dream.

* * *

It started that first morning in the hospital, the day after Boxing Day, and it's never stopped, not for a single day since. You wake up and for those first few seconds, minutes, you forget; forget you are injured; forget you are finished –

Forget you will never smell the dressing room again. Never put on a clean new kit. Tie on those shining boots and hear the roar of the crowd –

The roar when the ball hits the back of the net; the roar when you score –

The applause. The adoration. The love.

You wish you could see your wife. You haven't seen her in days —
Not since Boxing Day. Not since they brought you here.
No one is telling you anything. Not a bloody thing —
You'd get up and go find her yourself, except you can't.
Then on the fifth day, the door opens and there's your wife —
'I've been in bed,' she says. 'I've had a miscarriage.'

★ ★ ★

They take us on a tour, me and my kids and the press. Down more corridors. Round more corners. Past the lounges and the boxes. The suites and the clubs. The treatment rooms and the dressing rooms. Then they take us all out onto the pitch itself —

They stand me out there, out there in the centre circle —

The green blades of grass. The white chalk lines . . .

My arms raised aloft, a scarf in my hands —

I hate this place, this spiteful place.

Up this corridor. Round this corner. Down the next corridor. The next corner. The boys at my heels. To the office. The empty desk. The empty chair. *Don's office. Don's desk. Don's chair.* Four walls with no windows and one door, these four walls between which he etched his schemes and his dreams, his hopes and his fears. In his black books. His secret dossiers. His enemy lists —

Don didn't trust people. Didn't like people. He dwelled on people. Hated people. He put them in his black books. His secret dossiers —

His enemy lists. Brian Clough on that list.

Me. Top of that list —

This the office. The desk. The chair. In which he schemed and in which he dreamed, with his hopes and with his fears. In his books. His dossiers. His lists. *To exorcise the doubts.* The codes and the road maps. To obsession. To madness. To here —

Here in this office, where they sat upon his knee.

Mrs Jean Reid stands in the doorway. My boys looking at their feet.

'Any chance of a cup of tea, love?' I ask her.

Mrs Jean Reid says, 'The directors are waiting for you upstairs.'

'For me?' I ask. 'Why?'

'For the board meeting.'

I take off my jacket. I take out my handkerchief. I place it on the seat of the chair. *His chair.* I sit down in the chair behind the desk. *His desk.* I put my feet up on the desk –

His chair. His desk. His office. His secretary –

'They are waiting for you,' says Mrs Jean Reid again.

'Let them wait,' I tell her. 'Now how about that cup of tea, duck?'

Mrs Jean Reid just stands and stares at the soles of my shoes.

I knock on the desk. *Don's desk.* I ask, 'Whose is this desk, love?'

'It's yours now,' whispers Mrs Jean Reid.

'Whose was this desk?'

'Mr Revie's.'

'I want it burnt then.'

'Pardon?' exclaims Mrs Jean Reid.

'I want this desk burnt,' I tell her again. 'The chairs and all. The whole bloody lot.'

'But . . .'

'Whose secretary are you, duck?'

'Yours now, Mr Clough.'

'Whose secretary were you?'

Mrs Jean Reid bites her nails and stems her tears, inside her resignation already penned, just waiting to be typed up and signed. On my desk by Monday –

He hates me and I hate him, but I hate him more, more and more –

'Change the locks as well,' I tell her on our way out, the boys with their eyes on the floor and their hands in their pockets. 'Don't want the ghost of troubled Don popping in now, do we? Rattling his chains, scaring my young ones.'

* * *

The scenery changes. The pain remains. Stagehands bring on the furniture in boxes. Bring you home in an ambulance. In on a stretcher. You have suffered a complete tear of the cruciate and medial ligaments. More serious than a broken leg. There is no satisfactory operation. For three months you lie at home on your red G-Plan settee with your knee bent in plaster and your leg up on the cushions, smoking and drinking, shouting and crying –

You are afraid, afraid of your dreams; your dreams which were once your friends, your best friends, are now your enemies, your worst enemies –

This is where they find you, in your dreams. This is where they catch you –

The birds and the badgers. The foxes and the ferrets. The dogs and the demons. Now you are frightened. Now you run –

Laps of the pitch, up and down the steps of the Spion Kop. The fifty-seven steps. Thirty times. Seven days a week from nine in the morning. But you keep your distance from the dressing room. The fifty-seven steps. You prefer the beach at Seaburn. Thirty times. The beach and the bar. Seven days a week from nine in the morning. Running –

Scared. Frightened –

Scared of the shadows. The figures without faces. Without names –

Frightened of the future. Your future. No future.

But day by day you find your feet again. You cannot play, not yet. You cannot play, so you coach. For now. The Sunderland youth team. It keeps you out of the pubs and the clubs, out of bed and off the settee. Keeps your temper too. Coaching. Teaching. Five-a-sides. Six-a-sides. Crossing and shooting. You love it and they love you. They respect you. The likes of John O'Hare and Colin Todd. Young lads who hang on your every word, every one of them, every single word. You take the Sunderland youth team to the semi-finals of the FA Youth Cup. You pass the FA coaching examination. You bloody love it –

But it's no substitute. It's still second best –

Your future. Still second best.

★ ★ ★

Round the corner. Down the corridor. Up the stairs. To the board-room. The battlefield. The wooden double doors. There are windows here, behind these doors, but only here. Matching curtains and carpets. Matching blazers and brass:

Manny Cussins. Sam Bolton. Bob Roberts. Sydney Simon. Percy Woodward; *Alderman* Percy Woodward, the vice-chairman –

Half Gentile, half Jew; a last, lost tribe of self-made Yorkshiremen and Israelites. In search of the promised land; of public recognition, of acceptance and of gratitude. The doffed cap, the bended knee, and the taste of their arses on the lips of the crowd –

The unwashed, applauding them – not the team, only them – them and their brass.

Keith Archer, the club secretary, is hopping from foot to foot, clapping his hands. Patting my lads on their heads, ruffling their hair.

Cussins and Roberts, smiles and cigars, and would you like a drink?

'Bloody murder one,' I tell them and plonk myself down at the head of the table, the top table.

Sam Bolton sits down across from me. Bolton is an FA councillor and vice-president of the Football League. Plain-speaking and self-made, proud of it too –

'You've probably been wondering where your trainer is?'

'Les Cocker?' I ask and shake my head. 'Bad pennies always turn up.'

'Not this one,' says Bolton. 'He'll be joining Mr Revie and England.'

'Good riddance to bad rubbish,' I tell him.

'Why do you say that, Mr Clough?'

'He's a nasty, aggressive little bugger and you've still got plenty to go round.'

'You'll be needing a trainer though,' says Bolton.

'Jimmy Gordon will do me.'

'Derby will let him go, will they?'

'They will if I ask for him.'

'Well, you'd better bloody ask them then, hadn't you?'

'I already have,' I tell him.

'Have you now?' asks Bolton. 'What else you been up to this morning?'

'Just looking and listening,' I tell him. 'Looking, listening and learning.'

'Well, Clough, you've also got eight contracts to look at.'

'You what?' I ask him. 'Revie's left me eight bloody contracts?'

'He has that,' smiles Bolton. 'And one of them is for Mr John Giles.'

They all sit down now; Cussins, Roberts, Simon and Woodward.

Woodward leans forward. 'Something you should know about Giles . . .'

'What about him?' I ask.

'He wanted your job,' says Woodward. 'And Revie told him it was his.'

'Did he now?'

'Too big for his boots,' nods Woodward. 'The pair of them; him *and* Revie.'

'Why didn't you give it to him?' I ask them. 'Done a good job with the Irish.'

'It wouldn't have gone down well with Bremner,' says Cussins.

'I thought they were mates?' I ask them. 'Thick as thieves and all that.'

They all shake their heads; Cussins, Roberts, Simon and Woodward –

'Well, you know what they say about honour and thieves?' laughs Bolton.

'Bremner's the club captain,' says Cussins. 'Ambitions of his own, no doubt.'

I help myself to another brandy. I turn back to the table –

I clear my throat. I raise my glass and I say –

'To happy bloody families then.'

★ ★ ★

This is the last goal you will ever score. September 1964. Eighteen months since your last. Sunderland are now in the First Division. Home to Leeds United. You put the ball through the legs of Jackie Charlton and you score –

The only First Division goal of your career –

The last goal you will ever score.

Your sharpness gone. You cannot turn. It's over. The curtain down. You are twenty-nine years old and have scored 251 league goals in 274 games for Middlesbrough and Sunderland. A record. A bloody record in the Second Division. Two England caps. In the fucking Second Division –

But it's over. It's over and you know it –

No League Championships. No FA Cups. No European Cups –

The roar and the whistle. The applause and the adoration –

Finished for ever. Second best. For ever.

Sunderland Football Club get £40,000 in insurance as compensation for
your injury. You get £1,500, the sack from coaching the youth team, and an
education that will last you a lifetime –
You have a wife. Two sons. No trade. No brass –
That's what you got for Christmas in 1962. You got done –
Finished off and washed up, before your time –
But you will never run a pub. You will never own a newsagent's shop –
Instead, you will have your revenge –
That is how you shall live –
In place of a life, revenge.

★ ★ ★

These are the studios of Yorkshire TV. Of *Calendar*. Of their Special –
Clough Comes to Leeds.

Austin Mitchell is in a blue suit. I'm still wearing my grey suit but
I've changed into a purple shirt and a different tie; always pack a spare
shirt, your own Brylcreem and some toothpaste. Television has taught
me these things.

Austin looks into the camera and says, 'This week we welcome
Brian Clough as manager of Leeds United. How will his outspoken
personality fit in with Leeds, and what can he do for this team, this
team that has won just about everything?'

'Leeds United have been Champions,' I tell him and every household in Yorkshire. 'But they've not been good Champions, in the sense
of wearing the crown well. I think they could have been a little bit
more loved, a little bit more liked, and I want to change that. I want to
bring a little bit more warmth and a little bit more honesty and a little bit more of me into the set-up.'

'So we can expect a bit more warmth, a bit more honesty and a bit
more Brian Clough from the League Champions,' repeats Mitchell.

'A lot more Brian Clough actually,' I tell him. 'A lot more.'

'And hopefully win a lot more cups and another title?'

'And win it better, Austin,' I tell him. 'I can win it better. You just
watch me.'

'And the Leeds set-up? The legendary back-room staff? The legacy of the Don?'

'Well, I'll tell you one thing: I had great fears of that lucky bloody suit of his, in the office when I walked in. You know, the one he's had for thirteen years? I thought, if that's there, that's going straight in the bin because not only will it be old, it'll smell . . .'

'You're not a superstitious man then, Brian?'

'No, Austin, I'm not,' I tell him. 'I'm a socialist.'

Day Two

September 1965. The Chase Hotel, York. Five pints and five whiskies playing hide and seek in your guts. Jobless and boozing, fat and fucked, you are in hell. You'll play one more match for Sunderland. Your testimonial in front of a record 31,000 fans. Ten grand in your pocket. But it won't last. Jobless and boozing. Not at this rate. Fat and fucked. Not unless Peter says yes –

Peter Taylor. The only friend you've ever had. Peter Taylor –

He was a Probable and you were a Possible for Middlesbrough back in 1955. Their second-choice keeper and their fourth-choice striker –

But he liked you then. He believed in you then. He talked to you about football. Morning, noon and night. Taught you about football. He brought out the best in you. Moral courage. Physical bravery. The strength to run through brick walls. He brought out the worst. The arrogance. The selfishness. The rudeness. But he still liked you when you became club captain. Believed in you when the rest of the team despised you, when they plotted and petitioned the club to get rid of you –

And you need him now. That belief. That faith. More than ever –

'I've been offered the manager's job at Hartlepools United,' you tell Peter. 'And I don't much fancy the place, the club or the man who's offered me the bloody job but, if you come, I'll take it.'

But Peter is the manager of Burton Albion. Burton Albion are top of the Southern League. Peter has his new bungalow. His wife and kids settled. Peter is on £41 a week and a three-year contract. His wife shakes her head. His kids shake their heads –

But Peter looks at you. Peter stares into those eyes –

That desire and ambition. That determination and arrogance –

Peter sees the things he wants to see. Peter hears the things he wants to hear –

'You'll be my right arm, my right hand. Not an assistant manager, more a joint manager. Except they don't go in for titles at Hartlepools, so we'll have

to disguise you, disguise you as a trainer.'

'A trainer?' he asks. 'I'll drop down from being a manager to a trainer?'

'Aye,' you tell him. 'And the other bad news is that they can't afford to pay you more than £24 a week.'

'£24 a week,' he repeats. 'That means I'll lose £17 a week.'

'But you'll be in the league,' you tell him. 'And you'll be working with me.'

'But £17 is £17.'

The five pints find the five whiskies. The five pints catch the five whiskies – You put £200 on the table and tell him, 'I need you. I don't want to be alone.'

You're going to spew if he refuses. You're going to die if Pete says no.

'I'll come then,' he says. 'But only because it's you.'

Peter Taylor. The only man who ever liked you. Ever got on with you –

Your only friend. Your right hand. Your shadow.

★ ★ ★

They are waiting for us again. My youngest lad and me. The crows around the floodlights. The dogs around the gates. They are waiting for us because we are late again, my youngest lad and me –

Thursday 1 August 1974.

Bad night, late dreams; faceless, nameless men; red eyes and sharpened teeth.

Half an hour arguing with my boys over breakfast; they don't want to go to work with me today. They didn't like it there yesterday. But my youngest lad feels sorry for me. My youngest lad gives in. My wife takes the eldest and my daughter into Derby to get their new school shoes. I have a slice of toast and don't answer the telephone. Then my youngest lad and me get in the car and drive up the motorway –

The boots and the blades that marched up and down this route . . .

To the crows around the floodlights. Dogs around the gates –

Roman legions and Viking hordes. Norman cunts and royalist whores . . .

The press. The fans. The steady, grey rain. The endless, grey sky –

The emperors and the kings. Oliver Cromwell and Brian Clough.

I park the car. I get out. I do up my cuffs. I don't look at my watch. I get my jacket out of the back. I put it on and ruffle my youngest lad's hair. He's looking across the car park –

Up the banking. To the training ground –

Hands on their hips in their purple tracksuits, waiting. Their names on their backs, whispering, whispering, whispering –

Bastards. Bastards. Bastards.

Jimmy Gordon comes down the steps. Jimmy says, 'Can I have a word, Boss?'

I've known Jimmy Gordon since I was a player at Middlesbrough. *Doesn't work hard enough on the field*, he once wrote in a report on me. Jimmy didn't like me much then. He hated me. Thought I was a right bloody show-off. Big-headed. Selfish. He once told me, *Instead of scoring thirty goals a season, why don't you score twenty-five and help someone else to score fifteen? That way the team's ten goals better off.* I didn't listen to him. I wasn't interested. But I was when I went to Hartlepools. First job I had, I tried to get Jimmy to come and coach for us. But Jimmy wasn't interested. That changed when we got to Derby. I spent five hours round his house –

He said, 'Why me? All we do is argue.'

'That's why I want you,' I told him.

Five hours later, Jimmy still didn't like me. But he had his price. Everybody has. So I found him a house and I got the chairman to pay a £1,000 interest-free deposit on it –

But Jimmy still didn't like me much then. Jimmy still doesn't like me much now. Jimmy looks around the room –

'What the bloody hell are we doing here?' he asks me –

I'm sat in that office. *Don's office.* In that bloody chair. *Don's chair.* Behind that fucking desk. *Don's desk.* My youngest on my knee. *To cheer me up.* A brandy in my hand. *To warm me up* –

'They'll never forgive you,' says Jimmy. 'Not after all the things you've said. They never forget. Not round here.'

'That right, is it?' I laugh. 'So why did you agree to come and join me then?'

'Much as I don't like you,' he smiles, 'I don't like to think of you in trouble.'

I finish my brandy. I ask him, 'You want a lift tomorrow morning?'

'So I can drive you back?'

I pick my lad up off my knee. I put him down. I wink at Jimmy –
'Best not keep them waiting any longer,' I tell them both.

* * *

Welcome to the edge of the world. To Hartlepools –

*You can drop off the edge of the world at Hartlepools. On the beach at Seaton
Carew. Bottom of the entire Football League and up for re-election again –*

Many men will never know. Many men will never understand –

*Heaven is here. Here where the Victoria Ground was cursed by a Zeppelin
bomb, here where the roofs now leak and there are buckets in the boardroom to
catch the rain, where the stand is made of wood and the terraces are covered in
chicken feathers, where the chairman is a five-foot millionaire who made his
money as a credit draper and who bugs your office and your house, and where
the players are adulterers, drunks, thieves and gamblers who play in their street
socks. This is heaven here –*

For you and Pete, together again and working again –

The youngest manager in the Football League –

You on £40 a week, Pete on £24 –

The bucket-and-sponge man –

'*We're in the shit good and proper, make no mistake,*' says Pete. '*We'll be
asking for re-election at the end of the season. Bound to finish bottom. Lower
if we could. Something's got to be done about this lot and done fucking quick.*'

But it's you who paints the stand. Who unblocks the drains. You who cuts
the grass. Who empties the rainwater from the buckets. You who goes round the
colliery clubs. Who sits in committee rooms and stands on stages, asking for
donations. You who borrows hand-me-down training kits from Sheffield
Wednesday. Whose wife does the typing. You who takes your Public Service
Vehicle Licence so you can drive the team bus. Who organizes the cars to
Barnsley when you can't afford a coach. You who buys the team fish and chips.
Who goes without wages for two months –

The newspapers, the photographers and the television cameras, all there to
witness and record the whole bloody show. The pens, the tape recorders and the
microphones, all there for that big bloody open mouth of yours:

'*Age does not count. It's what you know about football that matters. I know*

I am better than the five hundred-odd managers who have been sacked since the war. If they had known anything about the game, they wouldn't have lost their jobs. In this business you've got to be a dictator or you've no chance, because there is only one way out for a small club: good results and then more good results –

'How hard it is to get them results, few people will ever know.'

Should I talk the way you want me to talk?

The bloody microphones and that bloody mouth of yours –

Say the things you want to hear?

Infecting the press. Inspiring the players. Infuriating the chairman –

This is the start of it all. This is where it all begins –

That new accent. That new drawl –

Hartlepools, 1965.

★ ★ ★

Pre-season. Fun and games. The 1974–75 season begins for real in sixteen days. Before that Leeds United, the League Champions, will play in three friendly matches and in the Charity Shield at Wembley against Liverpool, the FA Cup holders. The first friendly is at Huddersfield Town on Saturday, the day after tomorrow –

'Enough pissing around,' I tell them. 'Let's have a few games. Seven-a-sides.'

Hands on their hips, the first team shift their weight from foot to foot.

'Bloody get on with it,' I tell them. 'Come on, get fucking moving.'

The team turn to look at Syd Owen, stood at the back with his hands on his hips –

Syd shrugs. Syd spits. Syd says, 'Hope no one gets hurt.'

'Thank you, Sydney,' I shout back. 'Now come on! Two teams.'

They take their hands off their hips but they still don't move.

'For fuck's sake,' I shout. 'Harvey over there, Stewart here. Reaney there, Cooper here. McQueen there, Hunter here. Bremner there, Cherry here. Lorimer there, Giles here. Bates there, Clarke here. Madeley over there, and I'll be here. Jimmy gets the whistle. Now let's get fucking going –'

They amble about, pulling on bibs, kicking balls away, scratching their own.

Jimmy puts the ball down in the centre circle of the practice pitch.

'We'll kick off,' I tell him, tell them all.

So Jimmy blows the whistle and off we go –

For hours, hours and hours, I run and I shout, but no one speaks and no one passes, no one passes until I finally get the ball and am about to turn, about to turn to my left with the ball on my right foot, on my right foot when someone puts me on my arse –

Flat on my arse like a sack of spuds, moaning and groaning in the mud.

I look up and I see my youngest lad, my youngest lad watching and worried. I get up and I see them watching, watching and whispering –

'I told you someone would get hurt,' smiles Syd. 'Bloody told you.'

No one is laughing. But they will, later. In the dressing room and in the bath. In their cars and in their houses, when I'm not there.

★ ★ ★

You start to keep clean sheets. You start to build from the back. Even win away from home. You finish seventh from the bottom of the Fourth Division in your first season, 1965–66, and this is how your chairman says thank you –

'I can't afford two men doing one man's job any more.'

You open the autobiography of Len Shackleton, Clown Prince of Soccer, *to page 78. You show the blank page to Mr Ernest Ord, millionaire chairman of Hartlepools United:*

The Average Director's Knowledge of Football.

'Piss off,' you tell him. 'Pete's going nowhere.'

'You're getting too much publicity and all,' says Ord. 'You'll have to cut it out.'

'Piss off,' you tell him again. 'This town loves it. Loves me.'

'My son will handle publicity,' says Ord. 'You just manage the team. You manage it alone and all.'

'Pete's staying put,' you tell him. 'And I'll say what I want, when I want.'

'Right then,' says Ord. 'You're both sacked then.'

'We're going nowhere,' you tell him –

This is your first battle. Your first of many –

You go to Conservative Councillor Curry. You tour the clubs. You get shipyards and breweries to pay players' wages. You raise the £7,000 that the club owes the chairman. You are never out of the local papers. Never off the local telly –

'It's him or me,' you tell the board. The press. The fans. 'Him or me.'

Mr Ernest Ord, millionaire chairman of Hartlepools United, resigns –

Your first coup. Your first blood –

1–0.

* * *

I shower, bathe and dress alone. Except for my youngest lad. Then down the corridors, round the corners, back to the office, *his office*, to wait for Jimmy; Jimmy taking fucking for ever. I look at my watch. It's not there. I look in my pockets. But it's bloody gone –

Maurice Lindley puts his head round the door. No knock –

Maurice Lindley, assistant manager of Leeds United, right-hand man to the Don, another one of the Don's backroom boys along with Les Cocker and Syd Owen, Bob English and Cyril Partridge, another one that the Don left behind . . .

Maurice Lindley puts a thick file marked *Top Secret* down on that desk, *his desk*. Maurice says, 'Thought you'd be wanting to see this.'

Maurice Lindley, football's master spy, in his trench coat and his disguises.

I look down at that file on that desk. *Top Secret*. I ask him, 'What the hell is it?'

'Dossier on Huddersfield Town,' says Maurice. 'The bloody works.'

'You're joking?' I ask him. 'It's a bloody testimonial. A fucking friendly.'

'No such thing,' says Maurice. 'Not round here. Don didn't believe in friendlies. Don believed in winning every game we played. Don believed –'

There's a knock on the office door. My youngest lad looks up from his pens –

'Who is it?' I shout.

'It's me, Boss,' says Jimmy. 'I got it.'

I get up from that bloody chair. From behind that fucking desk.

Jimmy comes in, brown parcel in his hands. He passes it to me. 'There you go.'

'What about the petrol?' I ask him.

'It's in the boot of the car.'

'Good man,' I say and unwrap the brown paper parcel –

I unwrap the parcel and I take out an axe –

'Stand well back,' I tell them all. 'Look out, Maurice!'

And I swing that axe down into that desk, *his desk, Don's desk . . .*

I swing it down and then up, up and then back down again –

Into his desk and his chair. Into his photos and his files . . .

Again and again and again.

Then I stop and I stand in the centre of what's left of that office, panting and sweating like a big fat black fucking dog. Maurice Lindley gone. Jean Reid too. Jimmy bloody Gordon and my youngest little lad flat against one wall –

I'm a dynamite-dealer, waiting to blow the place to Kingdom Cum . . .

Then Jimmy and my youngest help me gather up all the pieces of the desk and the chair, all the photos and the files, all the bloody dossiers and every other fucking thing in that office, and we take it all outside and pile it up in the far corner of the car park, and then I go to the boot of Jimmy's car and take out the Castrol and pour it all over the pile, then I light a cigarette and take a couple of drags before I throw it on the pile and watch it all bloody burn –

To Kingdom fucking Cum –

Burn. Burn. Burn.

★ ★ ★

You saved Hartlepools from re-election in your first season. Now you have taken them to eighth in your second. You have also had a third child, a girl –

But these are not the things you will remember about Hartlepools United.

You don't hear this story until ten years later, but it haunts you; it haunts you here and it haunts you now –

Ernest Ord turned up at Peter Taylor's door in his Rolls-Royce and he told Peter, 'I've come to give you a warning. Your mate has finished me and one day he'll do the same to you. Mark my words, Taylor. You mark my words.'

Haunts you here. Haunts you now.

Day Three

I have been in the shadows here, in the corridors and round the corners. I have been in the wings, with the crows and with the dogs. Heart racing and legs shaking. My tongue still, my mouth closed. Ears back and eyes open. Under grey skies –

I have kept my own counsel . . .

No kids with me today. Not today. Today there are things to do. Things to say. Not things for kids to hear. For kids to see. Under grey skies –

Until today; Friday 2 August 1974.

The first team traipse down the embankment from the training ground to the car park, their studs across the tarmac. The team stand around the black cinders in the far corner of the car park. Their hands on their hips, their names on their backs, they move their boots through the white ash. Under grey skies –

'Players' lounge,' I tell them. 'Ten minutes.'

★ ★ ★

Two families by the seaside. The Royal Hotel, Scarborough. Oh, you do like to be beside the seaside. You are happy here, with your ice cream and your deckchair. Your wife and your three kids. You are a home bird and a happy bird now. The fear of unemployment and the need to booze, both are gone for now. Evil Ernest Ord has been vanquished and Hartlepools have finished eighth from the top this season –

There is a new roof upon the stand. Thanks to you. Modern floodlights too –

It is 1967 and things are on the up. You are happy here, but Peter is not –

Your very best pal. Your right hand. Your shadow . . .

Restless and jealous, his ear to the ground and his lips to the phone –

The bucket-and-sponge man on £24 a week –

'Look, we took Hartlepools only as a stepping stone to something better, and now that something has come along. You know yourself that it's been a hard slog at Hartlepools and, personally, I've had a bellyful of it. I know we can never pick the perfect time to go, but I think this is the right move for us.'

The sun goes behind the clouds and the rain starts to come down, to pour down, in buckets and buckets, buckets and spades, in spades and spades –

The deckchairs folded up and the ice creams melted –

'Just meet him,' says Pete. 'Listen to what he has to say. Can't hurt, can it?'

* * *

The players' lounge, Elland Road. Deep in the West Stand, off the main corridor. Round another corner. Two doors and a well-stocked bar. Low ceiling and sticky carpet. Easy chairs and no windows, only mirrors. Mirrors, mirrors, on the walls. The smell of shampoo and Christmas aftershave as they file in from the dressing room in their denim and their leather, with their gold chains and their wet hair, teasing and touching, picking and pinching, a gang of apes after a fuck, they form a circle, their heads as low as their knees in their easy chairs, they spread their legs and touch their balls and try not to look my way –

My Way, indeed.

They are internationals, the bloody lot of them. Medals and trophies galore, every last fucking one of them –

These big, hard men in their tight, new clothes –

These big, hard and *dirty* men. These big, hard, dirty, *old* men –

These old and *nervous* men. Their best years behind them now –

They are worried men. Frightened men. Just like me.

I pick a chair. Turn it round. I sit astride it, arms across the back, and I say a little prayer –

The Prayer to be said before a Fight at Sea against any Enemy . . .

I say the prayer and then I begin, begin to say my piece:

'You lot might be wondering why I haven't said much this week. The reason is I have been forming my own opinions. That is what I like to do. I don't like listening to other people. But now I've formed my opinions and so, before I start working with you lot, there are a

26

few things that need to be said about each of you –

O Most powerful and glorious Lord God . . .

'Harvey, you're an international and an improvement on Gary Sprake,' I tell him. 'But not much of one. The best teams are built on clean sheets. Clean sheets come from good keepers. Good keepers mean safe hands. So safe hands is what I want from you or I'll go find myself a safer pair somewhere else.'

The Lord of hosts, that rulest and commandest all things . . .

I turn to the two Pauls, Madeley and Reaney. I tell them, 'Mr Madeley, you've played in every bloody position bar the fucking keeper. Obviously Don couldn't make up his mind. But I reckon it's time you made a position your own, either that or I'll do it for you and that might mean the bloody bench or the transfer list. Mr Reaney, you've had one broken leg, missed one Cup Final and one World Cup – you're not getting any younger, so look after yourself because in my opinion you deserve more bloody caps than the ones you've had.'

Thou sitest in the throne judging right . . .

'No one in the game likes you,' I tell Hunter. 'And I think you want to be liked.'

Bites Yer Legs shrugs his shoulders and shakes his head. 'I don't give a fuck.'

'I think you do.'

'I'm an established England international,' he says. 'I really don't give a shit.'

Therefore we make our address to thy Divine Majesty in this our necessity . . .

'Mr William Bremner – you're the captain and you're a good one,' I tell him. 'But you're no good to the team and you're no good to me if you're suspended. I want discipline from my teams and, as the captain, I expect you to set the example.'

That thou wouldst take the cause into thine own hand . . .

'And you'd do well to follow that example,' I tell Lorimer. 'Because you know how I feel about you. How you harangue referees. How you fall over when you've not been touched. How you make a meal out of every tackle to try and get the other player booked. How you protest when you have nothing to fucking protest about –'

'Nothing to protest about?' he says. 'Them tackles that some of your lads at Derby gave me? You expected me just to stand for that the whole bloody game?'

And judge between us and our enemies . . .

'As for you and the amount of injuries you've had,' I tell Eddie Gray. 'If you'd been a bloody racehorse, you'd have been fucking shot.'

Eddie Gray looks up at me, looks up at me with tears in his eyes. Eddie Gray says, 'Didn't an injury end your career?'

'Yes,' I tell him. 'It bloody well did.'

'Then you ought to understand how I feel.'

Stir up thy strength, O Lord, and come and help us . . .

I turn to Michael Jones. I tell him, 'Same goes for you, young man.'

For thou givest not always the battle to the strong, but canst save by many or few . . .

'Irishman, you're another one with a terrible bloody reputation,' I tell John Giles. 'God gave you intelligence, skill, agility and the best passing ability in the game. These are qualities which have helped to make you a very wealthy young man. What God did not give you was them six studs to wrap around someone else's knee.'

'So bloody what?' he says. 'People kick me, I kick them back.'

'Just remember,' I warn him. 'It's not my fault you didn't get this job.'

'Relax, will you?' he says. 'I didn't want the job then and I don't want it now.'

O let not our sins now cry against us for vengeance . . .

I point at McQueen and Jordan. I tell them, 'You've both been to the World Cup and, McQueen, you've had a good one. I liked what I saw but I want to see more of it.'

But hear us thy poor servants begging mercy, and imploring thy help . . .

'Mr Cooper and Mr Bates, they tell me you're both finally fit again. Thank God! You'll get your chance to prove yourselves to me tomorrow. Make sure you bloody do!'

That thou wouldst be a defence unto us against the face of the enemy . . .

'Sniffer,' I tell Allan Clarke. 'You scored eighteen goals last season. I want fucking nineteen this season. At least fucking nineteen! Understood?'

Sniffer grins. Sniffer nods. Sniffer Clarke salutes.

Make it appear that thou art our Saviour and mighty Deliverer . . .

I turn to the last three. I tell them, 'Cherry, young Gray, Taff Yorath – it's a long season ahead of us, lots of games ahead of us – so train hard, keep your noses clean, do things my way and you'll have your chances. Up to you to make sure you bloody take them chances when they do come along.'

My way –

'Gentlemen, I might as well tell you now. You lot may have won all the domestic honours there are and some of the European ones but, as far as I am concerned, the first thing you can do for me is to chuck all your medals and all your caps and all your pots and all your pans into the biggest fucking dustbin you can find, because you've never won any of them fairly. You've done it all by bloody cheating.'

Through Jesus Christ our Lord . . .

'And there's one other thing,' I tell them all, tell every last fucking one of them. 'I don't ever want to hear the name of Don bloody fucking Revie again. Never ever again. So the next player who does mention that bloody name again will spend his working week with the fucking apprentices. Learning his lesson, whoever he bloody is, no matter who he fucking is –

'Now bugger off home, the lot of you.'

Amen.

★ ★ ★

You meet the chairman of Derby County at a hotel at Scotch Corner. Peter waits in the car. Len Shackleton makes the introductions. This Sam Longson is another self-made millionaire, another blunt and plain-speaking man who drives a Rolls-Royce. His money from haulage. Proud of it. Proud of Derby County too. But Derby County are in the Second Division and going nowhere. Their only cup won back in 1946. Third Division North Champions in 1957. Nothing since. Nowhere since. They have just finished seventeenth in Division Two and Sam Longson has just sacked their manager, Tim Ward. Now Longson is getting hate mail. Now Longson is shitting himself –

'That'll soon be a thing of the past,' you tell him. 'And I'll be the reason why –'

Then you start telling him why. Never stop telling him why. Never shut up.

Three hours later, Longson is so excited he won't be able to sleep tonight.

You go out to the car. Peter has the window down. Peter asks, 'How did it go?'

'Job's mine,' you tell him. 'Bloody mine!'

He's as happy as Larry. Pleased as punch. Then he says, 'What about me?'

* * *

Down the corridors. Round the corners. The empty corridors. The dark corners. The office is bare; just *his* old telephone and Jean Reid's resignation letter on the floor by the door. I pull my kit bag across the carpet towards me and take out an unopened bottle of Martell. I light a cigarette and pick the price off the brandy –

£3.79 – Wineways.

Tomorrow is Saturday. Away at Huddersfield. My first game here –

Fuck. Fuck. Fuck . . .

I haven't got a clue who to pick. I haven't got a clue what to say –

Not a fucking one. Not a fucking one.

There are voices and feet outside the door. Laughter, then silence –

Down the corridors. Round the corners . . .

I get up off the floor. I open the door –

Nothing. No one.

I don't believe in God. But I do believe in doubt. I do believe in fear.

Day Four

You drive down to a meeting with the Derby County directors at the Baseball Ground. The job's yours but it still has to be ratified and confirmed by the full board, according to Sam. You've got the wife with you, the three bairns in the back of the Rover. You drop them by the swings in Normanton Park. You tell the wife you'll be back within the hour. You drive on to the Baseball Ground.

Sam Longson is waiting for you with the rest of the board: Sidney Bradley, Harry Paine, Bob Kirkland and three others who say nothing and whose names you do not catch. Turns out the board have been overwhelmed with applications for the job, least that's what they're telling you. Turns out they have a shortlist of four —

Alan Ashman, Billy Bingham, Tommy Cummings and you —

Turns out the job's not quite yours —

The Derby board do not even offer you a drink, so you help yourself.

'My injury finished me as a player and took away the thing I loved most in this world,' you tell them. 'But it did give me an early start in management at Hartlepools. Re-election had become an annual event for them, but I changed that. I cut the playing staff down. I got rid of the players who were crap. I brought in one or two who were slightly better than crap. Hartlepools finished eighth at the end of this season. I also built them a new stand as well as a new team and have left them solvent. But I didn't do it alone. I couldn't have done it without Peter Taylor, and I want him here with me at Derby. We come as a pair or not at all.'

They shuffle their papers and fiddle with their pens, these worried rich men.

'Me and Peter Taylor can turn this club around. We can guarantee you that you'll not finish as low as you have this season and, more to the point, we can get the public off your backs. But we can only do it together —

'Me and Peter Taylor!'

They are interested now, these worried rich men, thinking of walking the streets of Derby without abuse, thinking of holding their heads up high again with their wives on their arms, thinking of finally getting the appreciation they deserve. They nod in the direction of their chairman, these worried rich men –

They have been overwhelmed by you, the shortlist down to one –

'I remember when you played here with Sunderland,' says Sam Longson. 'Pointing here, pointing there. Shouting at this one, shouting at that one. Telling everyone what to do. Lot of folk said you were arrogant, but I said you were a leader. That's what we need here: a leader.'

'And that's what you'll get,' you tell him. 'I promise you that. But I want a contract because you've got seven directors here and, within a month, at least one of them will want us gone. I promise you that and all.'

'Mr Clough,' says Longson. 'Your salary shall be £5,000 a year and your assistant's shall be £2,500. Furthermore, £70,000 will be available for new players and you shall both have contracts, don't you worry about that.'

Eight hours later you get back to Normanton Park; your boys are asleep on the swings, your wife and daughter curled up on a bench.

★ ★ ★

Saturday's come, with Saturday's stink. The sweat and the mud, the liniment and the grease. The steam and the soap, the sewer and the shampoo. The beer and the wine, the spirits and the cigars –

It's only a friendly, only a testimonial. But it's still a game, still my first.

I watch them climb up the steps onto the coach with their paperback books and their packs of cards and I count the hearts –

Not one among them.

No one speaks and no one smiles. But the journey to Leeds Road, Huddersfield, is supposed to be a short one.

I sit down next to Bremner. I ask him, 'You get my telegram, did you?'

'What telegram?' he says.

'The one I sent from Majorca,' I tell him. 'The one I sent inviting you and your family to join me and mine for a few days in the sun. The one in which I said how proud I was to be the new manager of Leeds United.'

'No,' he says and looks back down at his paperback book –

The Beautiful Couple.

I am first off the coach and the reception is warm. I sign autographs for the kids and shake hands with their dads –

It's only a friendly, only a testimonial.

Through the doors. Down the corridors. Round the corners. Up the stairs. Into the boardroom. Into the bar. Into the spirits –

The handshakes and the backslaps –

Then Jimmy is in my ear –

'They're waiting,' he whispers. 'They want to know who's playing.'

'Bring them up here,' I laugh. 'Get a few pints down them.'

'Come on, Boss,' he pleads, his eyes wide and his palms out –

I finish my drink. I light another fag. I follow him out of the boardroom. Down the stairs. Round the corner. Down the corridor –

To the doors of the visitors' dressing room. To the sound of silence –

I put out my fag. I take a deep breath. I open the door –

To the visitors' dressing room. To the stink of Saturday –

'Stewart, Reaney, Cooper, Bremner, McQueen, Hunter, Lorimer, Bates, Clarke, Giles and Madeley,' I tell them and leave them, leave them to their dressing room. Their silence. The stink of Saturday –

'Mr Clough?'

I turn round; Bates stood in the corridor outside the dressing room.

'You bloody deaf, are you, young man?' I ask him. 'You're playing. Now go and get your fucking boots on.'

'I know,' says Mick Bates. 'But where do you want me to play? I'm usually in midfield but, with both me and Paul Madeley playing today, I was wondering if I should play further up, in front of Johnny Giles and Billy Bremner?'

'Look, you'll do what I bloody tell you and play where I fucking say,' I shout. 'Now fuck off back in there and get your bloody boots on before I change my mind and have you fucking cleaning them all next bloody week!'

I walk off down the corridor. Round the corner. Up the stairs –

I take a seat in the stands to watch the game. My first game as manager of Leeds United. The Champions of England. But they are not my team. Not mine –

33

They go a goal behind. Then the Irishman volleys one back –

I look at my watch. It's not there. Still missing.

Half-time, I'll take off Norman Hunter and stick on Trevor Cherry and then they'll pass better and score a winner, but I'm already looking through my address book –

Because they are not my team. Not mine. Not this team, and they never will be –

They are his team. *His Leeds.* His dirty, fucking Leeds and they always will be.

Not my team. Never. Not mine. Never. Not this team. Never –

They are not Derby County. Never Derby County.

★ ★ ★

There's a beard and a smell about Peter when he answers the door, dark rings around his eyes and fresh whisky on his breath.

'Lillian's not bloody left you, has she?' you ask him.

'You never called,' he says. 'I thought you'd forgotten about us.'

'Forgotten?' you laugh. 'I didn't get back to the bloody house till midnight.'

'So?' he says.

'So, what?' you ask.

He wipes his mouth and he says, 'Don't make me beg, Brian. Please . . .'

'Beg?' you laugh. 'You'll never beg again. We're in! Bloody in!'

'Both of us?' he says. 'They agreed to take me and all?'

'Course they bloody did,' you tell him. 'Me and you.'

He's still smiling but now he's asking, 'How much?'

'£2,500 a year, with £70,000 for new players.'

'£2,500 a year each?'

'With £70,000 for new players,' you tell him again, and now he's jumping up and down on his doorstep and hugging you like you've both just come up on the bloody pools, and you're opening up the carrier bag in your hand and taking out the two bottles of champagne and the packets of cigars –

'We're on our way,' he's shouting. 'You and me; Clough and Taylor!'

Day Five

Sunday is the loneliest bloody day of the fucking week for the manager of a football club. The manager's office on a Sunday bloody morning, the loneliest fucking place on earth if you lost the day before –

Leeds won yesterday – just, thanks to Michael Bates – but I'm still the only one here today in this empty office, on this empty corridor, under this empty stand –

No one here today but me. No one here but me. No one but me –

In this empty ground, in this empty city, this empty land –

No wife. No kids. No Peter Taylor –

No fucking Taylor. No Judas –

Just me and the ghost of troubled Don –

Behind every door. Down every corridor. Round every corner.

I leave the office. *His office.* I walk down the corridors. *His corridors.* Round the corners. *His corners.* Down the tunnel. *His tunnel.* Out into the light and onto the pitch –

I take my cigs, I take my drink. Across the blades, across the lines –

This cigarette which takes the skin off my lip. This drink which dulls the sting. Every single blade of grass of consequence, every single line of chalk an authority –

Upon the empty, deserted pitch beneath the empty, deserted stands –

This pitch where I played and only won, where I've managed and only lost, beneath these stands where I've heard them jeer and heard them swear, heard them whistle and heard them boo.

It starts to spit. To piss it down again. I take my cigs. I take my drink. I leave that pitch. I leave those stands. I walk back down the corridors. Round the corners and through the doors. To the office –

His fucking office.

I should be at home with my wife and my kids, carving the roast and digging the garden, walking the dog and washing the car –

Not sat here in this office in my brand-new chair behind my brand-new desk, standing back up then sitting down again, picking up the phone and putting it back down, thinking about the week just gone and the one to come, planning and scheming, plotting and dreaming; every ground in the land, every manager the same –

Not home with the wife. Not home with the kids –

For when you're there, you wish you weren't . . .

No Sunday roast. No English garden –

When you're not, you wish you were –

Just a fat dog and a dirty car –

Because I'm never there. I'm always here –

Here in my brand-new chair behind my brand-new desk on the phone to Des Anderson, assistant manager at Derby County. I know they're still not happy, the players there. Not since we left. I know they'd all jump at the chance to play for me again –

John McGovern first. Then the entire first team, if I had my way –

My Way, indeed –

'How much?' I ask Des.

'£150,000.'

'Fuck off,' I tell him. 'You've got him on the bloody transfer list and playing in the fucking reserves.'

'Dave needs the money,' he says. 'It's as simple as that.'

'For what?' I ask him. 'I left him the best fucking team in bloody Europe.'

Des sighs. Des says, 'He wants Duncan McKenzie.'

'Who?'

'This lad at Forest. Twenty-eight goals last season. On a one-man strike now.'

'For what?'

'A better club,' laughs Des.

I put down the phone –

Who the fucking hell is Duncan McKenzie? Taylor would know, know everything about him. Especially a Nottingham lad. Chapter and verse. But he's not bloody here –

Fucking Taylor. Fucking Judas.

And he won't be at the Goldstone Ground either. Not on a Sunday. Not Taylor. So I call his house, his brand-new fucking flat beside the seaside. No answer –

Fucking Taylor. Fucking Judas.

Mike Bamber will have taken them all out for a slap-up Sunday lunch at his hotel. The Courtlands Hotel. Taylor and his family. Bamber and his –

Oysters and smoked salmon. Champagne and caviar –

Dora Bryan on the next table. Bruce fucking Forsyth.

I pour myself another large Martell. The name on my cig pack –

Duncan McKenzie.

Whoever the fuck this McKenzie is, Dave Mackay wants him for Derby County, and if Dave Mackay wants him for Derby County, I want him for Leeds –

My Leeds. My new Leeds.

I get out my address book. I pour another Martell, light another cig and pick up the phone again. I make a few calls. Take folk from their roasts and their gardens –

Their dogs and their cars.

He's a popular lad this Duncan McKenzie. Bloody Tottenham want him as well. To replace Martin Chivers. Fucking Birmingham too. Very popular for a lad who quit football a month ago and has only trained with his local amateur side. Popular enough for Dave Mackay to have already offered Alan Brown £200,000 for him. Popular enough for Alan Brown to have rejected it and all –

Popular enough for Brian Clough and my new Leeds United.

I drive back down to Derby on an empty stomach and an empty motorway. I show my face in the Midland Hotel and then out at the Kedleston Hall Hotel, where one thing leads to another, one drink to another, and I know I'm going to be late back home again, to another roast burnt, another garden overgrown, to another fat dog in another dirty car –

No son to my parents. No husband to my wife. No father to my kids –

But you can never bring it home –

Never. Never. Never –
Bring it home –
Ever.

Day Six

Derby County say they have a tradition. But it's not much of one; of enter-
tainment, not success, bar the 1946 FA Cup-winning side of Jack Nicholas,
Raich Carter and Peter Doherty. Derby County say they have a history. But
not much of one; relegated from the First Division in 1953; relegated from the
Second in 1955. Back now in the Second Division. But only just. Derby
County also say they have a curse. But not much of one; just the old belief that
the club was cursed by the gypsies who were turned off the site of the Baseball
Ground, them and every other club –

Curses. History. Tradition –

Derby County don't know the meaning of the bloody words, not in the
fucking Midlands. Middlesbrough, Sunderland and Newcastle, these are the
places where curses, tradition and history mean something; in the north-east.
You already think you might have made a mistake leaving home, leaving home
and coming here.

Your very first game as manager of Derby County is on the 1967 pre-season
tour of West Germany. Derby County are rubbish. Bloody rubbish. Utter
fucking rubbish –

Now you know you have made a mistake, now you know you should have
stayed at Hartlepools, should have stayed at home.

Sam Longson is stood beside you and Peter on the touchline –

'What do you expect me to do with this bloody lot, Mr Chairman?'

Sam Longson lights another cigar. Sam Longson says, 'It's in your hands.'

'Good,' you tell him. 'In that case, I'll sack the fucking lot of them.'

★ ★ ★

I can't get out of bed. Not with this head. This job. I can hear the wife
and the kids downstairs. The dog barking at the radio. But I can't get

out of bed. I reach for my watch, but it's not there. Sod it. I get out of bed, get washed and get dressed. I go downstairs –

'What time did you get in last night?' asks the wife.

'Too late,' I tell her.

She rolls her eyes and asks us, 'Do you want any breakfast?'

I shake my head. I tell her, 'I best be off.'

'Drive carefully,' she says. 'And call if you're going to be late.'

I nod and turn to the boys. 'Who wants to go to work with their dad today?'

The boys look down at their hands. Their fingers and their nails.

My wife comes up behind me. My wife kisses me on the cheek. My wife says, 'Don't force them, love. Not if they don't want to.'

'And what if I don't want to?'

She looks at me. She shakes her head. She starts to speak –

'Just kidding,' I tell her and open the front door. 'Just kidding.'

* * *

A manager is always at his strongest in his first three months at a club. Get all the unpleasant stuff out of the way then, because you're never stronger than in your first three months. Things like that are hard work to other managers but they are not hard work to you. Things like discipline, coaching and training. You have got your mind set on football and you know just how to approach it. Doesn't matter if it's Manchester United or Liverpool. Leeds United or Derby County –

You tell the players that they have three weeks to make an impression on you or they're out. Three weeks later, you sack sixteen of the playing staff, the chief scout, four groundsmen, the secretary, the assistant secretary, a couple of clerks and the tea ladies. You take down the photographs of Jack Nicholas, Raich Carter and Peter Doherty –

No more tradition. No more history. No more curses –

You want a bloody revolution. You want a future. You want it now.

You stand up before the Rotary Club of Derby and you tell them, and the newspapers, and the television cameras, 'Derby County under me will never finish as low as they did last season –

'I promise you they will always finish higher than seventeenth.'

The manager's office on a Monday morning and it all starts again. Building, building, building. To Saturday. Like Taylor used to say, if you're wrong on a Monday then you're wrong on a Saturday. But Taylor isn't here. Not today. Today there's just a pile of shit on my brand-new desk. A pile of shit and no secretary. A pile of shit that includes hate mail, death threats and the promise of legal action from Don Revie –

For the things I said, the many public things I said –

'On that show you did last Friday?' asks Jimmy Gordon.

'Aye,' I tell him. 'Didn't think they could get *Calendar* down at Lancaster Gate.'

'Don's house is only round the corner,' says Jimmy. 'He's back all the time.'

'Why do you think I'm getting the fucking locks changed,' I tell him.

★ ★ ★

'I've seen one,' Peter tells you and off you set, no questions asked, because this is how it works, you and Peter, this is the chemistry, the magic –

Observe. Expose. Replace –

This is Peter's talent; spotting players. This is Peter's hard work, how he earns his brass; travelling down to Devon on a Saturday in August to watch Torquay United vs Tranmere Rovers; to watch a centre-forward vs a centre-half; to watch Jim Fryatt vs Roy McFarland; to sneak out of the ground to find a phone box to ring you up – at the club, in a pub, at your home – and say, 'I've found one.'

Because that's all it takes, three little words, and off you set –

Derby to Liverpool. Liverpool to Tranmere.

The directors' box at Prenton Park is overflowing with managers and scouts. They all ask you, 'Who you after then, Brian?'

The Tranmere manager knows the moment he sees you both. Dave Russell says, 'Don't beat around the bush now, lads, it's my young centre-half that's brought you all the way up here, isn't it, lads?'

You both nod. You say, 'You can't kid a kidder.'

'Well then, you'll both be happy to know that he's available for the right price. How much you got to spend, lads?'

You cough. You take out your handkerchief. You tell him, '£9,000.'

'Fuck off,' he laughs –

This is how it begins. How it always begins –

When you get to £20,000 you ask Dave Russell if you can use his phone, 'Because this is getting so bloody high that I'll need sanction from the chairman.'

You go over to his desk. You pick up the phone. You dial an empty office. You plead down the line to the ringing bell, 'Please, Mr Longson. £24,000. That's what they're asking . . .'

'They might want more . . . That's your limit, I understand . . . I'll tell him then. £24,000 and not a penny more . . .'

You hang up on the ringing phone. You look over at Dave Russell –

You know Dave wants more. You know you could go as high as £50,000 –

But he doesn't and he never will.

You tell Dave, 'You heard the chairman; £24,000. Not a penny more.'

Dave Russell sighs. Dave Russell shrugs his shoulders –

You shake hands with Dave. But then Dave says –

'If he wants to go to Derby, that is.'

'Course he bloody will,' you tell him. 'Don't you fucking worry about that.'

It's gone midnight as you drive through the Mersey Tunnel. You park outside a small terraced house and bang on its door. But Roy's not here. His father tells you to try such-and-such a club where he sometimes goes. Roy's not there either. You drive back to the small terraced house and bang on its door again. Roy's here now but Roy's in his bed. You get his father to bring him downstairs in his red-and-white striped pyjamas.

'These gentlemen are from Derby County,' Dave Russell tells young sleepyhead. 'I have agreed a fee with them, Roy. So, if you want to go – and you don't have to – but, if you want to go, you can become a Derby County player.'

But he doesn't want to play for Derby. He wants to play for Liverpool –

For Bill Shankly.

Roy has spent his childhood on the Kop; his adolescence waiting for the call –

But Bill's not called. Peter Taylor and Brian Howard Clough have.

'I don't care how long you take or how many questions you want to ask. We are going to create one of the best teams in England and I'm not going *anywhere until you decide you want to be a part of that team.'*

Roy's father remembers you; remembers one of the goals you scored –

'It was a beauty,' he tells his son. 'Even the Kop chanted his name and, if Brian Clough wants you for Derby County this much, I think you should go.'

You take out a contract. You take out a pen. You put it in Roy's hand –

Peter has the eyes and the ears, but you have the stomach and the balls –

Not Peter and not Bill Shankly –

Brian Howard Clough.

You get back home with the dawn. You ring the Evening Telegraph *–*

You get the home phone number of the Sports Editor. You get him out of bed –

'I've got a scoop for you,' you tell him. 'I've just signed Roy McFarland.'

'Who the fuck is Roy McFarland?' he asks. 'And what bloody time is it?'

* * *

No one says good morning. No one says hello. I stand at the edge of the training pitch and watch Jimmy put them through their paces –

Running. Running. Running.

I call Frank Gray over. I tell him, 'Need to have a chat about your contract.'

'Been nice knowing you,' shouts one of them –

Running. Running. Running.

But no one laughs. No one says another word.

* * *

You have bought Roy McFarland and you have bought John O'Hare from Sunderland. You have got rid of some of the deadwood and you win the opening game of the 1967–68 season against a Charlton side managed by Bob Stokoe –

'Come on,' Stokoe once laughed at you, laughed at you in the mud, in the mud and on your knees, on your knees that were shattered and shot, fucked and finished for ever –

Bob Stokoe who told the referee, 'He's fucking codding is Clough.'

You win that game but lose the next. Win the next and then the next –

Lose the one after that but win the next and the next again –

This is how it goes, this life of yours –

Win one, lose one. Win the next –

*The performances improve and the attendances increase, but if the perform-
ances deteriorate then the gates go with them –*

Then you'll be next, you know that –

You'll be next, fucked and finished for ever.

★ ★ ★

I don't knock and they don't offer me a drink, so I help myself. Then I sit down, spark up and tell them, 'I've seen one.'

'One what?'

'Player, name of Duncan McKenzie,' I tell them. 'And tomorrow I'm going to buy him from Nottingham Forest for £250,000.'

'Now just one bloody minute,' says Bolton.

'We haven't got one,' I tell them.

'One what?'

'One minute or, for that matter, one centre-forward.'

'Now just a –'

'Allan Clarke is bloody suspended and Jones is fucking injured,' I tell them all. 'So I don't know who you think is going to score you the goals you'll need to retain the league or win you the European Cup.'

'There'll have to be a discussion,' says Bolton. 'We know nothing about this Duncan McKenzie and you're asking us to part with a quarter of a million bloody quid.'

'Twenty-eight goals last season,' I tell him. 'What more do you need to know?'

'I'd like to know who else you're planning to buy?' asks Percy Woodward.

'A goalkeeper and a centre-half,' I tell him. 'This team needs rebuilding from the back. This team needs a new spine.'

'And who would this new spine be then?'

'Peter Shilton and Colin Todd.'

'And what about Harvey and Hunter?' asks Bolton. 'They are both full internationals.'

44

'So are Shilton and Todd.'

'But are they for sale?' asks Cussins.

I laugh. I tell him, 'Everyone's for sale, Mr Cussins. Surely you know that?'

'Quite a long list you've got there,' says Bolton. 'Papers also say you're interested in Derby's John McGovern.'

'You shouldn't believe everything you read,' I tell them. 'But he's a good player. Known him since he was a lad.'

'We have Billy Bremner,' says Bolton. 'We don't need John McGovern.'

'You might be right,' I tell him. 'You might be wrong. But you pay me to be right every Saturday and I'm telling you, you need new players because some of the lot you've got have bloody shot it.'

'They're the League Champions,' says Woodward.

'Last season,' I tell him. 'Last season.'

'Look,' says Cussins. 'The first priority is the contracts of the players we have. The ones we want to hang on to. There are still eight to be signed.'

'These contracts?' I ask them. 'Why weren't they done before I got here?'

'It was difficult,' says Cussins. 'What with the World Cup and the close season.'

'Rubbish,' laughs Percy Woodward. 'Bloody rubbish. Revie was too scared. Didn't want to break up the family.'

'Not a very happy family now,' I tell them. 'Some very worried men out there.'

'What about our friend John Giles?'

'Not my friend,' I tell them.

'But have you . . .'

'Have I done your dirty work?' I laugh. 'Is that what you want to know?'

'Brian, Brian,' says Cussins. 'It's not like that. John Giles has been a loyal servant for this club and an important part of our success. But . . .'

'But you'd like me to help you get shot of him?'

They don't say yes. They don't say no –

They dare not.

Twenty years ago, this lot would have been selecting the side then sacking the manager when they lost. Things haven't changed; they never blame themselves for anything bad and they never say thank you for anything good –

Directors.

★ ★ ★

Peter shuts his little black book. Peter puts out his fag. Peter says, 'I know just the player. Just the club.'

This time you and Peter go and do your shopping at Nottingham Forest –

Pete spends half his bloody life here. Never out the fucking place. Home-town boy; even played twice as an amateur for Forest's first team against Notts County, a home-town derby in a wartime league.

Pete has two names at the top of his Nottingham shopping list:

Alan Hinton and Terry Hennessey.

Forest won't sell Hennessey. Not yet. But Forest don't seem too sorry to see the back of Hinton; dropped by England, over the hill, say the press, he's being given the bird by his own supporters, week in, week out –

Gladys, *they shout.* Where's your fucking handbag?

You couldn't give a shit; Peter says he's got pace and a left foot that can shoot and cross with equal accuracy, and that he can do both under pressure –

That's all you need to know, all you need to hear.

You tell Hinton to come to the Baseball Ground for a chat and then you walk him round and round and round the cinder track as night comes down and the lights go on –

'You're destined to play for us,' you tell him. 'So don't miss your chance.'

It's well after midnight when you track down the Forest chairman to the Bridgford Hotel. He wants £30,000 for Hinton. You lie and tell him Hinton wants a grand for himself. The Forest chairman agrees to £29,000 and you're laughing as you hang up; it's the principle of the thing –

Never give the bastards what they want.

You pay £29,000 and Forest boast to your directors about how they've done you, how they've off-loaded a passenger –

What colour's your fucking handbag, Gladys?

You couldn't give a fuck; four years from now, then you'll see who's laughing.

But three months later you're still winning and then losing, winning and then losing, and you're still receiving hate mail –

Sidney Bradley, the vice-chairman, summons you and Peter to the carpet of his office. Sidney Bradley says, 'I'm not happy with the way you two are operating.'

You've only been in the place five bloody minutes and already they want fucking rid. Shot of you both. You go to Sam Longson and you tell him, 'You are the only chairman I can work with. You are the saviour of Derby County.'

Uncle Sam pulls you close. Tight. Uncle Sam puts his wings around you –

Then Uncle Sam kisses you better. Now Uncle Sam will protect you –

The son he never had.

★ ★ ★

The Monday press conference. The post-mortem. The long rope –

'I don't have any disputes on my hands and I don't think there will be any problems because I've never had any trouble over players' contracts in the past, but I still feel that they should be signed, sealed and delivered long before a new manager takes over and certainly before 5 August. The last thing I wanted to do when I arrived here was to start by having to talk contracts with men I'd never met.'

'What about reports that Mr Revie is taking legal advice over the remarks you made on last Friday's *Calendar* programme?'

'Listen to me,' I tell him. 'Did you see that programme?'

The gentleman of the press nods.

'And?'

The gentleman stammers. The man stutters and shits himself.

'Anyone who saw that programme,' I tell him and the whole fucking lot of them, 'can make up their own minds and, as far as I'm concerned, Revie can have fifty transcripts of the broadcast if he wants them. Did you get all that down?'

The gentleman of the press nods.

'Rest of you lot?'

The rest of the gentlemen of the press nod too.

'You don't want me to say it again. Bit more slowly?'

The gentlemen of the press shake their heads now.

47

'Good work,' I tell them. 'Now if you'll excuse me, my wife's got my tea on.'

★ ★ ★

You've gone from fifth to thirteenth and seen all hope of promotion slide away with you. The only good news is your cup form. You beat your old club Hartlepools, then Birmingham City, Lincoln City and Darlington to reach the semi-finals of the League Cup, where you'll face Leeds United, home and away. Leeds United who, coincidentally, you've also been drawn against in the third round of the FA Cup. So, between 17 January and 7 February 1968, you'll be playing Leeds United three times –

Leeds United and Don Revie, an inspiration to you and Peter –

Leeds United and Don Revie who went from the Second to the First Division as Champions in 1964 to become runners-up in the First Division and the FA Cup in 1965, First Division runners-up again in 1966 and runners-up in the Inter-Cities Fairs Cup final of 1967 –

United and County, sleeping giants in one-club towns; Leeds steeped in rugby and Derby steeped in cricket; sleeping giants awoken by men who were among the finest, most skilful and most neglected players of their day –

Don Revie was also born in Middlesbrough. Just like you –

Peas in a pod, you and Don. Peas in a pod –

Born just seven years and some streets apart.

The club and the whole town is excited at the prospect of these games –

Just like you. Unable to sleep. Unable to eat. Back at the ground at the crack of dawn to sweep the corridors, to clean the baths and polish the pegs –

You're first at the door when the Leeds team bus arrives at the Baseball Ground, the players filing off, Don in his huddle with Les Cocker, Maurice Lindley and Syd Owen.

'Welcome to Derby, Don,' you say. 'Pleasure to meet you. I'm Brian Clough.'

But Don doesn't acknowledge you, introduce himself or even say hello –

Don stays away from the boardroom, out of the bar. Don heads straight down the corridor, down to the dressing room, the visitors' dressing room –

To stare into the mirror, the mirror, mirror on the dressing-room wall, combing his hair and saying his prayers, combing his hair and saying his prayers,

48

combing his hair and saying his prayers –

Don doesn't see you in the tunnel. Don doesn't see you on your bench –

Don rocking back and forth on the visitors' bench in the visitors' dug-out, rocking back and forth in his lucky blue suit and his old car coat –

From the very first whistle of the game to the very last one –

Rocking back and forth as his team niggle at your heels and pull at your shirts, clipping ankles and catching thighs, all elbows and knees to your fingers and thumbs –

Fingers and thumbs and a needless handball from Bobby Saxton to give away the penalty that Johnny Giles blasts into the back of your net –

Bobby Saxton will not play for Derby County again. Not play for you again. Never, never, never play again.

But at the very final whistle you stick out your own hand and you tell Don Revie, 'Well done, Don. See you next week.'

And this time Don Revie takes that outstretched hand but he looks right through you as he shakes it, shakes it, shakes it, looks right through you to the mirror, the mirror, mirror on the dressing-room wall, a comb in his hand and a prayer on his lips, a comb in his hand and a prayer on his lips, a comb in his hand and a prayer on his lips –

That he will win and you will lose. He will win and you will lose –

The rituals observed, the superstitions followed, all Don's prayers are answered.

You travel up to Elland Road twice in two weeks and twice in two weeks you are well beaten and you travel back down to Derby with nothing –

Nothing but ambitions fuelled; hearts hardened and lessons learnt –

Losing 2–0 in the FA Cup to goals from Lorimer and Charlton, then losing 3–2 in the second leg of the semi-final of the League Cup –

Two Derby goals that you know, in your hardened heart of hearts, flatter you and flatter Derby County in front of Elland Road –

In front of Leeds United, in front of Don Revie –

'Bit lucky there,' says Don. 'Thought God might be smiling on you.'

'I don't believe in luck,' you tell Don. 'And I don't believe in God.'

'So what do you believe in then?' asks Don Revie.

'Me,' you tell him. 'Brian Howard Clough.'

* * *

Just the three of us now; me, *his* shadow and *his* echo –

In the empty stadium, beneath the empty stand, off the empty corridor, the three of us in *his* old bloody office in my brand-new chair at my brand-new desk on *his* old fucking phone –

The spit from his lips. His tongue. The breath from his mouth. His stomach –

My brandy. My cigarette. My call –

Bill Nicholson ranting down the line about Martin Chivers; about modern footballers; about Mammon and greed –

'John Giles could be just the man you need,' I tell him. 'Be able to groom him. Mould him. Done a fine job with the Republic. Just what the Spurs need . . .'

Bill Nick's not keen, but Bill agrees to meet Giles. To talk to him.

I hang up, pour another brandy and light another cig, in my brand-new chair at my brand-new desk in *his* empty old office, off *his* empty old corridor, beneath *his* empty old stand in *his* empty old stadium –

Just the three of us: me, *his* shadow and *his* echo –

I walk out into the corridor. Round the corner –

Down the tunnel and out onto that pitch –

My brandy in one hand, my cigarette in the other, I stand in the centre circle again and look up into the dark, empty Yorkshire night –

Don't take it out on this world –

This night has a thousand eyes but just one song.

* * *

'It's easy to be a good manager,' Harry Storer *always used to say. 'All you have to do is sign good players.'*

Harry Storer was right. Harry Storer was always bloody right –

It's players that lose you games. Players that win you games –

Not theories. Not tactics. Not luck. Not superstition. Not God. Players –

You pick them, but they play. They win, they lose or they draw –

Not you. Not the manager. Them. The players –

You have kept the likes of Kevin Hector and Alan Durban. You have brought in the likes of John O'Hare, Roy McFarland and Alan Hinton –

You have tasted Elland Road. You have tasted the Big Time. But now it's back to the Second Division. Back to Portsmouth, Millwall, Huddersfield and Carlisle.

Derby County win a few games. Derby County lose a few –

Peaks and ruts. The hate mail comes. Ruts and peaks. The hate mail goes –

But there are still men like Fred Wallace; there are always men like Fred Wallace, standing on the terraces, behind the dug-out, outside the dressing room, in the corridors, in the boardrooms and at the bars –

'Dropped another place,' he tells you. 'Fifth from bottom now.'

Men who want you to fail. Men who want you to lose. Men who wish you dead. Men like Fred Wallace. There are always men like Fred and there are always doubts –

There are doubts in 1968 and there'll be doubts in 1978 –

Doubts and broken promises:

Derby County fail to win any of their last six games. Derby County lose their very last match at home to Blackpool. You have lost nineteen games in the 1967–68 season, scored seventy-one goals but conceded seventy-eight, and you have finished the season eighteenth in Division Two; one place lower than last season, last season when Derby sacked Tim Ward; two places lower than you promised the Rotary Club of Derby –

Promised the newspapers and the television, the town and the fans –

Broken promises and broken hearts –

Meanwhile, Hartlepools United have been promoted to Division Three –

Broken hearts and salted wounds –

Your glass breaks against his lounge wall, you are drunk and crying, shouting: 'Least we'd have fucking won something.'

'But we'd still be in the bloody Third Division,' says Peter.

You shake your head: 'This rate, we'll fucking pass them on our way down.'

'Brian, listen to me,' he says. 'Hartlepools was just a bloody stepping stone, always was and always will be. This time next year we'll be promoted as fucking Champions. And that'll just be the start of it. You wait and you see.'

You look up. You dry your eyes. You ask him, 'Do you promise me, Pete?'

'Cross my heart,' he nods. 'Cross my heart, Brian.'

'If you promise,' you tell him, 'then I believe you –'

Promises made and hearts healed –

Peter puts his arms around you, and your wives pick up the pieces.

Day Seven

Impeachment, impeachment, impeachment and the return of George bleeding Best. *Bestie.* Turning out for Dunstable Town and beating Manchester United 3–2. I've got a smile on my face and the radio on as I drive; a smile on my face until I see him, see Bestie by the side of the road, larger than life, any life –

His head full of demons; his own throat cut . . .

To sell them Brylcreem. Double Diamond beer and pork sausages.

They hate flair round here. Hate and fucking loathe it. Drag it out into the street and kick it in its guts, kill it and hang it from the posts for all to mock and see, from the motorway and the railway, from the factories and the fields, the houses and the hills –

Elland Road, Leeds, Leeds, Leeds –

Yorkshire. Nineteen seventy-four –

His own throat cut –

There is always a war coming, and England is always asleep.

★ ★ ★

You are bloody lucky not to have been sacked. Fucking lucky. Except you don't believe in luck. Talent and hard work. That's what you believe in. Ability and application. Discipline and determination. That's what got you from Clairville Common to Great Broughton. From a fitter and turner at ICI to centre-forward at Middlesbrough Football Club and then captain of Sunderland. That's what got you your 251 league goals in 274 games, got you your eighteen hat-tricks, your five four-goal hauls, and that's what's going to save you and Derby County –

That's what's going to get you what you want –

Ability and application. Discipline and determination –

No such thing as luck. No such thing as God. Just you, you and the players –

Peter reads out the pre-season team sheet; names like McFarland, O'Hare, Hector and Hinton. Peter puts down the team sheet. Pete says, 'Just two things missing now: a good bloody keeper and a bit of fucking experience.'

'And where are we going to find them?' you ask him. 'Not round here.'

'Don't you worry,' says Peter. 'I know just the keeper and just the man with the experience we need.'

★ ★ ★

There's another friendly tomorrow, another away game, my second game in charge. I stand at the far edge of the training pitch and watch them practising their set pieces, their corners and their free kicks –

Like clockwork.

Jimmy Gordon comes over. He says, 'Thought we'd knock it on the head, if that's all right with you, Boss?'

I look at my watch. It's not there.

'Half eleven,' says Jimmy. 'Anything you want to say to them before we finish?'

I shake my head. I tell him, 'What's to say?'

Jimmy shrugs his shoulders. He starts to walk back towards the team.

'Jimmy,' I call after him. 'Ask Eddie Gray to come over here, will you?'

Eddie's played in just one of the last forty-five Leeds games. He's in his purple tracksuit with his name on the back, sweating and out of breath. He says, 'Mr Clough?'

'Boss to you,' I tell him and then I ask him, 'You fit?'

'I think so,' he says.

'Think's no good to me,' I tell him. 'I want you to know so.'

'Well then, I know so,' he laughs. 'I know so, Boss.'

'Good lad,' I tell him. 'We'll give you a run-out tomorrow night then.'

Eddie sprints back over to his mates as someone shouts, 'You off and all then?'

★ ★ ★

'Me go and sign Dave Mackay? You must be bloody joking, or fucking drunk?'
you told Peter.

'You've pulled off bigger things than this,' he lied. 'Just go and try.'

'He's off into management,' you told him. 'Hanging up his boots.'

'It's only 99 per cent certain,' Peter lied again.

And so off you set. Just you. Not Pete –

You in your car to sign Dave Mackay –

Dave Mackay, the legendary Scottish wing-half with Tottenham Hotspur –
Tottenham Hotspur, the legendary 1960–61 double-winning Spurs –

The double-winning Spurs of the legendary Bill Nicholson.

So here you are at White Hart Lane, London. Been here since half seven
this morning. You want to speak to Bill Nicholson, but no one knows who you
are. Never heard of you. No one gives you the time of day. So you sit in your
car in their car park with the radio and the cricket on and you wait; wait and
wait and wait, in the car park in your Sunday best, wait and wait and wait
until you see Bill Nicholson –

Bill Nick, manager of Tottenham Hotspur, an inspiration and an idol to you.

'I've come to sign Dave Mackay,' you tell him.

'As far as I know,' says Bill Nick, 'Dave's off back to Edinburgh tomorrow.
He's off home to Hearts to become assistant manager.'

'Can I have a word with him?'

The phone is ringing in Bill Nick's office. Bill turns and, as he leaves me,
he says, 'Mackay's training, but you're welcome to wait.'

So you wait again, wait and wait and wait, in the passageway outside the
office, you wait and wait and wait until you hear the studs and then the voices.

Dave Mackay is older than you and he looks it. He marches straight up to
you. Hand out. Grip firm –

'Dave Mackay,' he says. 'And who the bloody hell are you?'

'My name's Brian Clough and I once had the pleasure of playing for
England against you in an Under-23 match,' you tell him.

'I do remember you now,' laughs Dave Mackay. 'You had a beautiful black
eye, a right bloody shiner.'

'Well, I'm the manager of Derby County now and I'm building a team
there that will be promoted this season and be First Division Champions in
three years.'

'Congratulations,' laughs Dave Mackay again. 'Now what can I do for you?'

'You can sign for Derby County,' you tell him. 'That's what.'

'No chance,' he says. 'I'm off home to Hearts tomorrow as assistant manager.'

'Tell you what then,' you smile. 'You go off and get yourself a nice hot bath and then we'll have a nice little chat about it. Never know your luck.'

But luck's got nothing to do with it. No such thing as luck −

Dave Mackay has his bath and then Dave Mackay takes you into the players' lounge at White Hart Lane, London. It is immaculate. Ladies in aprons bring you tea and sandwiches in china cups and on china plates. Then Dave Mackay takes you out onto the pitch at White Hart Lane and sits you down on the turf by the corner flag −

The stands and the seats immaculate. The sun shining on the pitch −

It is a beautiful place. It is a beautiful day.

'Derby is a sleeping giant,' you tell Dave Mackay. 'But since I arrived at the place, the crowds have already jumped to 20,000. The town backs me, the fans back me and, more importantly, the board back me 100 per cent. There's money for class and for skill and the wages to pay players with both; players like you and players like Roy McFarland.'

'Roy who?' asks Dave Mackay.

'McFarland,' you tell him. 'He's the next England centre-half, I'm telling you. Forget Jack Charlton. Forget Norman Hunter. Their days are numbered, mark my words. Alan Hinton, he's another of mine. Great winger and, now he's with us, he'll be back in that England side, Ramsey or no bloody Ramsey. And Kevin Hector? You must have heard of Kevin Hector?'

'Vaguely,' says Dave Mackay. 'Didn't he play for Bradford Park Avenue?'

'He did that,' you tell him. 'But now he's with us and you just can't stop the lad scoring goals. Not for love nor money.'

'Where did you finish last season?' asks Dave Mackay.

'Eighteenth.'

'Eighteenth?' he laughs. 'I'm very sorry, Brian. But I just wouldn't come to you. Not for ten thousand quid. Sorry.'

'I'll give you ten thousand quid, here and now, in cash.'

'No chance,' he laughs again. 'I'm off to Hearts tomorrow. That's that.'

'What would you come for then?' you ask him. 'If not ten grand?'

'I'd consider fifteen.'

'I can't get fifteen.'

'Then you're wasting your time,' he says. 'You might as well get off home.'

You look at Dave Mackay sat in the sunshine on the pitch at White Hart Lane, with its players' lounge and its china cups and its china plates; Dave Mackay, the greatest wing-half of his day; Dave Mackay, about to hang up his boots for a seat on the bench and a manager's suit –

You look at Dave Mackay and you tell him, 'I can get you fourteen thousand and, better than that, I can keep you playing.'

Dave Mackay looks down at the grass on the pitch at White Hart Lane, then up at the stands and the seats, and then Dave Mackay sticks out his hand and says, 'Done.'

* * *

In *his* corridors, in *his* shadows, they are waiting again; Maurice Lindley and Syd Owen –

Behind my back. Under their breath. Behind their hands. Through gritted teeth, they whisper –

'He's never really going to buy this lad McKenzie, is he?'

'Turn this place into a bloody circus,' they murmur –

'A bleeding pantomime,' they hiss.

I slam *his* door, I turn my key. In *his* office, at my desk –

I pick up *his* phone, I dial –

'Is that Duncan McKenzie?'

'Yes, this is he.'

'This is Brian Clough speaking,' I tell him. 'Now listen to me, you go get your coat and your skates on because you're coming to meet me at the Victoria Hotel in Sheffield. Half an hour and you'd better not be bloody late. And Duncan?'

'Yes, Mr Clough?'

'Bring a bloody pen because you're fucking signing for Leeds United today.'

* * *

You leave London behind. Thank Christ. *You drive straight back to the Baseball Ground.* Home sweet home. *You sing and shout all the way –*

Nailed it. Nailed it. Nailed it.

Peter is waiting. Pete is wondering, 'Any luck?'

'Fuck luck,' you tell him. 'He'll be here tomorrow to put his pen to our paper.'

'I don't bloody believe it,' shouts Peter. 'Never thought you had a prayer.'

'Fuck your prayers and all,' you tell him. 'Just believe in me. Brian Clough.'

'I do,' says Pete. 'You know I do.'

★ ★ ★

Duncan McKenzie is waiting for us in the posh lobby of the Victoria Hotel, Sheffield. He's looking at his watch, biting his nails and chain-smoking. I walk across that lobby and tell him, 'Forget Derby County. Forget the Spurs. You're coming to Leeds for £200 a week.'

Before he can reply or light another fag, I take him by his hand and waltz him into the bar. Duncan doesn't drink, but he will do today –

Champagne –

'Congratulations,' I tell him. 'You're my first signing for the new Leeds United. *My* Leeds United; honest and sincere, playing with flair and with humour, winning with style but winning the "right" way and winning the admiration of Liverpool fans, Arsenal fans and Derby fans, Tottenham and Birmingham fans –

'Because of THE WAY WE PLAY,' I tell him once, twice, three times.

Duncan McKenzie lights another cigarette and says, 'Yes, Mr Clough.'

'There'll be no more codding referees. No more haranguing referees. No more threatening referees. No more bloody bribing referees either,' I tell him.

Another cigarette, another 'Yes, Mr Clough.'

'No more *dirty* fucking Leeds!'

'Yes, Mr Clough.'

'And Duncan . . .'

'Yes, Mr Clough?'

'You call me Boss from now on.'

'Yes, Boss.'

I order another bottle of champagne. I go for a pee. I come back and change seats. I move round the table and sit down next to Duncan. I put my arm round him. I tell him, 'You're going to be my eyes and ears in that dressing room.'

'Yes, Boss.'

'My eyes and ears.'

'Yes, Boss.'

'They hate me,' I tell him. 'Despise me. And they'll hate you too. Despise you. But we'll be here long after they've all gone.'

'Yes, Boss.'

'Do you know why they hate me?' I ask him. 'Why they'll hate you?'

'No, Boss. Why?'

'Because we're not like them,' I tell him. 'Because we don't fucking cheat like them. Because we play fair and we win fair.'

'Yes, Boss.'

'Do you know how many bloody goals I scored when I was playing?'

'I'm sorry, Boss, I don't.'

'Two hundred and fifty-one,' I tell him.

'That's great, Boss.'

'You know how many fucking games that took me? League games?'

'I'm sorry, Boss, I don't.'

'Have a guess.'

'But I'm sorry, Boss, I –'

'Go on, have a bleeding guess.'

'Three hundred.'

'Two hundred and seventy-four,' I tell him. 'Just 274. Now what do you fucking think about that then?'

'Is that a record, Boss?'

'Course it bloody is,' I tell him. 'You know anyone else who's scored 251 goals in 274 league games, do you? Bobby bloody Charlton? Jimmy fucking Greaves? They score that many bloody goals in so few fucking games, did they? Did they bloody hell. So course it's a fucking record and it'll always be a fucking record because there'll never be another one like me. Never. Ever. Not you. Not no one. Now drink up because we're off to meet the press –'

'But I'm not drinking, Boss –'

I put the champagne glass back in his hand and tell him, 'You fuck-ing are now.'

★ ★ ★

'Dave,' Peter says to Mackay, 'the gaffer's got a wee bit of a shock for you.'

Mackay is sat in your office with his accountant and his solicitor –

The signed contract is in your drawer. The pen back in his pocket –

There is a smile on your face. A smile on his face –

£250 a week, plus promotion bonuses –

Dave Mackay is on £16,000 a year –

More than George Best and Denis Law. More than Bobby Moore –

You have the most expensive player in the entire Football League –

Now you're going to turn him into the best.

Peter locks the door. Takes the phone off the hook –

Dave Mackay stops smiling. Dave Mackay asks, 'What kind of shock?'

'He wants you to play a different role here,' says Peter.

'What kind of role?'

'The boss wants to play you as a sweeper.'

Dave Mackay looks across the desk at you. Dave says, 'I can't do it.'

'Listen to me. We've got this young lad here called Roy McFarland,' you tell him. 'He's the best centre-half in the league. He's that quick that your pace won't be needed. So I want you to drop off him. Then you'll be able to see everything –'

'Use your loaf and your tongue,' says Pete. 'Let the young lads do the running.'

'They need a captain; someone with experience; someone to tell them when to hold it and when to pass it. That's you, Dave.'

Dave Mackay is full of doubts. Fears. Dave Mackay is shaking his head.

'You'll control the game,' you tell him. 'We'll win the league. We promise you.'

'Look,' he says, 'I cover every blade of grass.'

'You're a stone overweight,' you tell him. 'And a year older than me.'

'Every blade of grass,' says Dave Mackay again. 'That's my game.'

'That was then,' you tell him. 'This is now.'

★ ★ ★

'Apart from Leeds United,' Duncan McKenzie is telling the press in the Victoria Hotel, 'I also spoke to Spurs and Birmingham City. But when Mr Clough here, whom I had not met before, when he came to see me, I was very flattered and so naturally I chose Leeds United. I think the move will also improve my chances of playing for England.'

'What do you feel about Leeds paying £250,000 for you?'

'It's a rather inflated market in football these days and you just have to live with these high fees. But it's not a problem for me.'

'What do you feel about your rivals for a first-team place? The likes of Allan Clarke, Mick Jones and Joe Jordan?'

'I know I will have to fight hard for my place at Leeds United. I do not expect anything gift-wrapped or on a plate for me. I never have.'

'Brian?' they ask me. 'Anything you want to add?'

'Duncan is a superb acquisition to the Leeds squad. He is a highly intelligent young man and among the things that have appealed to me about him were his approach to the game and his desire to score goals. I am delighted that he has joined Leeds but, of course, I have known about him for some time. After all, I lived next door to him, as it were, when I was manager at Derby.'

'Were there any problems?' they ask. 'Any problems signing him?'

'None,' I tell them. 'Because when anyone gets the chance to join Leeds United and Brian Clough there are never any problems.'

'Will he be in the squad for the Villa game tomorrow night?'

'I doubt that,' I tell them. 'He'll meet the rest of the players tomorrow morning.'

'Duncan?' they ask again. 'How do you feel about meeting the rest of the team and joining the League Champions? Are you nervous?'

'They have proved themselves to be Britain's top side for the last five or six years.'

I give him a nudge to his ribs. A wink and tell him, 'Apart from when I was at Derby County, that is.'

Duncan blinks. Duncan smiles. Duncan says, 'Apart from Derby County, yes.'

The press take their notes. The press take their photos –

The press finish their drinks and I order some more –

I look at my watch. It's not there –

'What time is it, lad?' I ask McKenzie.

'Half past eight, Boss,' he says.

'Fucking hell,' I tell him and the bar of the Victoria Hotel. 'The meal!'

'What meal, Boss?' asks McKenzie.

'None of your bloody business,' I tell him. 'You get yourself off home to bed. I'll see you at half eight tomorrow morning at Elland Road. And Duncan?'

'Yes, Boss?'

'You'd better not be fucking late.'

★ ★ ★

You take Dave Mackay on a tour of the Baseball Ground. The dressing rooms and the training pitch, off the ring road, with its old railway carriage where the players change for the practice matches. Dave Mackay is thinking about White Hart Lane, about the china cups and the china plates, about the cups he's won and the medals he owns –

Dave Mackay is full of doubts again. Fears. Dave is shaking his head again –

'You'll win the league?' he asks. 'You promise me, do you?'

'Cross our hearts,' you tell him. 'Cross our hearts.'

★ ★ ★

'You're fucking well late,' hisses Sam Bolton as I take my seat at the table. The top table. The Harewood Rooms. The Queen's Hotel –

The directors, the players, the coaching staff, the office staff, even the bleeding tea ladies; the entire Leeds United family and their wives and their husbands on their Big Night Out.

'I've lost my watch,' I tell him. 'Or someone's nicked it.'

'Food's finished,' says Sam Bolton. 'Folk are just waiting for you.'

I stand up. I straighten the cuffs of my shirt and I tell them, 'I feel like a bloody intruder at a party you have all worked for over the past year. It is a great pity that Don Revie and Les Cocker are not here to enjoy it because they are the men who won the Championship with

61

you. Not me. But it will be my turn next year. Mark my words.'

I sit back down. I light another fag. I pour myself another drink –
I listen for the sound of a pin drop, drop, dropping.

Day Eight

You have bought Dave Mackay to be your sweeper. You have bought Pete's old mate Les Green from the Southern League to be your keeper. You know that this time the final pieces are in their places. You know that this time the traditional pre-season optimism is well-founded, built on bloody rock, rock, rock –

Rock, rock, rocks like Dave Mackay and Les Green.

You can't wait for the first game of the new season, can't fucking wait –

Away at Blackburn Rovers. Roy McFarland scores. But so do they –

You draw 1–1. One point. Away from home. Not bad.

Back at home you play Blackpool. John O'Hare scores. But so do they –

You draw 1–1 again. One point again. But at home. Not good.

You go to Bramall Lane. To Sheffield United. You don't score. But they do –

You lose 2–0. No points. Bad, bad, bad; you are eighteenth in Division Two. Eighteenth again and on sinking shifting, fucking sand, sand, sands –

There are tears again and there are broken glasses. Then Peter puts out his fag and Peter gets out his little black book and Peter says –

'I know just the player. Just the club.'

★ ★ ★

Nothing is ever the way they say it is. Nothing is ever the way you want it to be. John Giles knocks on *his* door. John Giles sits down opposite my desk. He says nothing. He just sits. He just waits –

'I've had Bill Nick on the phone this morning,' I tell him.

The Irishman smiles, brushes the tops of his trouser legs and asks me, 'You sure now you didn't call him?'

'Why would I do that?'

'Because you want me gone,' he smiles.

'Why would I want you gone, John?'

63

'Because you hate me,' he smiles. 'Can't stand the sight of me.'

'Look, what's said is said,' I tell him. 'But the past is the past to me. Finished.'

'That'd be very convenient for you,' he says.

'Look, I've told you before,' I tell him again. 'You have intelligence, skill, agility and the best passing ability in the game.'

'But you'd still be glad to see the back of me, now wouldn't you?'

'Look,' I tell him. 'There are things I don't like about your game and I've told you to your face what they are, but I've nothing against you as a person. I admire what you've done with Ireland and so does Bill Nicholson. That's why he called.'

'And so what did Mr Nicholson say?'

'He said he'd like to talk to you about going to Spurs as assistant manager.'

'Still playing as well?'

'Yes.'

'Nice to know someone thinks there's life left yet in these old legs of mine.'

'I've never said you've shot it,' I tell him. 'Never said that.'

'It's written all over your face, man.'

'Are you interested in talking with Bill Nicholson or not?'

'Of course I'm interested,' he smiles. 'Who wouldn't be?'

'How about this then?' I tell him. 'No need for you to travel with the team to Villa tonight. You stay up here and give Bill Nicholson a call. Have a chat with Bill and with your family. Arrange a time to go down and meet him, see the lay of the land.'

'That's very kind of you,' he says. 'But I'll travel with you all the same tonight.'

★ ★ ★

You are in the dug-out at Leeds Road, Huddersfield. You are losing 2–0 again. You will have taken just two points from a possible eight. You are filled with doubts. Fucking racked with fear. But then something happens; something bloody special happens –

Your team are under pressure in their own six-yard area. The team look like conceding a third. The ball comes to Mackay. Mackay puts his foot on the ball –

'Kick it! Shift it!' shouts Jack Burkitt beside you. 'Get fucking rid!'

'Shut up, Jack,' says Peter. 'This is what we bought him for. This is what we want him to do. To put his foot on it. To pass it out. To lead and teach by example –'

Mackay plays the ball out and defence becomes attack –

Defence becomes attack. Defence becomes attack –

'We'll buy Carlin tomorrow,' whispers Peter. 'Then we'll be on our way.'

* * *

I get on the coach last and make Allan Clarke shift so I can sit next to Billy Bremner again. I try and make chit-chat. To break the ice. But Billy Bremner doesn't give a fuck about President Nixon or George Best. He's not interested in Frank Sinatra or Muhammad Ali. He doesn't want to talk about the World Cup, about playing against Brazil. Doesn't want to talk about his holidays. His family full stop. Bremner just looks out of the window and smokes the whole way down to Birmingham. Then, as the coach pulls into Villa Park, he turns to me and he says, 'If you're looking for a pal, Mr Clough, you can count me out.'

* * *

When you went to Bramall Lane last week, when you went to Sheffield United and they beat you 2–0, you blamed it on Willie Carlin. You've had enough of going to places like Sheffield bloody United and losing 2–0 because of players like Willie fucking Carlin –

You've had enough of failure. Doubts. Had enough of disappointment –

Had enough of Willie fucking Carlin, hard little Scouse bastard –

Dirty little bugger of a bloke, had enough, enough, enough –

'But you'll do for me,' you tell him. 'If you do as you're bloody told.'

'I'd rather play for fucking Leeds,' he tells you.

'You'd fucking fit right in and all,' you laugh. 'But they don't bloody want you, do they, Willie?'

'They bloody might,' he says. 'You don't fucking know that.'

'Well, I don't see Don fucking Revie sat here, do you?'

'I don't know what I see.'

'Well, I know what I see,' you tell him. 'I see a five-foot-four dirty little bastard who spends half the fucking match arguing with the referee and who's been booked eighteen bloody times and sent off another three fucking times for his trouble. Now that won't do for me because you're no good to me suspended. But if you behave yourself and keep that great big bloody Scouse gob of yours shut, I'll get you a bloody Championship medal to go with all your fucking bookings and sendings-off.'

'And what if I can't behave myself? What if I don't fucking want to?'

'You will,' you laugh. 'Because I'm not asking you, I'm fucking telling you.'

★ ★ ★

I'm down in the dug-out for this game. This testimonial. This centenary game at Villa Park. Jimmy and me with Stewart, Cherry and Johnny fucking Giles for company –

My one and only plan before the game to make sure Johnny bloody Giles doesn't get a fucking kick, but then Madeley has to come off and so on goes John –

Thank fuck for Allan Clarke, two great goals; one with his head from a Reaney cross, the other sliding into a low centre from the Irishman. The rest of the match is the same old *dirty* Leeds; McQueen gets booked, then Cooper gives away a penalty – saved by Harvey – then Hunter gives away another, but the Villa lad misses. Half-time I tell Jimmy to take off Harvey and Hunter and stick on Stewart and Cherry while I go for a drink and a chat in the top of the stands with Jimmy Bloomfield, the Leicester manager –

We talk about Shilton, swaps and trades. We talk about money –

'Not bad that one you've got,' says Jimmy Bloomfield.

'Harvey? You're bloody joking?' I ask him. 'He's fucking shit.'

'He saved that penalty well enough.'

'You can have him,' I tell Jimmy. 'If you like him so much, him and two hundred grand, and I'll take Peter Shilton off your hands.'

'He'll get you the bloody sack, will Shilton,' says Jimmy. 'He's trouble.'

'Then he's my kind of fucking trouble,' I tell him.

Dirty Leeds concede a goal but still win 2–1 –

Not a bad start; two games, two wins –

'Not a bad bloody start at all,' says Jimmy Bloomfield as we shake our hands and say our goodbyes and head down the stairs, round the corners and down the corridors.

★ ★ ★

There is always one game in every season, one moment in that game, that one moment in that one game in the season when everything can change, when things can either come together or fall apart for the rest of the season, that one moment when you know you will win this game and then the next and the next, when you know you will have a season to remember, a season never to forget –

The Football League Cup, third round replay; Wednesday 2 October 1968 –

Derby. Derby. Derby. Derby. Derby. Derby –

This is one of those nights you will never forget. This is one of those nights when everything comes together and stays together, one of those nights when everything changes, everything turns –

Derby. Derby. Derby. Derby. Derby. Derby –

You went down to Stamford Bridge last week where Chelsea were unbeaten in twenty home games. You went down to Stamford Bridge and you took everything Chelsea could throw at you and you held them 0–0, held the likes of Bonetti, Hollins and Osgood –

Now you've brought them back here, here to the Baseball Ground, here where there's no running track around the pitch, here where you hear every cheer and every jeer from the 34,000 crowd, here where there's no place to hide –

Derby. Derby. Derby. Derby. Derby. Derby –

'No fucking hiding place,' you tell the Derby dressing room. 'Not tonight; tonight we're going to see who's fucking who out there.'

Derby. Derby. Derby. Derby. Derby. Derby –

Green. Webster. Robson. Durban. McFarland. Mackay. Walker. Carlin. O'Hare. Hinton. Hector –

Derby. Derby. Derby. Derby. Derby. Derby —

That one moment when everything can change, when things either come together or fall apart for the rest of the season, that one moment comes in the twenty-sixth minute of the first half, comes when Houseman jumps a Carlin tackle and slips the ball across to Birchenall, who shoots into the top corner of the net from thirty yards out and puts you a goal down —

Derby. Derby. Derby. Derby. Derby. Derby —

This is that one moment, that one moment when you look into the eyes of the players out on that pitch, you look into their eyes and down into their hearts and you listen to the noise of the crowd, the thundering noise of 34,000 hearts up in those stands and you listen for the eleven hearts out on that pitch, and you hear those hearts beating as one, and you know that this is the moment you have been waiting for, that one moment when everything changes, when no one gives up, when no one goes home, when no one hides —

Derby. Derby. Derby. Derby. Derby. Derby —

From the twenty-sixth minute to half-time, from half-time to the seventy-seventh minute, no one hides, no one goes home and no one gives up, not the players and not the crowd, and then, in that seventy-seventh minute, Carlin races through the middle and back-heels the ball for Mackay to hit home from thirty yards out, and everyone knows, everyone knows now —

Derby. Derby. Derby. Derby. Derby. Derby —

Everyone knows now that when Hutchinson breaks for Chelsea, then Walker will be there for you, not once but twice, and that then Walker will burst forward down the left and cross for Durban to head past Bonetti —

Derby. Derby. Derby. Derby. Derby. Derby —

And everyone knows now that you haven't finished yet, that when Bonetti and Hector both go for the same ball that Hector will get there first to make it 3–1 in the eighty-first minute, because everyone knows now that everything has changed, that everything has turned, everything has come together —

Derby. Derby. Derby. Derby. Derby. Derby —

The things you've done and the things you've said; the fists you've raised and the bruises you've kissed. Everything has finally come together and will now stay together —

Derby. Derby. Derby. Derby. Derby. Derby —

That this will be a season to remember, a season never to forget —

Derby. Derby. Derby. Derby. Derby. Derby –

'What a wonderful display by the team and how wonderful our supporters were,' says the chairman. 'This is a night I shall remember as long as I live.'

Derby. Derby. Derby. Derby. Derby. Derby –

'I was delighted for the players,' you tell the press, the cameras and the whole wide world. 'This was easily the best performance since I have come to Derby.'

* * *

I stand in the corridor at Villa Park. I finish my fag and I take a deep breath. Then I open the door to the visitors' dressing room –

The place goes dead. The players looking at their sock tags; their vain bleeding sock tags with their numbers on; those bloody tags they throw to the home crowd after every game like Roman fucking gladiators or something. Then Norman Hunter pipes up, 'Brilliant pass that, Gilesy. Beautiful ball for Clarkey. Put it on a plate for him. Lovely.'

'Forget that fucking pass,' I tell him. 'What about the way Clarkey stuck it in?'

Bites Yer Legs shakes his head. Irishman smiles. Sniffer basking –

'That was class,' I tell him. 'And don't you forget the Irishman wouldn't have even been on that bloody pitch if Madeley kept himself in better fucking nick.'

'Played a blinder though,' says Bites Yer Legs. 'A fucking blinder.'

'Better make the bloody most of him then,' I tell him. 'Destined for bigger things, aren't you, Irishman?'

'There's nothing bigger than playing,' says Giles. 'You know that, Mr Clough.'

The players are watching us now; whispering and wondering.

I leave them to it. I stand outside in the corridor. I light a fag. I listen –

'No respect,' I hear them say, 'for the traditions of Leeds United.'

Duncan McKenzie walks past in his posh new suit. McKenzie turns and says, 'They weren't bad, were they? I thought Johnny Giles was ace.'

'Fuck off,' I tell him. 'You can bloody walk back to Leeds for that.'

* * *

The Chelsea game has brought a swagger to your side. To the whole club. To the whole bloody town. But you know in your heart of hearts that it is Dave Mackay who has brought that swagger to this side. This whole club. This whole fucking town. Not you –

In your heart of hearts.

You switch training to Tuesdays so Dave can have Sundays and Mondays off to take care of his tie shop back down in London. You put him up at the Midland Hotel for the rest of the week and move Roy McFarland in there to keep him company while Dave drinks his fill from Monday night through to Thursday night. But then Dave doesn't touch another drop from Friday morning through to Saturday teatime –

This man is *Derby County. The foundation and the cornerstone –*

And you're the first to recognize this; the first to treat him as such –

You chat to him while the rest of the team run their laps. You bring him into the team talks with an easy, 'What do you think, captain?'

Together you, Peter and Dave Mackay turn this team from part-timers into full-timers; no more afternoon golf, no more selling insurance door to door –

Morning after morning, you drum the basics into them –

'Keep the ball down. Play it forward. On the ground. To feet. Hold it. Pass it. Score! Win the ball back. Keep the ball down. Play it forward. On the ground. To feet. Hold it. Pass it. Score! Win the ball back . . .'

And you don't just tell them how to do these things, you sodding well show them, scoring in every single six-a-side match, then changing with your *lads, bathing with* your *lads, and joking with* your *lads –*

This is good bloody management. This is you and Pete at your best –

Spotting the talent, buying the talent and then handling that fucking talent –

Insulting that talent. Humiliating that talent. Threatening that talent –

Hurting that talent and then kissing it fucking better again –

Again and again, bringing out the bloody best in folk –

In that fucking talent, that's you and that's Peter.

Day Nine

I don't believe this. I get out of my car. *Don't fucking believe this.* I slam the door. *Bastards.* I lock it. *Who the fucking hell do they think they are?* I put my jacket on. *Bastards. Bastards. Bastards.* I walk across the car park. *Lazy fucking bastards, the bloody lot of them.* Up the banking to the training ground and I ask Jimmy Gordon, Jimmy who's picking up the balls and putting them back in their bags, ask Jimmy, 'Where the fucking hell are they?'

'They've finished up. They've all gone for their soap downs and their massages.'

'Get them back out here,' I tell him. 'I'm the fucking manager here. I decide −'

'But you weren't −'

'I wasn't what?'

'Nothing,' says Jimmy. 'You're right, Boss. You're right.'

'I know I am,' I tell him. 'Now you get them back out here and you fucking tell them from me, you tell them they finish when I say so. Not a moment before.'

'Boss, maybe it'd be better coming −'

'Do it,' I tell him. 'Or I'll fucking sack you and all.'

Jimmy does it and, ten minutes later, there are sixteen very long faces in sixteen dirty purple tracksuits out on that training pitch; sixteen long faces until Duncan McKenzie, the new boy, gets hold of the ball and runs with it at Bites Yer Legs −

'Nutmeg, Norman!' he shouts out and plays the ball through Hunter's legs −

Everyone is laughing now, even Hunter. Even Bremner. Even Giles −

I clap my hands. Jimmy blows his whistle. The laughter stops.

'Now before you all go off for your lovely hot baths,' I tell them, 'before you all piss off in your lovely new suits and your lovely flash cars to your lovely new houses and your lovely young wives, you can all get down on your bloody hands and knees and look for my fucking watch!'

★ ★ ★

You and the team have three days' relaxation at your Marlow HQ. You and the team go down to London on a luxury team coach. You and the team spend a night at one of the capital's finest hotels. You and the team have your breakfasts in your beds. You and the team arrive to a splendid reception from your travelling fans at Selhurst Park. You and the team go and get changed. Then you and the team run out onto that pitch and beat Crystal Palace 2–1 with goals from Roy McFarland and Willie Carlin –

You beat high-flying Crystal Palace and you go top, top, top –

This is the day, this is the day, this is the day –

The day Derby go top of Division Two –

Saturday 30 November 1968.

Everything about you and Derby County has First Division stamped all over it; your preparation, your luxury coach, your choice of hotels, the style of your play and the manner of your victories –

You have lost only once in the league since you went to Leeds Road and were beaten by Huddersfield Town. Just once in the league since that day –

Just once since Willie Carlin joined.

Following that victory over Chelsea, you also went to First Division Everton and drew 0–0 in the fourth round of the League Cup. Then you brought them back to the Baseball Ground and beat them 1–0; another night to remember in a season never to forget. Next you got Swindon in the fifth round but you could only draw at the Baseball Ground. Swindon then beat you at their place and so now you're out of the League Cup –

You took your eye off the ball. Took your eye off the ball. Your eye off the ball –

You were bloody angry at the time, fucking furious at the time, but not now –

Not now everything about you has First Division stamped all over it. Not now you are favourites to go up. Not now you are favourites to go up as Champions –

Not now you've gone from eleventh to first in just three months –
Not now you've been named Manager of the Month –
Not now you're top, top, top of Division Two.

★ ★ ★

Under the stand. Through the doors. Round the corner. I'm walking down the corridor towards Syd Owen. He walks past me without a word, without a look. Then he says behind my back. Under his breath. Behind his hand. Through gritted teeth, Syd says something that sounds like: '*Anything to do with peacocks is fatal . . .*'

I stop. I turn round. I ask, 'You what?'

'There was a phone call for you.'

I ask him, 'When?'

Syd's stopped now, turned round and is facing me in the corridor. 'Yesterday.'

I ask him, 'Where was I?'

'How I should I know?' he laughs. 'Probably off selling or buying someone.'

'What time?'

'Morning, afternoon,' he shrugs. 'Not sure.'

'Well, who was it?'

'I can't remember.'

'But you answered it?'

'Oh, aye.'

'Where? Which phone?'

'The one in the office.'

'*My* office?'

'It is now,' he laughs again.

'What were you doing in *my* office?'

'I was looking for the Matthewson file,' he says. 'For Saturday.'

'The *what* file?'

'The file on Bob Matthewson,' he says, slowly.

'And who the fucking hell is Bob Matthewson when he's at home?'

'You mean you don't know?' he asks.

73

'Course I don't fucking know, Syd,' I tell him. 'That's why I'm fucking asking you who the bloody hell he is.'

'No one special,' he smiles. 'Just the referee for Saturday.'

'You've got bloody files on the fucking referees?'

'Course we have,' he says. 'What do you think we are, amateurs?'

'Why?'

'Turn a game can a referee,' he says. 'Specially if you know how to help him.'

'Well, I told you,' I tell him again, 'I burnt all them fucking files with his desk.'

'Lucky we've got copies then, isn't it?'

I walk down the corridor towards him, my finger out and pointing straight at him. 'I don't need files on referees and I don't need files on other teams and I don't need you in my office and I don't need you to answer my phone for me. Is that clear?'

'Their scream forebodes rain and even death . . .'

'You what?' I ask him again. 'Is that clear?'

'Crystal,' says Syd. 'Crystal.'

★ ★ ★

'You're fucking shit,' you tell him –

Tell Green. Tell Webster. Tell Robson. Tell Durban. Tell McFarland. Tell McGovern. Tell Carlin. Tell O'Hare. Tell Hector. Tell Hinton –

You tell the lot of them, the bloody lot of them except Dave Mackay –

'Utter fucking shit. And, worse than that, you're a fucking coward. The only fucking time you fucking ran out there was to find a new fucking hole to fucking hide in. So that makes you a fucking coward; a fucking coward to yourself, to your teammates, to me and the staff, to the club and the fans who pay your fucking wages, and to your own fucking moral sense of responsibility. So you're a fucking coward and you're fucking finished, you fucking cunt!'

You slam the dressing room door. Bang! You storm off down the corridor –

'A cunt and a coward! A cunt and a coward! A cunt and a coward!'

Peter puts his arm round him. Peter tells him, 'The boss didn't mean that.' Tells Green. Tells Webster. Tells Robson. Tells Durban. Tells McFarland.

Tells McGovern. Tells Carlin. Tells O'Hare. Tells Hector. Tells Hinton –
  He tells the lot of them, the bloody lot of them except Dave Mackay –
  'Didn't mean a word of it, you know that. The boss is just disappointed
because he has so much hope for you, so much belief in you. He knows you can
be the best player out on that park, so he's just upset because today you weren't,
because you let yourself down and you let him down. That's why he's angry,
angry because he cares about you, because he loves you, thinks the bloody world
of you. You know that, don't you?'
  And Green nods. Webster nods. Robson nods. Durban nods. McFarland nods.
McGovern nods. Carlin nods. O'Hare nods. Hector nods. Hinton nods –
  The lot of them nod, the bloody lot of them except Dave Mackay –
  It is 18 January 1969 and you have just lost 2–0 at Charlton –
  This is your first defeat in fourteen league games –
  You've got it down to a fine art, you and Peter –
  And you're still top of Division Two.

* * *

There's another set of feet outside the office, another knock –
  'What?' I shout.
  Terry Yorath opens the door slowly. Terry Yorath puts his head inside.
  'What do you want, Taffy?' I ask him.
  Yorath says, 'Is it possible to have a word please, Mr Clough?'
  'It's Boss to you, Taff,' I tell him.
  Yorath says again, 'Is it possible to have a word please, Boss?'
  'Yes,' I tell him. 'If you take your hands out of your bloody pockets.'
  Yorath takes his hands out of his pockets. 'It's about my contract.'
  'What about it?'
  Yorath puts his hands back in his pockets, then takes them out again
and says, 'It's run out, Boss. My contract . . .'
  'And?'
  Yorath says, 'And I was hoping I'd get a new one.'
  'Did you talk about a new contract with my predecessor?'
  Yorath nods. Yorath says, 'Yes, I did.'
  'And what did he say?'

Yorath wipes his mouth. Yorath says, 'He promised to double my wages, Boss.'

'To what?'

Yorath wipes his mouth again. Yorath says, '£250 a week.'

'£250 a fucking week! Why the bloody hell would he promise to do that?'

Yorath shrugs his shoulders. Yorath says, 'Because I played in more than thirty first-team games last season, I suppose. And because we won the title.'

'Who else knew about this promise?'

Yorath shrugs his shoulders again. Yorath says, 'Just the chairman, I think.'

'OK then,' I tell him. 'I believe you. You'll have your new contract by Monday.'

Yorath nods his head. Yorath mutters his thank-yous. But Yorath doesn't move.

'Something else on your mind is there, Taff?' I ask him.

'Wembley, Boss.'

'What about it?' I ask him.

'Will I be playing?'

'No,' I tell him.

'Will I be in the squad?'

'No,' I tell him again.

'So I won't be going down to London?'

'No,' I tell him for the third time.

Yorath looks up at me. Yorath asks, 'So what'll I be doing on Saturday, Boss?'

'You'll be turning out for the reserves at Witton Albion, Taff.'

★ ★ ★

You are on your way. You, Peter, Dave Mackay and Derby County –

These are the happiest hours of your life . . .

This old, unfashionable, run-of-the-mill, humdrum provincial little club is on the bloody up and the board and Sam Longson can't do enough for you –

The happiest hours and days of your life . . .

The keys to his cars. His holiday homes and his drinks cabinet. His wallet and his safe. Longson had had you in the York Hotel when you first came down to Derby; then he moved you over to the Midland, the hotel where you later set up Dave and Roy, the hotel that's now a home from home for you and the whole bloody team; Longson then helped you and your wife and children find a house just outside Derby, a home of your own –

The happiest hours, days and weeks of your life . . .

You sweep the terraces and you sign the players. You take the training and you do the mail. You clean the baths and you water the grass. You talk to the press and you talk on the telly. You walk the pitch every Sunday morning and you plot, plot, plot and plot –

The happiest hours, days, weeks and months of your life . . .

Plot to stay top. Plot to go up. Plot to stay up. Plot –

The happiest times of your life.

* * *

I have locked the office door. Put a chair against it. I have opened a new bottle of Martell. Lit another fag. Tomorrow Leeds will have to travel to London. For the Charity Shield; the First Division Champions vs the FA Cup holders; Leeds United vs Liverpool. The first time the Charity Shield has ever been played at Wembley; the first time it's ever been shown on television. The new curtain-raiser for the new season. The brainchild of Ted Croker, the new Secretary and self-styled Chief Executive of the Football Association, despite the protests of both Leeds United and Liverpool –

Two years ago, when Derby County won the title, I refused to take part in the old Charity Shield; pissed them off no end, the FA, the Derby board, the fucking lot of them. Two years ago, I sent Derby on their pre-arranged pre-season tour of Germany instead –

This year there's no escape. No escape at all –

Three o'clock or thereabouts on Saturday afternoon, I will have to lead out that team at Wembley. *His* team. Not mine. Three o'clock, I will have to stand side by side with the great Bill Shankly. It will be

Shankly's last bow, having retired in July. His last chance to lead out a team of his at Wembley –

The Wembley Way. The twin towers. The Empire Stadium. The tunnel. The National Anthem. The handshakes. The presentations. The crowd. The kick-off . . .

Three o'clock. Three o'clock –

And I'll wish I wasn't there, anywhere but there.

Day Ten

There have been alarms and there have been scares. There have been insults and there have been threats. Broken cups and slammed doors. Doubts and fears. But you were top in February and you were top in March and you're still top now in April –

You beat Fulham 1–0 and you beat Bolton 5–1 –

You are guaranteed promotion with four games still to go, four games that could also see you promoted as Second Division Champions, four games starting with a 1–0 victory over Sheffield United, a 1–0 victory that opens up a seven-point lead over Crystal Palace and means Palace need to win all of their final four games while you need just two points from your last three games to be Champions, two points from your last three games starting today –

Saturday 12 April 1969.

You and the team are back down in London. Back down on your luxury team coach to one of the capital's finest hotels, back down to your breakfasts in your beds and another splendid reception from your travelling fans, this time on Cold Blow Lane, this time outside the Den –

There is a moment of panic, a moment of doubt, when it turns out you've brought the wrong kit, when it turns out you'll have to play in the Millwall away kit –

'It's a bloody omen,' says Jack Burkitt. 'A bad bloody omen.'

'Bollocks,' you tell him. 'You're talking fucking bollocks.'

You run out onto the pitch at the Den in the Millwall away kit and the Millwall players line up to applaud you, applaud your promotion –

But it's not promotion you're thinking about today –

Two bloody points and that fucking title is all you're thinking about today and from the kick-off you control the match, you take it by the scruff of its bloody neck and never let it fucking go, not to Millwall, not to their fans, not to the bloody acrobatics of their keeper King, not to the fucking dust and wind that bellows round Cold Blow Lane –

Nothing is going to stop you. No way. Not today. Bloody nothing –

Not Millwall. Not their fans. Not their keeper –

Not the dust and not the wind. Not today:

Mackay rolls a short free-kick to Webster. Webster runs down the right wing. Webster crosses to McFarland. McFarland heads it back across their goal to Carlin and Willie nods it home to score the only goal of the game –

Short, sweet, simple fucking football and you are the Champions –

The Champions of Division Two –

You are the Champions.

★ ★ ★

Leeds will stay at the Royal Garden Hotel in Kensington tonight and so we are due to leave Elland Road for London this afternoon. But the team still trains this morning while I do contracts; Madeley, Allan Clarke and Frankie Gray. The only two contracts not yet signed are those for Giles and Yorath. Then there is the press conference –

That length of rope with which to hang yourself. That knife. That gun . . .

'There have been no moves whatsoever for Shilton,' I tell the pens and the pads. 'I've made no offer and no enquiry and, although I've contemplated buying Peter Shilton a million times before, I have not done so while I have been at Leeds.'

They chew the ends of their biros and they ask, 'What about all the rumours?'

'Nobody is going from this club in exchange deals or any other deals until I have been here a very long time. Nobody has asked for a transfer, nobody wants to go and nobody is going. I have two goal-keepers with whom I am delighted.'

They scratch their chins and they ask, 'Why hasn't Giles signed his contract yet?'

'I have not yet seen him about his contract,' I tell them. 'That's all there is to it.'

They blow their noses and they ask, 'What are your feelings about tomorrow?'

'The game gives us a terrific chance to get away to a good start,' I tell them. 'You cannot have tougher opposition than Bill Shankly and Liverpool, and everybody will be going like bombs. We have trained hard all week, got on with our jobs, made a signing and are all now looking forward to the match.'

Liar, liar, I'm thinking. They're thinking, *Your whole body's on fire.*

The press conference over, I show my face to the directors then I change my gear, get my suitcase from the office and go out to the coach. They are all sat there in their Sunday best, smoking and sulking, whispering and waiting for me, with their paperback books and their packs of cards. I make Sniffer shift again so I can sit next to Bremner again. Billy rolls his eyes and lights another fag –

'You don't fucking give up, do you?' he says.

'Never,' I tell the man –

This the man I watched and commentated on for ITV at the World Cup this summer, captaining his country, beating Zaire 2–0, drawing with Brazil, drawing with Yugoslavia, sticking it up the press boys, this the man who *was* Scotland, this man who sits beside me now and stares out of the window at the rain and the motorway, this man who Revie thought of as a second son, this man who would run through fire for Don, who walks on water for the people of Leeds, the people of Scotland, this man beside me now, lighting another fucking fag and pretending to read a bloody paperback book until he turns to me, until he finally turns to me and asks –

'You ever play at Wembley did you, Mr Clough?'

The cunt. Cunt. Cunt –

Halfway down the M1, the coach stops at a service area. Everyone gets off for a coffee and a piss. It's raining hard as I walk across the car park to the foyer –

The fucking cunt. Cunt. Cunt –

I come out of the toilets and they're all stood around the one-arm bandits, signing autographs and getting kisses off the waitresses –

The cunts. Cunts. Cunts –

'Come on,' I tell them. 'Let's all go for a walk around the car park.'

'Walk?' spits Bremner. 'I've never been for a fucking walk in my life.'

'Get going,' I tell them. 'Stretch your legs, you lazy buggers!'

They stare at me and, for one moment, they look like they won't go. But then Captain Bremner opens the door and leads them one by one out into the rain and the car park, leads the League Champions around the service-station car park –

In the rain. In their Sunday best. In the rain. In their polished shoes –

'Good man, Billy,' I tell him as I catch him up. 'Stretch them legs.'

'Fuck off,' he hisses at me. 'I'm getting bloody soaked here.'

'I thought you lot bloody loved these kinds of communal activities,' I tell him. 'Round of golf. Bit of bingo. Carpet bowls. Thought that was all part of Don's appeal? Togetherness. One for all and all for one. One big happy family.'

'You're right,' says Bremner. 'One big happy family; till you fucking turned up.'

* * *

The very last game of the season. The very last game in the Second Division –

Saturday 19 April 1969 –

Home to Bristol City. Home in front of 31,644 fans. Home as Champions. You've had your hair cut, your suit pressed and your shoes shined –

The players, your players, do a lap of honour while Bristol stand on the pitch and wait for the game to begin, the mauling to begin –

The midfield of John McGovern, Alan Durban and Willie Carlin are in their element with a first-half hat-trick from Durban, plus one from Kevin Hector, and then one from Alan Hinton which is the pick of the five –

Dave Mackay clips the ball forward to Willie Carlin. Carlin takes the ball into the box then back-heels the ball to Alan Hinton. Hinton runs onto the ball and never stops, never breaks stride, just lashes it with his left foot into the bottom corner of the net –

Unstoppable. Unstoppable. Un-fucking-stoppable –

Green. Webster. Robson. Durban. McFarland. Mackay. McGovern. Carlin. O'Hare. Hector and Hinton.

Dave Mackay goes up the steps. Mackay picks up the trophy –

The Second Division Championship trophy –

Mackay holds it aloft in his right hand –
The crowd roars. The crowd chants –
'Derby! Derby! Derby!'

You stand before the chairman, the directors and the board, stand before them with your players and your trophy, the sound of the crowd ringing around the Baseball Ground, ringing around the whole of the bloody town –

This time last year there were 20,000 here to see you lose to Blackpool. The year before 11,000. This time last year Dave Mackay thought he'd played his last game. Today there are 32,000 here. Today you are Champions –

You shake Dave's hand. Peter pats Dave's back –

Dave Mackay is one year older than you; umpteen medals, cups and caps heavier than you, he will be named joint Footballer of the Year for this season –

But you are still smiling from ear to bloody ear –
Still smiling from ear to fucking ear –
The chairman too. The board –
The whole fucking town.

* * *

They are not my team. Not mine. Not this team, and they never will be. They are his team. *His Leeds.* His dirty fucking Leeds, and they always will be. Not my team. Never. Not mine. Never. Not mine. Never. Not this team. Never –

It is gone midnight and I cannot sleep. I've drunk too bloody much again and I've got a thumping fucking headache. The hotel room is too hot and the pillows are too hard and I miss my wife, I miss my kids and I wish I wasn't me, Brian Howard Clough. Not for tonight and not for tomorrow. I get out my address book. I pick up the phone. I dial his number and I wake him up:

'Who is this?'

'It's Brian Clough,' I tell him.

'What the hell do you want, Brian? It's past midnight.'

'I know,' I tell him. 'I'm very sorry to wake you up like this.'

'Are you drunk, man? What's wrong with you?'

'This is your team,' I tell him. 'I want you to lead them out at Wembley.'

83

'Pardon?'

'You won the league,' I tell him. 'You lead them out tomorrow.'

'You've got the job now, Brian,' says Don Revie. 'It's your privilege.'

* * *

The sky is dark but clear, the stands empty but for the rubbish and the echoes. The crowd have all gone home or to the pub, to celebrate the Second Division Championship; the start of the Golden Age. But not you –

You stand in the mouth of the tunnel at the Baseball Ground and you watch Dave Mackay practising with your eldest and your youngest, kicking ball after ball after ball into the wooden shooting box, a little wooden target area beneath the old main stand –

Put it in a box, hide it in a tree, the tallest tree you can see . . .

Ball after ball after ball, ball after ball after ball –

Because this is the happiest day of your life . . .

Because this is the first thing you have ever won and, like your first pair of boots, your first kiss and your first car, you'll never forget the hours of this day –

Saturday 19 April 1969.

Day Eleven

Bill Shankly walks out of the Wembley tunnel alone, out onto the Wembley pitch, out to a massive ovation from the whole of the Wembley stadium, the Leeds fans as well as the Liverpool ones –

You'll never walk alone.

Then Revie takes his salute from the pitch, from both sets of fans –

Marching on together –

Revie in his lucky blue suit; his match-day suit –

Fingers crossed for his team, his boys.

I turn to Bremner in the tunnel, turn to see if he's applauding his old boss, but Billy's looking at his boots. Billy's been in a fucking rotten mood from the moment we got him up; cursing at breakfast, cursing at lunch. Having a go at the receptionist, the waiter, the coach driver and half the bloody team. Maybe it's the heat. Maybe it's London. The occasion. Now he walks out behind me, dragging that League Championship trophy down the tunnel and across the pitch, leading out the glummest faces ever seen at Wembley. I turn to Shanks and his Liverpool side and I applaud him as we walk from the tunnel to the touchline, the team he built behind him, the team Revie built behind me –

Harvey	Clemence
Reaney	Smith
Cherry	Lindsay
Bremner	Thompson, P.
McQueen	Cormack
Hunter	Hughes
Lorimer	Keegan
Clarke	Hall
Jordan	Heighway

Through the noise of 67,000 people clapping and cheering, I ask Bill, 'How many times have you done this, sir?'

But Shankly does not reply, his head high, his eyes fixed –

On this one last match. His last ever match . . .

Fixed on the future. Fixed on regret –

Regret. Regret. Regret.

From the kick-off, Bremner and the Irishman nip and snap at Liverpool's heels, but it's Sniffer who gets the first blood; a four-inch gash in Thompson's shin. Then the Irishman receives a dose of his own medicine from Tommy Smith. This is how it starts –

The 1974 FA Charity Shield; Liverpool vs Leeds –

Dirty, dirty Leeds, Leeds, Leeds . . .

Every kick and every touch, with every trip and every punch –

This is what you think we are, they say. *This is who you say we are . . .*

Then this is what we are, they shout. *This is who we are . . .*

Dirty, dirty Leeds, they sing. *Dirty, dirty Leeds, Leeds, Leeds . . .*

His eyes in the stands. Behind my back. *His* eyes in that suit –

Dirty, dirty Leeds, Leeds, Leeds.

This is how it starts and that is how it will finish; Bremner and the Irishman kicking Liverpool up the arse –

Up the arse and in the balls. Particularly Kevin Keegan –

Keegan who dodges behind Hunter and Cherry with ease to lash in a shot that Harvey cannot hold, that lets Boersma knee the ball into the net on twenty minutes. From then on it's all Liverpool; Heighway and Callaghan running rings around Hunter and Cherry. Thank Christ for Paul Reaney on the right and Eddie Gray on the left because the rest of them are bloody shite –

This is what you think we are. This is who you say we are . . .

Then this is what we are. This is who we are.

Off the pitch and out of the light, down the tunnel and down the corridor, in the half-light and the full stench of their Wembley dressing room at half-time, I tell them, 'The first fifteen minutes, you were all over them. Then Bremner and the Irishman here, they decided to give Keegan the freedom of the fucking park and now you're losing, losing because of Kevin bloody Keegan and these two clowns, these two clowns and their lack of bloody concentration and their lack of fucking responsibility, their complete bloody abdication of any fucking sense of responsibility.'

* * *

You have built an ocean liner out of a shipwreck. You have played forty-two games. You have won twenty-six of them. Drawn eleven and lost five. You have scored sixty-five goals in those forty-two games and conceded just thirty-two. Those twenty-six wins and eleven draws have brought you sixty-three points and the Second Division Championship; promotion to the First Division –

You can't wait for the new season to start –

You can't, can't, can't fucking wait.

Just one little thing spoils this time and this place for you, and that one little thing is Leeds United and Don Revie winning the First Division Championship, and to make this one little thing much, much worse, the press are forever comparing Leeds and Derby: the clean sheets; the Scottish engine rooms of Bremner and Mackay; the Middlesbrough-born managers, Revie and yourself, cut from the same cloth; the list goes on and on –

But you are not Don Revie and you will never be Don Revie. Never –

'Whatever people say you are, that is what you're not.'

Derby County are not Leeds and you are not Revie –

You are a dynamite-dealer, waiting to blow the First Division to Kingdom bloody Cum, the whole fucking game, because this is who you are –

Brian Howard Clough, thirty-four, and a First Division manager –

Brian Howard Clough and nobody else –

An ocean liner out of a shipwreck.

* * *

Fifteen minutes into the second half, Kevin Keegan hustles the Irishman from behind and Giles whips round and punches Keegan in the face with his right fist. *They will burn the grass.* Giles, the player-manager of the Republic of Ireland; John Giles, the would-be assistant manager of Tottenham Hotspur; Johnny Giles, the should-be manager of Leeds United. *Turn this grass to ash.* The referee gets out his book. Keegan pleads for leniency on behalf of Giles. The Irishman stays on the pitch but goes in the book. *Turn this field to dust.* Minutes later, Bremner and Keegan collide during a Leeds free-kick. *They will salt this earth.* There is a sea of fists, kicks to the heels and digs to the ribs. *Leave this ground as stone.* Keegan flies round and swings out at Bremner. *Barren and fallow for ever.* Bob Matthewson sends them both off –

Dirty, dirty Leeds, Leeds, Leeds . . .

His eyes in the stands. Behind my back. *His* eyes in that suit.

Bremner and Keegan walk along the touchline. It is a long, lonely walk to a deserted, empty dressing room. Bremner and Keegan strip off their shirts, the white number 4 and the red number 7; shirts they should be proud to wear, these shirts they throw to the ground –

This is what you think I am, says Bremner. *This is who you say I am . . .*
Shirts any lad in the land would dream of picking up, of pulling on –
Then this is what I am, shouts Billy. *This is who I am.*

But not Billy Bremner. Not Kevin Keegan –

His eyes in the stands, behind my back.

No one learns their lesson; Jordan fights with Clemence, and McQueen goes in to sort it out like a fucking express train. *Dirty, dirty Leeds, Leeds, Leeds.* To add injury to the insults, Allan Clarke is carried off with torn bloody ligaments –

His eyes in that suit, behind my back.

Ten minutes after that, Trevor Cherry heads home an equalizer; first right thing he's done all afternoon. But no one's watching. Not now; now minds are racing, events and pens. The game goes to penalties; the first time the Charity Shield has ever gone to penalties, no more Charity, no more sharing of the Shield. The penalties go to 5–5. Harvey and Clemence make a goalkeepers' pact to each to take the sixth penalty for their side. David Harvey steps up. David Harvey hits the bar. Ray Clemence stays put –

Callaghan steps up. Callaghan converts the sixth penalty –

Liverpool win the 1974 Charity Shield –

But no one notices. Not now –

Now two British players have been dismissed from Wembley –

The first two British players ever to be dismissed at Wembley –

Now they're going to throw the fucking book at them – *at us* – for this. The fucking book. Television and the Disciplinary Committee will see to that. You can forget Rattin. There will be those who want Leeds and Liverpool thrown out of the league. Their managers too. Bremner and Keegan banned for life –

Heavy fines and points deducted –

On the panels. In the columns –

In *his* eyes. In *his* eyes.

The stadium empties in silence. The tunnel. The corridors and the dressing rooms.

No one is sat next to Bremner on the coach out of Wembley. I sit down next to him. I tell him, 'You'll pay your own bloody fine out of your own fucking pocket and, if I had my bloody way, you'd fucking pay Keegan's fine and all.'

'You ever play at Wembley did you, Mr Clough?'

'You can't do that to me,' says Bremner. 'Mr Revie always paid all our fines.'

'He's not here now, is he?' I tell him. 'So you'll pay it yourself.'

'You ever play at Wembley did you, Mr Clough?'

Bremner looks at me now and Bremner makes his vow:

In loss. In hate. In blood. In war –

Saturday 10 August 1974.

Day Twelve

'You ever play at Wembley did you, Mr Clough? You ever play at Wembley, Mr Clough? You ever play at Wembley?'

You played there just the once. Just the once but you know it should have been a lot more, a lot, lot fucking more; you were sure it would have been and all, after Munich in 1958 and the death of Tommy Taylor, the effect it had on Bobby Charlton. You know it would have been a lot, lot more too, had it not been for your own bloody coach at Middlesbrough, your own fucking directors; everybody telling the selectors you had a difficult personality, that you spoke your mind, caused trouble, discontent. Still, they couldn't not pick you, not after you played a blinder for England in a 'B' international against Scotland in Birmingham, scoring once and laying on two more in a 4–1 victory. You were bloody certain you would go to the World Cup in Sweden then, fucking convinced, and you were picked for the Iron Curtain tour of Russia and Yugoslavia in May 1958, just one month before the World Cup –

That number 9 shirt down to just Derek Kevan and you.

The night before the tour, you were that nervous that you couldn't sleep. You got to the airport three hours early. You hung around, introduced yourself –

But no one wanted to know you. No one wanted to room with you –

'Because he bloomin' never stops talking football. Drives you bleeding barmy.'

But Walter Winterbottom, the England manager, sat next to you on the flight east. 'I want you to play against Russia,' he told you. 'Not Derek. You, Brian.'

You believed him. But you didn't play. England lost 5–0.

'I want you to play against Yugoslavia,' he told you the next day. 'You, Brian.'

You believed him again. But again you didn't play. This time England draw 1–1, thanks to Derek fucking Kevan.

After the Yugoslavia game, Walter sat you down and Walter spelt it out for you. 'You won't be going to the World Cup, Brian,' he told you. 'Not this time.'

You didn't believe him. You had travelled to Russia. You had travelled to Yugoslavia. You hadn't had a single kick. Not a touch. Not a single one –

'I scored forty-two goals in the league and cup this last season,' you told Walter. 'They bloody count in the fucking matches we play for Middlesbrough but apparently it's not enough for you lot, not nearly enough . . .'

The manager and the selectors shook their heads, their fingers to their lips –

'Don't burn your bridges, Brian. Bide your time and your chance will come.'

You'd bide your time, all right. You'd take your chances –

Five in the first match of the 1958–59 season; five against the League of Ireland for the Football League; four on your twenty-fourth birthday –

There was public clamour and press pressure now. But you still had to bide your time for another year until you finally got your chance –

Until you were picked to play against Wales at Cardiff.

You forgot your boots and spilt your bacon and beans all down you, you were that nervous, that nervous because that was what it meant to you, to play for your country –

And now that is all you can remember about your England début at Ninian Park; how bloody nervous you were, how fucking frightened –

But, eleven days later, you were picked to play against Sweden at Wembley –

'You ever play at Wembley did you, Mr Clough? You ever play at Wembley, Mr Clough? You ever play at Wembley?'

The dreams you'd had of that turf, at that stadium, in that shirt, for that badge; the goals you'd score on that turf, at that stadium, in that shirt, for that badge, in front of your mam, in front of your dad, in front of your beautiful new wife, but that day –

28 October 1959 –

You hit the crossbar and laid on a goal for John Connelly, but it wasn't enough. You were heavily marked and you couldn't escape. You found no space –

'His small-town tricks lost on the big-time stage of Wembley Stadium.'

On that turf, at that stadium. For that badge, in that shirt –

The Swedes took you apart; the Swedes beat you 3–2; it wasn't enough –

Not enough for you. Not enough for the press. Not enough for Walter –

'How can I play centre-forward alongside Charlton and Greaves?' you told him. 'We're all going for the same ball! You'll have to drop one of them.'

But Walter loved Bobby. Walter loved Jimmy. Walter did not love you –

Walter dropped you and so those two games, against Wales at Cardiff and Sweden at Wembley, those two games were your only full England honours –

'You ever play at Wembley did you, Mr Clough? You ever play at Wembley, Mr Clough? You ever play at Wembley?'

Two-hundred and fifty-one bloody league goals and two fucking caps.

Twenty-four years old and your international career over, the next morning you boarded the train to Brighton with the rest of the Middlesbrough lads. You did not score in that game either. The day after, Middlesbrough travelled up to Edinburgh to play the Hearts. For six hours you sat in a compartment with Peter and you analysed your England game. No cards. No drink. Just cigarettes and football, football, football –

Football, football, football and you, you, you –

Because you knew then you would return –

Return as the manager of England, the youngest-ever manager of England; because you were born to manage your country; to lead England out of that tunnel, onto that pitch; to lead them to the World Cup –

A second, a third and a fourth World Cup –

Because it is your destiny. It is your fate –

Not luck. Not God. It is your future –

It is your revenge.

Day Thirteen

Bed, breakfast and ignore the papers. Shower, shave and ignore the radio. Kit on, car out and ignore the neighbours. Goodbye family, goodbye Derby. Hello motorway, hello Monday fucking morning; the Monday fucking morning after the Saturday before –

Leeds and Liverpool disgrace Wembley; soccer stars trade punches . . .

Here comes that fucking book, thrown at them – at us all – with a vengeance. There's even talk of fans having Bremner and Keegan charged with breach of the peace; all they need now is a willing bloody magistrate, a hanging fucking judge –

Well, here I bloody am; ready and more than fucking willing . . .

The players should have had the day off today. To recover from Saturday and to rest for Tuesday. But not after Saturday. Not after what they've put me through; the headaches they've given me and the headaches I've got coming; the board meetings and the press conferences; the bloody team to pick for tomorrow night and the fucking contract to write for that bloody Irish fucking shithouse –

I hate bloody Mondays, always fucking have.

★ ★ ★

Time does not stand still. Time changes. Time moves fast. Derby must not stand still. Derby must change. Derby must move fast –

The cast remains the same but the scenery changes and the Ley Stand goes up, towering over the Pop Side and the Vulcan Street terracing; it should be the bloody Brian Clough Stand because it would never have left the fucking drawing board had it not been for you, because it was you who raised the expectations of the town, who raised the demand for tickets in the first place. You who envisioned a new stand to take the capacity of the Baseball Ground to 41,000, who looked at the original plans and saw there wasn't enough space. You who then went to see the managing director of Ley's steel factory, who told him you wanted eighteen inches of his property for your new stand. You who promised to build him a new fence and move back his pylons, who told him to fuck off at the mention of compensation; that his compensation would be the name of the new stand and season tickets for life. You who's still got plans to buy all the houses on the opposite side of the ground, because it's only you who can see further than 41,000, who can see gates of 50,000, can see gates of 60,000, see the First Division Championship, the FA Cup, the European Cup . . .

It's only you who has the stomach for this job, who has the balls –

No one else, not Peter, not Longson either, just you –

You and your stomach. You and your balls.

It's been sixteen years since Derby were in the First Division and the expectations are such that the demand for tickets still cannot be met. Priority is given to folk willing to buy tickets for not one but two seasons. Behind the scenes there are some changes too –

Jimmy Gordon replaces Jack Burkitt as trainer and coach –

'It's a ready-made job,' says Jimmy. 'The players are here and the discipline is here. The Boss's job is to determine the method of playing and my job is then to get it going on the field.'

Time does not stand still. Time changes. Time moves fast –

So Derby changes. Derby moves fast –

You pushing and pulling, pushing and pulling her all the way, all the way up the hill, up the hill to the very top, and you'll never forget those first few weeks at the top, those first few weeks in the First Division, that first Saturday –

Home to Burnley, Burnley who finished mid-table last season. Home, in front of 29,000 supporters. That'll change with the results. Soon be gates of 40,000 or more; 40,000 or more to watch your team, your boys:

Green, Webster, Robson, Durban, McFarland, Mackay, McGovern, Carlin, O'Hare, Hector and Hinton.

You're lucky to draw 0–0 and you would've lost had it not been for the quick reflexes of your keeper Les Green, who saves a penalty –

But it's not luck. Not today. Not ever –

You play good methodical football; on the ground, to feet, passed forward –

You are not out of your depth. You have no vertigo here –

Not today; this first Saturday, these first few weeks, this first month: the first Tuesday away at Ipswich and your first win. Down to Coventry the following Saturday for a draw. Home to Ipswich again and another win. More draws against Stoke and Wolves. Then the 2–0 win away at West Brom –

Next comes the trip back up to Hartlepools in the League Cup –

Time has stood still here. Time has not changed here. Not moved fast:

Still more weeds than grass on the pitch at the Victoria Ground, still as even as a cobbled street, still no floodlights until the eightieth minute. But Hartlepools throw themselves into the match and at half-time it's only 0–0 –

Second half and McFarland and Carlin score, but Hartlepools pull one back before Hinton finishes things off with a penalty –

This is how far you have come. This is who you are now:

You are named England's Manager of the Month for August. You are given a £50 cheque and a gallon bottle of Scotch whisky:

'His Derby County team is probably the first side since Ipswich under Alf Ramsey or Leeds under Don Revie to make such an immediate impact on the First Division,' says the spokesman for the sponsors of the award. 'Clough has succeeded in restoring genuine enthusiasm to one of the great traditional strongholds of football and in re-establishing the soccer prestige of Derby County and the Midlands.'

You go on to beat Everton 2–1 in front of the Match of the Day *cameras. Then Southampton 3–0 and Newcastle 1–0 away, and you are still unbeaten. Next come Tottenham and the 5–0 win in front of a record gate of just under 42,000 –*

Easy. Easy. Easy, *they chant.* Easy. Easy. Easy –

The Tottenham of Jimmy Greaves and Alan Mullery. Of Bill Nicholson –

'They humiliated us,' says Bill Nicholson. 'They are very talented and they don't just run, they know where to run and when. Dave Mackay? If I wanted all this to happen for anybody it would be him. Six Dave Mackays and you wouldn't need anybody else. An inspiration to everybody and a credit to the game. One of the all-time greats.'

'I am happy for the team because everybody played so well,' says Dave Mackay. 'Not because it was Spurs we beat but because you can't be anything but happy when you are in a team which plays like that. It is the best we have played since I came here.'

And you? The Biggest Mouth in Football? What do you say?
'You don't need to say anything after that. I was very proud of the lads.'
This is how far you've come. This is who you are. This is where you are –
The First Division, the very top. You don't ever want to leave here.

* * *

The sun never shines at Elland Road. Not on the training ground.
Not since I've been here. No wonder the kids don't want to come to
work with me. The wife too. Just wind and shadow, mist and rain;
dogshit and puddles, purple tracksuits and purple faces –

They've had enough of me and I've had enough of them –

But they've made their beds. Their own fucking beds:

'I'm only going to say this once,' I tell them. 'I don't care what you
were told before, what little tricks and little tactics, little deceits and
little cheats your old manager and your old coaches taught you, but
there's no room for them in my team. None whatsoever. So there'll be
no repetition of the kind of things that went on at Wembley on
Saturday. None whatsoever. I was embarrassed to be associated with
you, with this club, the way some of you – most of you – behaved, and
I'll not have it. Not at this club, not while I'm the manager –

'So any repetition and you'll not only be finding the money to pay
your own bloody fines, you'll also be finding another fucking club to
play for and all!'

* * *

You bring your team, your boys, to Elland Road on Saturday 25 October
1969 to play the Champions, the First Division Champions.

This will not be the same as last year. Not the same as those three cup
defeats. This time you are in the First Division too –

This time will not be the same –

This time he will notice you. This time he will respect you.

But suddenly things have not been going as well for you. Perhaps things had
been going too well for you, perhaps you were becoming complacent; you were

the last unbeaten side in Division One until you lost to Wednesday, then you drew with Chelsea and Palace and lost at home again to Manchester City. Now Robson is out injured and the rest of the team are only playing thanks to cortisone injections –

Cortisone to mask the pain, to mask the bloody fear, to mask the fucking doubt: Derby County have not won a game since you beat Manchester United 2–0 – Beat Manchester United with Charlton, Best and Kidd –

But that was then and this is Leeds, Leeds, Leeds:

Sprake. Reaney. Madeley. Bremner. Charlton. Hunter. Lorimer. Clarke. Jones. Bates and Gray –

Leeds United, First Division Champions, 1968–69.

There are 45,000 here at Elland Road to watch them beat you 2–0 with two trademark Leeds United goals; the first from Clarke as the linesman flags for a foul throw from Bremner; the second three minutes later as Bates plays the ball forward to Clarke, who is at least three or four yards offside –

But the flag stays down and the goal goes in.

At half-time your team, your boys, protest. You tell them to shut their bloody mouths. You tell them to listen and fucking learn:

'They are ruthless,' you tell them. 'They fight for every ball. They brush off every challenge. Now I want to see your courage and I want to see them defend.'

Leeds don't get a sniff for the entire second half. Not a single one. But you don't get a goal either. Not a single one –

In the tunnel, Revie shakes your hand. Revie says, 'You were unlucky.'

'There's no such thing as luck,' you tell him. 'No such thing, Don.'

* * *

The Irishman puts the top back on his new pen, puts his pen back in his jacket pocket. The club secretary picks up the new contract, puts the contract in his drawer.

'Pleasure doing business with you, gentlemen,' says the Irishman.

'Likewise,' I tell him.

He laughs. 'You wanted me gone and you still do and you might yet get your wish. But you're also smart enough to know you need me now, now with all the injuries and the suspensions you've got, the start of the season upon you. You'll be bloody glad of me come Saturday, sure enough.'

'Sure enough,' I tell him.

'Be bleeding ironic though if Mr Nicholson agrees terms with us before then, now wouldn't it, Mr Clough?'

'You read my mind,' I tell him.

★ ★ ★

You still have not won again, not won again since 4 October; already there are the doubters and the gloaters, on the terraces and behind the dug-out, outside the dressing room and in the corridors, the boardrooms and the bars, the ones who were right all along, who knew it wouldn't last, just a flash in the pan, another false dawn, all this talk of a Golden Age, a Second Coming at Derby County –

But however loud the voices in the stands and in the streets, in the newsrooms and the boardrooms, they are never louder than the ones inside your head –

The voices that say the same, the voices that say you've shot it –

'You're all washed up, Brian. You're finished, Clough.'

These are the voices you hear morning, noon and night; every morning, every noon and every night. These are the voices you must silence; the voices you must deafen:

'I will win, I will not lose. I will win, I will not lose . . .'

On 1 November 1969 Bill Shankly's Liverpool come to the Baseball Ground: Lawrence. Lawler. Strong. Smith. Yeats. Hughes. Callaghan. Hunt. Graham. St. John and Thompson; their names are a poem to you, their manager a poet –

'Win. Win. Win. Win . . .'

But you have been too long at this master's knee; now the pupil wants to give the teacher a lesson, needs to:

'Win. Win. Win . . .'

The first goal comes from McGovern after quarter of an hour; from the right-hand edge of the penalty area, he hits the ball with the outside of his right foot, curving it around a mass of players and inside the far post.

The second goal comes forty-seven seconds later; Hector takes the ball off Strong's toes, races into the box and puts it between Lawrence and the near post.

'Win. Win . . .'

For the third, McGovern turns the ball inside to Durban so he can deliver the pass that sends Hinton clear, who, just as the challenge comes in, chips the ball towards the far post for Hector to bury.

On sixty-eight minutes, Hector turns again, leaving Strong behind again, and passes to the overlapping Durban, who sends a low ball across the goalmouth that O'Hare back-heels into the net. But up goes the linesman's flag, followed by 40,000 cries of injustice, but not from your team, not from your boys –

Your boys just get on with it and, one minute later, Hector is through again and on for a hat-trick but, with only Lawrence to beat, he rolls it to O'Hare, who puts it into an empty net.

'I will win!'

'It is no disgrace to be beaten by Derby,' says Shankly. 'When they play well, they'll beat anybody.'

You will beat Liverpool again at Anfield in February, but there's only one game on your mind, only one voice in your head from now to then –

The return of Leeds United and Don Revie.

* * *

'Any discipline that might be taken will be taken in private.'

'So you *are* saying there will be *some* disciplinary action against Bremner?'

'I'm not saying yes, I'm not saying no,' I tell them. 'I'm simply saying that anything that might be done will be done in private.'

'But, but, but . . .' they stammer, stammer, stammer –

I already know their faces, already know their names and their papers; what time they have to have their copy in by and what time their presses roll; what they like to drink, when they like to drink it and how much they like to drink of it. And they already know just what to ask me and what not; what to write and what not; because I practically write their sodding copy for them; do their bleeding jobs for them –

And they bloody love me for it. Fucking love me –

Every time I open my mouth.

99

These should still be the happiest days, weeks and months of your life, but behind the scenes, upstairs and down, there is always doubt, always fear and always trouble –

Always trouble, round every corner, down every corridor.

In November 1969 the club secretary resigns, unable to cope with the demands of the First Division, unable to cope with the demands of the chairman and the board, the manager and the assistant manager.

The manager and the assistant manager –

Mistakes have been made. Books not balanced. Contracts not signed –

On promotion to the First Division, you and Peter were offered new contracts, new contracts that included no incentive clauses, new contracts that remain unsigned –

You have taken Derby County to the First Division –

You have been named as Manager of the Month –

'But I am still interested in any job going,' you tell the press, and the press know there is a vacancy at Barcelona. The press know Barcelona are interested in you. The press put two and two together. The press write another headline:

Clough and Taylor in Barcelona talks.

You confirm nothing. You deny nothing.

Coventry City are interested in you. Birmingham City are interested in you –

'We want a dynamic young manager,' says the Birmingham chairman. 'And Brian Clough obviously comes into that category.'

Birmingham offer you three times your Derby salary. Peter has already packed his bags and bought his ticket to Birmingham. Or Coventry. Or Barcelona –

But there is always doubt. There is always fear. Always Uncle Sam –

Sam Longson reads the headlines. Sam Longson shits his pants. Sam Longson locks you and Peter in the boardroom –

Sam Longson promises you whatever you want –

You and Peter sign the new contracts. Different contracts.

'The understanding, kindness, honesty and trust you have shown Peter and I since we came to Derby makes it impossible for us to leave the club,' you tell Uncle Sam. 'And I am looking forward to many years of good relationship and success (not forgetting the hard work) with you.'

Uncle Sam pulls you closer. Tighter. His wings around you –

'I will do anything necessary to keep you here,' he tells the son he never had.

'Then get bloody rid of that board; Bradley, Payne, Turner and Bob Kirkland. Those men are against us, against our ways, stood in our way.'

Uncle Sam nods his head. Uncle Sam stuffs banknotes into your pockets –

The board give you a new contract. The board give you a pay rise (and about bloody time too). Not Peter. But Peter doesn't know that. Doesn't know that you now get an annual salary of £15,000; double that of the Archbishop of Canterbury –

'I can only say that the Derby ground is full, but the churches are empty.'

★ ★ ★

Under the stand, through the doors. I'm walking round that bloody corner again, down that fucking corridor again, towards Syd Owen and Maurice Lindley. They walk past me without a word. Then Syd says behind my back. Under his breath. Behind his hand. Through gritted teeth, Syd says something that sounds like, 'So long as they were kept, the daughters of the house would have no suitors for their hands . . . '

I stop. I turn round. 'Pardon?'

'Your phone is ringing.'

'What? When?'

'Just now,' Syd says. 'Just as we were walking past the office. Maurice was all for nipping in and answering it for you, and he would have as well, but I told him that you told us not to, didn't you?'

'Still might be ringing though,' says Maurice Lindley. 'If you hurry, you might just catch it.'

Round the corner, down the corridor, I walk towards the office. I can hear the phone still ringing. Ringing and ringing and ringing. I get out my keys. I unlock the door. I get to the desk –

I pick up the phone –

The line is dead.

★ ★ ★

You can't sleep a wink. You have been waiting for this day since 25 October last year. You've been waiting for this fixture all season –

Easter Monday; 30 March 1970; Derby County vs Leeds United.

You have not lost since QPR in February. Not since you signed Terry Hennessey from Nottingham Forest for £100,000. You are right up there now, a top-five finish on the cards. Fairs Cup place. You are doing well –

But not as well as Leeds United. Not as well as Don Revie, OBE –

Leeds United are second in the league, in the semi-finals of the European Cup against Celtic, in the FA Cup final against Chelsea and on the verge of an unprecedented treble –

Leeds, Leeds, Leeds; marching on together:

David Harvey, Nigel Davey, Paul Peterson, Jimmy Lumsden, David Kennedy, Terry Yorath, Chris Galvin, Mick Bates, Rod Belfitt, Terry Hibbitt, Albert Johanneson –

It is their reserve side and the 41,000 fans jeer as the Leeds team is announced; the Baseball Ground has been cheated and they want their money back, and you'd bloody well give it to them if only you fucking could –

You are seething, fuming and looking for Revie. You find him in a huddle with Les Cocker, Lindley and Owen and you let him have it, both barrels:

'Listen to that fucking crowd,' you tell him. 'They came here to see the League Champions. Paid their hard-earned brass to see the fucking Champions. Not Leeds United fucking reserves. You've cheated these folk. The people of Derby. My team.'

'Take it up with the FA,' says Revie. 'Day after bloody tomorrow, we play Celtic in the semi-final of the European Cup and if you were in my shoes you'd do the same.'

'Never,' you tell him. 'Never.'

You field your strongest side. You easily beat them 4–1, but the crowd continues to jeer for the full ninety minutes. They even slow-hand-clap your Derby –

And you don't bloody blame them. You can't and you won't.

The FA will fine Leeds and Revie £5,000 for this, for failing to field their strongest side, and your hate will be as crisp and complete as Leeds United's season will be barren and bare, finishing second to Everton, losing to Celtic in the semi-finals of the European Cup and to Chelsea in an FA Cup final replay –

'But if you were me,' says Revie in the tunnel, 'you'd have done the same.'
You ignore his hand and tell him, promise him, 'I'll never be you, Don.'
Two months later, Revie is named Manager of the Year –
For the second successive season.

★ ★ ★

The door is locked and the chair against it; a cig in my mouth and the phone in my hand:

'Mr Nicholson?' I ask. 'Brian Clough here.'

'Afternoon, Mr Clough,' says Bill Nicholson. 'What can I do for you?'

'Well, it's about John Giles –'

'What about him?'

'Well, about him coming to you –'

'I hope you're joking with me? After Saturday?'

'Saturday?'

'I was at Wembley, Mr Clough. Giles was worse than Bremner. Ten times worse. He should never have stayed on that pitch.'

'That's your final word, is it?'

'You can take it as that, aye.'

I hang up. I get out my address book. I pick up the phone –

'Brian Clough here,' I tell Huddersfield. 'Can I speak to Bobby Collins please?'

★ ★ ★

There is always doubt, always fear, and always trouble –

Round every corner. Down every corridor. Behind every door. In every drawer.

Four days after you beat Leeds United reserves, four days after that win guarantees you a place in the Fairs Cup, a place in Europe, the joint League and FA commission into the bookkeeping at Derby County makes its report; the Derby County books have been inspected by the joint League and FA commission because there have been administrative blunders. Big bloody blunders. Huge fucking blunders –

Tickets oversold. Books unbalanced. Contracts unsigned. Illegal payments made.

The joint League and FA commission find Derby County guilty of eight charges of gross negligence in the administration of the club; of failing to lodge the contracts of three players with the League; of varying the contracted payments to players during the season; of paying £2,000 to Dave Mackay Limited for programme articles; and of paying lodging allowances to your apprentices instead of their landladies –

Every technicality. Every little thing –

'The offences enumerated in the charges were admitted by the representatives of the club. The commission, therefore, finds the club guilty of the offences with which they have been charged and, as a result of the investigation of the charges, the commission has reached the conclusion that there has been gross negligence in the administration of the club, for which the members of the board must accept some responsibility. Taking the offences as a whole, the commission has imposed a fine of £10,000 and has further decided that the club be prohibited from playing in European competition during the season 1970/71 and also from playing any friendly matches against a club under the jurisdiction of any other National Association prior to April 30, 1971.'

The FA and the League have thrown the book at you – with a vengeance – and have imposed the heaviest penalties in the history of English football: a £10,000 fine and a one-year ban from European football and the loss of £100,000 in European revenue –

'A terrible injustice,' says the Mayor of Derby.

But this is personal, you know it is; because of the things you've written – Because of the things you've said, in the papers and on the telly:

'Trouble has blown up because I've been so open in my criticism of Alan Hardaker, the League Secretary. It seems you cannot say that he has too much power.'

But every cloud has its silver lining and this is just the ammunition Longson needs:

'For some time now,' Sam Longson tells the local press and the national press, 'I have not agreed with the policy and approach of some of the directors. In fact, I asked the chairman to resign last November and told him we wanted a stronger man. He talks of a united board, but the truth of the matter is that three of them, Mr Paine, Mr Turner and Mr Kirkland, have not spoken to me for about six months.'

Longson asks for the resignations of Paine, Turner and Kirkland –

Payne, Turner and Kirkland ask for the resignations of Longson, Peter and you –

You phone Birmingham City. Birmingham City rub their hands –

The very first Keep Clough at Derby campaign begins –

There can only be one winner –

Harry Paine resigns. Ken Turner resigns. Bob Kirkland resigns:

'When I became a director of Derby County Football Club,' writes Bob Kirkland, 'I assumed certain responsibilities. To discharge these responsibilities, it is necessary to be kept informed of all major decisions within the club. I regret to say that I feel that I have not been kept informed and particularly with regard to the matters which gave rise to the recent inquiry by the Football Association and the Football League. I must make it quite clear that these matters only came to my knowledge at the conclusion of the investigation. I felt it my duty to remain on the board so as not to prejudice the result of the inquiry, but in view of the deep divisions on the board which have now been revealed, I feel that I must now tender my immediate resignation as a director.'

There's only one winner; only ever one winner –

Brian Howard Clough.

* * *

'You're home early,' says my wife. 'Not like you. Are you feeling all right?'

'You want me to go back out? Find a pub?' I ask her.

'Don't be daft,' she says. 'It's a nice surprise.'

'Make the most of it,' I tell her. 'I'll be away a bit this week.'

'You've got enough shirts, have you?'

'I'll get by,' I tell her.

She walks over to me. She puts her arms around my neck and asks, 'Will you?'

'I'll have to,' I tell her. 'Not much choice, have I?'

'Never say that,' she says. 'You've always got us. You know that, don't you?'

'What do you think keeps me sane?'

'I don't know,' she smiles. 'Thought you said it was football that kept you sane.'

'Not any more,' I tell her. 'Not any more.'

Day Fourteen

Cassius Clay becomes Muhammad Ali. The Quarrymen become the Beatles. Lesley Hornby becomes Twiggy and George Best becomes Georgie Best –
 Superstar.
 It is a new world. It is a new England –
 The colour supplements. The colour televisions. The brand-new papers. The Sun. *The columns and the panels. The columns and panels that need opinions. Minds with opinions. Mouths with opinions –*
 A mind and a mouth like yours, open wide.
 Open wide, just like your arms and your wallet.
 Your wife is not keen. Peter neither. But Sam Longson is –
 'You have something big to offer football,' Uncle Sam assures you.
 The summer of 1970; Alf Ramsey and England are in Mexico for the World Cup, losing twenty-odd pounds a game and struggling for air. You are in the television studios of Independent Television, getting hundreds of quid a game and struggling for breath on a panel with Malcolm Allison; Big Mal and Big Head –
 You are television panellists. You are television pundits –
 You open your mouths. You speak your minds –
 You are controversial. You are confident –
 Making names for yourselves –
 A new name for yourself –
 Cloughie.

* * *

I've been stood here for an hour watching them go through their paces, through their practices; here in the shadow of this ground, here under this sickening sky. Tonight's game is at Southampton, the last so-called friendly before the season starts –

Have to fly down as well –

I don't want to go; not one single part of me. I'd pay good money to get out of it.

Bites Yer Legs comes up to where I'm stood –

'I'm a bit worried about the way we dealt with the corners on Saturday,' he says. 'We've got to get that right and I wondered if you had any thoughts?'

'You're professional fucking footballers,' I tell him. 'Sort it out your-selves.'

★ ★ ★

In the 1969–70 season, Derby County finished fourth; fourth in your first sea-son in the First Division. You played forty-two league games, won fifteen at home and seven away; you scored sixty-four goals and conceded thirty-seven; you had a total of fifty-three points at the end of the season, thirteen less than Everton, the Champions, four less than Leeds in second, two less than Chelsea in third, but two more than Liverpool and eight more than Manchester United. Derby finish fourth; Derby should be in Europe next season; in the Inter-Cities Fairs Cup –

But Derby are not. Derby have been banned. But despite the ban from Europe. Despite the boardroom fights. Despite these dark clouds and ominous signs, hopes are still high for the new season, the 1970–71 season –

Hopes on the pitch. Hopes off the pitch. Hopes upstairs. Hopes downstairs –

A new club secretary has been appointed, has been appointed by you –

You didn't ask the board. You didn't ask Uncle Sam. You didn't ask Peter and you didn't ask your wife –

You just told them all that you had appointed Stuart Webb –

Stuart Webb comes from Preston North End. Stuart Webb is young –

Webby has immaculate suits. Webby has business aspirations –

Burning ambitions. Burning, scolding ambitions –

Webby wants to be in total control of the administration of the club, to expand the promotions, to revive the supporters' club, the Junior Rams, to ini-tiate awards nights –

He wants to do for Derby off the pitch what you have done on the pitch –

Stuart Webb wants to be you. Stuart Webb wants to be Brian Clough –
Webby wants to be Cloughie.

You can't blame him. Nobody can –

Everybody wants to be you. Everybody loves you; fathers and sons, wives and daughters. Young and old, rich and poor. Because hopes are high in the poor houses, hopes are high in the posh houses –

Hopes you have raised. Hopes you must fulfil.

Manchester United have come to the Baseball Ground for the big pre-season game; the 1970 Watneys Cup final. In front of 32,000 –

Live on television. Live because of Manchester United:

Stepney. Edwards. Dunne. Crerand. Ure. Sadler. Morgan. Law. Charlton. Kidd and Best (with Stiles on the bench) –

The one and only Manchester United, with Law, Charlton, Kidd and Best.

But it's your team, your boys, who score four, who hammer in shot after shot, who produce four- or five-man moves with simple first-time passes, it is your team, your boys who find the space, who carve open their defence –

Time after time after time.

Later, the men from Manchester will say this was just a friendly; just another pre-season game; an inconsequential warm-up. But you know there are no such things as friendlies –

Because you know you cannot switch it on and switch it off.

You sit in your dug-out and you watch Denis Law limp off, Kidd and Best fade and Bobby Charlton look so very, very tired, and then you look at your team, your boys; every one of them giving you 100 per cent, because they know you cannot switch it on and switch it off; because they know football is a game of habit; because they know that habit should be winning –

You've raised hopes. Hopes you must fulfil –

And you will; you, Peter, Sam and Webby –

The Golden Age here at last.

* * *

In the Yorkshire boardroom, the Yorkshire curtains drawn. Judgement hour is upon them, upon us all. The FA Secretary and the FA Disciplinary Committee have concluded their four-hour meeting down in London. The Leeds board have received the FA statement –

I help myself to a large brandy and take a seat next to Bremner.

Manny Cussins takes out the statement and, in a solemn tone, reads it aloud: 'Bremner of Leeds and Keegan of Liverpool will each be under suspension for three matches with effect from August the twentieth unless an application for a personal hearing is made by the players . . .'

Cussins pauses here and looks up at Bremner –

Bremner shakes his head.

'Both Bremner of Leeds and Keegan of Liverpool will also be charged separately under FA Rule 40 A7 for bringing the game into disrepute by their actions following being sent off the field of play. Both players, their managers and a representative of each respective board are ordered to attend a meeting at FA headquarters on Friday with Mr Vernon Stokes, the chairman of the FA Disciplinary Committee.'

Cussins puts the statement to one side. The eyes of the board are on me now –

I light a cigar. I take a nip of brandy. I turn to William Bremner and I tell him, 'They're going to hang you out to dry for this, you stupid bastard.'

★ ★ ★

Despite the high hopes, despite the Watneys Cup, there are always the dark clouds and ominous signs; heavy over you, but heavier still over Peter, worried and shitting bricks –

'We're short of pace,' he says, over and over. 'We'll go down without pace.'

Brick after brick after brick; day after day after day –

This is how the 1970–71 season starts; Peter anxious again, screwing up his Sporting Life, *chain-smoking and biting his nails, having those dreams again, those nightmares that tell him you've shot it, he's shot it, his days of doubt, his nights of fear –*

Only doubts and only fears. No succour, no supper.

Peter thinks you should both have gone to Greece last March; gone to Greece to work for the Colonels for £20,000 a year plus a £10,000 signing-

on fee, all tax-free. Peter would have gone, but there was no job for Peter without Brian. In your secret room at the Mackworth Hotel, Peter had begged and pleaded with you to take the job –

'I'm not meddling with dynamite,' you told him and that was that.

Peter thinks you should both have gone to Birmingham last April; gone to Birmingham to work for Clifford Coombs. Peter would have gone, but there was no job for Peter without Brian. Again in your secret room at the Mackworth Hotel, Peter had pleaded and Peter had begged, begged and pleaded, pleaded and begged –

Barcelona. Greece. Birmingham. Coventry. Anywhere but here –

'But I'm happy here,' you told him then, tell him now. 'We're on a good thing.'

But Peter's never happy with your lot; the grass is always greener and your own nothing but a field of weeds and stones; nothing but weeds and stones –

'We're short of pace,' he says, again and again. 'And we'll go down without it.'

'Did all right last season,' you tell him. 'If it's not broken . . .'

'And if we go down,' he says, 'who'll want us then, Brian?'

* * *

I hate fucking flying and this lot don't make it any bloody better; they don't talk or joke, don't drink or smoke, they just sit and stare at the backs of the chairs in front of them. The safety instructions. Me and all –

I think about my wife. I think about my kids . . .

In the sky over England, up among the bloody birds and the clouds, no one feels invincible. Not up here. Not even me. Not without a drink or a fag in my hand. Up here everybody's mortal, full of regret, wishing they were back down there with their feet upon the ground, making things right, making things good, making things better –

They'll be having their tea, my wife and my kids, watching a bit of telly . . .

Never flew with Middlesbrough. Never flew with Sunderland –

Then it'll be bathtime and bedtime, a story if they're good . . .

Never would have if we'd stayed at bloody Hartlepools –

Goodnight, sleep tight; lights out and sweet dreams . . .

Never would again if I had my way. Never would again –

Sweet, sweet dreams.

★ ★ ★

Observe. Expose. Replace. Observe. Expose. Replace –

This is what Peter does; what Peter does for his money; does to feel worth-while; to feel needed; important. Stuart Webb's been in Peter's ear; he's been telling him about this lad at his old club; this young Scot at Preston North End. So Peter goes to see Archie Gemmill and ninety minutes later Peter is on the telephone to the Baseball Ground –

'I've seen one,' he tells you. 'Get Longson's cheque book up here fast.'

You drive up to Preston. You meet Alan Ball, father of England's Alan Ball, the manager of Preston North End. You agree to pay £64,000 for Gemmill –

If Gemmill will agree to join you (which he will; they always do).

Peter goes back home now, needed and important, his job done –

Now your job starts. You go round to Gemmill's house. Two minutes inside this house and you know your work has only just begun; you can sense another club, the League Champions Everton, are in here; you can hear it in Gemmill's voice, see it in his eyes, smell it on his clothes. And then there's Gemmill's wife; Betty's seen you on the telly and she's not keen on what she's seen, that mouth, those opinions. Betty's also pregnant and against any other changes in her life –

Two minutes in here and you know you'll not be going home tonight. So you roll up your sleeves, march into their kitchen and get stuck into the washing-up.

'I'd like to sleep on it,' says Archie Gemmill.

'Good man,' you tell him. 'I'll kip in your spare room, if you don't mind.'

The next morning Betty cooks you bacon and eggs while Archie signs the contract between the marmalade and the ketchup –

A job well done, that's you.

You go back to the Preston ground. You break the news to Ball; Ball doesn't look too sad. Ball thinks he's pulled a fast one –

'He's not the player you think he is,' says Ball. 'Your mate's fucked up.'

You don't listen to him; you don't give a fuck. You and Peter, you know players. Nobody else knows players, just you and Peter –

'You're not making any friends, you and your mate,' says Ball –

You don't bloody listen; you don't give a flying fuck –

It's all water off a duck's back to you.

You go back to Derby. You sell Willie Carlin to Leicester. You let Peter tell
him. Hold his hand. Hold his heart —
Inject it full of cortisone. Dry his tears —
All water off a duck's back.

* * *

There are 15,000 at the Dell for this bloody Ted Bates testimonial
match; the last of these fucking dress rehearsals. Clarke, Madeley and
Yorath haven't made the trip and so I play Terry Cooper and Eddie
Gray from the start to see how they'll hold up for Saturday. I also play
Hunter in the first half as well, even though he's suspended for
Saturday, play him because I've got a couple of prospective clubs in the
stands here to have a look at him, Cherry, Cooper and Harvey. Flog
those four for starters, get shot of the Irishman, buy Shilton, Todd,
McGovern and O'Hare and then I'll be halfway there —

But now I'm still back in the stalls; back in the stalls with the season four days off.

In the dug-out, under his breath, Jimmy Gordon asks, 'What's
wrong, Boss?'

'What do you mean? What are you talking about?'

'You're not even watching them,' he says. 'Eyes are on the roof of
the stand.'

'Fuck off,' I tell him. 'You do your job and I'll do mine.'

There are just two good things about this game: the behaviour of
the players, for bloody once, and Duncan McKenzie's first goal for the
club, a fifteen-yard shot inside the far post. He also misses a hatful of
chances, but at least he's got one under his belt —

Just two good things in ninety fucking minutes of football —

It's not enough. Jimmy knows it. I bloody know it —

There is something wrong.

The players know it too. They feel it in their boots —

The season starts in four days. The season starts away from home.

* * *

It is Halloween 1970, and Peter looks like death. You know how he feels:

You have played fourteen games so far this season and won just four of them. You have been beaten at home by Coventry, Newcastle, Chelsea and Leeds –

Leeds, Leeds, Leeds:

You never had a kick, never had a bloody touch. Never had any fucking confidence either. Just cortisone. Norman Hunter man of the match, a colossus, the Leeds defence outstanding, with goals from Sniffer Clarke and Peter Lorimer –

Leeds went two points clear at the top. You dropped four places down –

Now you've just lost 2–0 to Arsenal. Now you are twentieth in the league.

Peter is stretched out on the treatment table at Highbury. He looked terrible on the coach here from Paddington and looked no better in the dug-out next to you –

'I'd give anything to stay here,' he tells you.

'Come on,' you tell him. 'You're taking the team to Majorca tomorrow.'

Peter opens his eyes. His bloodshot eyes. Peter looks up at you –

You're not going to Majorca. Not this time. It's half-term holidays for the kids and you're going to spend the week with them and your wife.

You'll not be going home to pack; you'll not be driving back down to Luton Airport; you'll not be flying to Majorca at three in the morning –

That'll be Peter, with his pains in his chest, with his doubts and his fears –

Not you. Just Peter. Peter and the team.

★ ★ ★

I'm first on the coach. The coach back to the airport. Least there'll be drink on this plane. The plane back to Leeds –

Leeds, Leeds, fucking Leeds.

I'm first off when it lands. First back on the coach to Elland Road. First off again. The players stumbling back to their cars in the dark, them that can still walk. But there's no car and no walking for me; a taxi waiting outside Elland Road to take McKenzie and me back to the Dragonara Hotel –

Situated next to Leeds City Station and the closest modern luxury hotel to the Leeds United ground. For party rates please contact the sales manager . . .

Part of the Ladbroke Group.

I sit on my modern luxury bed in my modern luxury hotel room. I stare out of the modern luxury window at the modern concrete city of Leeds –

Motorway City, City of the Future.

I reach over the modern luxury bed and I switch on the modern luxury radio. But there's no Frank Sinatra. No Tony Bennett. No Ink Spots and no more bloody brandy either. I get off my modern luxury bed and walk down the modern luxury corridor and bang on the door of a modern luxury footballer –

Bang and bang and fucking bang again –

'Who is it?' shouts Duncan McKenzie. 'It's one o'clock in the morning.'

'It's Cloughie,' I tell him. 'I want to see you down in reception.'

He's a good lad is Duncan. Duncan won't argue. Duncan will come.

'Give us five minutes then,' he shouts back. 'I need to get dressed, Boss.'

'Don't make it any bloody longer then,' I tell him.

Reception is deserted but for a terrible fucking draught and some horrible bloody music which the receptionist can't seem to turn off. I have an argument about the music and the bar being closed but I still manage to order a pot of tea and then sit down with my feet up to wait for McKenzie –

'Took your bloody time,' I tell him. 'Worse than a fucking woman.'

McKenzie sits down. McKenzie takes out his fags.

'Don't ever let me see you get off a plane in that condition again,' I tell him.

'What do you mean? What condition?'

'Don't play daft with me, lad. You were fucking rat-arsed!'

'But I don't drink, Boss,' he says. 'I'd only had a couple of tonic waters.'

'Good job I've only ordered you a cup of bleeding tea then, isn't it?'

'Yes, Boss,' he says and puts out one cig and lights another –

'And give us one of them while you're at it,' I tell him.

He hands me a cigarette and holds up a light –

I take a drag and ask him, 'Who were you sat with on the plane back?'

'I can't remember now,' McKenzie says. 'Trevor Cherry, I think.'

'What did he say about me?'

'Pardon?'

'Come on,' I tell him. 'What was bloody Cherry saying about me?'

'We didn't talk about you,' he says. 'Just small talk. Mutual friends.'

I know he's lying. I know they talked of nothing but Cloughie.

'You've settled in well,' I tell him. 'They trust you. Now what are they saying?'

'Nothing.'

'Fuck off,' I tell him. 'You're supposed to be my eyes and ears in that bloody dressing room. Now what are they fucking saying about me?'

'Nothing. Honest, Boss,' he pleads. 'Just worried about their futures. Nervous –'

'Course they're all fucking nervous,' I tell him. 'They're all fucking old men; over thirty the bloody lot of them.'

'They just want to play well –'

'Fucking shut up about them, will you?' I tell him. 'What about me? No one understands my position. No one understands the mess Revie left them in and put me in; no contracts, over-the-hill the lot of them. Team had shot it and he knew it. No chance in hell they can win the European Cup. That's why he fucked off and took the England job. You think he'd have walked out on a team that he thought was going to win the European Cup? The fucking European Cup? That man? Never in a month of bloody Sundays. They've fucking shot it; he knew it and I know it. Half them bloody players fucking know it and all; know it in their boots; know it in their hearts. But now it's my job to tell them, tell them what they already bloody know but don't want to fucking hear.'

He's a good lad is Duncan. Duncan won't argue. Duncan will nod.

'Thank Christ I got you,' I tell him. 'Now bugger off.'

Duncan stands up. Duncan smiles. Duncan says, 'Goodnight, Boss.'

'Fuck off,' I tell him. 'Before I give you a bloody kiss goodnight.'

But Duncan doesn't move. 'Boss, can I ask you one question?'

'If you give us another fag.'

Duncan hands me one, then asks, 'What did you think of my goal?'

'It was good,' I tell him and Duncan smiles –

A right broad Cheshire Cat of a grin –

Just like my eldest. Just like my youngest –

'Almost bloody good enough to make up for the other hundred fucking sitters you missed. Now get off to bloody bed, you've got fucking training tomorrow morning!'

★ ★ ★

It is the early hours of Saturday 9 January 1971. You are home to Wolves this afternoon. You are lying awake next to the wife –

You cannot sleep. You cannot dream –

You thought things had been on the up again; the draws with Liverpool and Manchester City, the wins over Blackpool and Forest. But then you lost at home to West Ham and away at Stoke, drawing 4–4 with Manchester United at home on Boxing Day –

4–4 when you'd been leading 2–0 at half-time; you blame Les bloody Green for that. Blame fucking Pete; it was Peter who brought him from Burton Albion with him; Taylor who's kept defending him, paying off his gambling debts, fending off the paternity suits, lending him money and keeping him in the side when he's cost you games.

You hear the phone ringing. You get out of bed. You go downstairs –

'You won't see me today,' says Taylor. 'I've not slept a bloody wink. I feel like fucking death. I think I've got cancer.'

'Be at the ground in half an hour,' you tell him.

'It's no good,' he says. 'I've had it.'

'I want you there not later than nine,' you tell him and hang up –

I feel like death. I feel like death. I feel like death.

You get out your address book and the phone book and you start to make the calls; to call in favours, to trade on your fame; to pull strings, to get what you want –

The best possible care for Peter.

You get the X-ray department of your local hospital to open on their weekend. You get the best doctor in Derby to come in, to bring a cancer specialist with him.

You pick Pete up at the ground. You drive him to the hospital –

And then you wait, wait in the corridor, wait and pray for Pete.

'He's had a heart attack,' the doctor says. 'Probably about eight weeks ago.'

'The Arsenal game,' you tell Pete. 'Remember how you were?'

'When was that?' asks the doctor.

'October thirty-first,' I tell him. 'We lost 2–0.'

'Well, that certainly fits,' says the doctor. 'Now you need to drive him home slowly and make sure he stays there.'

'We've got a match against Wolves this afternoon,' says Pete. 'I can't.'

'You've got no match. Nor will you have for several weeks,' the doctor tells Pete. 'It's important that you rest completely.'

You both thank the doctor, the consultant, the specialist and the X-ray department. Then you drive Pete home slowly and see him into his house, making sure he stays put.

Back at the ground, you drop Peter's old mate Les Green; drop him after 129 consecutive league and cup appearances; drop him and tell him he will never play for Derby County or Brian Clough again –

You play Colin Boulton in goal. You lose 2–1 –

It's your twelfth defeat of the season.

Day Fifteen

I wake up in my modern luxury hotel bed in my modern luxury hotel room with an old-fashioned fucking hangover and no one but myself to blame –

No one but myself and Harvey, Stewart, Lorimer, the Grays, Bates, Clarke, Hunter, McQueen, Reaney, Yorath, Cherry, Jordan, Giles, Madeley, Bremner, Cooper, Maurice bloody Lindley and Sydney fucking Owen.

Two wins, one draw and one defeat (on penalties) and I should be happy; if this was for real, Leeds would have five points from four games, four games away from home, and I would be happy; not ecstatic, not over-the-moon but not gutted; not sick-as-a-parrot, just happy. But this is not for real –

For real is Saturday. For real is away at Stoke.

I get out of bed. I have a wash and a shave. I get dressed. I go downstairs to see if I can still get any breakfast. I sit in the deserted dining room and stare at my bacon and eggs, my tea and my toast, trying not to throw up again –

This is not real life. Not the life I wanted –

Those days gone. These days here –

Not the life for me.

★ ★ ★

January 1971 is a miserable month; Peter's still at home ill, Sam still on his holidays; no one here but you and Webby, and you're already regretting appointing Stuart bloody Webb as club fucking secretary; too bloody big for his bloody posh boots is Stuart Webb.

Folk had been coming up to the ground all morning for tickets for the cup tie against Wolves; almost sold the bloody lot; got a carpet of fucking cash, the apprentices stuffing it into plastic bags and wastepaper baskets, anything and anywhere to get it out the way. Now here's this bloody johnny-come-lately of a secretary, a secretary you fucking appointed, here he bloody is giving you the third fucking degree –

'The ladies in the office say there were four whole bins full of cash,' he says. 'There's three here; now where's the fourth?'

'How the bloody hell should I know?' you tell him.

'Well, someone said you took one home at lunchtime, for safe keeping.'

'Who the fucking hell told you that?'

'It doesn't matter who told me,' he says. 'What matters is where the cash is.'

'Exactly,' you tell him. 'So stop bloody yapping and start fucking looking!'

'All right,' he says. 'I will and I'll get the police to help me, shall I?'

'All right, all right,' you tell him. 'It's at home. I'll bring it in tomorrow.'

'Why did you take it home?'

'Because, one, you won't give us a key to the bloody safe and, two, it's safer in my house than in this fucking office and, three, I can do what the bloody hell I want here because I'm the fucking boss – not you. You're a secretary and you answer to me.'

Stuart Webb shakes his head. Stuart Webb slams the door on his way out.

Peter is still ill, Sam still on his holidays –

Suddenly, this is a lonely place.

★ ★ ★

The taxi drops me at the ground. Training has already finished, the players gone home. But through the doors. Under the stand. Round the corner. Down the corridor. Bobby Collins is waiting for me –

Bobby Collins, former captain of Leeds, now manager at Huddersfield –

'You're bloody late,' he says as I show him into the office. 'Huddersfield Town might not be in the First Division, Mr Clough, but I'm still a busy man and I don't like to be kept fucking waiting.'

I pull open a drawer. I take out a bottle of Scotch. 'Drink?'

'Not just now, thank you very much.'

I pour myself a large one and ask him, 'Now do you want Johnny Giles or not?'

'Of course I bloody want him,' he says. 'Who fucking wouldn't?'

★ ★ ★

January was bad but February could be worse. Pete is still fucking ill; the whole town ill now. Rolls-Royce in collapse. Thousands out of work. The Derbyshire Building Society on the verge of bankruptcy. The whole fucking town. That's why Derby County FC must be on the mend. That's why you start to win some matches again, away at Ipswich and West Ham. For the whole town. You lose at Everton in the cup, but you then beat Palace and Blackpool. That's why you also go shopping. For the whole fucking town. No Peter to hold your hand this time either. But this time you know exactly who you want. This time you go back to Sunderland for Colin Todd –

You coached this lad in the Sunderland youth team; the Almighty Todd –

'He's too expensive,' you tell the press. 'We're not interested.'

You don't ask Peter. You don't ask the chairman. You don't ask the board –

You are the manager. You are the man in charge. You are the Boss –

You sign the players. You pick the players. Because it's you who sinks if they don't swim. No one else. That's why you don't ask. That's why you just do it –

This time you break the British transfer record; £170,000 for a defender; £170,000 as Rolls-Royce collapses, the whole town, the whole fucking town –

But you've also done it for them; for the whole bloody town –

To cheer Derby up; the whole fucking town.

Longson is in the Caribbean. The tactless old twit. You send him a telegram:

'Signed you another good player, Todd. Running short of cash, love Brian.'

In Colin Todd's first game you beat Arsenal 2–0 and you're hailed a hero again. The next game is away against Leeds. Revie tries to get it postponed because of a flu epidemic in the Leeds United dressing room. You're having bloody none of that and, fucking surprise surprise, only Sniffer Clarke is absent from the Leeds eleven. Norman Hunter's certainly not absent and eventually ends up in the book as Revie and Cocker leap out of their dug-out, arms flapping, shouting and carrying on as if Norman really were bloody innocent. But fifteen minutes from the end Lorimer fucking scores and sends Leeds seven points clear of Arsenal and Derby back to the drawing board –

You lose to Liverpool, Newcastle and Nottingham bleeding Forest and do not win a single bloody game in the whole of fucking March –

Fear and doubt. Drink and cigarettes. No sleep. That's March 1971 –

It is your worst month as a manager. Your loneliest month.

But then Peter finally comes back to bloody work and you finally get a fucking win, at home to Huddersfield. You lose again at Tottenham but then you do not lose again; you beat United at Old Trafford and Everton at home –

But it's not enough for Peter; Peter's had a long time alone in the house with his Raceform; a long time alone to think; to brood and to dwell –

'Longson slipped you a £5,000 rise, didn't he?'

'Who fucking told you that?'

'Answer the bloody question,' Peter says. 'Am I right or am I wrong?'

'I want to know where you got your bloody information.'

'That doesn't fucking matter, Brian. What matters to me is that you took a £5,000 rise, that you took it eighteen fucking months ago, and that you've never said a bloody word about it to me. I thought we were partners, Brian.'

'Pete, listen –'

'No, you listen, Brian,' he says. 'I want my share of the cake.'

'Pete –'

'I want my share of the fucking cake, Brian. Yes or no?'

★ ★ ★

'Bobby Collins thinks that Giles is the player to do Huddersfield proud, but Giles will be very much involved in my squad for Saturday's game at Stoke. That is my priority now. So Johnny Giles, at the moment, is absolutely necessary to Leeds United. If the situation changes, Bobby Collins will be the first to be informed.'

'What do you think about the comments made by Kevin Keegan's father that if Johnny Giles hadn't punched Keegan then none of this would have happened?'

'It's only natural for a father to stick up for his own son; I'd do the bloody same for my two lads and I hope you'd do the same for yours.'

'But do you blame Giles for the whole affair? Believe he started it?'

'How it all started is a mystery to me. We shall just have to wait until we get the referee's report to get things sorted out. But I did feel very sorry for Kevin Keegan.'

'Will Billy Bremner be appealing?'

'No.'

'What do you think of the decision by the FA to call this meeting of representatives of the Football League, the Professional Footballers' Association, linesmen, referees and managers to study ways of improving behaviour on the pitch?'

'I'm all for cleaning up the game, you gentlemen know that. But I wouldn't want to see it done on the back of Billy Bremner.'

'You still intend to play Bremner on Saturday?'

'Of course I bloody do.'

'And you'll be accompanying Bremner to London on Friday?'

'I don't think I've any fucking choice, have I?'

★ ★ ★

These have been a bad few months but at least Pete is back at work. He's still not happy; still after his slice of cake, but at least he's back at work, back doing what he's paid for. Pete has found another one; another ugly duckling, another bargain-bin reject. He's been down to Worcester three times to watch Roger Davies in the Southern League. He's offered Worcester City £6,000 but Worcester have put up their price; Worcester know Arsenal, Coventry and Portsmouth are all in the hunt now –

Now Worcester want £14,000 for Roger Davies.

'Is it definitely yes?' you ask Pete.

'It's definitely yes,' he says, and so you get in your car and drive down to Worcester to meet Pete and sign Roger Davies for £14,000 –

'I hope you're right about Davies,' says Sam Longson to Pete when you all get back home to Derby. '£14,000 is a lot of money for a non-league player.'

'Fuck off,' replies Pete and walks out of the room and out of the ground.

You follow Pete home; knock on his door; let yourself in. You pour him a drink; pour yourself one; light you both a fag and put your arms around him.

'You shouldn't let the chairman upset you,' you tell him.

123

'Easy for you,' sniffs Pete. 'The son he never had, with your £5,000 raise.'

'Right, listen, you miserable bastard, why did we buy Roger fucking Davies?'

'You doubting me and all now?' he shouts. 'Thanks a fucking bunch, mate.'

'I'm not bloody doubting you, Pete,' you tell him. 'But I want to hear you tell me why we went down to Worcester City and bought a non-league player for £14,000.'

'Because he's twenty-one years old, six foot odd and a decent fucking striker.'

'There you go,' you tell him. 'Now why didn't you say that to Longson?'

'Because he questioned my judgement; questioned the one bloody thing I can do: spot fucking players. I'm not you, Brian, and I never will be – on the telly, in the papers – and I don't bloody want to be. But I don't want to be questioned and fucking doubted either. I just want to be appreciated and respected. Is that too much to ask? A little bit of bloody respect? A little bit of fucking appreciation every now and again?'

'Fuck off,' I tell him. 'What was the first thing you ever said to me? Directors never say thank you, that's what. We could give them the league, the European Cup, and you know as well as I do that they'd never once say thank you. So don't let the bastards start getting under your skin now and stop feeling so fucking sorry for yourself.'

'You're right,' he says.

'I know I am.'

'You always are.'

'I know I am,' you say. 'So let's get back to work and make sure next season we bloody win that fucking title. Not for any fucking chairman or any board of bloody directors. For us; me and you; Clough and Taylor; and no one else.'

★ ★ ★

I am on my hands and my knees on the training ground, looking for that bloody watch of mine in the grass and the dirt. But the light is going and I'm sure one of them fucking nicked it anyway. There's a ball in the grass by the fence. I pick it up and chuck it up into the sky and volley it into the back of the practice net. I go and pick it out of the back of the net. I go back to the edge of the penalty box and chuck it up into the sky again, volley it into the back of the net again,

again and again and again, ten times in all, never missing, not once. But there are tears in my eyes and then I can't stop crying, stood there on that practice pitch in the dark, the tears rolling down my bloody cheeks, for once in my fucking life glad that I'm alone.

* * *

This has been a bad season; a season to forget. But today it's almost over. Today is the last game of the 1970–71 season. Today is also Dave Mackay's last game –

1 May 1971; home to West Bromwich Albion –

West Brom who last week helped put pay to the ambitions of Leeds United and Don Revie; Leeds United and Don Revie who have lost the league by a single point to Arsenal; Arsenal who have not only won the league but also the cup and become only the second-ever team to win the Double –

Tottenham being the only other team. Tottenham and Dave Mackay.

Two minutes from the end, from the end of his last match, a match Derby are winning 2–0, and Dave Mackay is still rushing to take a throw-in; still clapping urgently, demanding concentration and 100 per cent –

He has played all forty-two games of this season. Every single one of them.

Then the final whistle of his final match comes and off he goes, running from the pitch with a quick wave to the 33,651 here to see him off, off down that tunnel, down that tunnel and he's gone –

Irreplaceable. Fucking irreplaceable.

Derby County have finished ninth, scoring fifty-six and conceding fifty-four, drawing five at home and five away, winning sixteen and losing sixteen –

The symmetry being no bloody consolation whatsoever –

Because there is no fucking consolation –

No consolation for not winning –

That's irreplaceable.

* * *

I don't go back to the Dragonara. Not tonight. I go back home to Derby. Past the Midland Hotel. Past the Baseball Ground. But I don't stop. Not tonight –

Tonight, I get back to the house, the lights off and the door locked. I put away the car and I go inside the house. I put on a light and I make myself a cup of tea. I switch on the fire and I sit down in the rocking chair. I pick up the paper and I try to read, but it's all about Nixon and resignation, resignation, resignation:

'I have never been a quitter. To leave office before my term is complete is abhorrent to every instinct in my body . . . '

I put down the paper and I switch on the telly, but there's nothing on except documentaries and news programmes about Cyprus, Cyprus, Cyprus:

Deceit and division; division and hate; hate and war; war and death.

I switch off the telly and I switch off the fire. I wash up my pots and I switch off the lights. I go up the stairs and I clean my teeth. I look in my daughter's room and I kiss her sleeping head. I look in my sons' room and my eldest one says, 'Dad?'

'You still awake, are you?' I ask him. 'You should be asleep.'

'What time is it, Dad?' he asks me.

I look at my watch, but it's not there. I tell him, 'I don't know, but it's late.'

'You going to bed now, are you, Dad?'

'Course, I am,' I tell him. 'I got work tomorrow, haven't I? You want to come?'

'Not really,' he says. 'But will you tell us a joke? A new one?'

'I don't think I've got any new jokes.'

'But you've always got jokes, Dad,' he says. 'You know loads of jokes.'

'All right then,' I tell him. 'There's this bloke walking about down in London and suddenly London gets hit by an A-bomb . . .'

'Is this the joke, Dad?' he asks me.

'Yes,' I tell him. 'Just listen . . .'

'Is it a funny joke?'

'Just listen to me, will you?' I tell him again. 'So there's this bloke walking about and London gets hit by an A-bomb and now this bloke is the only man left in the whole of London. So he walks around and around London, the whole of London, and it takes him four or five days, until finally he realizes that he must be the only person left in the whole of London and he suddenly feels very, very lonely because there's nobody else to talk to. Nobody else but him. So he decides that he's had enough, that he doesn't want to be the only man left, and so he climbs up to the top of the Post Office tower . . .'

'The Post Office tower's all right then, is it, Dad?'

'What do you mean?'

'After the bomb,' he says. 'It's still all right, still there, is it?'

'Yes, it's fine,' I tell him. 'Don't worry about the Post Office tower. So anyway, this bloke, he climbs all the way up to the top of the Post Office tower and then he jumps off the top and he's falling down, down and down and down, the sixteenth floor, the fifteenth floor, the fourteenth floor, and that's when he hears the phone ringing!'

'When?'

'When he's passing the fourteenth floor!'

'But you said everybody else was dead?'

'But they're not. That's the joke.'

'I don't get it, Dad,' he says.

'That's good,' I tell him. 'I hope you never do.'

Day Sixteen

Times change. Faces change. One season ends and another one starts –

New season, new hope, and your first game of the 1971–72 season is at home to Manchester United; a crowd of over 35,000 and a pre-match thunderstorm. It is also your first game without Dave Mackay; Roy McFarland injured as well.

Half-time and you're two down; soft goals from Law and Gowling, both from Charlton corners. Soft, soft fucking goals. You go into that bloody dressing room and you let them have it, both fucking barrels:

'Fucking rubbish the lot of you. You might as well get dressed and bugger off home now, the bloody lot of you. Useless every last fucking one of you. First day of the bloody season and you're playing like this; first fucking day. You bloody lose today and you'll lose every fucking day and you'll be doing it in empty grounds and all. There are over 35,000 folk here to see you, bloody paid to see you, good money, hard-earned fucking money; you think they'll be back next week? Will they bloody hell. Now get out there and show all them 35,000 folk and that team of old men and so-called superstars what you're bloody made of, how you earn your big wages, and if you're still losing at that final fucking whistle don't bother coming back into work on Monday morning because you'll not have a bloody job to come to. Be the real world for the lot of you –

'Now fuck off, out of my sight!'

Five minutes later, Hinton floats a ball into their box; Wignall charges in and goes up with Stepney for it; the ball runs loose and Hector stabs it in. Ten minutes after that, Hennessey robs Georgie bleeding Best and passes the ball out to Hinton, who sends in another centre for O'Hare to head against the crossbar and Wignall to then bury. That's how it ends, 2–2.

'Carry on playing like that and they'll get me the sack,' you tell the world. Times change, faces change but the doubt remains. The fear remains –

Round every corner. Down every corridor –

Every match, every day, the doubt and then the fear.

I hate injured players. I don't want to hear their bloody names. I don't want to see their fucking faces. I stay out of the treatment rooms. I stay out of the bloody hospitals. I can't stand the fucking sight of them –

'I'm not taking you to Stoke,' I tell Eddie Gray, and then I watch his face fall; this face that has taken so much pain; worked through it; smiled through it all; the initial breaks and the many operations; the verdicts and the second opinions; the frustration and the depression; the rehabilitation and the therapy; the training and the cortisone –

I watch it fall to the floor and crawl across the carpet to the door.

Here is where League Championships are won and lost; here at Leeds Road, Huddersfield. Not White Hart Lane. Not Anfield or Highbury. Not Old Trafford in front of 50,000 crowds and the television millions –

Here, in this filthy Yorkshire town on a filthy Saturday in November in front of 15,000 filthy Yorkshire folk calling you every filthy fucking name they can bloody think of; here is where Championships are won, won and lost –

And Derby have just lost. 2-bloody-1. You look around this filthy fucking dressing room, these filthy fucking players, soaked to their bloody skins and covered in filthy fucking Yorkshire mud –

And you ask Colin Boulton, 'You want to get me the fucking sack, do you?'

'No, Boss,' he says.

'Well, you fucking will because you're a useless cunt of a keeper.'

You ask Ronnie Webster, 'You want to get me the fucking sack, do you?'

'No, Boss,' he says.

'Well, you fucking will because you're utter fucking shite. Bloody rubbish.'

You ask John Robson, 'You want to get me the fucking sack, do you?'

'No, Boss,' he says.

'Well, you will because you're the worst fucking defender I've ever seen.'

You ask Colin Todd, 'You want to get me the fucking sack, do you?'

'No,' he says. 'I don't.'

'Well, the amount of bloody money I fucking paid for you, I must have been

bloody pissed out of my fucking skull. You can't even bloody keep on your fucking feet.'

You ask McFarland, 'You want to get me the fucking sack, do you, Roy?'

'No,' he says.

'No, what?'

'No, Boss. I don't want to get you the sack.'

'Well, I don't fucking believe you,' you tell him and then turn to Terry Hennessey, 'You want to get me the fucking sack and all, do you?'

'No, Boss,' he says.

'So where the bloody hell were you this afternoon? You might as well have fucking stopped at home, use you were to me out there.'

You ask John McGovern, 'You want to get me the fucking sack, do you, John?'

'No, Boss,' he says.

'Well, you remember that open goal, that open bloody goal you should have stuck that fucking ball in?'

'Yes, Boss.'

'Well, that looked like a deliberate miss to me, to get your manager the sack.'

'I'm sorry, Boss,' he says. 'It wasn't.'

'Fuck off,' you tell him and turn to Archie Gemmill. 'You want to get me the fucking sack and all, do you, Scotsman?'

'No, Boss,' he says.

'Come on, admit it,' you tell him. 'You liked it better back in the Third Division, didn't you? Come on, admit it.'

'No, I didn't,' he says.

You shake your head and turn to John O'Hare and ask him the same question: 'You want to get me the fucking sack, do you?'

'No, Boss,' he says.

You point at Hinton and ask O'Hare, 'You know how many centres he sent in?'

'I'm sorry, Boss,' he says.

'No, you're not,' you tell him. 'Or you'd be out there now fucking practising.'

You ask Kevin Hector, 'You want to get me the fucking sack, do you?'

'No, Boss,' he says.

'Really?' you ask him. 'Didn't bloody look like that to me. Not when they took the lead and you had that chance – not chance – that fucking sitter when

you landed flat on your bloody arse. They'll be laughing about that in Huddersfield all fucking season.'

You turn to Alan Hinton. You tell him, 'You played well, Alan. Thank you.'

You leave them to Peter; for Peter to kiss them all better. You step out into the corridor and light a fag; there's Sam Longson, your chairman –

'Did you hear all that?' you ask Uncle Sam.

'You can't talk to people like that,' says Longson.

'Can't I?' you ask him. 'You just bloody watch me.'

★ ★ ★

'Jones injured. Gray injured. Bates injured. Yorath injured. Clarke suspended. Hunter suspended. The odds are already stacked against us,' I tell them as I pour the drinks –

For Harry from the Yorkshire Post. *For Ron from the* Evening Post –

'I'd have liked to have had a full squad available against Stoke because it is essential for us to start the season well. But being under strength does not mean I will abandon my open-play policy –'

Another round –

'Attack is my only policy –'

And another –

'This Saturday, every Saturday –'

And, go on then, twist my arm then, one last one for the road then –

'I cannot play the game any other way.'

★ ★ ★

The day after Boxing Day 1971 and you lose to Leeds. Again –

Again, just when you were beginning to believe; after losing at Huddersfield, you'd beaten Manchester City at home, then lost at Anfield but beaten Everton at home. You were beginning to believe again; to banish the doubt and the fear, slowly –

But then you come to Elland Road. Again. The doubt and the fear. Again –

You saw the doubt and the fear in the eyes and the hearts of your players, saw the doubt and the fear when Gemmill was downed early on, saw their eyes

*and their hearts go down with him. But today you don't swear; today you
don't shout or strip the walls of the visitors' dressing room. Today you will buy
them steak and pints on the way back to Derby. You will sit next to them on
the coach, put your arms around them and tell them that they are the best players in the country, the very best –*

*Because your team, your boys, do not pull shirts, do not nudge people in
the box, do not protest every decision, feigning innocence and then outrage –*

Because your boys do not lie and your boys do not cheat.

*But tonight you will still not sleep; tonight you'll still sit in your rocking
chair and stare at that league table and those fixtures to come. Tonight you will
still not close your eyes because tonight you'll see this game again, again and
again and again, over and over and over. But you still will not see the way Leeds
outwitted you on the flanks, still will not see your lack of any decent tackles, of
any physical presence, will not see the licence you gave to Lorimer and Gray –*

Tonight you will still see your team lose, but still lose only to cheats.

*You still will not see Gray beat Hennessey; you still will not see his one-
two with Bremner; you still will not see Gray's low shot into the goal. Nor will
you see Gray's crossfield pass to Bremner; Bremner's centre for Lorimer to score.
You still will not see Gray beat Webster and his pass to Lorimer; you still will
not see Lorimer change feet to shoot and score the third:*

'Leeds have a nasty habit of reminding Derby how far they have yet
to go.'

*You will still not sleep. You'll still sit and you'll stare at that league table and
those fixtures to come, again and again and again, but all you will see is the
look on Revie's face as that whistle went and the teams left that field, over and
over and over –*

The look on that face, the handshake and the smile, and that field –

That field of loss. That field of hate. That field of blood –

You will still not sleep, but you still will dream –

Of that field of war.

* * *

'Brian here,' I tell Lillian. 'Is Pete there?'

'Brian, it's two o'clock in the morning,' she says. 'He's asleep.'

'I'm sorry,' I tell her. 'I haven't got a watch.'

'Go to bed, Brian,' she says. 'I'll get him to call you first thing.'

'But I really need to speak to him now.'

'Has something happened, love?' she asks. 'Are you all right?'

'No, I'm not.'

'Where are you?' she asks.

'I'm in the sodding Dragonara Hotel in Leeds.'

'What are you doing there?' she asks. 'Get yourself back home.'

'I can't; I've got to take Billy bloody Bremner down to London in the morning.'

'But you'll be able to go straight home after that, won't you?'

'No,' I tell her. 'We're travelling to Stoke tomorrow night.'

'But you'll be home on Sunday, won't you?' she says. 'It's not long.'

'Six nights a week I used to be round your house,' I tell her. 'Remember that? And you two just married; you must have been sick of the sight of me.'

'No, Brian,' she says. 'We never were.'

'Pete and I'd always be going off somewhere to scout some game in the Northern League and then we'd bring back fish and chips. Do you remember?'

'Yes, Brian,' she says. 'I remember.'

'Rea's Ice-cream Parlour?' I ask her. 'Remember that place?'

'Yes, Brian,' she says again. 'I remember.'

'All gone now,' I tell her. 'The ice-cream parlours and the coffee bars.'

'I know, love.'

'Do you remember when me, you and Pete went to see *Saturday Night, Sunday Morning* at the pictures? That was a good night, wasn't it?'

'You liked that film, didn't you?'

'I bloody loved it,' you tell her. '*Don't let the bastards grind you down.*'

'You used to say that all the time.'

'And what about that time we went to hear Harold Wilson speak? Remember that? One of the clubs in Middlesbrough, it was. Barely fifty bloody folk to hear him and all; the future Prime Minister of Great Britain. Pete's idea. You remember that?'

'I remember you going,' she says. 'But that was just you and Peter, love.'

'You know I'd give my right arm for it to be like that again. Just me and him. This bloody lot here, they wouldn't stand a chance if it was me and him, the two of us. There'd be no more ganging up, no more whispering, no more conspiring behind my back. Me and Pete, we'd bloody sort them out, show them who was fucking boss.'

'I'll go and wake him for you,' she says. 'You need to talk to him –'

'Don't,' I tell her. 'Not now. It's too late.'

'If you're sure?' she says. 'But you get yourself off to bed then.'

'But how are you?' I ask her. 'How's Brighton? The children?'

'We're all well,' she says. 'Peter's very busy, of course, but the new flat's nice. Lovely view. Wendy likes her job too, settled in very well. But you don't want to hear about all that. You get yourself to bed and Peter will call you tomorrow.'

'I won't be here.'

'Hang on,' she says. 'He's coming downstairs now. I'll put him on.'

'Brian?' says Peter. 'What's wrong? It's half two in the morning.'

'Name your price,' I tell him. 'You can have whatever you want, but just come. We'll be able to sort this place out together. We'll be able to clean it up, to turn it around. We'll be able to put them in their fucking place. Stop all their whispering and conspiring, their plotting and scheming, their lying and cheating. Me and you, just like before –'

'Brian –'

'Tomorrow.'

'Brian –'

'It's too much for me,' I tell him. 'I need you up here, Pete.'

'There's no point kidding you,' he says. 'I'll not come to Leeds.'

'Then that's me and you finished,' I tell him and I hang up.

* * *

The Leeds defeat was a turning point. Again. You have now beaten Chelsea, Southampton, Coventry and Forest. You have beaten Notts County 6–0 in the FA Cup. You have given away tickets to striking miners. You are Cloughie. You can do what you want –

Football manager one week, prime minister the next.

Manchester United are in Nottingham. Frank O'Farrell is there to sign Ian Storey-Moore. Storey-Moore is a left-winger; fast, direct and twenty-eight years old. Nottingham Forest have accepted a £200,000 bid from United. O'Farrell and the Forest secretary have gone up to Edwalton Hall to finalize the deal with Ian Storey-Moore. Then Pete hears the deal is breaking down over Storey-Moore's personal terms –

Pete says, 'This one's ours, Brian.'

You pick up the phone. You dial Edwalton Hall. You catch Ian Storey-Moore –

'Cloughie here,' you tell him. 'Stay where you are, I'm coming over.'

You and Pete drive over to Nottingham. You make him an offer he can't refuse; Ian Storey-Moore will play for Derby. Not United –

Ian Storey-Moore signs blank forms –

The only thing missing is the signature of the Forest secretary.

Longson calls you. Longson asks you, 'Are you sure you're in order?'

'He wants to play for Derby County,' you tell him. 'So I've bought him.'

You take Ian Storey-Moore to the Midland Hotel, Derby. You introduce him to his new teammates. Before the home game against Wolves, you parade him around the Baseball Ground in a Derby County shirt as your new player. Your new player waves to the crowd. Your new player sits up in the directors' box to watch Derby beat Wolves 2–1.

Then you drive him back to the Midland Hotel after the game –

You lock him in a room with his wife, a nice room –

You cross your fingers. You hope for the best –

But Forest won't sign the transfer forms:

'I am absolutely staggered and distressed at the performance of Nottingham Forest Football Club this morning. They are depriving the game of the dignity it deserves, and I will not have Derby County brought into any disrepute by anyone in football.'

Sir Matt Busby buys Mrs Ian Storey-Moore a bouquet of flowers –

Ian Storey-Moore joins Manchester United.

You are outraged. You send a four-page telegram in protest to Alan Hardaker and the Football League Management Committee. Your chairman sends a second telegram disassociating himself from you and your protest –

You are outraged, fucking outraged –

Outraged and out for revenge, again.

Day Seventeen

I don't think I've slept; not since I hung up on Peter. Just lain here; eyes closed, thinking. Next news there's my old mate John Shaw from Derby banging on the hotel door:

'Do you fancy some company for the trip down to London?' he asks.

'I'm booked on the bloody train with Billy Bremner, aren't I?'

'Sod him,' he says. 'I'll drive you. Meet him at the FA.'

That's what we do then. We drive down to London –

Day before the season starts. Day before our first game –

Drive down to London, thanks to Billy Bremner, talking politics and unions, socialism and football, wishing it was a one-way trip –

'I hate them,' I tell John. 'I hate managing them. But what can I bloody do? They're filthy and they cheat. They've got it off to a fine art. If the pressure's on, someone goes down in the penalty area to give them time to regroup. Then one of them gets boot trouble, which is just an excuse for the trainer to pass on messages from the bench. You wouldn't believe what they're capable of . . .'

'Need to get you back to Derby County,' says John. 'Back where you belong.'

'Either I'll bust them or they'll bust me.'

★ ★ ★

April Fool's Day 1972, and Leeds United have come to you; 39,000 crammed inside the Baseball Ground to see you versus Revie.

Don's been up to his old tricks again too, telling anyone who'll listen that there'll be no Giles today; John ruled out with a troublesome strain. But then, surprise surprise, come three o'clock and here comes Johnny Giles –

It makes no odds. No difference today –

Today you will not lose. Not today –

Not on this field. Not today:

You create chance after chance as Robson hustles Bremner and O'Hare turns Charlton time after time to score twice, the second cannoning back off Sprake and going in off Hunter for an own goal. It is the first time you have beaten Leeds since that Easter when Revie fielded his reserves; but these were not his reserves today –

Today you have beaten Leeds United. Beaten Don Revie –

Today you go top; top of the First Division:

'Brilliant, indefatigable and utterly ruthless; Brian Clough and Derby County did not so much beat Revie and Leeds at the Baseball Ground as massacre them . . .'

You have beaten Leeds. You are top of the table. You resign –

You, Peter and Jimmy. The three of you resign –

'For want of a bit more money –'

* * *

'Now you let me do the talking,' says Sam Bolton when we meet. 'You're here to listen.'

Bremner of Leeds and Keegan of Liverpool don't even get to listen. They are made to wait outside the FA, so it's Brian Clough and Sam Bolton vs Bob Paisley and John Smith in front of Vernon Stokes, Harold Thompson and Ted Croker of the FA, here at Lancaster Gate, in the Corridors of Power, with the portraits on the walls:

Her Majesty the Queen and HRH the Duke of Kent; the patron of the Football Association and the President of the Football Association –

Power and money; money and power –

The Honorary Vice-Presidents; the Life Vice-Presidents; the plain old Vice-Presidents; the letters after their names, the titles before them; the Dukes, the Earls, the Air Marshals, the Generals, the Admirals, the Field-Marshals, the Majors and the Aldermen; the Right Honourable this and the Right Honourable that –

These are the men who run the game, who control English football –

These men with their money; these men with their power –

The money to appoint people. The power to sack people –
The money to select people. The power to drop them –
To fine and suspend them –

'You're here to listen.'

'Both clubs agree that the conduct of certain players in the match was deplorable and cannot be tolerated. Both realize that the good name of their club is involved, quite apart from the image of the game. The FA understands that both clubs are taking strong disciplinary action against the players concerned and the two who were sent off will also be dealt with by the FA in accordance with the agreed procedure. They will also face an FA disciplinary commission on charges of bringing the game into disrepute.'

'You're here to listen.'

'Our disciplinary work is costing us £30,000 a year, over and above the cost of maintaining a disciplinary department. We have better ways of spending this money.'

'You're here to listen.'

'We have to show that we will take disciplinary action against misdemeanours on and off the pitch; everyone agrees this has to be done.'

'You're here to listen.'

'I am not pessimistic about the future of football. We showed a slight improvement in the number of disciplinary cases last season but we have to increase that rate of improvement. No one is expecting no fouls to be committed on a football field. What we are trying to get rid of is dissent, and we want an acceptance of disciplines.'

'You're here to listen.'

'Leeds's disciplinary record was so much better last season than in the year before that they have obviously made a considerable effort to put their house in order.'

I stop listening. I start telling them, 'Eighty-four players will miss the opening-day fixtures due to suspensions from last season. Players like Stan Bowles and Mike Summerbee. Players like Norman Hunter and Allan Clarke.'

'I told you to listen,' says Bolton after the meeting. 'Told you to keep it bloody shut for once.'

'Let me give you some friendly advice, Mr Bolton,' I tell him. 'Never tell me what to do and then I'll never have to tell you what to do. Now take me back to Leeds.'

* * *

On 11 April 1972 your resignations are accepted by the Derby County board.

You've lost to Newcastle and drawn with West Brom. You held dressing-room inquisitions. Then you went to Sheffield and beat United 4–0 away –

You are still top. But you're still gone –

You, Pete and Jimmy. To Coventry.

Except Coventry City are getting cold feet now; their chairman has had the champagne on ice too long and the warmer his champagne gets, the colder his feet.

Three hours after your resignations are accepted, you and Pete drive out to Sam Longson's pile. You bring one of your tame directors with you.

'Do you really want to be remembered as the chairman who lost the best team in football management?' you ask Sam Longson. 'When Derby County were top of the league? The Championship within touching distance? Derby's first ever Championship. European glory on the horizon? Is that how you want to be remembered? As the chairman who gave it all away? Is that what you want, Mr Chairman?'

'For want of a bit more money,' adds Pete.

Sam Longson shakes his head. Sam Longson asks, 'But it's too late, isn't it? You've already signed with Coventry, haven't you?'

You put your arm around Sam and tell him, 'It's never too late, Mr Chairman.'

'For want of a bit more money,' adds Pete again.

'I told them they couldn't bloody have you,' says Longson. 'I told them hands off. But Coventry told me you wanted away from Derby –'

'No, no, no,' you tell him. 'Home is where this heart is; right here beside you.'

'They'll tell Coventry City to go to hell,' says your tame director –

'For want of a bit more money,' says Pete for the third time.

Longson dries his eyes, blows his nose and asks, 'How much will it take?'

'All we're asking,' you tell him, 'is for you to match their offer.'

Longson takes out his cheque book and asks, 'Which is?'

'An extra five grand for me, three for Pete and one for Jimmy,' you tell him.

Longson nods his head and signs the cheques while you pour the drinks.
In your car in his driveway, Pete asks, 'What if the old twit finds out?'
You stop looking at your cheque and ask him, 'Finds out what?'
'Finds out that Coventry had already pulled out of the deal.'
'So what if he does,' you tell Pete. 'What's he going to do? Sack us?'

★ ★ ★

It's late and pissing it down, and we're late and pissed off when we finally arrive at the hotel alongside the M6 near Stoke. The team get off the coach and walk towards the entrance and the reception, the warmth and the light. I call them back outside –

'Where do you think you're going?' I ask them. 'Get out here, the lot of you.'

They march back down the hotel steps, into the rain and into the night.

'This way,' I tell them and lead them round to the back of the hotel.

They stand there in their suits and their ties, in the rain and in the night, on the hotel lawn, and they listen, they listen to me:

'Tomorrow it all starts again; the first game of the season. I've won a League Championship and you've won a League Championship and so, no doubt, you all think you know what it bloody takes to win the fucking League Championship. Well, you don't, because you won your titles through deceit and deception. This season you're going to win the league my way; honestly and fairly. Now last season you played forty-two league games and you won twenty-four, drew fourteen and lost four; well, this season you'll play forty-two games and lose only three. Last season you scored sixty-six goals and you let in thirty-one; well, this season I want you to score more than seventy and let in less than thirty. And, if you do it my way, not only will you win the league, not only will you win it honestly and fairly, you'll also win the hearts of the public, which is something you've never fucking done before.'

In their suits and their ties, in the rain and the night, they listen:

'Not only the league title either; this season we're going after everything in sight. If Leeds United are entered for a competition, we'll be playing to win that competition. There'll be no reserve teams in the League Cup, no second-string teams in a Leeds shirt, not under Brian Clough. Because I won't settle for second best for my team. It is not in my nature. I am after excellence in all things and that includes every game we play –

'Every single fucking game, starting tomorrow. Right?'

There's silence on the hotel lawn from the suits and the ties, in the night and in the rain, so I ask them again and ask them louder than before, 'Right?'

'Right,' they mumble and they mutter.

'Right what?' I ask them.

'Right, Boss,' they say, in their suits and their ties, in the rain and in the night –

Under their breath, through gritted teeth.

'Right then,' I tell them. 'Let's go get our bloody dinners then.'

★ ★ ★

You easily beat Huddersfield Town 3–0 to stay top with just two games to go. You are now certain to finish in the top four; certain of a place in the UEFA Cup; certain of that, at the very least –

Just two games to go; two games, against Manchester City and against Liverpool. City, who are third, away; Liverpool, who are fourth, at home –

Two games to stop Leeds, two games to win the league.

On 22 April 1972 you travel to Maine Road, Manchester. It is the last home game of the season for Manchester City; Manchester City who are managed by your TV mate Malcolm Allison; Malcolm Allison who has just spent £200,000 on Rodney Marsh; Rodney Marsh who scores in the twenty-fifth minute and wins a second-half penalty, which Francis Lee converts. You have your chances too, but you also have your nerves –

Manchester City go top and you drop down to third:

	GP	W	D	L	GF	GA	Pts
Manchester City	42	23	11	8	77	45	57
Liverpool	40	24	8	8	64	29	56
Derby County	41	23	10	8	68	33	56
Leeds United	40	23	9	8	70	29	55

Now there is just one game to go for you in the league –

Home to Bill Shankly and Liverpool.

But before Bill Shankly and Liverpool, you have one other match: the second leg of the Texaco Cup final against Airdrieonians –

It is not the FA Cup. It is not the League Cup. But it is a cup.

You drew the first leg 0–0 in Scotland back in January. It was a hard bloody game and you know the return game will be a physical one too; you also know some of your squad will be called up for internationals and you still have to play Liverpool –

Bill Shankly and Liverpool.

You are forced to field five reserves. Not through deceit. Not through deception. Not like Don. This is through necessity. Sheer necessity. Roger Davies is one of those reserves and he scores, to Pete's delight. But Airdrie take the Derby man in every tackle and it is another hard and bloody night, but you win 2–1 –

You have won the Second Division Championship, the Watneys Cup and now this; the 1971–72 Texaco International League Board Competition –

It is not the FA Cup. It is not the League Cup. But it is a cup –

'It doesn't matter what Derby win,' you tell the newspapers and the television, 'just as long as we win, and it'll set us in good store for Liverpool and the league title.'

Day Eighteen

The Liverpool game has been moved to the first of May; your favourite day of the year. But you are not a superstitious man; you do not believe in luck –

'Not over forty-two games,' you tell the world. 'There's no such thing.'

But if you beat Liverpool today, you'll still have a chance of the title –

If Liverpool do not win their last game. If Leeds lose theirs.

But first Derby have to win; to beat Bill Shankly, Kevin Keegan and Liverpool; Bill Shankly, Kevin Keegan and Liverpool, who have taken twenty-eight out of the last thirty available points; who have not been beaten since the middle of January; who have conceded just three goals since then; who still have a game to go after this, away at Arsenal, still one more game; something you do not have; something you do not need.

'This is it,' you tell the dressing room. 'The last game of our season. The best season of our lives. The season we will win the League Championship. Enjoy it.'

It's an evening kick-off, but the sun's still shining as the two teams are announced, as the record 40,000 crowd gasp at your selection; you have named sixteen-year-old Steve Powell for the injured Ronnie Webster.

The score is still 0–0 at half-time. Your team, your boys, exhausted –

Exhausted by the tension of it all; the tension which crawls down from the fans on the terraces to the players on the pitch; the tension which crawls from the players to the referee; from the referee to the bench, to Peter and to Jimmy, to Bill Shankly and his Boot Room, but not to you; you put your head around the dressing-room door:

'Beautiful,' you tell them. 'More of the same next half, please.'

In the sixty-second minute of your forty-second game, Kevin Hector takes a throw on the right to Archie Gemmill; Gemmill runs across the edge of the Liverpool area and slips the ball to Alan Durban; Durban who leaves the ball with a dummy for John McGovern; McGovern who scores; John McGovern, your John McGovern, your boy –

The one they like to blame. The one they love to jeer —

1–0 to John McGovern and Derby County:

Boulton. Powell. Robson. Durban. McFarland. Todd. McGovern. Gemmill. O'Hare. Hector and Hinton; Hennessey on the bench with Pete, Jimmy and you; Cloughie, Cloughie. Cloughie.

	GP	W	D	L	GF	GA	Pts
Derby County	42	24	10	8	69	33	58
Leeds United	41	24	9	8	72	29	57
Manchester City	42	23	11	8	77	45	57
Liverpool	41	24	8	9	64	30	56

Bill Shankly shakes your hand and tells you it should have been a penalty, a clear penalty when Boulton floored Keegan, but well done all the same —

He still thinks he can go to Arsenal and win the league, you can see it in his eyes. Read him like a bloody book. But you know —

Know, know, know, know, know, know, and know —

Liverpool will not win their last game and Leeds, two days after a Cup Final against Arsenal, will lose at Wolverhampton Wanderers —

'But if my Derby side can't win it,' you tell the newspapers and the television, tell Revie and Leeds United, 'then I'd want Shanks and Liverpool to have that title.'

★ ★ ★

I haven't slept. Not a bloody wink. I've just sat on the edge of the hotel bed. The whole fucking length of the night. Looking at the empty glass on the bedside table. Next to the phone which never rings. Failing to make it move. Not a single fucking inch. Not one. Listening to the footsteps in the corridor. Up and down, up and down. For the key in the door, the turn of the handle. But the sun is shining now and Saturday's come. The first Saturday of the new season. The first Saturday for real. Police patrol the centre of Stoke in pairs, their German shepherd dogs straining on their leather leashes. For real —

Leeds United are coming to town. Leeds United are coming to town . . .

The first Saturday of the new season; the first game of the new season.

I stand by the door to the coach and I watch the team board the bus for the trip to the Victoria Ground. Harvey and Hunter get on; Hunter who is suspended anyway –

'You'll not be doing this much longer,' I tell them. 'It'll soon be Peter Shilton and Colin Todd, not you two.'

Harvey and Hunter don't say anything, they just take their seats on the team bus.

The coach through the streets, fists against the side, gob against the glass . . .

I stand up at the front of the team bus as we drive to the ground and I tell them, 'I've got a bit of bad news for you, gentlemen. There will be no pre-match bingo today. No carpet bowls either. Now I know you're all fond of your bingo and your bowls, but I'm afraid those days are gone. Just football from now on, please.'

The fists against the side, the gob against the glass . . .

The players say nothing, in their club suits and their club ties with their long hair and their strong aftershave, their heads and their shoulders in their books and their cards.

The gob against the glass.

The coach arrives in the car park. The team and I run the gauntlet of autograph-hunters and abuse, and I leave them to get changed and head for the private bar; I'll not be bothering with a team talk. Not today. There's no point. I've just stuck the team sheet on the dressing-room wall and I'll let them sort it out for themselves –

They're professional fucking footballers, aren't they?

I've brought in Trevor Cherry for Hunter and I'm also starting with Terry Cooper; his first league game in two years, first league game since he broke his leg on this very ground; a chance for both Cherry and Cooper to prove themselves –

Prove themselves in front of the watching scouts from Leicester and Forest.

Ten to three and I finish my drink. I walk back down the stairs. Round the corner. Down the corridor. I stand by the dressing-room door and I stare at each one of them:

Harvey. Reaney. Cooper. Bremner. McQueen. Cherry. Lorimer. Madeley.

Jordan. Giles and McKenzie.

I stare at each one of them and I wonder how much they want to win this game –

How much do they really, really want to win this fucking game?

I stare into their eyes and know I can make them win or lose this game –

Win or lose it with the flick of a switch.

Half-time and it's 0–0; half-time and I flick that switch:

'Do you want to win this bloody game?' I ask the Irishman –

'What about you?' I ask Bremner. 'Fucking suspension hasn't started yet.'

Five minutes into the second half, Terry Cooper gets a booking and Bremner misses a tackle and Leeds are a goal down –

Three down by full-time.

The press are waiting, the television too:

'We played enough good football to win three bloody matches,' I convince them. 'In the first half hour we played well enough to be three up. I'm not saying Stoke didn't deserve to win – I'd never say that – but it could have gone either way and I do feel very sorry for the lads, very sorry –

'They wanted to win so badly.'

I'm the last on the bus and the driver gives me another dose of West Riding charm. I sit down at the front next to Jimmy, head against the window, and then the team begins to applaud me, the whole coach clapping me –

Slowly; very, very slowly –

'I feel very sorry for the lads.'

Just like the big fat fucking smile that's growing across my lips, across my face.

★ ★ ★

Leeds are still 10–11 favourites; Liverpool 11–8; Derby County 8–1.

But there's a whole week to wait, and you don't like waiting, so you go on holiday; Peter takes the team to Cala Millor, Majorca, for a week in the sun.

You make bloody sure the press know that's where Derby have gone; fucking sure Revie and Leeds know that's where Derby have gone; sunning themselves in Majorca, the bets laid at generous prices and the champagne on ice –

'No sweat,' Pete keeps telling the team. 'The Championship is ours.'

You don't go to Spain, not this time. You take your mam, your dad, your wife and your kids to the Island Hotel, Tresco, in the Scilly Isles. You pretend not to care about the Championship, not to be interested, but you think of nothing else –

Nothing else as you build sandcastles with the kids on the beach –

Nothing else; Liverpool and Shankly you could get over. Perhaps. But not Leeds and Revie. Never. Not again. Not Revie. That team. But you know in your heart of hearts, your darkest heart of hearts, you know that Don will have prepared his dossiers, will have laid out his lucky blue suit, filled the envelopes full of used banknotes, had a chat with the referee and packed the bingo cards and the carpet bowls –

Nothing left to chance.

On the Saturday night at the Island Hotel, you hear Leeds have beaten Arsenal to win the Centenary Cup final. Leeds are now just one game away from a cup and league double; Arsenal now no competition for Liverpool.

Last week you were certain it would be you who won the title. You just knew –

Now you're not so sure, the sandcastles washed away each day by the tide –

These tides of doubt and tides of fear, these seas of doubt and fear.

Monday night, nine o'clock, the phone at the Island Hotel starts to ring –

Liverpool have drawn with Arsenal and Leeds have lost at Wolves –

You kiss your mam, your dad, your wife and your kids; you order champagne for the guests and the staff of the Island Hotel and pose for the Sun on the beach –

On the beach in the tides of champagne, the seas of champagne –

Champagne in the Scilly Isles. Champagne in Majorca. Champagne in the boardroom at Highbury where Old Sam has gone to watch Liverpool and Shankly lose –

'Keeping the management and winning the title,' Old Sam Longson declares. 'What more could the people and fans of Derby ask for?'

Three bottles of champagne. Three separate bottles of champagne –

Derby County are the 1971–72 First Division Champions –

Those final league placings for ever on your wall –
It is a beautiful night; Monday 8 May 1972 –
And fear is dead. Doubt is dead –
Long live Cloughie!

THE SECOND RECKONING

First Division Positions, 18 August 1974

		P	W	D	L	F	A	Pts
1	Man. City	1	1	0	0	4	0	2
2	Middlesbrough	1	1	0	0	3	0	2
3	Stoke City	1	1	0	0	3	0	2
4	Carlisle United	1	1	0	0	2	0	2
5	Liverpool	1	1	0	0	2	1	2
6	Wolves	1	1	0	0	2	1	2
7	Newcastle Utd	1	1	0	0	3	2	2
8	Arsenal	1	1	0	0	1	0	2
9	Ipswich Town	1	1	0	0	1	0	2
10	QPR	1	0	1	0	1	1	1
11	Sheffield Utd	1	0	1	0	1	1	1
12	Derby County	1	0	1	0	0	0	1
13	Everton	1	0	1	0	0	0	1
14	Coventry City	1	0	0	1	2	3	0
15	Burnley	1	0	0	1	1	2	0
16	Luton Town	1	0	0	1	1	2	0
17	Birmingham C.	1	0	0	1	0	3	0
18	Chelsea	1	0	0	1	0	2	0
19	**Leeds United**	**1**	**0**	**0**	**1**	**0**	**3**	**0**
20	Leicester City	1	0	0	1	0	1	0
21	Tottenham H.	1	0	0	1	0	1	0
22	West Ham Utd	1	0	0	1	0	4	0

I have come to turn the stones –
Eleven round stones to place one upon another, one after another –
On the Cursing Stone.
One after another, one on top of another, I place them stones –
But if one should slip, if one should fall, the curse will fail –
But I place my stones. Then I say your name –
'Brian.'

Day Nineteen

I wake up on Sunday morning at the Dragonara with another bloody hangover, of booze and dreams, thinking how fucking ungracious they are; never ever been gracious in defeat have Leeds United; always had their excuses have Leeds; always the poor tale –

Runners-up in the league and the cup in 1964–65; runners-up in the Inter-Cities Fairs Cup, 1965–66; two disallowed goals in the FA Cup semi-final against Chelsea and runners-up in the Inter-Cities Fairs Cup again in 1966–67; finally winners of the Inter-Cities Fairs Cup and also of the Football League Cup in 1967–68, but lose the semi-final of the FA Cup through a Gary 'Careless Hands' Sprake howler; finally League Champions in 1968–69 but go out of the Inter-Cities Fairs Cup in the quarter-finals; 1969–70, they finish second in the league, runners-up in the FA Cup final and are knocked out of the European Cup in the semi-finals by Celtic, blaming 'fixture congestion', 'injuries' and Gary Sprake; 1970–71, they go out of the cup to Fourth Division Colchester and claim only to have lost the league thanks to a referee called Ray Tinkler, who allowed an offside West Brom goal to stand, though they manage to pull themselves together to win the Inter-Cities Fairs Cup for a second time; then, in 1971–72, they are made to play their first four home games away from Elland Road – because of the pitch invasion following the West Brom game and because of the comments made by Revie and his chairman, Woodward – and that season they do win the cup but lose their very last game of the season at Wolverhampton Wanderers, Derby County winning the league –

Derby County and Brian Clough.

'There were no congratulations from Revie,' I tell the Turkish waiter over a very, very late breakfast. 'It was always Leeds had lost the title, never Derby had won it.'

No congratulations. No well done. No nice one. No good for you, Brian . . .

'I tell you, it still makes me seethe; the things they wrote in the papers, the things they said on the telly; that Derby had won the title by default. Default? Fucking idiots. How can you win a league fucking title by default? You tell me that, Mehmet?'

The waiter shakes his head and says, 'You can't, Mr Clough.'

'Bloody right you can't,' I tell him. 'You know that and I know that; you can't win a title by default, not over forty-two fucking games, you can't. We had a fine team who had achieved the best results over a season of forty-two games and so we were the Champions. Not Leeds. Not Liverpool. Not Manchester City –

'Derby bloody County and Brian bloody Clough, that's who.'

Just hard feelings. Ill will. Hostility and enmity –

And a police investigation.

'Nothing was ever proved mind,' I tell the waiter. 'But where there's smoke there's fire, and old Don certainly knows how to light a fire.'

The waiter smiles and says, 'Fires are dangerous things, Mr Clough.'

'Exactly, Mehmet,' I tell him. 'But you've got to remember that Revie and Leeds only needed a point; just one single fucking point and that title was theirs. The league and cup double. They'd just won the cup, don't forget that. Beaten Arsenal only forty-eight hours before. The bookies still had Leeds as 10–11 favourites for the title, Derby right out at 6–1. And don't forget Liverpool; Shanks and Liverpool were still in the race. The atmosphere was white hot, apparently. The atmosphere at Molineux before the Wolves game. There were allegations of bribery, you know?'

The waiter looks confused. He asks, 'That the bookies bribed the Wolves?'

'No, no, no,' I tell him. 'It was in the *Sunday People*; Sprake, their own former fucking keeper, putting it about that former Leeds United players had been in the Wolverhampton dressing room, having a word or two, asking Wolves to go easy and throw the match for £1,000; having a word or two with the referee and all, offering cash in an envelope for a penalty in the Wolves box, and – this is the fucking irony of it all – Leeds actually had a decent penalty appeal turned down, apparently. Handball, clear handball. Bernard Shaw was the player's name, I think. Blatant penalty, from what I hear. But you know what I think? I think all Don's chickens came home to roost that night because of all the rumours and what-have-you, the rumours of a fix, they probably made the referee think twice before giving Leeds anything. Referee doesn't want people saying that he turned a blind eye or gave a penalty for an envelope under the table, does he? But then, and this is what really got to me, then while the FA and the CID are sniffing around, the Director of Public fucking Prosecutions and all, while they're all sniffing around, Don's on the bloody box and in the fucking papers crying the bloody poor tale again; fixture congestion, injuries, suspension, bad refereeing and bad bloody luck –

'Anything and anybody but themselves –'

'It's just too much. We should have had at least three penalties. When you get decisions like that going against you, what can you do?'

The waiter still looks confused. The waiter repeats, 'Bad luck?'

'Bad luck? Bad luck my fucking arse. There's no such bloody thing as bad luck, bad luck or good, not over forty-two games. If Leeds United had been better than Derby County then Leeds United would have won that title and not Derby County. But Leeds lost nine games and we lost eight, so Leeds finished second and we finished first –

'Champions! End of bloody story.'

Mehmet the waiter picks up my empty coffee cup and nods his head.

'Last two seasons haven't been much better for them, have they?' I tell Mehmet. 'In 1972–73 they lost to bloody Second Division Sunderland in the FA Cup final and then to AC Milan in the Cup Winners' Cup final. They might have won the league last year but, since Revie took them over, they've lost three FA Cup finals and two semi-finals; three European finals and two semi-finals; and they've "just" missed out on the league eight bloody times, runners-up five fucking times. What do you say about that, Mehmet?'

Mehmet shrugs his shoulders and says again, 'Bad luck?'

'Bad fucking luck my arse,' I tell the man again. 'I'll tell you what it is, shall I? It's because they've been so fucking hated, so absolutely despised by everybody outside this bloody city. Everybody! Do you know what I mean?'

Mehmet shrugs his shoulders again, then nods again and says, 'Everybody.'

'Just think about it,' I tell him. 'All those bloody times Leeds "just" missed out on a league title or "just" lost a cup final, you know why? I'll tell you why, shall I? Because every team they met, in every bloody match they ever played, they hated Leeds, they despised them. That Monday night at Molineux, that night in front of fifty-odd-thousand of their own supporters, there was no way Wolves were going to go easy on Leeds, no way they were going to throw the match; no way because they hated Leeds United, they despised Leeds United. Their keeper Parkes, players like Munro and Dougan, these players had the game of their lives and I'll tell you why, shall I? Because there's not a team in the country, not a team in Europe, who does not want to beat Don Revie and Leeds United. Not one. That's all they dream about, playing Don Revie and Leeds United and beating Don Revie and Leeds United. That's all I dream about, playing Don Revie and Leeds United, beating Don Revie and Leeds United –

'You'd be the bloody same, Mehmet, if you were me.'

Mehmet the waiter looks confused. Mehmet the waiter shakes his head and says, 'But you're the manager of Leeds United now, aren't you, Mr Clough?'

Day Twenty

You have won the 1971–72 League Championship; you have beaten Shanks and Liverpool; you have beaten Revie and Leeds –

You are the Champions of England.

The summer months see the builders back to the Baseball Ground, now you're in the European Cup; there has been work on the Osmaston End and on the Normanton Stand; new, pylon-mounted floodlights are also erected, now your games will be shown in colour at home and abroad –

Now you are the Champions.

But all your dreams are nightmares and all your hopes are hells, the birds and the badgers, the foxes and the ferrets, the dogs and the demons, the wolves and the vultures, all circling around you, the clouds and the storms gathering above you, above the new pylon-mounted floodlights, your pockets filled with lists, your walls defaced with threats, your cigarettes won't stay lit, your drinks won't stay down.

The parties and the banquets, the civic receptions and the open-top bus tours, the parades and the photographs; the Championship dinner that no other club dare attend; the Charity Shield you'll never defend –

Every one a pantomime, every one a lie –

You can't stand the directors and the directors can't stand you:

'The threat to me comes from the faceless, nameless men in long coats with long knives who operate behind closed doors.'

There is a war coming; a civil bloody war.

★ ★ ★

No need for nightmares. Not today . . .

Every day I wake up and wonder if I'll ever win again; Hartlepools, Derby and Brighton, every day I wondered if I'd ever win again. But today I wake up and for the first time wonder if I'll ever bloody *want* to win again; if I'll ever give a fuck again –

Monday 19 August 1974.

I have a shit. I have a shave. I get washed and I get dressed. I go downstairs. The boys are already out in the garden with their mates, having a kick about in the dew. My daughter's at the table, colouring in. My wife puts my breakfast down in front of me and moves the newspaper away, out of my sight. I reach over and I bring it back –

No need for nightmares, that's what I told the press on Saturday and that's their headline for today, and that's what I'll tell them again; today and every fucking day –

'But what'll you tell yourself?' asks my wife. 'Tell my husband?'

* * *

There's been trouble all your life, everywhere you've ever been, one crisis after another; one war after another. This time, this trouble, this war starts like this:

'I'm not bloody going then,' you tell the Derby board. 'Simple as that.'

'It's the pre-season tour,' says Sam Longson. 'Holland and West Germany; your own suggestion. The reason you won't let Derby compete in the Charity Shield.'

'You're still going on about that, are you?'

'I'm not going on about it,' says Longson. 'But you're not making any sense.'

'Listen,' you tell him. 'The tour was arranged long before we won the title.'

'When you were saying we couldn't win it,' says Jack Kirkland –

The Big Noise from Belper, that's what Pete calls Jack Kirkland; made his pile in plant hire but thinks he knows his football; plans to turn the Baseball Ground into a sports complex; plans that need big gates and your transfer money, the money you've put in their coffers with those 33,000 gates you've brought them, money you need to spend to bring them more big gates or you'll get the sack –

But Jack Kirkland doesn't give a fuck about that; Jack Kirkland is the brother of Bob Kirkland; Bob Kirkland who you and Pete forced to resign –

Now Jack Kirkland, the Big Noise from Belper, is out for a seat on the board; a seat on the board and your head and Pete's on a pole –

Jack Kirkland is out for revenge.

'*No bloody pleasing you, is there?' you ask him. 'One minute I'm arrogant and conceited, next minute you're throwing my humility and honesty back in my face.*'

'*If you can't stand the heat,' begins Kirkland –*

'*The point is –' interrupts Longson . . .*

But two can play at that game and so you tell him, 'The point is either my family comes on this bloody trip or I don't fucking go.'

This is how it goes, round and round, until Longson has had enough:

'*This is a working trip, not a holiday,' he shouts. 'And I am ordering you in no circumstances to take your wife and kids with the team to Holland or West Germany.*'

'*You're ordering me? Ordering me?' you ask him, repeatedly. 'Ordering me? Who the fucking hell do you think you are?*'

'*The chairman of Derby County,' he says. 'Chairman before you came here.*'

'*That's right,' you tell him. 'You were chairman of Derby County before I came here, I remember that; when Derby County were at the fucking foot of the Second Division, when nobody had heard of them for twenty years and nobody had heard of Sam bloody Longson ever. Full stop. I remember that. And that's where you'd still fucking be if it wasn't for me; at the foot of the bloody Second Division, where nobody remembered you and nobody had heard of you. Just remember, there would be no Derby County without me, no league title, no Champions of England; not without Brian Clough –*

'*Just you remember that, Mr bloody Chairman.*'

Longson sighs and says again, 'You're not taking your family on a working trip.'

'*Then I'm not fucking going,' you tell him –*

And you don't. And that's how it starts; this trouble, this war, this time.

★ ★ ★

Ten minutes after that final whistle on Saturday I'd taken the call from Elland Road; Eddie Gray had pulled up during the Central League reserve match, limped off –

'*If you'd been a bloody racehorse, you'd have been fucking shot.*'

157

Injuries and suspensions, bad decisions and bad bloody luck –
The Curse of Leeds United.

Through the doors. Under the stand. Round the corner. Down the corridor. I'm sat at that bloody desk in that fucking office, wondering what the fuck I'm going to do on Wednesday against Queen's Park bloody Rangers, who the fuck I should play, who the fuck I should not, who the fuck I'm going to be *able* to play, when Jimmy Gordon puts his head around the door and his thumb up –

'You're fucking joking?' I ask him.

'No joke,' says Jimmy. 'Sale of the century time.'

★ ★ ★

Peter is on the pre-season tour of Holland and Germany with the team and the directors. You are at home in Derby with the wife and the kids –

It is August 1972.

This is when the Football League Management Committee make their report, their report into your conduct in the Ian Storey-Moore transfer fiasco:

'The Committee considered evidence both verbally and in writing from Nottingham Forest, Derby County, the player and from the League Secretary. It transpired that, although the player had signed the transfer form for Derby County, this form was never signed by Nottingham Forest and the player could not remember having signed a contract for Derby County. It was admitted that the League Secretary had informed the club secretary of Derby County that, until the transfer form was completed by Nottingham Forest, the player was not registered with Derby County. The Committee was satisfied, therefore, that by taking the player to Derby and announcing publicly that he was their player, while he was still registered with Nottingham Forest, Derby County had committed a breach of Football League Regulation 52(a).'

The Football League Management Committee fine Derby £5,000 –
Because it's Derby County. Because it's Brian bloody Clough –
Because of the things you've said. The things you've done –
Because you won't play in their Charity Shield –
Because you won't keep it bloody shut.
This is how the 1972–73 season starts for the Champions of England:

158

Not with the Charity Shield, not with the Championship dinner, but with Peter, the team and the directors in Holland playing ADO of the Hague, while you, the wife and the kids are at home in Derby with your reprimands and with your fines –

The whole bloody world at war with you; you at war with the whole bloody world.

★ ★ ★

'Now just you wait one bloody minute, Clough,' says Sam Bolton.

'There isn't a bloody minute,' I tell him and I stand up.

'Sit down,' he says and he means it. 'Enough bloody stunts. It's not your brass you're spending, so you'll bloody well sit down and shut up until this meeting is over and we tell you whether or not we've accepted or refused your request for transfer funds.'

I roll my eyes and tell him, 'There's a match on Wednesday night.'

'I know that,' says Bolton.

'Well then, do you know how many players you have available to play?'

'That's your job, Clough,' he says. 'Not mine.'

'Exactly,' I tell him. 'Now you're talking some bloody sense, Mr Bolton. So if it's my job to know how many players are available, then it's my job to go out and bloody buy some more if we've got three players suspended, two with long-term injuries and countless bloody others with short-term ones. Isn't it now?'

'I don't think anybody doubts your motives,' says Cussins, the peacemaker.

'Oh really?' I ask him. 'It doesn't bloody sound like that to me.'

'I just think,' he says, 'that perhaps the Derby County way of doing things and the Leeds United way of doing things are probably quite different.'

'I would bloody well hope they are,' laughs Bolton.

'What do you mean by that?' I ask him.

'Come on, Clough,' says Bolton. 'World and his wife knows how you treated Sam Longson and rest of them mugs on Derby board. You had them all round your little bloody finger, eating out of palm of your hand, didn't you now?'

'So what?' I ask him. 'I won the title for them, didn't I? Took them to the semi-finals of the European Cup. They were forgotten when I took them over, were Derby. Yesterday's men they were. Now look at them; household name now Derby County.'

'I know *you* are,' smiles Bolton.

I look at my watch but I've not got one, so I just ask them outright, there and then, 'I want John McGovern and I want John O'Hare. Derby want £130,000 for them –

'Yes or no?'

★ ★ ★

You are the Champions of England and this is how you start the defence of your title on the opening day of the 1972–73 season:

Down at the Dell, you draw 1–1 with Southampton in front of the lowest gate of the day; the lowest gate of the day to see the Champions of England, see the Champions of England miss chance after chance. The only good thing you take back to Derby is the performance of John Robson in the back four. Three days later, you draw again at Selhurst Park. In another disappointing game, your best player is again John Robson.

This is how you start the defence of your title, as Champions of England, with draws against Southampton and Crystal Palace. But it doesn't worry you, not much –

Not with all the other things on your plate and on your mind; on your mind and on the box; on the box with your new contract from London Weekend Television for On the Ball, On the Ball *and in the papers; in the papers and in your columns; your columns for the* Sunday Express:

The FA Cup should be suspended for a year to give England the best possible chance in the World Cup. I feel I am the best manager to handle George Best; he's a footballing genius and I'm a footballing genius, so we should be able to get along well enough. I'll actually be leaving football shortly. I fancy a job outside the game; one which would give me more time with my family. I'm thinking of telephoning Sir Alf and offering to swap jobs for a year. Unfortunately the chairman has refused to give me time off to accompany England on their winter tour of the West Indies. I think I would like the supreme job of dictating football. I would halt league football in March to give the national side three months' preparation for the World Cup finals.

★ ★ ★

Just one call, that's all it takes. Jimmy to Dave. Just one call and I'm on my way. From Elland Road to the Baseball Ground.

I get Archer, the club secretary, to drive while I sit in the back with Ron from the *Evening Post*; bit of an exclusive for Ron this, put a few noses out of joint, but Ron and the *Post* have been good to me; kept me company at the Dragonara; kept me from my bed, my modern luxury hotel bed; never one to say no to a drink is our Ron from the *Post*.

Teatime and I'm sat down with Dave Mackay in *my* old office; Dave in *my* old chair at *my* old desk, pouring the drinks into *my* old glasses.

'You weren't ever tempted to burn that bloody desk, were you, Dave?'

'Oh, aye,' he tells me. 'The way the fucking players went on about you, on and on about you. Fucking Cloughie this, fucking Cloughie that. Like you'd never left the fucking building, felt like you were fucking haunting the place.'

'So why didn't you burn the bloody stuff?' I ask him. 'Have fucking done?'

'Be a waste of a good desk,' he laughs –

In my chair. At my desk. In my office. The tight Scottish bastard.

From the Baseball Ground to the Midland Hotel, where John and John are waiting. Not waiting in the lobby. John McGovern and John O'Hare are in the bar –

These are my boys and my boys know me.

'Champagne,' I tell Steve the barman. 'And keep it bloody coming, young man. Because tonight it's on Leeds United Football Club.'

★ ★ ★

Chelsea beat you 2–1 in your first home game of the season; your first home game in defence of your title, in front of 32,000. You play with frenzy and anxiety, bookings and dissent; no retention and no penetration, no calmness and no method. You have lost faith in yourselves; faith in yourself.

There's also trouble on the terraces, fighting among the fans for the first time, police dogs and police sirens up and down the side streets, trouble and fighting –

Off the pitch and on the pitch; in the boardroom and in the dressing room; upstairs and downstairs; round every corner, down every corridor.

You will beat Manchester City and you will climb to twelfth in the league before the end of August 1972. But before the end of August 1972 the press already have a new title for Derby County: Fallen Champions –

Last year's men managed by last year's man; Farewell Cloughie.

Peter takes you to one side. Peter says, 'Sell John Robson.'

'What you talking about?' you ask him. 'He's just got a Championship medal; played in all but one of our games last season, not put a foot wrong this season.'

'Fuck him,' says Pete. 'We're talking about the European bloody Cup, Brian. Not resting on our fucking laurels. Robbo's got his medal, now let's get rid.'

Pete's had his ear to the ground, got out his little black book, lips to the phone; Leicester City have been flashing the cash; buying Frank Worthington for £150,000 and signing Denis Rofe at full-back for £112,000 –

'Where does this leave David Nish?' asks Pete.

'On his way to Derby County perhaps?'

Pete nods. Pete pats you on the back. Pete says, 'Go do your stuff, Brian.'

★ ★ ★

The press switch on their microphones and pick up their drinks –

'I could not let down the Leeds supporters in the type of quality players they are used to. We were faced with an absolute crisis for Wednesday night with Allan Clarke, Norman Hunter and Billy Bremner under suspension, Terry Yorath recovering from enteritis, Eddie Gray out of action after breaking down in the reserves with thigh trouble, Mick Jones recovering from a knee operation and Frank Gray going down with influenza.

'So I am absolutely delighted to get McGovern and O'Hare, for the type of players they are and the type of people they are. They are both players of character and skill and they give me cover at a time when injuries and suspensions are a real problem.'

– the press put down their drinks. The press pick up the telephones.

* * *

You did not make an appointment. You did not telephone. You do not wait in line and you do not knock. You just walk straight into the Leicester City board-room and tell them, 'I've come to buy your full-back.'

Len Shipman, the chairman of Leicester City and the president of the Football League, is not impressed. Shipman says, 'This is a very important meeting and you can't just come barging in here, uninvited.'

'Very good,' you tell him. 'I'll wait outside, but you'll still be skint.'

You don't care; don't give a fuck. You're going to buy David Nish for £225,000 whether Leicester like it or not; whether Derby like it or not –

'Derby County – the Biggest Spending Club in the League!'

Derby County do not like it. Sam Longson says, 'That's a hell of a lot of money to spend on a full-back with no caps; a full-back who won't even be eligible for the opening European Cup games. A hell of a lot of money to spend without even asking.'

'There wasn't the time,' you lie. 'There were other clubs knocking.'

'Look, Brian, we've always done our best to provide cash for Peter and yourself. But where is the consultation, where is the conversation? The respect and the trust?'

'Like I told you, no time.'

'But the board firmly believes we could have got Nish for considerably less than the £225,000 you paid for him, had we been consulted.'

'I telephoned, didn't I?'

'From the hotel bar,' says Longson. 'Drunk as a lord.'

'We were celebrating a job well done.'

'I will bite my tongue,' he says. 'And I will swallow my pride as best I can.'

'You do that then,' you tell him. 'You do that, Sam.'

* * *

It is late when I get a taxi from the Midland Hotel back to the house. I make it go past the Baseball Ground on the way, the long way home –

'Never should have done what they did to you,' says the driver. 'Outrageous.'

'Did it all to ourselves,' I tell him. 'It was all bloody self-inflicted, mate.'

'I don't know about that,' says the driver. 'But it wasn't right, I do know that.'

'You're a good man,' I tell him.

'Not right,' he says again. 'Everybody knows that. You ask anybody.'

'Not in Leeds,' I tell him.

The driver stops the taxi outside the house. He turns round to face me in the back. He asks, 'What did you go there for, Brian? They don't deserve you. Not Leeds.'

★ ★ ★

Kirkland stops you and Peter in the corridor outside the visitors' dressing room at Carrow Road; stops you after you've just lost to Norwich City on David Nish's début for Derby County; Derby County, the Champions of England, now sixteenth in the league; Jack Kirkland stops you and says, 'That's your lot.'

'Our bloody what?' says Peter.

'Big-money signings like Nish,' Kirkland says. 'That's your lot.'

'The influx of players must never stop,' says Peter. 'It's a club's lifeblood.'

'No more transfusions then,' Kirkland laughs. 'That's your lot.'

'Fuck off,' shouts Peter. 'Fuck off!'

'No chance,' Kirkland winks. 'Be you two gone before me, I promise you.'

Day Twenty-one

My car is still at Elland Road, so Jimmy Gordon comes to the house for me at half eight and then we go to pick up McGovern and O'Hare from the Midland.

'Be able to run a bloody bus service soon,' laughs Jimmy. 'The Derby Express.'

'Fucking hope so,' I tell him. 'The sooner the bloody better and all.'

★ ★ ★

Four days after losing to bottom-placed West Bromwich Albion, on a day when you, the Champions of England, are still sixteenth in the league table, despite having beaten Liverpool but still having lost four out of eight games, winning just twice and scoring only six goals, on this day you take your European bow. Not in the Inter-Cities Fairs Cup; not in the Cup Winners' Cup; but in the Holy Grail itself, the European Cup.

Only Jock Stein and Celtic, Busby and United have drunk from this cup; this cup that you dream of, that would make the nightmares cease –

The doubts and the fears; give what you want above all else –

Because this is what you want and this is what you'll get.

It is 13 September 1972 and you are at home to Željezničar Sarajevo of Yugoslavia in the preliminary round; two legs, home and away, winner takes all.

'Forget West Bromwich fucking Albion. Forget Everton. Forget Norwich and forget Chelsea,' you tell the Derby dressing room. 'Anybody can play against West Bromwich Albion. Against Everton, Norwich and bloody Chelsea –

'But this is the European Cup. The European fucking Cup. Only one English team a year plays for this cup. Tonight we're that team –

'Not Liverpool. Not Arsenal. Not Manchester United. Not Leeds United –

'Derby fucking County are out there, on that pitch and in the history books –

'So you go out there, onto that pitch, into those history books, and you fucking enjoy yourselves because, if you don't, it might never bloody happen to you again.'

★ ★ ★

Under the stand and through the doors and round the corner, I am walking down and down and down that corridor, past Syd Owen and past Maurice Lindley, when Syd says behind my back and under his breath, behind his hand and through gritted teeth, he says something that sounds like, 'The fucking hell did he buy them for?'

I stop in my tracks. I turn back and I ask, 'You what?'

'Pair of reserves,' agrees Maurice. 'Reserves.'

'They couldn't even get a fucking game at Derby bloody County,' says Syd.

'They're internationals,' I tell them. 'Both with Championship medals.'

'Championship medals?' asks Maurice. 'When was that then?'

'Nineteen seventy-bloody-two,' I tell him. 'And you fucking know it.'

'They didn't really win them then, did they?' says Syd. 'Not really.'

'So what did they bloody do then?' I ask him. 'Fucking find them?'

'Yes, you could say that,' smiles Maurice.

'In a way,' laughs Syd.

'They'll show you their medals,' I tell them.

'But medals won't do them much good tomorrow,' says Maurice.

'You what?' I ask him. 'What you talking about now?'

'They can't play,' says Syd. 'No chance.'

'Course they fucking can,' I tell him. 'Why the fuck wouldn't they?'

'Because they're not really fit, are they?' says Maurice. 'Not really.'

'They should fucking fit right in here then, shouldn't they?' I tell them and turn my back to go, go down that corridor, round that corner.

'There's one other thing,' says Syd behind my back and under his breath, behind his hand and through gritted teeth. 'Training –'

I stop. I turn. I ask, 'What about it?'

'It's a bit of a shambles,' says Maurice.

'How is it a bit of a shambles?'

'There's a game tomorrow, you know?' says Syd. 'Against QPR –'

'I have seen the bloody fixture list, Sydney,' I laugh. 'Don't worry.'

'But we do worry,' says Maurice. 'Neither you nor Jimmy Gordon have said or done a single thing about how QPR will play. Not a thing –'

'Don would've had the bloody reserves playing in the Rangers way,' says Syd. 'Had the first team playing against them; looking out for this, looking out for that.'

'Bollocks,' I tell them. 'They're professional fucking footballers; they don't need all that bullshit. Just stop Bowles, that's all you fucking need to know about QPR.'

'That's madness,' says Maurice. 'Madness . . .'

'Well, I think you *are* mad,' Syd tells me. 'Fucking crackers. I really do.'

'Well, while we're at it then,' I tell them both, 'there's one or two things I want to say to the pair of you. First off, I don't have to justify myself to either of you. Not how and when I conduct training. Not who I buy or who I pick to play. Second, if you don't like that, or you don't like me, think I'm mad, think I'm crackers, then – as far as I'm concerned – you can sling your fucking hooks, pair of you –

'And bugger off!' I shout. 'Now are we clear?'

'Are we clear?' I ask them. 'Are we?'

Syd Owen just looks at me. Syd Owen just stares at me. Then Syd Owen says, 'You're right, Mr Clough. You don't have to justify yourself or your actions to Maurice or me. Not to us, you don't. But, come tomorrow night, there'll be 40,000 folk here, 40,000 folk whom you will have to justify yourself to. Make no mistake.'

'Not forgetting the eleven men you send out on that park,' adds Maurice Lindley. 'Not forgetting them.'

★ ★ ★

You beat Željezničar Sarajevo 2–0 in the first leg at the Baseball Ground, under your new, pylon-mounted floodlights; not only did you beat them, you tore their morale to shreds, such was your dominance, the magnificence of your display, of Hennessey and of McGovern. Fucking shame only 27,000 turned up to watch it –

Fucking shame you then went to Old Trafford and were beaten 3–0 by the worst Manchester United team in years. Fucking shame you only trained with the team for thirty minutes that week. Fucking shame you spent most of that week on the motorway or on the train, up and down to London Weekend Television. Fucking shame no one is speaking, speaking to each other, listening to each other:

'My terms are simple. If someone wants to employ me, they take me as I am. If, after five years, they can't take me as I am, then the whole world has gone berserk.'

There are 60,000 here tonight in the Kosevo Stadium for the return leg among the trees and the hills of Bosnia and Herzegovina, the mosques and the minarets; 60,000 sons of Tito with their hooters and their sirens –

'Europe is an adventure,' *you tell the team.* 'Like a bonus, a holiday. So let's make bloody sure we fucking enjoy it, enjoy it and bloody win it!'

Within quarter of an hour, Hinton and O'Hare have made it 2–0, 4–0 on aggregate, the game as good as over. But Željezničar Sarajevo do not go gracefully into the Balkan night; they trip and they kick, on that rough, rough pitch, in that heavy, heavy Yugoslavian mud; they are worse than Leeds United, worse than the sons of Don Revie –

The sons of Tito burn their newspapers, the sons of Tito light their rockets –

But you win and their press say, 'See you in Belgrade next May.'

Belgrade. Next May. The 1973 European Cup final.

★ ★ ★

Bremner doesn't knock. Bremner opens the door and says, 'You wanted to see me?'

'Yes,' I tell him. 'Have a seat, Billy. Pull up a pew, mate.'

Bremner doesn't speak. Bremner sits down in the chair and he waits.

'You're out for the next three games,' I tell him. 'Possibly longer?'

Bremner still doesn't speak. Bremner just sits in the chair and waits.

'Now I don't know what your thoughts are about this,' I ask him, 'but as team captain and a natural leader, it would be a bloody shame to lose your presence in the dressing room, as well as on the pitch, for these three games.'

Bremner still doesn't speak. Bremner still just sits in his chair and waits.

'I'd like you to be here for the home games at least,' I tell him. 'I'd also value your input in the team talks; over lunch, in the dressing room, and on the bench with me.'

Bremner stands up. Bremner says, 'Is that all?'

* * *

Europe gives you hopes. Europe gives you dreams –

You start to win domestic games; beating Birmingham and Tottenham, drawing with Chelsea in the League Cup. You are set to play Benfica in the next round of the European Cup; Benfica and Eusebio, five-time finalists, twice winners of the cup; your hopes and your dreams made real –

But there is always doubt. There is always fear. Always trouble –

The childish vendettas and the mischief, the back-biting and the politics –

The directors are in the chairman's ear, asking about Peter; what does he do, how does he do it, how much do we pay him for it, and do we really need him?

Then the chairman is in your ear about Peter; what exactly does he do, how exactly does he do it, how much exactly do we pay him, do we really, really need him, and how about a bit of extra money for you in your new contract, the extra money and the new contract that could be yours –

If there was no Peter Taylor.

Then the club secretary whispers in Pete's ear about you; about how you don't support Peter in the boardroom, about how you murder him and plot to dispose of him, about how you're never there but always on the box and in the papers, about the bit of extra money in the new contract that could be coming your way if there was no Peter, or the bit of extra money and new contract that could be for Peter –

If there was no Brian Clough.

There is always doubt and always fear. There is always trouble, always tension. Tension and trouble; fear and doubt; war, war, war and then, right on cue –

As if by magick, here come Leeds, Leeds, Leeds.

* * *

Under the stands. Under the stands. Under the stands. Under the stands. There is a half-eaten cheese sandwich on the desk, my address book open beside it –

Every manager I've ever met, every trainer, coach and scout . . .

'Take your bloody pick,' I tell them down the telephone –

Forest. Leicester. Birmingham. Everton. Stoke and even Carlisle . . .

'Harvey. Cooper. Cherry. Giles. Hunter,' I tell anyone who'll listen –

Ipswich. Norwich. Luton. Burnley. Wednesday and bloody Hull . . .

'Take your fucking pick,' I tell them, beg and plead with them –

Every manager I've ever met, every trainer, coach and scout.

The half-eaten cheese sandwich, my address book and an empty, drained glass. Under the stands. Under the stands. Under the stands. Under the stands –

'Where's my fucking watch?'

* * *

Longson has been summoned to a meeting of the Football League Management Committee, another bloody meeting of the Management Committee, another fucking meeting to discuss you. The Football League Management Committee tell Longson that Derby County Football Club will face severe disciplinary action and severe fines, even more severe disciplinary action and even more severe fines, if their manager does not modify his criticisms on the television and in the papers, his criticisms on the box and in his columns, his criticisms of the Football League and the Football Association –

Longson shits his fucking pants. Longson goes into hospital.

The birds and the badgers, the foxes and the ferrets, the dogs and the demons, the wolves and the vultures, they circle and gather with the black clouds and the winter storms as your new, pylon-mounted floodlights creak and groan over the Baseball Ground in the wind and the weather, creak and groan and threaten to collapse, to fall.

The football then comes as a relief; a relief from the childish vendettas and the mischief, the back-biting and the politics; comes as a relief even if it's at Leeds, Leeds, Leeds –

It is 7 October 1972 and you are on the Derby coach to Elland Road, Leeds.

You are the Champions of England, not Leeds United; Derby County fin-
ished first, Leeds United finished second; you won and they lost; Daylight
Robbery, *say Don Revie and Leeds, Leeds, Leeds United, again and again*
and again –

Daylight Robbery. Daylight Robbery. Daylight Robbery.

There is a point to prove for both sides today, a point and a lot of bloody
needle. But when you stand up at the front of that coach, when you stand up
to count the hearts on board today, you can sense the doubt and smell the fear,
the trouble and the tension –

There is no John McGovern today. No Terry Hennessey –

In their place you'll play Peter Daniel in midfield; an experiment. But, in
your heart of hearts, you know Elland Road is no place for experiments, no
place at all –

On that field of loss and field of hate, that field of blood and field of war.

The Derby coach pulls into Elland Road, to fists banged on its side, to
scarves up against its glass, and the players whiten, their hearts sink and you're
a goal down –

A goal bloody down before you've even got off the fucking coach.

Two long halves and ninety minutes later, Derby County have lost 5–0
thanks to two from Giles and one each from Bremner, Clarke and Lorimer –

'They didn't even play that fucking well,' says Pete. 'They're not that good.'

But you're not listening; you've had enough of him, the team, the game –

These fields of loss and fields of hate, these fields of blood and fields of war.

★ ★ ★

The long rope. The sharp knife. The loaded gun. The press here, here
to watch me parade McGovern and O'Hare, here to listen to me
parade my lies and my deceits:

'I stick by what I said a fortnight ago, that nobody will be leaving
Leeds for a long, long time. Invariably when people talk about unloading they mean the very players you would least want to let go. I can
honestly say that unloading any of these players has never come into
my mind. The two new signings were out of necessity. I am very
conscious of the fact that Leeds United are the Champions and that I

cannot afford to bring any ragtag and bobtail players here. They have to be the right type of man as well as good players, and I am sure McGovern and O'Hare are tailor-made for this club.'

A question from the front: 'Any news about Eddie Gray?'

'It could be another lengthy spell out,' I tell them. 'And obviously there's a question mark over the lad's fitness.'

A question from the back: 'There have been reports of behind-the-scenes rows between yourself and Syd Owen; have you any comment to make on these reports?'

'These reports are disgraceful,' I tell them. 'Utterly disgraceful. I have never had differences with anyone at the club staff-wise, none whatsoever. Syd has worked like a slave for me since the day I took over. He is totally honest, he is dedicated and exactly the type of man to get on with me.'

A question from the side: 'So absolutely no one at all is leaving Elland Road?'

'There's a job for everyone here,' I tell them. 'Even me.'

★ ★ ★

You go to Portugal to watch Benfica. To spy. You don't take Peter. You take your wife and kids instead. You are glad to go. To get away. You've had enough of England. Had enough of Derby fucking County too; their bloody directors and their fans; their ungrateful directors and their ungrateful fans:

'They only start chanting at the end, when we're a goal up,' you tell the papers. 'I want to hear them when we're losing. They are a disgraceful lot.'

Benfica are shit too and are lucky to draw –

You have no doubts. Have no fears –

Not about the Eagles of Lisbon –

You know you can win –

Know you will win.

★ ★ ★

I never learn; never bloody learn. Never did and never fucking will.

Back in the bar at the Dragonara when I should be back at home in Derby with my wife and my kids. Here in the bar with Harry, Ron and Mike; blokes I'd never met two weeks ago, never even bloody heard of, now my new best mates and pals for life –

'A drink for all my friends,' I shout. 'Another fucking drink, barman.'

On the chairs and on the sofas of the Dragonara Bar –

'Play "Glad to Be Unhappy",' I shout at Bert the pianist. '"Only the Lonely".'

On the tables and on the floors –

'"In the Wee Small Hours of the Morning".'

On the chairs and on the sofas. On the tables and on the floors. In the lift and in the corridor. In my modern luxury hotel room, in my modern luxury hotel toilet –

Because I never learn; never bloody learn; never did and never fucking will; why I failed my eleven-plus and haven't got a certificate to my name, not a bloody one; why I scored 251 goals in 274 games but won only two England caps and not any fucking more –

Why I won the Second Division and the league titles; why I reached the semi-finals of the European Cup and why one day very soon I'll win the bloody cup itself –

Because I never learn; never bloody learn. Never did and never fucking will –

Because I'm Brian bloody Clough. Face fucking down on the floor tonight –

The future bloody manager of England, face fucking down on the floor.

Day Twenty-two

Here is Europe again; your hopes and your dreams. The hopes and the dreams that keep you here, home to Benfica –

Derby County vs Benfica in the second round of the European Cup.

You can't sleep. You can't eat. You don't believe in luck. You don't believe in prayers, so you can only plot, only plot and scheme:

You had the groundsman pump half the river Derwent onto the pitch the night before, turning the Baseball Ground into a bog. You have Kevin Hector carried down the narrow corridor into the treatment room. You have the team doctor pump Kevin Hector full of cortisone an hour before kick-off; the hour before the Eagles of Lisbon are supposed to feast upon the Rams of Derby –

The press have given you no chance. The press have written you off:

Hard luck, Cloughie, *they all write.* This time you're out of your class.

Pete pins up these cuttings in the dressing room; this is where you and Pete are at your best, in the dressing room, beneath these cuttings, with ten minutes to kick-off. You've asked Pete to run through their players, who to watch for and what to watch them for, something you never usually do, never usually give a fuck about. Tonight's no different. Pete looks down at the piece of paper in his hand then he looks back up at your team, your boys, and he screws up that piece of paper –

'No sweat,' *he says.* 'You've nothing to worry about with this lot.'

Pete's right, you're right; this is one of those nights you've dreamt of; one of those nights you were born and live for, and, despite your comments, despite your criticisms, over 38,000 people are here to share this night with you, this night when you sweep aside Benfica and Eusebio from the first minute to the last, from the minute McFarland climbs above their defence to head home Hinton's cross, from the minute McFarland nods down another Hinton cross for Hector to score with a left-foot shot into the top corner, from the minute McGovern takes hold of a Daniel lob to score from the edge of the area, from

174

the first minute to the last –

'Unbelievable,' Malcolm Allison tells you at half-time. 'Fucking unbelievable.'

You put your head around that dressing-room door and you simply tell them, 'You are brilliant, each and every one of you.'

Boulton. Robson. Daniel. Hennessey. McFarland. Todd. McGovern. Gemmill. O'Hare. Hector and Hinton –

Derby County; your team, your boys.

Tonight is everything you've ever dreamed of. Everything you've ever worked for. Everything you were born and live for. Plotted and schemed for –

Tonight is vindication. Tonight is justification –

Tonight is your revenge, revenge, revenge –

Tonight is Derby County 3, Benfica 0 –

25 October 1972 –

Tonight you have only one word for the press after this game, one word for your team, your boys, and tonight that word is 'Magical'.

* * *

This is another of *his* traditions, another of *his* bloody routines, another of *his* fucking rituals. Tonight is my first home game at Elland Road; home to Queen's Park Rangers. But we don't meet at Elland Road; we meet at the Craiglands Hotel, Ilkley –

Fucking Ilkley; middle of the moors, middle of bloody nowhere.

A little light training and a little light lunch; bit of bingo, bit of bowls; chat with the coaches and a discussion with Don; then back to Elland Road –

'Every home game,' says Maurice Lindley. 'Been this way for a long time.'

'Well, it's the last fucking time,' I tell him. 'They'd be better off having an extra couple of hours at home with their wives and kids, not sat around on their arses up here, twiddling their bloody thumbs or gambling their fucking wages away, waiting and worrying like a load of little old ladies.'

'It's valuable preparation time,' says Maurice. 'Helps them focus on the game.'

'It's a waste of bloody time and a waste of bloody money,' I tell him. 'It cost me a fucking fortune to get up here in that bloody taxi.'

'The lads won't like it,' he says. 'They don't like change. They like consistency.'

'Tough fucking shit then,' I tell him and head inside the place to the deserted, silent restaurant; deserted but for the first team, sat staring into their tomato soup, waiting for their steak and chips.

Billy Bremner's here, Sniffer and Hunter too, even though all three are suspended. I go up to Billy Bremner, put an arm around his shoulder, pat him on his back and say, 'It's good of you to come, Billy. Much appreciated. Thank you, Billy.'

Billy Bremner doesn't turn round. Billy Bremner just stares into his soup and says, 'Didn't have much fucking choice now, did I, Mr Clough?'

★ ★ ★

Derby travel to the Estadio da Luz in Lisbon for the second leg on 8 November 1972. You don't train. You don't practise. You grill sardines and drink vinho verde –

DRINKMANSHIP, *screams the* Daily Mail. *They're right:*

Just four days ago you went to Maine Road and Manchester City hammered you; off-sides, own goals and fucking Marsh again. You conceded five against Leeds. Three against Manchester United. Now four against City –

'And they didn't even play that well,' Pete said. 'They're not that good.'

'Just like you then,' you snapped back. 'Because that's all you ever say.'

The doubt. The fear. The trouble. The tension.

You went round later. You knocked on his door. You shouted through his letterbox. You waited until he put down his Nazi history books and finally answered his front door. Then you kissed and made up, and now here you are, side by side again, in Lisbon –

In the Estadio da Luz with 75,000 Benfica fans; with the walls and walls of bodies, the walls and walls of noise; the waves and waves of red shirts, the waves and waves of red shirts from the first whistle to the last –

But your team, your boys, they stand firm and Boulton has the game of

176

his life, saving time after time from Eusebio, from Baptista, from Jordao, until half-time comes and the Eagles of Lisbon begin to fall to the ground, time against them now –

The Mighty Rams of Derby against them now –

No fear. No doubt. No trouble. No tension.

There are whistles at the end, but not for you, not for Derby County, whistles and cushions hurled onto the pitch of the Estadio da Luz, but not for you and Derby County –

In the last twelve seasons of European football, only Ajax of Amsterdam have ever stopped Eusebio and the Eagles of Lisbon from scoring, only Ajax and now Derby –

For you and Derby there is applause. For you and Derby there is respect –

For you and Derby there are the quarter-finals of the European Cup.

* * *

The team bus brings us back to Elland Road for half five and there are already folk about, queuing for their tickets and buying their programmes, eating their burgers and drinking their Bovril. I hide in the office, down the corridor and round the corner, through the doors and under the stand. I hide and I listen to the feet above me, climbing to their seats and taking their places, sharpening their knives and poisoning their darts, clearing their throats and beginning to chant, chant, chant; chant, chant, chant –

Leeds, Leeds, Leeds. Leeds, Leeds, Leeds. Leeds, Leeds, Leeds –

I put my head on the desk. My fingers in my ears. I close my eyes. In that office. Down that corridor. Round that corner. Through those doors. Under that stand and under their feet, feet, feet –

There's a knock on the door. It's John Reynolds, the groundsman –

'There you go, gaffer,' he says and hands me my watch. 'Look what turned up.'

'Fucking hell! Where did you find that?' I ask him.

'It was over behind the goals on the practice pitch,' says John. 'Bit mucky like, but I've cleaned it up for you. Nice bloody watch that; still going and all.'

'You're a saint,' I tell him and take out a new bottle of Martell from my drawer. 'And you'll have a seat and a drink with me, won't you?'

'Go on then, gaffer,' he smiles. 'Purely for medicinal reasons, of course.'

'Summer colds,' I laugh. 'They're the bloody worst, aren't they?'

John Reynolds and I raise our glasses and have our drink, and then John asks, 'Can I say something to you, gaffer?'

'You can say what you like to me, John,' I tell him. 'I owe you that.'

'Well, I know you want to make changes here,' he says. 'That one or two players and one or two of the staff might be on their way out but, if I were you, I wouldn't rush it, gaffer. Don't be in too much of a hurry, especially not here. They don't take easily to change, so just take your time. Rome weren't built in a day, as they say.'

I stare at John Reynolds. Then I stand up, stick out my hand and I tell him, 'You're a good man, John Reynolds. A good man and an excellent bloody groundsman. Thank you for your advice, for your friendship and for your kindness, sir.'

★ ★ ★

You never want to leave this place. You never want this feeling to finish –
The applause of the Benfica fans. The respect of the Benfica fans –
These nights you dream of, nights you were born and live for –
Drink and drink and drink and drink for.

In the restaurant, at the celebration, you stand up to speak, stand up and shout: 'Hey, Toddy! I don't like you and I don't like your fucking missus!'

There's no laughter, no applause and no respect now; just a cough here, embarrassed and muffled. Tomorrow you will telephone Mrs Todd. Tomorrow you will apologize and send her flowers. Tomorrow you will try to explain.

But tonight Longson hides his face while Kirkland taps his glass with his knife, slowly, slowly, slowly. Tap, tap, tap. Slowly, slowly, slowly –

'I am going to bury you,' Jack Kirkland whispers, his hate fresh upon his breath. 'Bury you,' he promises you –

You want to go home. You want to lock your door. You want to pull your curtains. Your fingers in your ears, your fingers in your ears –

You never want to leave your house again.

I am scared. I am afraid. Frightened and shitting bricks. I wish I had
my two boys here, here to hold my hand, to give it a squeeze. But
they're back home in Derby, tucked up in their beds under their
Derby County posters and their Derby County scarves, not here with
me tonight at Elland Road, here with me tonight in front of 32,000
Yorkshiremen. Tonight it's just me on my Jack bloody Jones in front of
32,000 fucking Yorkshiremen –

Tetley Bittermen, says the sign. *Join 'em . . .*

I take a deep breath and I swallow, I swallow and walk down that
tunnel, walk down that tunnel and out into that stadium, out into that
stadium to make my very, very long, long way to that bench but, as I
make my way to that bench, tonight these 32,000 Yorkshiremen in
Elland Road, tonight they rise as one to their feet and applaud me as
I make my way to that bench in the dug-out, and I wave to the crowd
and bow ever so slightly as I make my way, I wave and bow and then
take my seat on that bench in the dug-out, take my seat on that bench
as the manager of Leeds United; Leeds United, the Champions of
England –

Tetley Bittermen, says the sign. *Join 'em.*

'Welcome to Elland Road, Mr Clough,' shouts a man from behind
the dug-out. 'Best of luck,' shouts another, and Jimmy Gordon, Jimmy
in his brand-new Leeds United Admiral tracksuit with his bloody
name upon his back, he gives me a little nudge and a little wink, and
I glance at my watch, my watch that is back on my wrist, and for the
first time, the first time in a very long time, I think that maybe, just
maybe this might work out.

★ ★ ★

*The whispers. The whispers. The whispers. The whispers. The whispers. The
way things are going, you've got to keep winning games, keep winning games
otherwise that lot in the boardroom will slaughter you –*

Slaughter you. Bury you.

So that's what you do to Arsenal; you slaughter them, you bury them, 5–0;
McGovern (21), Hinton (37), McFarland (40), Hector (42) and Davies (47).

'I do not accept that was our best performance of the season,' you tell the
press and the cameras, the columns and the panels. 'That was at Goodison on
August the twenty-ninth when we lost 1–0 and you lot bloody wrote us off;
slaughtered and buried us. That's when the doubts crept in, the doubts and the
fears that we could play that well and still lose. Well, today those doubts and
those fears have been banished.'

It's over three years since you hit Tottenham for five, three years since you
and Dave Mackay slaughtered and buried Bill Nicholson and Tottenham.

Arsenal don't leave the visitors' dressing room for a full forty-five minutes
after the match, locked in –

Slaughtered and buried –

Just like you know you will be, you will be if you slip, if you lose –

If you ever take your bloody eye off that fucking ball.

* * *

Fifteen minutes into the game, Harvey moves to get his body behind
the ball, to take it on the first bounce, but the ball slips through and
under him, into the net –

Two games. Two defeats. No goals.

'Bad luck, lads,' I tell the dressing room. 'Didn't deserve to lose, not
tonight. There are things to work on tomorrow, things to take care of
before Birmingham; but we can sort it out on the training pitch and
get it right on Saturday. There's no need to panic and there's no need
to blame yourselves. Just a matter of confidence, that's all.'

'Aye-aye-aye,' mumbles Syd Owen from the back of the room.
'Never heard such a load of fucking rubbish.'

I bite my bloody tongue, bite it till it fucking bleeds, and I go outside, outside to the corridor, to the press and the cameras, the vultures
and the hyenas, and I tell them all:

'We did not play with confidence.'

'Aye-aye-aye. Never heard such a load of fucking rubbish.'

'We badly missed Bremner, Clarke and Hunter.'

'*Aye-aye-aye. Never heard such a load of fucking rubbish.*'

'I was very sorry for David Harvey, but it is essential he forgets it.'

'*Aye-aye-aye. Never heard such a load of fucking rubbish.*'

'We created enough chances, but we could not put them in.'

'*Aye-aye-aye. Never heard such a load of fucking rubbish.*'

'It is a bad start by anybody's standards, particularly by Leeds's standards.'

'*Aye-aye-aye. Never heard such a load of fucking rubbish.*'

'But we will be here in the morning, working like hell.'

'*Aye-aye-aye. Never heard such a load of fucking rubbish.*'

'This is all you can do. Goodnight, gentlemen.'

Then I walk away, away from the press and the cameras, the vultures and the hyenas, round the corner and down the corridor to the office, the telephone and the bottle:

If only you could see me here. If only you could hear me now . . .

I miss my wife. I miss my kids. I wish I wasn't here. I wasn't me –

If you could only hold me here. If you could only help me now . . .

The things I've bloody done. The things I've fucking said –

'*Never heard such a load of fucking rubbish.*'

All these things I've said and done.

★ ★ ★

You have been invited to speak at the Yorkshire TV Sports Personality of the Year dinner. You have not won it, just been invited to speak about the winner –

Mr Peter Lorimer of Leeds United.

The Sports Personality of the Year dinner is being held at the Queen's Hotel, Leeds. It is being screened by Yorkshire Television, who have organized it in conjunction with the Variety Club of Great Britain –

Mr Wilson, the former and future Prime Minister, is the guest of honour –

But he does not impress you, Wilson. Not these days. Just another bloody comfortable socialist, out to feather his own fucking nest, the nests of his mates –

'We're all out for good old Number One,' *you start to hum, you start to sing.* 'Number One's the only one for me . . .'

You are drunk when you stand up to speak; drunk and do not give a fuck:

'Right then,' you tell Harold Wilson and this roomful of Yorkshire tuxedos. 'I've had to sit here and listen to a load of crap for the last hour, so you lot can all sit here and wait for me while I go and have a bloody pee.'

You go and have your pee. You make your way back. You say your piece:

'Despite the fact that Lorimer falls down when he has not been kicked. Despite the fact that Lorimer demands treatment when he has not been injured. Despite the fact that he protests when he has nothing to protest about . . .'

The booing starts. The jeering starts –

'If you don't like it, if you can't take it, invite Basil bloody Brush next time –'

The chairs scrape and the evening ends –

'Boom-fucking-boom.'

THE THIRD RECKONING

First Division Positions, 22 August 1974

		P	W	D	L	F	A	Pts
1	Man. City	2	2	0	0	5	0	4
2	Carlisle United	2	2	0	0	4	0	4
3	Ipswich Town	2	2	0	0	2	0	4
4	Everton	2	1	1	0	2	1	3
5	Liverpool	2	1	1	0	2	1	3
6	QPR	2	1	1	0	2	1	3
7	Wolves	2	1	1	0	2	1	3
8	Newcastle Utd	2	1	1	0	5	4	3
9	Stoke City	2	1	0	1	4	2	2
10	Middlesbrough	2	1	0	1	3	2	2
11	Arsenal	2	1	0	1	1	1	2
12	Derby County	2	0	2	0	1	1	2
13	Leicester City	2	1	0	1	4	4	2
14	Sheffield Utd	2	0	2	0	3	3	2
15	West Ham Utd	2	1	0	1	2	4	2
16	Burnley	2	0	1	1	4	5	1
17	Coventry City	2	0	1	1	3	4	1
18	Chelsea	2	0	1	1	3	5	1
19	Birmingham C.	2	0	0	2	3	7	0
20	Luton Town	2	0	0	2	1	4	0
21	**Leeds United**	**2**	**0**	**0**	**2**	**0**	**4**	**0**
22	Tottenham H.	2	0	0	2	0	2	0

I curse you, I curse you, I curse you –
I throw handfuls of rue at the television set and I shout,
'I am the last truly Cunning person left!'
Beware! Beware!
She will eat you like air!
I throw handfuls of rue at the television set and I swear,
'May you rue this day as long as you live.'

Day Twenty-three

Here comes another morning; another morning after the defeat of the night before –

The sun is shining in my modern luxury hotel room, through the curtains and across the floor to the modern luxury hotel bed in which I haven't slept a bloody, fucking wink, just lain here replaying last night's match in my head, on the inside of my skull, reliving every touch and every kick, every pass and every cross, every tackle and every block, over and over, again and again, player by player, position by position, space by space, over and over, again and again, from the first minute to the last –

The things I saw and the things I missed –

The many, many bloody things I fucking missed –

It's just another morning; another morning when I wish I wasn't here.

★ ★ ★

You beat Manchester United 3–1 at the Baseball Ground on Boxing Day. Manchester United and Tommy Docherty. You move up to seventh and United go bottom. You'd thought it was a turning point, another turning point, like Benfica, like Arsenal. But you were wrong again. It was no turning point.

You pick up the phone. You dial Longson's number. You scream down that line: 'If Peter bloody Taylor isn't at fucking work by Friday, I shan't be going to Liverpool with the fucking team. I'll fucking walk out and all, I will!'

'What in heaven's name is wrong with you?' asks Sam Longson.

Money, money, money, that's what's wrong; that's all that's ever fucking wrong with Peter Taylor; money, money, money –

You hang up. You go round to Longson's house. You beg Longson to sack Taylor. You throw your drink at his kitchen wall when he refuses –

'I'm getting bloody nowhere with you fucking buggers!' you shout.

'But what's wrong?' asks Sam Longson –

Money, money, money, that's what's wrong; that's all that'll ever be fucking wrong with Peter Taylor; all that Peter ever goes on about, on and on about:

'I just want my slice of the cake,' he'd said again. 'Just my fucking slice.'

'You get your slice,' you told him. 'You get your slice and more.'

'Do I fuck.' he said. 'Where's my new bloody coat? My waste-disposal unit? Where are my fucking Derby County shares then, eh?'

'Your bloody what? What you fucking talking about now?'

'Don't fuck me around, Brian,' he said. 'Webby's told me all about it.'

'All right then,' you told him. 'You have the whole fucking cake if you want it, if that's what's fucking bothering you, because I can bloody do without it, without all this fucking bollocks. But I'm telling you this: you won't last a fucking minute, not a single fucking minute out there, on your own, in front of all them cameras, them crowds, you can't even buy a pair of bloody socks in town, you're that fucking afraid of being recognized, of someone speaking to you who you don't bloody know but, go on, if that's what you want, that's what you fucking want, you fucking take it because I'm telling you now, I've had enough, enough to fucking last me a bloody lifetime.'

That was ten days ago; the last you saw of him, saw of Pete; Webby phoned the next day and said Peter was feeling a bit chesty. Ten days ago, that was –

'A bit chesty?' you asked Webby. 'A bit fucking chesty?'

'Chesty, you know?' said Webby. 'Under the weather.'

'Under the bloody what?' you asked.

'The weather,' said Webby, again.

That was ten fucking days ago now; that's how this year begins –

This new year you'll wish had never happened –

Nineteen hundred and seventy-three –

The worst year of your life.

★ ★ ★

Under skies. Under bloated skies. Under bloated grey skies. Under bloated grey Yorkshire skies, I walk from the taxi straight up the banking and onto the training ground.

186

Six days into the new season and the team already look like they need a week off. But there are no weeks off, no days off now, not now; Birmingham at home on Saturday, the day after tomorrow. Queen's Park Rangers again, three days after that. No days off –

'They can get here on bloody time,' says Syd. 'Why can't he?'

'It sets a bad example,' adds Maurice. 'A very bad example, in fact.'

Jimmy jogs up to me. Jimmy in his Admiral fucking tracksuit. And Jimmy says, 'I think they've done enough for today, Boss.'

I shake my head. I shout, 'Let's start again. From the fucking top.'

From the fucking top with the running and the lifting, the passing and the shooting, the free kicks and the corners, the goal kicks and the throw-ins, the set plays to plan and the walls to build, attack against defence, defence against attack, attacks to sharpen and defences to stiffen, stiffen and make resolute under these skies. These bloated skies. These bloated grey skies. These bloated grey Yorkshire fucking skies.

* * *

Soon there will be European nights again, soon there will be sunshine again. No one walks away from Europe. No one walks away from sunshine. Taylor showed up in the snow at Anfield and you drew 1–1 on a miserable, miserable day.

'It's this bloody weather, Pete,' you told him. 'We're warm weather creatures, you and me. Marjorca, that's us. We ought to fucking migrate each bloody winter.'

'And the board will help us bloody pack,' said Pete. 'Way things are going.'

But then things, these things that are always going, these things start to look up; Derby go on a little run, a little run to keep you warm in these long, dark winter months. You beat West Brom in the league and then draw against Tottenham in the cup, going on to win the replay 5–3 after extra time –

Back from 3–1 down with just twelve minutes to go; back with a Roger Davies hat-trick; back to beat QPR 4–2 in the fifth round.

But all good things, these good things, must come to an end and you go and get Leeds United in the quarter-finals of the FA Cup. This means Derby have to play Leeds twice in two weeks, once in the league and once in the cup, and these are not just any two weeks; you have to play Leeds United four days before you meet Spartak Trnava in the quarter-finals of the European Cup;

then you have to play Leeds again, four days before the return leg against Trnava. If you were a superstitious man, you'd think Lady Luck had deserted you, turned her back against you —

But you're not a superstitious man and you never will be.

If you were a religious man, you'd think God had deserted you, turned his back against you. But you're not a religious man and never will be. You don't believe in God —

You believe in football; in the repetition of football; the repetition within each game, within each season, within the history of each club, the history of the game —

That is what you believe in; that and Brian Howard Clough.

★ ★ ★

The sharp knife and loaded gun. The long rope. The post-mortem. The press conference: Not since Leeds United returned to the First Division in 1964 have Leeds United lost their opening two games of the season —

'We are not gloomy,' I tell the press. 'We will just have to work harder.'

Not since Leeds United returned to the First Division in 1964 have Leeds United lost their opening two games of the season —

'Certain players have been badly missed,' I tell them.

Not since Leeds United returned to the First Division in 1964 have Leeds United lost their opening two games of the season —

'I am delighted that Clarke and Hunter will be available for Saturday.'

Not since Leeds United returned to the First Division in 1964 have Leeds United lost their opening two games of the season —

'We are not gloomy,' I tell the press again. 'We will just have to work harder.'

Not since Leeds United returned to the First Division in 1964 have Leeds United lost their opening two games of the season; the door and the exit. The corners and the corridors. The office. The long rope. The sharp knife. The loaded gun. The door. The exit.

★ ★ ★

The winter is almost gone and Europe is here again. But Europe will be gone too, if you do not win tonight. For these have not been a happy two weeks –

For the first time in Europe, you were drawn to play the first leg away, away in a small, provincial Czechoslovakian town that's home to Spartak Trnava:

'The Derby County of Czechoslovakia,' you joked, but it wasn't funny and you were lucky to lose only 1–0 to the Czech Champions, the Czech Champions four years out of the last five, seven years unbeaten at home in their own league and boasting 164 caps between them –

'That wasn't luck,' you told the press. 'That was our keeper, Colin Boulton.'

Four days before that game Don Revie and Leeds United had beaten you 3–2 at home in your own league; your much vaunted, talented and expensive Derby defence conceding two silly penalties and a daft goal in the course of being kicked, punched, grappled and wrestled off the park, Mick McManus-style –

'You should be in the book for that, Cherry,' you shouted from the side –

Tackle after tackle, foul after bloody foul, crime after fucking crime –

'McQueen!' you screamed. 'You're not fit to play in this bloody league.'

You were incensed, you were bloody outraged, you were fucking furious because you know exactly why Leeds played like this, why Revie told Leeds to play like this, because Derby won the league and they didn't, you did and he didn't –

Daylight Robbery. Daylight Robbery. Daylight Robbery –

Because you're in the European Cup and he's not –

'You're an animal,' you shouted and screamed. 'A fucking animal, Hunter!'

You did not shake Revie's hand after the game and you never will again.

Then, four days before this game tonight, ten days after you lost in Czechoslovakia, Leeds beat you again, beat you 1–0 at home in the FA Cup –

Fields of loss. Fields of hate. Fields of blood. Fields of war –

Fuck Lorimer. Fuck Revie. Fuck Leeds. Fuck them all.

There was no Hinton for these last three games. Tonight there's Hinton:

21 March 1973; Derby County vs Spartak Trnava –

The quarter-finals of the European Cup, second leg; nigh on 36,500 here at the Baseball Ground to see it –

See it. Hear it. Smell it. Taste it. Bloody touch and fucking feel it –

The tension. The tension. The tension. The tension –

Two goals or you're out of Europe, your hopes and your dreams buried, and while Alan Hinton might well be back for you, bloody Kuna is back for them –

The tension. The tension. The tension –

The fresh lines. The new ball –

The tension. The tension –

Two goals or out –

The tension, then the whistle and it starts, starts at long, long fucking last and you hope, you even pray, for an early goal, but it doesn't come and you know now Trnava are the best team you've played this year, better than bloody Benfica, better than fucking Leeds; they hold the ball, they keep it close and they don't let go, second after second, minute after minute, they don't let go, don't let go until Adamec does and Gemmill's there, there to take it away, away with a pass to McGovern, who centres it for Hector to hit low into that beautiful, beautiful fucking net and bring the scores level on aggregate, level at 1–1; level at 1–1 for two minutes, just two minutes until Hinton crosses and Davies is knocked to the ground in the box and the whole area freezes expecting the whistle, expecting the penalty, the whole area but for Hector, who leans back into that bouncing bloody ball to volley that fucking thing home from fifteen yards and from then, from then on you can only look at your watch, the only place you can stand to look –

Not at the bloody pitch, the pitch the last fucking place you can look –

Not at the pitch when Hector is brought down, not at the pitch when Davies is pushed over, not when the whole of the bloody Baseball Ground is screaming and screaming and screaming for a penalty; not when Boulton sends Martinkovic flying and the whole of the fucking ground goes silent, silent, silent, expecting a penalty for Trnava, a penalty that would bring the scores level again at 2–2, level at 2–2 but give Trnava an away goal, a penalty the referee does not see, just like you with your eyes on your watch, and so the fucking score stays at 2–1 and you –

You just look at your watch, just look at your watch, look at your watch –

The only place, the only place, the only place you can stand to look –

Not at Webster's last-ditch tackle, at Nish's vital, vital tackle –

You just look at your watch, just look at your watch –

Until finally, finally, finally Signor Angonese, the Italian referee, looks at his own watch and raises his right hand and slowly, slowly, slowly Signor Angonese, the lovely, lovely, lovely Italian referee, puts his beautiful, beautiful,

beautiful black whistle to his red, red, red lips and blows that final, final, final whistle that puts Derby County –

Derby fucking County. Derby fucking County into the semi-finals –

The semi-finals. The semi-fucking-finals of the European Cup –

Derby County. Not Leeds United. Derby fucking County!

Later that night, drunk and half-delighted/half-depressed, you telephone Don, phone fucking Don at his family home, just to make sure he knows –

'Just in case you fucking missed it,' you tell him –

'How did you get this number?' he asks. 'It's half two in the bloody morning.'

You hang up. You go upstairs. To the bedroom and your wife –

Then you hear the phone ringing again and so you turn back round and walk back down the stairs and pick up the phone and it's your older brother –

'We've lost our mam,' he tells you. 'We've lost our mam, Brian.'

* * *

I go home early. I don't give a shit. I kiss my wife. I kiss my kids. I take the phone off the hook. I put on an apron and I get stuck into the cooking. Bangers and mash, few sprouts and moans and groans from the kids, with lots of lovely thick bloody gravy; can't beat it. Then I do the washing up and put the kids in the bath. I read them their stories and kiss them goodnight. Then I sit down on the sofa with the wife to watch a bit of telly:

Nixon and Cyprus. Nixon and Cyprus. Nixon and Cyprus –

So my wife goes up to bed but I know I won't be able to sleep, not yet, not for a long time, so I stay up in the rocking chair and end up looking in the bloody paper again, the results spread out, working out a fucking league table on the back of one of my daughter's paintings, a league table for the first two games, a league table that leaves Leeds next to bottom, next to last, so then I go through the fixture list inside my head, inside my skull:

If Leeds win this game and Derby lose that game; Derby lose that and Leeds win this; if Leeds get five points from these three fixtures and Derby only three, then the league table will look like this and not that, that and not this, and so on, and so on, and so on –

Until the sun is shining in my house, through the curtains and across the floor, and it's just another morning; another morning when I wish I wasn't there –

I wish I wasn't going back there.

Day Twenty-four

You go back home to Middlesbrough to cremate your mam –
   The end of anything good. The beginning of everything bad . . .
   When you're gone, you're gone; that's what you believe –
   The end of anything good. The beginning of everything bad . . .
   No afterlife. No heaven. No hell. No God. Nothing –
   The end of anything good. The beginning of everything bad.
   But today, for once in your life, just this once, you wish you were wrong.

★ ★ ★

The board have called me upstairs, upstairs to their Yorkshire boardroom with their Yorkshire curtains drawn, upstairs to break their bad
news: 'The FA have ordered Clarke to appear before the Disciplinary
Committee, along with Bremner and Giles.'

'For what?' I ask them. 'That's unbelievable.'

'It is a bit of shock,' agrees Cussins. 'But –'

'It's more than a bloody shock,' I tell them. 'It's a fucking outrage
and an injustice. I'm not having any Leeds players put on trial by television. He wasn't even bloody booked, he wasn't even fucking spoken to by the referee, so the only reason they've called him down there
is because of them replaying his bloody tackle on Thompson, over and
over again, morning, noon and fucking night.'

'Brian, Brian, Brian,' pleads Cussins. 'Look, calm down –'

'I won't bloody calm down,' I tell them. 'I've only just got him fucking back so I'm buggered if I'm going to lose him again for another
three or four bloody matches, just because of fucking television.'

'Brian, Brian –'

'No, no, no,' I tell them. 'If this is what's going to happen, then I want the television cameras banned from the bloody ground, from Elland Road. If that's what it fucking takes to stop this kind of operation against me then –'

'I believe Mr Revie often felt the same way –'

'Fuck Don bloody Revie!' I shout. 'Ban them! Ban the television!'

'Those who live by sword,' laughs Bolton, 'die by sword.'

* * *

You are still in your tracksuit playing cards in the hotel bar in Turin, playing cards with the team – your team, your boys – twenty-four hours before the first leg of the semi-final of the European Cup.

There was a magpie on your lawn when you left your house for the airport. There was also one on the tarmac as you got off the plane in Turin. Now one's just flown into the window of the hotel bar. But you don't believe in luck. In superstitions and rituals –

You believe in football; football, football, football.

Pete comes down the stairs, down the stairs in his tuxedo –

'You not ready yet?' he asks. 'The dinner's in half an hour.'

'You go.'

'But it's a bloody dinner for us,' he says. 'All the Italian and British journalists are going to be there. We're the guests of fucking honour.'

'You go.'

'Brian, come on,' he says. 'You're making a bloody speech.'

'You make it.'

'You what?' he says. 'I've never made a fucking speech in my life.'

'Now's your chance then.'

'Come on, Brian,' he says again. 'You know I can't.'

'No, I don't.'

'We're going to be late,' he says. 'Stop playing silly buggers, will you?'

'You bloody go and you make the fucking speech for a change.'

'Don't do this to me, Brian,' he says. 'Please –'

'You wanted your slice of fucking cake,' I tell him. 'Now here it is.'

'Fuck off.'

'No,' you tell him. 'You bloody wanted it. Now you've fucking got it.'

'Please don't do this to me, Brian.'

'Do what?' you ask him. 'What?'

'Don't do this, Brian. Not in front of the team.'

'Why not?' you ask him. 'Don't you want them to see you for what you really are? A big fat spineless fucking bastard who can't go anywhere or do anything without me to hold his hand –'

Peter picks up a glass. Peter throws the whisky in your face –

'Fuck off! Fuck off!'

You jump up. You lunge at him –

'You fuck off! You fat cunt!'

The players leap up. The players pull you apart –

'Dinners. Speeches,' you're shouting. 'This is what it's all about. This is the fucking slice of cake you're after. This is what you're always going on about, fucking moaning on and on about. Now you run along. Don't be late –'

He lunges at you again, tears down his cheeks –

'Go on then,' you shout. 'Go on then, if that's what you want.'

'Fuck off! Fuck off!'

You are in your tracksuit fighting with Peter in the hotel bar in Turin, your best mate, your only friend, your right hand, your shadow, fighting with Peter twenty-four hours before the first leg of the semi-final of the European Cup –

The blood of a dead magpie running down the windows of the hotel bar –

The blood of your best mate running down the knuckles of your hand –

The first time you've spoken to anyone since your mam passed on.

* * *

Three hours and three phone calls later, Mr Vernon Stokes, the chairman of the FA Disciplinary Committee, tells Manny Cussins that, on reflection, he has decided it wouldn't be right to call Clarke of Leeds before the Committee as he was not cautioned during the match and, if he ordered Clarke of Leeds to appear, he would have to call up every player who committed a foul during the Charity Shield game.

I go downstairs to face the press, face the press with a smile on my face for once, with a smile on my face as they ask about the draw for the League Cup:

'I would have felt much better had we been drawn to play Huddersfield at home. They had a fabulous result in the first round, which proves they are no pushovers. Bobby Collins has obviously got things well organized over there.'

'Have you any further thoughts on your two games in charge so far?'

'Listen to me,' I tell them. 'Leeds lost three matches in a fortnight while they were on the crest of a wave going for the title. This kind of thing has happened before.'

'But you've said they play without confidence and yet they're the League Champions; how is it they can lack confidence?'

Because Don Revie made them believe in luck, made them believe in ritual and superstition, in documents and dossiers, in bloody gamesmanship and fucking cheating, in anything but themselves and their own ability –

'It's a vicious circle,' I tell them. 'Once Leeds get back to their winning ways, then their confidence will return and then there'll be no stopping them –'

'In the race for the title?' they ask.

'Leeds will be there or thereabouts, just as they have been for the last ten years.'

'But you said you wanted to win the title better,' they remind me. 'But the first time Leeds won the title in 1969 they lost only two matches the entire season.'

'Is that a question or a statement?' I ask them.

'Up to you,' they say.

'Well, they'll just have to win the next forty games then, won't they?'

'But how do you honestly feel?' they ask. 'Two games into the new season and with the League Champions still seeking their first point and their first goal.'

'Birmingham City are also still looking for their first point.'

'You're suggesting Saturday is a relegation battle then?'

'No.'

'Can you tell us anything about the team for tomorrow?'

'There's no room for Bates, Cooper or Jordan, I can tell you that.'

'There'll be some disappointed players in the dressing room then?'

'There will always be disappointed players in the dressing room, but these three players also know how delighted I've been with them so far, and Cooper and Bates will go into the reserves tomorrow, along with Terry Yorath, and continue to get practice. Jordan will be on the bench . . .'

'And McKenzie?'

'Young Duncan McKenzie has fallen foul of your Leeds United curse,' I laugh. 'He's injured himself and will have to watch the game from the stands.'

'Are you becoming superstitious, Brian?'

'Never.'

'Will you be saying the same tomorrow, if you lose again?'

'Look, my coming here has just magnified all this. I am not feeling the pressure and I don't want pressure on the team, either,' I tell them, the press and the television, their microphones and their cameras, their cameras and their eyes –

But there's something in their eyes, the way their eyes never meet mine; the way they look at me, the way they stare at me, but only when I look away; like I'm bloody sick or something, like I've got fucking cancer and I'm dying –

I feel like death. I feel like death. I feel like death . . .

Dying, but no one dare bloody tell me.

★ ★ ★

Half an hour before kick-off, Peter comes rushing into the dressing room, face red and eyes wide, shouting: 'He's in the fucking referee's dressing room again. I've just seen him go in. That's twice now.'

'Who is?' you ask him. 'Who?'

'Haller, their substitute,' says Pete. 'Just seen him go in with my own bloody eyes. That's the second fucking time and all. Talking fucking Kraut.'

'Forget it,' you tell him. 'Could be anything.'

'Could it hell,' shouts Pete. 'Haller's bloody German and so's the fucking referee, Schulenberg. It's not right. I'm telling you, they're up to something.'

'Fucking forget it, Pete,' you tell him again. 'Think about the match, the game.'

The first leg of the semi-final of the European Cup; 11 April 1973 –

The Stadio Comunale, the black and the white; the black-and-white flags of 72,000 Juventus fans; Juventus, the Old Lady herself, in black and white:

Zoff. Spinosi. Marchetti. Furino. Morini. Salvadore. Causio. Cuccureddu. Anastasi, Capello and Altafini –

'Dirty, dirty, dirty bastards,' Pete is saying, saying before you even get to the bench, before you even get sat down, before a ball has even been kicked.

For the first twenty-odd minutes, you ride the late tackles, the shirt-pulling and the gamesmanship –

'They're just bloody flinging themselves to the floor at the feet of the ref.'

The obstructing, the tripping, and the holding of players –

'Dirty, diving, cheating, fucking Italian bastards.'

Then Furino puts his elbow in Archie Gemmill's face. Gemmill trips him back, just a little trip, and Gemmill goes in the book –

'Fuck off, ref! Fuck off!' screams Pete. 'What about fucking Furino?'

Roy McFarland goes up for a high ball with Cuccureddu. McFarland and Cuccureddu clash heads. McFarland goes in the book –

'For what? For fucking what?' yells Pete. 'Fucking nothing. Nothing!'

Gemmill booked. For nothing. McFarland booked. For nothing –

'By their bent axis mate of a fucking Kraut referee.'

Gemmill and McFarland already booked in previous legs, this was the one thing you didn't want to happen tonight; the two players now suspended for the return leg, the one thing you didn't want to happen –

'And they fucking knew it,' says Pete. 'They fucking knew it.'

But it's almost the half hour, almost the half hour and still 0–0 when Anastasi beats Webster and Todd, beats Webster and Todd to feed Altafini, feed Altafini to make it 1–0 to Juventus; 1–0 to Juventus but then, two minutes later, just two fucking minutes later, and out of nothing O'Hare knocks the ball to Hector and Hector takes the ball into their box and shapes to shoot with his left but brings it inside and shoots, shoots with his right and suddenly, just two minutes later and out of nothing, it's –

1–1! 1–1! 1–1! 1–1! 1–1!

Salvadore and Morini beaten, Zoff on his arse, and the Stadio Comunale silent, those black-and-white flags fallen to the floor.

Causio misses a chance and blasts over the bar, Nish clears a shot off the line from Marchetti, but it stays 1–1 to half-time; half-fucking-time:

Haller, the Juventus substitute, is straight off their bench and walking off down the tunnel with Schulenberg, the referee –

'Look at that,' says Pete. 'How much more fucking blatant can you get?'

And Pete is straight off your bench and running down the tunnel after them –

'Excuse me, gentlemen,' he shouts. 'I speak German. Do you mind if I listen?'

But Haller starts jabbing Pete in his ribs, keeping Pete from Schulenberg, and shouting for the security guards, who shove Pete against the wall of the tunnel and pin Pete there while you and the players file past the mêlée towards the dressing room –

There is nothing you can do for Pete. Nothing now. Not now –

Now you have to get to the dressing room, get to the dressing room because this is where you earn your money. This is where you bloody live –

This is where you have to be, to be with your team, your boys –

'They are Third Division, this lot,' you tell them. 'Just keep your heads.'

But this is where things go wrong, thinking of Pete pinned up against the wall; this is where you make mistakes, thinking of Pete up against that wall –

Pete pinned up against the wall of that tunnel, his head lost –

Do you defend at 1–1? Do you attack at 1–1?

But Derby neither defend nor attack –

Your heads all lost.

Haller comes on for Cuccureddu in the sixty-third minute and everything changes; the end of anything good and the beginning of everything bad –

In the sixty-third minute of the first leg of the semi-final of the European Cup, Haller and Causio pass the ball across and back across the face of your penalty area, across and back across, until Causio suddenly turns and beats Boulton to make it 2–1 to Juventus in the sixty-sixth minute.

But 2–1 to Juventus is still not so bad; you still have Hector's goal, an away goal; 1–0 to Derby County in the return leg at the Baseball Ground and you'd be through; through to the final of the European Cup . . .

This is what you're thinking, what you're thinking just seven minutes from the end, just seven fucking minutes from the end as Altafini goes past two of yours and makes it 3–1 to Juventus, 3-fucking-1 and their flags are flying now –

Black and white. Black and white. Black and fucking white.

They are the better side, but that does not matter –

Because they are cheats and cheats should never beat:

199

'Cheating fucking Italian bastards,' you shout at their press and in case they didn't understand, then again more slowly: 'Cheating. Fucking. Bastards.'

'Cos' ha detto? Cos' ha detto?' they ask. 'Cos' ha detto?'

You are no diplomat. No ambassador for the game, the English game –

'I don't talk to cheating fucking bastards!' you shout.

No diplomat. No ambassador. No future manager of England –

'Cheats and fucking cowards!' you scream.

You hate Italy. You hate Juventus –

The Old Fucking Lady of Turin –

The Whore of Europe –

You will remember her stink, the stench of Turin; you will remember it for the rest of your days; the stink of corruption, the stench of decay –

The end of anything good, the beginning of everything bad –

And you will remember this place and this month –

Turin, Italy; April 1973 –

Everything bad –

You've lost your mam. You've lost your mam. You've lost your mam.

Day Twenty-five

There would have been superstition. There would have been tradition. There would have been routine. There would have been ritual. There would have been the blue suit. There would have been the dossiers. The bingo and the bowls. There would have been the walk around the traffic lights. The same route to that bench in the dug-out. There would have been no pictures of birds. No peacock feathers. No ornamental animals –

Saturday 24 August 1974.

Under the feet. Under the stand. Through the doors. Round the corners. Down the corridors. In the office with the door locked and a chair against it, I hang my daughter's picture of an owl upon the wall; hang it above the china elephant and the wooden horse; hang it next to the photograph of the peacock and the mirror –

The cracked and broken mirror.

There would also have been the envelopes full of cash. Under the table. Briefcases and boxes of notes. Hundreds and thousands. Unmarked and non-sequential. In a brown paper bag or on a back doorstep. That would have been the stink of Don's Saturday. The stench of Don's Saturday –

'Where's the money, Don? Where's it all gone?'

Under the feet and under the stand, through the doors and round the corners, down the corridors come their voices, knocking on the door, rattling at the lock –

'What is it now?' I yell. 'Who is it now?'

Through the keyhole Syd and Maurice whisper, 'It's us.'

'Bates and Cooper are out; Hunter and Clarke are back in; Jordan is on the bench; McGovern and O'Hare still starting. Now fuck off,' I shout. 'The bloody pair of you.'

Their laughter echoes and retreats down the corridors. Round the corners. Through the doors. Under the stands. Under the feet, climbing to their seats and taking their places, sharpening their knives and poisoning their darts, clearing their throats and beginning to chant, chant, chant; chant, chant, chant –

Leeds, Leeds, Leeds. Leeds, Leeds, Leeds. Leeds, Leeds, Leeds . . .

The stink of my Saturday. The stench of my Saturday –

Shit, shit, shit. Shit, shit, shit. Shit, shit, shit. Shit, shit, shit. Shit, shit, shit.

★ ★ ★

25 April 1973; the Baseball Ground; the second leg of the semi-final of the European Cup and the crowd of over 38,000 is almost on the pitch. The crowd packed in so bloody tight, tight and tense, the Baseball Ground is a fucking bear pit. You straighten your tie. You straighten your hair –

No Gemmill tonight. No McFarland tonight –

'They did for us in Turin,' you tell the dressing room. 'Now we'll do for them here tonight in Derby. Here tonight in our own house! Here tonight on our own field!'

Webster sends Zoff sprawling in the opening minutes; O'Hare shoots and Zoff saves again; Hinton's free kick forces another save from Zoff –

But the Old Whore's lips are sealed tonight; cold and dry, her legs are closed; she niggles at your players, she nips at your players, tickles and teases them –

Salvadore goes in the book, Spinosi and Altafini too –

The possession all yours, the resistance hers.

Finally, finally, there's a hint of thigh; the briefest, slightest glimpse of leg beneath the Old Whore's skirts; in the fifty-fourth minute Kevin Hector goes down. The whistle blows and Derby have a penalty. Alan Hinton steps up. Alan Hinton shoots –

Wiiiiiiiiiiiiiiiiiiiiiiiiiiiiiiiiiiiiiiiiiiiiiiiiiiiiiiiiiiiiiiiiiiiiiiiiiiiiiiiiiiiiiiiide!

'Fucking hell,' you shout. 'Fucking useless piece of fucking shit.'

You will eat Hinton for dinner, spit him out, prostrate on the dressing-room floor, this fucking useless piece of fucking shit, this fucking useless piece of fucking shit who has stolen victory from you, robbed you of the European Cup.

But you do not give up. Yet. You refuse to give up. Yet. You will never give up –

You look at your watch. You look at your watch. You look at your watch —
There is still time. There is still time. There is still time —
Until Roger Davies explodes and headbutts Morini —
Until Roger Davies gets bloody sent off —
'Fucking useless piece of fucking shit.'

This fucking useless piece of fucking shit, this fucking useless piece of fucking shit who has stolen victory from you, robbed you of the cup —

Down to ten men with twenty-four minutes to go.

Twenty minutes from the end, you take off Peter Daniel, stick on John Sims, your striker from your reserves; this is the extent of the hand you have to play —

Boulton saves from Anastasi. Boulton saves from Longobucco —

Your empty, empty bloody hand and then the empty, empty fucking sound of that last and final whistle as black-and-white arms punch the air —

Black-and-white flags flood onto the pitch —
Black-and-white chequered flags —
Pull you under, finish you off —
Finish and drown you.

You drew 0–0 with Juventus. You won thirteen corners and twenty-nine free kicks but it is no consolation; no consolation that only Manchester United have gone any further than you, only Manchester United have reached the final —

Only Manchester United have lifted that cup —
Drunk from that European Cup —
No consolation whatsoever.

No consolation that Juventus will be beaten 1–0 by Ajax of Amsterdam in the final in Belgrade next month. No consolation that the Portuguese referee, Francisco Lobo, will tell UEFA that an attempt was made to bribe him before tonight's game, that he was offered $5,000 and a Fiat car if he would allow the Italians to win the second leg. No consolation that five years ago you were losing at home to Hull City, in front of 15,000 people, sixteenth in Division Two —

It is no fucking consolation whatsoever —
There can be no consolation.

These days and these months, this year and this time will always be with you, never leave you, never leave you, never leave you —

The blackest two months of your whole life, months that still haunt and hound you, that will always haunt and hound you, always haunt and hound you —

March and April 1973; the end of anything good, the beginning of everything bad.

★ ★ ★

I go into the dressing room and the dressing room goes silent. I stare at David Harvey. I stare at Paul Reaney. I stare at Trevor Cherry. I stare at John McGovern. I stare at Gordon McQueen. I stare at Norman Hunter. I stare at Peter Lorimer. I stare at Allan Clarke. I stare at John O'Hare. I stare at John Giles and I stare at Paul Madeley –

'You're going to win today,' I tell them. 'You're going to win.'

Then I leave that dressing room and walk down that tunnel and out into that stadium and make my way to that bench in the dug-out, where I take my seat on that bench between Jimmy Gordon and Joe Jordan –

No one says, 'Afternoon, Cloughie.'

No one says, 'Best of luck, Brian.'

No one says anything; the crowd is quiet and down 9,000 on the corresponding day last season; it might be the holiday weekend; it might be the violence on the terraces at some grounds; it might be Leeds United's results so far –

It might just be me.

The doubt and the fear. That stink of Saturday. The whistle –

Birmingham have not come to defend. They have come to attack –

Four times they almost score. Through Francis. Through Burns. Through Hatton. Through Kendall. But four times they miss –

Hunter at the back. Hunter back from suspension. Hunter makes the difference –

McGovern has played better. McGovern has played worse –

O'Hare plays well beside Lorimer. O'Hare plays well beside Clarke –

Clarke up front. Clarke back from suspension –

Clarke makes the difference.

The Birmingham clearance hits the referee. The ball spins backwards into the path of a young, debutant Birmingham defender. Clarke is too quick for him –

1–0! 1–0! 1–0! 1–0! 1-fucking-fucking-0!

I'm off the bench and out the dug-out with a big, big kiss for Allan Clarke. A smacker, right on the chops –

No one in England could have scored it better than the way Clarkey did. It is one touch of class above all others –

Nothing lucky about it –

No blue suits. No dossiers. No bingo and no bowls. No ritual walks around the traffic lights or lucky routes to this bench in the dug-out. No envelopes full of cash. No gamesmanship or cheating –

Just football . . .

Not superstition. Not bloody ritual and not fucking luck –

Just good, clean, honest football.

'There will be no stopping us,' I tell the press. 'No stopping us now.'

THE FOURTH RECKONING

First Division Positions, 25 August 1974

		P	W	D	L	F	A	Pts
1	Carlisle United	3	3	0	0	5	0	6
2	Ipswich Town	3	3	0	0	4	0	6
3	Liverpool	3	2	1	0	4	2	5
4	Wolves	3	2	1	0	6	3	5
5	Everton	3	2	1	0	5	3	5
6	Arsenal	3	2	0	1	5	1	4
7	Derby County	3	1	2	0	3	1	4
8	Stoke City	3	2	0	1	5	2	4
9	Man. City	3	2	0	1	5	4	4
10	Middlesbrough	3	1	1	1	4	3	3
11	Chelsea	3	1	1	1	6	6	3
12	QPR	3	1	1	1	2	2	3
13	Newcastle Utd	3	1	1	1	7	8	3
14	Leicester City	3	1	0	2	5	6	2
15	Sheffield Utd	3	0	2	1	3	5	2
16	West Ham Utd	3	1	0	2	4	7	2
17	**Leeds United**	**3**	**1**	**0**	**2**	**1**	**4**	**2**
18	Burnley	3	0	1	2	4	7	1
19	Coventry City	3	0	1	2	4	7	1
20	Luton Town	3	0	1	2	2	5	1
21	Birmingham C.	3	0	0	3	3	8	0
22	Tottenham H.	3	0	0	3	0	3	0

I curse the man you are. I curse the land you have –
I go from field to field. I collect stone after stone –
I pile up the stones. I kneel by the stones –
'May every kind of mishap, may every kind of misfortune –
Fall on this man. Fall on this land.'
I rise up from them stones and I take up them stones –
And I hurl them here. And I hurl them there.

Day Twenty-six

You are out of the European Cup. You are out of the league title race. You are out of the FA and the League Cups. The only way Derby County can now qualify for next season's UEFA Cup is if Derby beat Wolverhampton Wanderers tonight and then Leeds United beat Second Division Sunderland in the FA Cup final tomorrow or Leeds beat AC Milan in the Cup Winners' Cup final. You beat Wolves. You do it in half an hour —

First Roy McFarland tucks in a ball from John O'Hare, next O'Hare centres for Roger Davies to lash into the roof of the net, then Davies pounces again to send home the rebound from a David Nish shot; the job done in half an hour, your eyes are on the roof of the stand, the fingers of grass on the pitch, the hands on the face of your watch —

Because these are the last few minutes of the 1972–73 season. The last few minutes you are League Champions. The final whistle will blow and Bill Shankly and Liverpool will be the new Champions, not you —

But who watches Bill Shankly on the box? Who reads his columns?

Does Mike Yarwood impersonate Bill Shankly on his show?

You know you annoy as many people as you amuse on the television; On the Ball *and* The Big Match. *They might kick the screen, they might kiss the screen, but you know no one switches it off while you're on. They bloody watch it. The same with your columns in the newspapers: the* Sunday Express *and the* Sun. *They might screw them up and stick them in their bin, they might cut them out and stick them on their wall, but you know no one turns the page. They bloody read them. The same with directors. You know you annoy as many directors as you impress. But you also know most would love to have you managing their club, know most would have you at the drop of a hat.*

Just like you annoy as many managers as you inspire. But you know they'd all like a bit of what you've got, have a bit of what you've got, give their right arm for it.

The same with the bloody players; you know there are more who loathe you than love you. But you know not one would ask for a transfer, over their dead fucking body –

You have seen the tears in their eyes. Heard their pleas for mercy.

Because on your day, on your day there is no stopping you. On your day, you can do no wrong; walk on water, then turn it into wine –

Just like today; even after you've been knocked down and robbed blind by Juventus, even after you've been cheated out of the European Cup, cheated out of your destiny by that black-and-white old whore, even after all that, you've still gone out and fucking won the last three bloody league matches of the season –

Still scored nine goals, still conceded only one, still got six points out of six –

Beating Everton 3–1, Ipswich Town 3–0, and now Wolves 3–0.

But now it all stops. The season over. Champions no more. Europe no more –

You have done your job. The season over. It is out of your hands now –

Your empty hands. No trophies. Your season now over –

Between the fingers, the fingers of grass –

In the soil. In the dirt. In the mud –

Everything bad, bad, bad –

It hits you anew every day. Every time you close your eyes, that's all you ever see, her face in the kitchen. In the doorway. In the garden. In her hat. In her nightie. In the hospital. You wish you'd buried your mam, not cremated her. Now there is no grave, no place to go. But if you had buried her, if there had been a grave, you'd go every Sunday –

But there's no place to go but here, here, here, here, here, here, here, here –

Here where the crowd's all gone home, here where there is no crowd –

No crowd. No trophies. No one. No one here now, now, now –

'I've lost my mam,' is all you can say, over and over –

No spirits here. No ghosts here. No saints here –

'I've lost my mam,' is all you can repeat –

Only devils are here. Only demons now –

'I've lost my mam,' all you can say –

Devils and demons. Here, now –

Now, now your mam is dead.

Day Twenty-seven

The sun is shining, the sky is blue, and it's a beautiful Monday morning in late August. The kind of day that makes you feel glad to be alive and glad to be English, glad of your family and glad of your friends, glad you've your health and glad you've a job; two away games this week, one in London and one in Manchester; Billy Bremner and Johnny Giles up before the FA Disciplinary Committee; but nothing can take this feeling away from me –

This feeling of victory. This feeling of winning . . .

I get washed and I get dressed; a good shave and a good suit; nice tie, clean shoes. I get out my other suit and get out my suitcase. I pack my razor and pack my toothbrush. Then I go downstairs, down to my family. The smell of bacon frying and bread toasting. The sound of eggs breaking and kettles boiling. I sit down at the table and I ask my eldest to pass me the sugar, and he knocks over the salt cellar, spills the salt my way, my direction –

Not superstition. Not bloody ritual and not fucking luck.

I get out the car. I put my suitcase in the back. I go back into the house. I kiss my wife and kids goodbye. I wave to them as I reverse out of our drive and blow them more kisses. I don't pick up Jimmy Gordon; don't pick up John McGovern or John O'Hare. Just me today, on the drive north. Just me on this beautiful Monday morning in late August, on my way to work with the radio on, listening to the news –

'Kevin started watching Blackpool two years ago. He went to all the home games. I wouldn't stop him going to matches but I've always told him: "Be careful, don't get into any trouble." I used to watch Blackpool myself, but the trouble on the Kop put me off and I don't go now. I think it's a disgrace. I feel sorry for those who are genuine supporters. They are going to have to do something about it. He was only fourteen years old.'

I switch off the radio as I come off the motorway. Round the bends and the corners to the junction with Lowfields Road and onto Elland Road. Sharp right and through the gates and I hit the brakes hard; there's a big black dog stood in the entrance to the car park. I hit the horn hard but this big black dog will not move. I start to reverse. I look in the mirror. I see the writing on a wall –

CROUGH OUT

* * *

Leeds were the shortest ever favourites to win the FA Cup. But Bob Stokoe –

The same Bob bloody Stokoe who looked down on you as you lay on that cold, hard Boxing Day ground and said, 'He's fucking codding is Clough.'

– Bob fucking Stokoe hates Don Revie even more than you and so Leeds United lose the FA Cup final to his Second Division Sunderland. Eleven days later, with Clarke and Bremner suspended, Giles injured and Revie supposedly on his way to Everton, Leeds lose the Cup Winners' Cup final to AC Milan in Greece –

We've been robbed, Leeds say. We've been cheated –

But so have Derby. Derby are not in Europe.

'Trust bloody Leeds,' you tell folk. 'I wouldn't be fucking surprised if they hadn't lost those bloody finals on fucking purpose! To keep Derby out of Europe!'

Leeds United have also been found guilty of 'persistent misconduct on the field'; Leeds United have been fined £3,000, suspended for a year –

This is the final straw. This is what you write in the Sunday Express:

Don Revie should have been personally fined and Leeds United instantly demoted to the Second Division after being branded the dirtiest club in Britain. Instead, the befuddled minds of the men who run soccer have missed a wonderful chance to clean up the game in one swoop. But the trouble with soccer's disciplinary system is that those who sit in judgement, being officials of other clubs, might well have a vested interest. I strongly feel that this tuppence-ha'penny suspended fine is the most misguided piece of woolly thinking ever perpetrated by the FA, a body hardly noted for its common sense. It's like breathalysing a drunken driver, getting a positive reading, giving him back his keys, and telling him to watch it on the way back home!

This article is the final straw for the Football League. You are charged with bringing the game into disrepute. This charge the final straw for Longson –

Your chairman is not speaking to you. You are in the dock. You are not in Europe. You lock the doors of your house. You pull the curtains and take the phone off the hook. You go up the stairs. You get into your bed and pull your covers over your head –

The 1973–74 season is but weeks away, days and hours away.

★ ★ ★

They are dirty and they are panting. The training almost finished, the practice almost done. The sun is still shining, but the rain is now falling. The sky black and blue, purple and yellow. No rainbows here. No smiles. I thought there might be some smiles today. Thought there might be some laughter. Now we are winning. But the only one smiling, the only one laughing is Allan Clarke –

'You going to give us a kiss every time I score, are you, Boss?'

'If that's what it takes to keep you scoring, I will. You big bloody poofter.'

'You'll have a pair of sore lips come May then,' laughs Sniffer again.

'I bloody well hope so,' I tell him. 'I fucking well hope so.'

But there are no smiles today from Harvey, Reaney, Cherry, McQueen or Hunter. No laughter today from Lorimer, Giles, Madeley, Jordan or Bremner –

No smiles or laughter from McGovern or O'Hare either.

★ ★ ★

You can see a way out; out of the failures on the pitch, the injustices off it –
Jimmy Hill has jumped ship to the BBC and ITV are desperate, the 1974

World Cup only a year away. ITV offer you a full-time job at £18,000 a year; £18,000 a year and no directors to deal with, no defeats to suffer –

No victories and no cups, no applause and no adoration, no love –

You want it and you don't. You don't and you do –

You take the job part-time. You will travel to London on Thursdays to record one show and travel down again on Sundays to record another –

You don't ask your wife. You don't ask Peter. You don't ask Longson or the board. You don't ask anyone. You are Brian Howard Clough –

Cloughie, *as the viewing millions call you –*

And Cloughie doesn't bloody ask folk –

Cloughie fucking tells them.

* * *

The Monday morning press conference; no long ropes and post-mortems today, only garlands and accolades, tributes and compliments:

On Birmingham City?

'Freddie Goodwin is not entitled to have lost three matches with his side,' I tell the press. 'He has an awful lot of talent and they are grafting like hell for him. They are by far, by far not the worst side in the league.'

On John O'Hare's début?

'He turned it on from start to finish all over the pitch,' I tell them. 'Just you wait until John's been here a few weeks.'

And as for Allan Clarke's goal?

'No one in England could have scored it better than the way Allan did,' I declare. 'It was one touch of pure class above all others.'

The rumours of departures and transfers?

'No one goes,' I repeat and repeat. 'No one bloody well goes.'

On the prospects for Leeds United and the season?

'There'll be no holding us now,' I tell the press. 'No stopping us.'

And tomorrow night away, down at Queen's Park Rangers?

'There'll be no holding Leeds United,' I tell them again and again. 'You just watch us bloody go.'

England will play Poland at Wembley in October. England must beat Poland to qualify for the 1974 World Cup in West Germany. It will be the nation's most important match since the 1966 World Cup final itself. You will be part of the ITV panel for this game.

Before England, Poland have a warm-up game against Holland; this will be a useful game for you to watch, as a member of the ITV panel –

The leading member. The one that makes folk switch on –

The one that keeps them bloody watching.

You tell Longson you are going to Amsterdam. You tell Longson you're taking Pete with you. You tell Longson that he can regard it as part of your holiday –

'This is a private matter then,' says Longson. 'And Derby will not pay for it.'

'Of course not,' you tell him. 'I wouldn't bloody dream of it.'

Then Sam Longson asks you, 'I wonder what you do bloody dream of these days, Brian?'

'What the hell do you mean by that?'

'Do you dream of Derby County?' he asks. 'Or do you dream of television?'

'What are you saying?'

'I'm not saying anything,' says Sam Longson. 'All I know is that a man cannot serve two masters. He will come to love the one and hate the other.'

'If I have to give up all of this, the television, then I'll resign, Mr Chairman.'

'Bloody well resign then,' laughs Longson.

'But if I do, Mr Chairman, you know it'll be curtains for you too.'

Longson spits on his hands. Longson rubs them together and then Longson says, 'Right then, Brian, we'll see, shall we?'

★ ★ ★

The cleaning lady is cleaning my office, under the desk and behind the door, whistling and humming along to the tunes inside her head –

'You know, I once sacked all the cleaning ladies at Derby.'

'What did you do that for then, Brian?' she asks me.

'For laughing after we lost.'

'Least you had a good reason then,' she says. 'Not like Mr Revie.'

'What do you mean?'

'Well,' she says, 'Mr Revie once sacked a lass here for wearing green.'

'Wearing green?'

'Oh yes,' she says. 'He thought green brought bad luck to club.'

'And so he sacked her?'

'Oh yes,' she says again. 'After we lost FA Cup final to Sunderland.'

'Just like that?'

'Yes,' she says. 'Just like that.'

The telephone on my desk starts to ring. I pick it up. I tell them, 'Not now.'

★ ★ ★

The new season, 1973–74; but this new season is no new start; no beginning and no end. Things just going from bad to worse; out of Europe, in the dock; your chairman out to sack you and your mam still dead; this is how the 1973–74 season starts –

You face Sunderland and Bob bloody Stokoe in the second round of the League Cup and a thousand bad fucking memories. But Derby have a two-goal lead by half-time. You outplay the winners of the FA Cup and conquerors of Leeds United for three quarters of the match. You are playing exhibition football.

Then Sunderland hit back and equalize with two goals. Now you will have to travel to Roker Park for a replay. Now no one would bet on Derby to win that game.

'Sheer lack of fucking professionalism!' you tell the dressing room. 'Your brains are still in Spain, sat on that fucking beach in the sun. The season's bloody started –

'Never take your eye off that fucking ball –

'Never play exhibition football –

'Always kill a game –

'Always win it –

'Always!'

★ ★ ★

Up the stairs. Down the corridor. Round the corner and through the doors. I'm late for the Monday lunch with the board. Late again. The board waiting in the club dining room, their bread all gone and their soup cold, their vegetables soft and their wine cheap –

I sit down. I light a cigar and I ask for a brandy, a bloody large one –

I thought there might be more smiles here. More laughter now –

'Someone died, have they?' I ask the dining room –

But the room is silent and stinks of cigarettes; the ashtrays full and the wine gone. The waiters clear away the club crockery and cutlery, the white linen tablecloths.

'What time is the team leaving for London?' asks Cussins, eventually.

'After this party breaks up,' I tell him, holding up my glass.

* * *

Your first two league games of the new season are against Chelsea and Manchester City. You win these first two games at home to Chelsea and Manchester City, win them both by one goal to nil. You have four points out of four. Not since 1961 have Derby County won the opening two games of a season, and that was in the Second Division. Not the First.

Then you draw 0–0 at Birmingham, defending in depth, adopting the very tactics you repeatedly castigate the England manager for, those negative tactics you repeatedly deplore on ITV and in your columns. There was also a clear, clear penalty; the most blatant, blatant one you have ever seen:

'The only good thing to come out of this was a clear demonstration of the discipline of the Derby County players,' you tell the world and his wife. 'I am sure that a certain other team who usually wear white, on the outside at least, I'm sure that particular team would have besieged the referee.'

You can say what the hell you want. You have five points out of six –

You do say what the hell you want. Twice weekly on the box –

Cloughie, that's you. Twice weekly. The hell you want.

* * *

I have been in the kit room. I have been among the socks and the straps, the shirts and the shorts, but I have found what I was looking for. I have changed out of my good suit and nice tie into my tracksuit bottoms and this old Leeds United goalkeeping jersey.

Down the corridors. Round the corners. Through the doors and into the car park. The team and their trainers are already sat on the bus waiting for me. I climb aboard and plonk myself down next to Syd Owen at the front of the coach –

'What do you think of this then, Sydney?' I ask him.

'Of what?'

'Of this?' I ask him again, pointing at this old Leeds United goal-keeping jersey.

'I think if the team have to wear suits when they travel, so should their manager.'

'But what do you think of the colour, Sydney?'

'Green?' he asks. 'I think it suits you, Mr Clough.'

★ ★ ★

You have five points from your first three games. The fourth game of the 1973–74 season is at Anfield against the League Champions; against Kevin Keegan and Liverpool, against Bill Shankly. Young Steve Powell and John McGovern force early saves from Ray Clemence, but then it's all Kevin Keegan, all Liverpool. Nineteen-year-old Phil Thompson scores the first of the night and his first for Liverpool; the first goal Derby have conceded in 305 minutes of First Division football. In the eighty-fifth minute of this game, Keegan scores a second with a penalty –

You have been beaten, well beaten, and outplayed –

Derby County drop from fifth to seventh place.

Eight days later, on Wednesday 12 September, Liverpool come to the Baseball Ground. Between these two games, you have beaten Everton in a game that some of the papers described as the very worst Derby County performance since you took over:

'A shambles of a match . . . the kind of match one wants to forget . . . a complete lack of application . . . Everton robbed by two decisions from a linesman.'

Peter pins these words to the dressing-room wall; no team talk tonight and, four days after one of your worst performances, you take apart the League Champions –

You attack. You attack. You attack –

'To go like this, from the macabre to the sublime,' say the newspapers now, 'means that Derby County are superbly managed. Nobody has ever doubted the ability of this team, but somebody had to make these players produce their best –'

Roger Davies stabs home a rebound after Kevin Hector's shot is blocked –

'That somebody is Brian Clough –'

Roy McFarland exchanges passes with Hector and fires in a well-taken strike –

'Last Saturday, one had to scratch around to find someone who had played even adequately. Last night, one could fill a book describing the fluid moves and the brilliant individual performances –'

Then Nish, Davies and Gemmill combine before Hector scores the third –

'Even Don Revie and Leeds United, gazing down with a three-point lead over the Rams, would have been pleased with McGovern, Powell and Gemmill.'

You've beaten the League Champions 3–1; beaten Kevin Keegan and Liverpool; beaten Bill Shankly; beaten and outplayed them –

Buried and slaughtered them.

You are on your way back to the top. Right back to where you belong –

It is Wednesday 12 September 1973.

* * *

There are no smiles on the team coach down to London. No smiles and no laughter. Just murmurs and whispers, packs of cards and paperback books. Bremner hasn't travelled with us; he'll be making his own way down tomorrow, ready for the FA Disciplinary Committee on Wednesday. I glance back down the aisle at Giles from time to time, the backseat boy, glance back to look for hints of doubt, hints of fear –

But the man doesn't give a fuck.

Not smiling, not laughing, he plays a hand of cards here, then reads another page of his paperback book, *The Exorcist*.

There are still no smiles as we check in at the Royal Garden Hotel, Kensington. No smiles and no laughter at the team talk with their timetable for tomorrow. The drinks and then the dinner. No smiles and no laughter. Just murmurs and whispers –

The early night for them and the late, late night for me –

The late, late night with no, no sleep –

No, no sleep but dreams of dogs –

Big black dogs that bark:

'Clough out!'

Day Twenty-eight

There is no beginning and there is no end. Things just going from bad to worse; worse and worse, week by week, worse and worse, day by day, worse and worse –

Longson wants his seat on the League Management Committee, his place on the plane when England travel abroad, a word or a wave from the Duke of Kent in the Royal Box at Wembley, dinner and drinks with Hardaker and Shipman –

Longson thought you were his passport to these places, his ticket to the top, and so he gave you the keys to his car and his bungalow at Anglesey, a waste-disposal unit for your kitchen and a Burberry suede coat for your back, presents for your kids and the photograph in his wallet of the son he never had –

'It's in the eyes, the power Brian has over the players, power he has over me.'

Now Longson wishes he'd never looked into your eyes, into the eyes of the son he never had; the son he no longer wants; this son he no longer speaks to.

So you dictate while Peter types:

'Due to the complete breakdown of communication, common sense and ability to have a reasonable discussion with the chairman, we find it impossible to work with Mr Longson for the good of Derby County any more. Would you please advise the best way to resolve this urgent problem?'

You both sign the letter, put the letter into an envelope and then the post.

★ ★ ★

The sun is not shining, the sky is not blue, and it's an ugly Tuesday morning in August 1974. The lack of sleep and the lack of dreams. The excess of nightmares and the excess of drink. The hangover and the call home. To the wife and to the kids. To say I love you and I miss you and wish I was there –

There, there, anywhere but here –
The Royal Garden Hotel, Kensington High Street, London.

★ ★ ★

There is no response. No answer to your letter. No beginning and no end. Things just getting worse and worse, day by day, worse and worse, hour by hour, worse and worse –

Jack Kirkland and Stuart Webb, the new director and the new secretary, have got their feet right under the table now, your table. Kirkland and Webby have unveiled their plans for a new 50,000-capacity stadium, a 50,000-capacity stadium with a sports and leisure centre attached, a 50,000-capacity stadium that means no more money for transfers, no more money for players and no more money for you.

You would protest to the chairman, but he is not speaking to you. You would protest to the board, but they are not speaking to you; no one is but Jack Kirkland:

'I'm going to give you some good advice,' he tells you. 'No matter how good you are, or how powerful you think you are, the chairman is the boss, then come the directors and the secretary, then come the fans and the players, and finally and last of bloody all comes the fucking manager.'

But you've already got your fingers in your ears and your eyes on the clock; hour by hour, minute by minute, things just getting worse and worse –

Fingers in your ears, your eyes on the clock –

There is no beginning. There is no end.

★ ★ ★

There is no one in the dining room when I get down there. Breakfast has finished. The waiters clearing away the cups and the plates. The team gone. I sit down and drain the last dregs from a cold pot of tea and scrape a last bit of butter over a cold slice of toast. The waiters watching me from the doors to the kitchen –

'Have a seat,' I tell them. 'Pull up a pew and let's have a chat.'

But the waiters stay where they are by the door to the kitchen, watching me.

'I'll tell you this story, shall I?' I ask them. 'Frank Sinatra was once in this bar late at night in Palm Springs, just him and the barman, the barman tidying up and getting ready to shut up shop for the night when, suddenly, the door opens and in runs this woman and says, "Excuse me! Excuse me! Do you have a jukebox in here?" And Frank Sinatra turns around and looks her right in the face and says, "Excuse me? What did you say?" And so the woman says again, "Do they have a jukebox in here?" So Frank looks around the room and then turns back to her and says, "Doesn't look like it but, if you want, I'll sing for you." And the woman says, "No thanks." And she turns and walks out. So, anyway, the barman is very embarrassed and he says, "She obviously didn't recognize you, Mr Sinatra." But Frank just shrugs and says, "Or maybe she did."'

The waiters walk over to my table by the window. The waiters have found their courage now, their pens and their pieces of paper –

'He met me, you know,' I tell them, as I sign my name for them –

'Who did?' they ask.

'Frank Sinatra.'

★ ★ ★

You have been told there is no money. You have been told not to buy any new players. You have been told there is no money for transfers. But you lose 1–0 at Coventry and you know you have to buy some new players. You make a telephone call. You drive down to London. To the Churchill Hotel.

'I hear you are interested in winning a Championship medal?'

'Who wouldn't be?'

'Someone who already had one.'

Bobby Moore smiles. Bobby Moore grins. Bobby Moore, captain of West Ham and England. Bobby Moore, World Cup winner and national treasure.

'Would you play for Derby County?' you ask him.

Bobby Moore lights another fag. Bobby Moore laughs, 'Why not?'

'That'll do for me,' you tell him and take him for lunch in the restaurant.

'I'm afraid,' begins the maître d'hôtel at the door, 'that Mr Moore is not dressed appropriately for our restaurant . . .'

'Listen to me,' you tell him. 'My team will never stay here again if my player can't sit in this restaurant, my player who has won the World Cup for this country, my player who has done more for this bloody country than any other person you have ever had in your fucking little restaurant!'

'I don't play for you yet,' whispers Bobby Moore.

'Shut up!' you tell him. 'You're my player. I'll ring Ron straight after lunch.'

* * *

The team will be training, having their rub-downs and their massages, lunch back at the hotel and then a short nap. I meet the London press in the hotel bar. I confirm that Madeley and McKenzie are still injured and will not play tonight. I admit that Yorath will. I deny any interest in Burnley's captain Dobson. I refuse to talk about Bremner and Giles and tomorrow's FA Disciplinary Committee. I have a couple of drinks with a couple of journalists and then a long, long lunch with David Coleman. Half an hour late back to the hotel, I go up to my room, throw my clothes in my case and take the coach with the team to Loftus Road.

* * *

You do not make an appointment. You do not telephone. You go straight to Upton Park. You do not wait in line and you do not knock on Ron Greenwood's door. You just walk right into his office and tell him, 'I'm here for a chat. Now, have you got any whisky?'

Ron Greenwood gets to his feet. Ron Greenwood gets you a whisky.

'Any water?' you ask him. 'I am driving.'

'The kitchen's just round the corner,' he tells you.

You go off to find the kitchen. You get the receptionist to take you up to the directors' box. You ask her all sorts of questions about West Ham United, about Ron Greenwood and Bobby Moore –

Twenty minutes later, you're back in Ron's office –

'I've been having a good look around this place,' you tell him. 'Isn't it lovely? All nice and spruce. You don't know how lucky you are, a nice place like this.'

'Glad you like it,' says Ron Greenwood. 'Was there anything else?'

'Yes,' you tell him. 'I want to sign Bobby Moore and Trevor Brooking.'

'You can't be serious, Brian?'

'Every man's got his price,' you tell him. 'And I'd make sure it was a nice big bloody price, with a nice big fucking piece of it for you and for Bobby and Trevor.'

'They're not for sale,' says Ron Greenwood.

'How about we start at £300,000 for the pair of them, plus your slice?'

'They're not for sale,' he says again.

'Well then, how about £400,000 for the pair of them, plus your slice?'

'Brian,' says Ron Greenwood, 'they are not for sale.'

'Well listen then, if I can't have Moore, can I have Brooking? Or how about this? If I can't have Brooking, can I have Moore?'

'They're not available,' he says again. 'But I'll pass your offer on to the board.'

'How about £500,000?' you ask. '£500,000 for the pair of them? Not forgetting your slice of the cake for all your toil and trouble. Can't say fairer than that, now can we, Ron?'

Ron Greenwood is on his feet again, the door to his office open –

'Any chance of another whisky then?' you ask him. 'One for the road?'

★ ★ ★

It's only six days since Queen's Park Rangers beat Leeds United 1–0 at Elland Road. My first home game, to a warm reception. Just six days ago, just last week. It feels like six years ago, another lifetime –

'This lot came to your house last week and they beat you,' I tell the visitors' dressing room at Loftus Road. 'They beat you in your own house, in front of your own fans; the League Champions, in their own house, in front of their own fans. They beat you because you couldn't handle Gerry fucking Francis. Yorath will handle him tonight so the rest of you can forget about him, because you won't see him. But remember this, the lot of you, every bloody one of you – they beat you in your own house last week, in front of your own fans. Now in my book there's only one bloody answer to something like that and I hope you don't need me to fucking tell you what that is – do you?'

They look up from their boots. From their socks and their tags.

Their eyes blank –

'Do you?'

They shake their heads. They nod their heads –

'Right then, well bloody well get out there and show me that fucking answer!'

They stand up from the benches. They file out of the dressing room –

Into the corridor. Down the tunnel. Onto the pitch –

The grass and the earth. The soil and the dirt –

The heavy, heavy mud.

* * *

Everyone has heard about your adventures in London; the chairman, the directors, the players and the fans. You made bloody sure they did. You might not have got Bobby Moore, you might not have got Trevor Brooking, but you still got what you wanted; no way for the board to refuse you transfer money now, so you got your new signing: Henry Newton for £120,000 from Everton –

And all this talk of new signings, of trips to London, of Bobby Moore and Trevor Brooking, all this talk means there's no need for a team talk today –

Saturday 22 September 1973; Derby County vs Southampton:

There's a penalty after seven minutes and, on the retake, Alan Hinton scores. Twenty minutes later, Roger Davies brings down a Hinton cross on his chest to score the second. Ten minutes after that, Hinton crosses again and this time Kevin Hector scores. Southampton pull one back before half-time, but it doesn't matter. Ten minutes into the second half, Hinton leaves two Southampton players standing and crosses again for Hector to make it 4–1. Southampton then pull another back, but again it doesn't matter. Hector sets up Davies for the fifth and then Davies sets up Hector for his hat-trick.

It is the first time Derby County have scored six since they beat Scunthorpe United in April 1963. Kevin Hector's hat-trick was also Derby's first in the league since 1969 and means Hector has now broken Jack Parry's post-war league scoring record with 107 goals in 287 games –

Derby County are now back up to second, Leeds United still first.

* * *

It was a good game, the best yet. They played for their pride and they played with their hearts. Especially in the first half as Lorimer, McGovern, Giles and Yorath passed the ball the length and width of the field, opening Queen's Park Rangers up so that Yorath scored one and McGovern had one cleared off the line by Terry Venables. Rangers then equalized early in the second half, but it was still a good game. The best yet –

'We have come on a ton tonight,' I tell the microphones and the pens, the cameras and the lights, on pitch and in the tunnel. 'And when you get it into perspective, when you remember we still have men like Bremner, McKenzie, Madeley and Jones out, it was marvellous. We should have really wrapped it up in the first half, we were that much on top. But at least there are no further injuries.'

It was a good game, the best yet. They played for their pride and they played with their hearts. But there are still no smiles on the team coach out of Loftus Road. No smiles and no laughter. Just the murmurs and the whispers, the paperback books and the packs of cards. I plonk myself down next to Syd Owen again –

'Do you think I should wear this every match day, Sydney?' I ask him.

'Wear what?'

'Wear this,' I tell him, pointing at my old green Leeds United goalkeeping jersey.

'Why?'

'I think it might just be my lucky jumper,' I tell him. 'My lucky colour.'

'I thought you didn't believe in luck, Mr Clough? In superstition?'

'Well, you know what they say?' I ask him. 'When in Rome . . .'

'Are you going to wear it tomorrow then?'

'Tomorrow?' I ask him. 'What's tomorrow?'

'Just the FA disciplinary hearing.'

★ ★ ★

You have been beaten 1–0 by Tottenham Hotspur at White Hart Lane, drawn at home with Norwich City and watched Henry Newton struggle in both

games. The board have refused Peter permission to write for the Derby
Evening Telegraph. *The board have refused your wife and Peter's wife tickets for the game at Old Trafford this Saturday.*

*It is Thursday and you are late again for the weekly board meeting. In your
absence, Sam Longson has called for your sacking –*

'For bloody breach of fucking contract?' *you repeat.*

'There is a clause in your contract,' *states Longson,* 'that requires you to give
your whole time and your whole attention to the affairs of Derby County
Football Club.'

'Hypocrites! Bloody hypocrites! When I was invited to sit on the last World
Cup panel, three years ago now, you lot bloody told me I must do it. And in
those days I even fucking took him with me,' *you tell them, rail at them, pointing at Longson –*

'And he bloody lapped it up, fucking loved it he did!'

'Stop him doing television,' *Peter tells them,* 'and you'll take away part and
parcel of his management job from him. That's unfair. Brian's right, you were
the ones who encouraged him in the first place. Egged him on.'

'Not me,' *says Jack Kirkland.* 'You'll not be laying that one at my door.'

'Well then, what about this?' *asks Longson and hands out a piece of paper –*

*It's an invoice for your expenses for your trip to Amsterdam; your trip to
Amsterdam to watch Poland play Holland, the warm-up for the England game –*

The England game you will be watching and speaking about for ITV.

'That's a mistake,' *you tell them.* 'A genuine mistake. The TV pays for that.'

*This time the board believe you. This time Sam Longson loses the vote to
sack you. You have lived to fight another day –*

But Jack Kirkland still has the last word:

'Stay off the bloody television and cut down the newspaper work,' *he tells
you.* 'And get on with the fucking job we're paying you for.'

It is Thursday 11 October 1973.

THE FIFTH RECKONING

First Division Positions, 28 August 1974

		P	W	D	L	F	A	Pts
1	Ipswich Town	4	4	0	0	7	0	8
2	Liverpool	4	3	1	0	6	2	7
3	Carlisle United	4	3	0	1	5	1	6
4	Everton	4	2	2	0	6	4	6
5	Man City	4	3	0	1	7	5	6
6	Derby County	4	1	3	0	4	2	5
7	Stoke City	4	2	1	1	6	3	5
8	Middlesbrough	4	2	1	1	5	3	5
9	Wolves	4	2	1	1	6	5	5
10	Chelsea	4	2	1	1	8	7	5
11	Arsenal	4	2	0	2	5	4	4
12	QPR	4	1	2	1	3	3	4
13	Sheffield Utd	4	1	2	1	5	6	4
14	Leicester City	4	1	1	2	6	7	3
15	Newcastle Utd	4	1	1	2	8	10	3
16	West Ham Utd	4	1	1	2	4	7	3
17	**Leeds United**	**4**	**1**	**1**	**2**	**2**	**5**	**3**
18	Coventry City	4	0	2	2	5	8	2
19	Luton Town	4	0	2	2	2	5	2
20	Burnley	4	0	1	3	5	9	1
21	Birmingham C.	4	0	1	3	4	9	1
22	Tottenham H.	4	0	0	4	1	5	0

First thing every morning, last thing every night –
I recite Psalm 109.
Twice a day for one whole year.
If I miss one morning, if I miss one night –
Then I die, not you –
But I am a Cunning Man. And I am a Clever Man –
And I never miss.

Day Twenty-nine

It's gone two in the morning when the bus drops us back at Elland Road and the taxi comes to take me to my modern luxury hotel. The bar is closed, the piano silent. I go up to my room and I pick up the phone to call my wife and kids, to call my brothers, to call John, Billy or Colin or any of my family and my friends not here with me tonight –

My mam and Peter.

I dial room service and I order champagne. Then I get out my pens and I get out my papers. I spread out the *Evening Post* and I start on the league tables and the fixtures. There's a knock on the door and the waiter wheels in the trolley –

The bucket and the bottle.

'Thank you very much,' I tell him. 'Now pick up that phone and call your gaffer and tell him you won't be back down for the next hour because Brian bloody Clough has requested the pleasure of your company and then go get yourself another glass, pull up a pew and raise that glass in a toast with me –

'To absent friends – fuck them all.'

* * *

No one speaks when you meet in the car park at the Baseball Ground. No one speaks as you get on the team bus. No one speaks on the drive to Old Trafford. No one speaks at all; the players don't speak; the trainers and the coaches don't speak; Jimmy and Peter don't speak; you don't speak; Longson and Webby don't speak; Kirkland and the other directors don't speak. No one speaks at all. No one says a single bloody word –

Things have come to this; month by month, week by week, day by day. Now things can't get any worse; the month is here, the week is here and the day is coming, the hour and the minute. Tick-tock, tick-tock, go the hands on your watch. Tick-tock –

This is the end, you think. This is the end. This is the end.

You and Peter stay with the team in the dressing room, your wives in the stands on scalped tickets, the ground filling up, the ground opening up –

Tick-tock, go the hands on your watch. Tick-tock.

You go down the tunnel with the team, your team, and out onto the pitch. You walk along the touchline. You look up into the stand for your wife. You see her in the stands. You put two fingers together and salute her with a wave. You take your place in the dug-out, on the bench, with Peter and with Jimmy –

Tick-tock, go the hands on your watch.

Just four minutes in and Forsyth underhits a back pass to Stepney, and Hector nips in and tucks the ball into the corner of the net. Just four minutes in and it's as good as over, good as over until the seventy-ninth minute when Kidd and Young hit the bar. But the score remains the same until the end –

This is the end, you think. This is the end.

'I know that Don Revie studies the league table every night,' you tell the press and the television. 'And I know he'll be looking at that table and thinking about Liverpool and Newcastle. But I also know one club will hit him right in the eye, and that club is Derby and this time I reckon we'll be ready for Don Revie and Leeds United when he brings them to the Baseball Ground on November the twenty-fourth.'

'You'll still be there then, will you?' they ask. 'Still the manager?'

Peter pulls you away. Peter takes you to one side. Peter says, 'Winning here doesn't happen very often. Let's take the wives upstairs to the boardroom.'

'I don't think it's a good idea,' *you tell him.*

'Come on,' *he says.* 'Might never happen again.'

Tick-tock, tick-tock, go the hands on your watch. Tick-tock –

'Go on then,' *you tell him,* 'but I'm not staying more than half an hour.'

So Peter goes off and finds your wives and then the four of you go upstairs to the Manchester United boardroom, the Manchester United boardroom where Longson and Kirkland and all the other Derby brass are having the time of their bloody lives, with their cigars in their hands and their wives on their arms, the time of their lives until you four walk in and the Manchester United boardroom goes quiet, silent –

Tick-tock, go the hands on your watch. Tick-tock.

But then the glasses clink, the coughs come and the conversations start back up.

'This must be the first time you've been in here?' asks Louis Edwards as he cracks open another bottle of champagne. But Peter is already pulling you away, already taking you to one side and saying, 'Time we were going back down.'

'Fuck off,' you tell him. 'We've only just bloody got up here.'

'But I don't like it here,' he says. 'Not my kind.'

'Looks like someone wants a word with you though,' you tell him, and Peter glances back to see Jack Kirkland crooking his finger, beckoning him over.

'No one bloody crooks their fucking finger at me,' hisses Peter.

'Just go and see what the twat wants and then we'll get off,' you tell him –

Tick-tock, go the hands on your watch.

But as Peter is walking across the Manchester United boardroom towards Jack Kirkland, Longson is walking up to you and, in front of your wife and in front of the room, Sam Longson asks, 'Did you make a V-sign at the Manchester United directors?'

'Did I do what?'

'Did you make a V-sign at Sir Matt and the Manchester United directors?'

'No.'

'They say you did.'

'Well, I didn't.'

'I want you to apologize.'

'No.'

'I'm not asking you to apologize,' says Longson. 'I'm telling you to apologize.'

'Fuck off.'

The chairman of Derby County Football Club stares into your eyes as your wife looks down at the devils in the carpet and you glance at your watch –

It has stopped.

Longson turns and walks away as Peter comes back across the Manchester United carpet. Peter is also red-faced. Peter also has tears in his eyes. Peter takes Lillian by her arm. Peter leads her out of the Manchester United boardroom –

You turn to your wife. You tell her, 'We're going.'

No one speaks on the coach back to Derby; the players don't speak; the trainers and the coaches don't speak; Jimmy and Peter don't speak; you don't speak; your wives don't speak; no one speaks at all –

No one says a single fucking word –

It is Saturday 13 October 1973, and you know this is the end.

★ ★ ★

The sun is shining, the sky is blue, but it's still another bloody ugly Yorkshire morning at the arse-end of August when I wake up in my modern luxury hotel bed in my modern luxury hotel room, feeling like fucking dogshit, and reach over the pens and the papers, the league tables and the fixtures to switch on the modern luxury radio beside the bed:

'*Yesterday Mr Denis Howell, the Sports Minister, chaired the so-called Soccer Summit to hammer out plans for dealing with hooliganism after the stabbing to death of a fourteen-year-old Blackpool supporter last Saturday. Afterwards Mr Howell said that players would also be required to tighten up their conduct on the pitch:*

'"*We have expressed the view that the FA, in dealing with misconduct, must express the seriousness of the situation and the determination we have to get this problem under control and conquer it in the interests of football and the sporting public.*"

'*Later this morning, Billy Bremner, of Leeds United and Scotland, and Kevin Keegan, of Liverpool and England, will appear before the FA Disciplinary Committee in London, accused of bringing the game into disrepute by pulling off their shirts after being sent off in the FA Charity Shield at Wembley earlier this month.*'

I switch off my modern luxury radio and lie back in my modern luxury hotel bed and thank fucking God that I left Maurice in London to accompany Bremner and Giles –

Thank fucking God, this once.

★ ★ ★

The coach drops you all back at the Baseball Ground. You call taxis for your wives and then you and Peter go up the stairs to your office –

'*He wants to know exactly what my job is,*' rails Peter. '*Can you fucking believe the cunt? He's only been on the board two fucking minutes and he*

234

wants to know what my bloody job is. Wagging his fucking finger at me in front
of all them folk. First thing Monday bloody morning, the bastard tells me. Well,
I'm not going, Brian. I'm bloody off. No one wags their fucking finger at me.'

You open up your office. You switch on the lights. You go inside –
The security grille has been pulled down over the bar.
You walk over to the grille. You rattle it –
It's been locked.

* * *

There is no training today and the car park is empty when the taxi
drops me at the ground. It'll fill up soon enough; as soon as the FA
Disciplinary Committee announces its verdict. I see John Reynolds
up on the practice pitch. I jog up the banking and onto the pitch –

I hold up my wrist and my watch and I tell him, 'Still going strong,
John.'

'That's good,' he says.

I nod and I smile and I ask him, 'How are you this morning then,
John?'

'I'm working,' he says and walks away.

* * *

You pace and you pace, up and down your carpet. Back and forth, you pace
and you pace. The walls getting closer and closer, the room getting hotter and
hotter. It is Sunday lunchtime and you can hear the church bells pealing, smell
the Sunday joint cooking. Roasting. Peter is sat on your sofa. Peter is smoking.
You pick up the phone. You telephone Longson at his home –

'Can I have your permission to sack Stuart Webb? He's locked the bar.'

'I know,' Longson tells you. 'Stuart was acting on my instructions.'

'He was what? Why? What's going on?'

'You just get on with managing the team,' he tells you and hangs up.

You put down your telephone. Slam it down. Break it –

Peter is sat on your sofa. Peter is crying –

It is Sunday 14 October 1973.

Under the stands. Through the doors. Round the corners. Down the corridor to the office. I unlock the door and I switch on the lights. The telephone is ringing. I pour a drink and I light a fag and I pick up the phone:

'You best come up here,' says Cussins. 'The verdict's in.'

I finish my drink. I put out my cigarette. I switch off the lights and I lock the door. Down the corridors and round the corners. Up the stairs and through the doors –

The Yorkshire boardroom, the Yorkshire curtains, the board silent and subdued, grim and stony-faced. The ashtrays filling up –

'Both Bremner and Keegan have been fined £500 each and suspended from today until September the thirtieth,' says Manny Cussins.

'September the thirtieth?' I repeat. 'That's over a bloody month.'

'The viewing public were shocked and offended by what they saw,' says Cussins. 'The FA were let down. Mr Stokes and the Committee felt they had no choice.'

'What about Giles?'

'Both John Giles and Tommy Smith were giving a good talking to,' says Cussins. 'But no further action was taken against either of them.'

'How many games will Bremner miss?' asks Percy Woodward.

'Eight,' I tell him. 'Including the first leg of the European Cup.'

'Eight?' repeats Cussins.

'Not forgetting the three he's already missed, so that's eleven in all.'

'We'll survive,' says Woodward. 'It's happened before.'

'A hundred and forty-two days out of the last ten years,' I tell them.

'But this is the first trouble Bremner's had in over four years,' says Woodward. 'Mr Revie worked very hard to improve discipline.'

I light a cigarette. I say nothing.

Then Sam Bolton says, 'You should have been there.'

'At the FA? Why?'

'Paisley was there with his players.'

'So bloody what?' I tell him. 'What Bremner did was nothing to do with me and I'll not be associated with it.'

'He's your player,' says Bolton. 'Your captain.'

'It wouldn't have made any bloody difference whether I was there or not.'

'Not to fine or suspension,' says Bolton. 'But it might have made a bloody difference to player himself and rest of his bloody team.'

'Bollocks,' I tell him, tell them all, and I leave the room. Through the doors. Down the stairs. Round the corners. Down the corridors. I unlock the door and I switch on the light. There is a note on the floor under the door to say Bill Nicholson called.

* * *

Peter comes out of his meeting with Jack Kirkland and says, 'I don't think there is any place for me here now. It's Hartlepools all over again, trying to get at you through me.'

'They think we're too big for our boots,' you say and hand Peter the letter – The letter that arrived this morning. The letter from Longson – First class. Recorded delivery:

Dear Mr Clough,

Henceforth each and every newspaper article and television appearance must be approved by the board. If you repeat or continue after receipt of this letter any breach of your obligations under your agreement with the club, the board will assuredly take the only course which you will thereby leave open to them. I should add that they will do so with some reluctance but without hesitation.

Yours sincerely, Samuel Longson

'What are we going to do?' asks Peter.

'We're finishing,' you tell him. 'That's what we're going to do.'

You pick up the phone. You call Longson –

'You've got what you wanted,' you tell him. 'We're calling a special board meeting tonight and we're resigning.'

'There'll be no board meeting tonight,' he tells you. 'I'm not driving all the way into Derby just for you two buggers. Put your resignations in writing and give them to the board tomorrow morning.'

You put down the phone. You look round the office –

At Peter. At the journalists and the mates who've gathered here –

'You're a bloody journalist so you can type, can't you?' you tell the bloke from the Evening Telegraph, *and Gerald Mortimer from the* Derby Evening Telegraph *nods.*

'Good,' you tell him. 'Then take this down:

'Dear Mr Longson,

'Thank you for your letter, which was delivered to me today. I have studied it carefully and have come to the conclusion that this, coupled with the other events of the past three months, leaves me with no alternative course of action. I wish therefore to inform you and the board of directors that I am tendering my resignation as manager of this club and wish this to come into effect immediately.

'Yours sincerely, Brian Clough.'

Gerald Mortimer stops typing. The office is silent. The security grille locked –

'Right, Peter,' you tell him. 'You're next.'

★ ★ ★

I drive back down to Derby early. I kiss my wife and I kiss my kids. I lock the door and I take the phone off the hook. I have dinner with my wife and my kids. I wash the dishes and I dry them. I bath my kids and I dry them. I read them stories and I kiss them goodnight. I watch television with my wife and I tell her I'll be up in a bit. Then I switch off the television and I pour another drink –

I get out my pens and I get out my papers –

The league table and the results. The league table and the fixtures –

But the results never change. Never. The table never changes –

Until it's almost light outside. Again. Morning here now –

This won't work. That big black fucking dog again –

'Clough out!' he barks. 'Clough out! Clough out!'

Day Thirty

You've spent the whole night doing the rounds; house to house, pub to pub, club to club; gathering your support and rallying your troops, your heart already heavy with regret but your head still light with injustice and rage, injustice and rage, injustice and rage . . .

First you met with Phillip Whitehead, your friend and local MP –

'Don't give the board the chance to overthrow you,' he told you. 'Because that's what they want, what they're waiting for. Only resign if you genuinely don't want the job and you're satisfied that the sacrifice will be worth it . . .'

Injustice and rage. Injustice and rage . . .

Then off you flew again, off in your club car to meet Sir Robertson-King, the President of Derby, at his local pub in Borrowash –

'Are you sure about what you're doing?' he asked you.

'No, I'm not sure,' you told him. 'But I can't carry on working in that atmosphere. Now, if you took the chair . . .'

'Let's see how it goes at the board meeting tomorrow then.'

Injustice and rage. And regret . . .

Now night is day, tomorrow today, and the morning of the board meeting here, your children looking at you with worry in their wide eyes, worry on their open mouths, for the things they've seen, the things they've heard –

The things they feel but do not understand.

* * *

I'm late out of bed, late to get washed, late to get dressed, late down the stairs and late out the door. Jimmy is picking me up this morning, Jimmy already parked waiting outside, Jimmy with his hand on his horn, and the first thing he says when I open the door is, 'You hear about Bill Nick, Boss?'

'What about him?'

'He's resigned.'

'What?'

'You didn't know?'

'No.'

'It's in all the papers, all over the radio.'

'Why?'

'Poor results and modern players, that's what they're saying.'

'What about modern chairmen and modern directors?'

'Never mentioned them,' laughs Jimmy. 'But, seriously, I think it was Rotterdam. I don't think he's ever got over that. He told Dave Mackay that he was physically sick, he was that scared. You know his own daughter was there in the stadium when all the Spurs fans were rioting. Dave was there and all and he says he's never heard owt as sad as the sound of Bill Nick making his appeals over the loudspeakers for them to stop fighting.'

'I don't know about that,' I tell Jimmy. 'But I do know one thing . . .'

'What's that, Boss?'

'Never resign,' I tell him. 'Never ever resign.'

Then we pick up the Johns. Four big men in one small car –

No conversation. No chat. No banter. No jokes. No radio. Nothing –

Just four men on their way to Leeds. On their way to work.

★ ★ ★

You have prior engagements, prior to the board meeting, engagements you intend to keep; so you drive miles and miles out of Derby to open a new shop for an old friend, then you drive miles and miles back into town to visit some elderly patients at a hospital –

And at the shop and at the hospital, the customers and the patients, the staff and the doctors, they all shake you by your hand and say, 'Don't go, Brian. Please don't.'

And you clasp their hands and nod your head and thank them for their hands and for their words, and tell them, 'I don't want to go.'

Then you drive to the Baseball Ground and park your Derby County club car in the space reserved for the Derby County club manager and walk through the press and the television, the pens and the microphones, the cameras and the lights, past a group of night-shift workers from Rolls-Royce who pat you on your back and plead with you, 'Please don't bloody go, Brian. Please don't fucking go.'

And you clasp their hands and nod your head and thank them for their pats and for their pleas, and tell them, 'I don't want to go.'

Then you disappear inside the Baseball Ground, you disappear.

★ ★ ★

In the rain and in the sun, under the black and blue, purple and yellow Yorkshire skies, it should be business as usual today, training as usual for everyone. The club secretary has issued a statement on behalf of Leeds United:

'Billy will be training with the rest of his teammates as he has done over the past fortnight when he has also been under suspension.'

But the press and the television still want more, the pens and the microphones, the cameras and the lights, still waiting for me as we pull into the Elland Road car park, as I slam the door of Jimmy's car, as I do up my cuffs and tell them all:

'I am not saying a word about the FA decision. Not a word.'

★ ★ ★

Up the stairs. Through the doors. Round the corners. Down the corridors, Pete already here; smoking his cigs and biting his nails in the antechamber –

'Where have you been?' he asks. 'I thought you weren't going to show.'

'I had things to do,' you tell him. 'Now let's get in there.'

'We've got to wait out here.'

'For what?'

'For them to consider our resignations.'

'If they've got things to say, they can bloody well say them to my fucking face,' you tell him and walk towards the boardroom doors –

'Please don't,' Pete says, Pete begs. 'It'll just make things worse.'

*So you turn back from the doors and sit down next to him and light a cig
of your own, staring at the clock on the wall and the potted plant by the doors;
and you know you've made a big mistake, sat out here, smoking your cig, waiting your turn, remembering all the bloody things you know you should have
said, all the fucking things you know you should have done, all them bloody,
fucking things you had forgotten –*

Then the doors open and Longson shouts, 'Right, you two, let's have you in!'

*But before you're even halfway into the room, before you've even sat down,
you've already told them: 'Accept our resignations.'*

'Now wait, Brian,' says Sir Robertson-King. 'We'd like you to reconsider.'

*But Longson is quick too, quick to say, 'He's resigned and he wants us to
accept his resignation, so I propose we accept it and have bloody done!'*

*'Now just you listen to me,' you tell him, tell them all. 'We've only resigned
because of him, him and his narrow-minded ways. Everything I've ever done
has been for the good of Derby County, everything! And that includes the television and the newspapers, the television and the newspapers that helped put
Derby County on the bloody map, that put you all on the fucking map. And
so I won't be told by him – not by him or by the FA or by the League or by
anybody – what I can or cannot write and what I can or cannot say. But if this
board withdraw his daft ultimatum and banish that bugger from our sight and
just let us get on with our job of winning the league and then the European
Cup, of taking on every single thing in the game and of creating a footballing
dynasty here at Derby County, then we will withdraw our resignations.'*

*The board nod their heads. The board mutter. The board will put it to the
vote. The board ask you and Peter both to wait outside again –*

*Outside with the clock on the wall. The potted plant by the doors. The doors
that quickly open again so they can call you back in:*

'Your resignations have reluctantly been accepted,' smiles Jack Kirkland –

*Only Sir Robertson-King and Mike Keeling have voted against accepting
your resignations. Now Mike Keeling resigns, along with your own secretary.*

'Don't even think of a settlement,' Longson tells you. 'You're getting nowt!'

You stand in the centre of the room, naked and beaten, with Peter beside you.

'Leave your car keys on the table and get out now,' barks Longson.

*In the centre of the room, naked and beaten before the board, their eyes down
on the table, their fingers at their mouths, their feet shuffling and eager to leave –*

242

'Not one of you has the guts to stop this?' you ask them. 'Not one of you?'
But their eyes stay down on the table, their fingers at their mouths –

'Cowards!' you bark at them all and turn to the doors, the doors and the exit, the exit and the antechamber; through the antechamber and down the corridor, down the corridor and into the executive lounge you go –

'I want you out of the ground,' Longson is shouting. 'Both of you, now!'
Into the heat of the lights, the gaze of the cameras, and the . . . Action!

Daggers drawn, pistols poised, you stand at one end of the lounge and Longson stands at the other; Longson telling the press and the television, the pens and the microphones, the cameras and the lights, telling them all how your resignations have been accepted, accepted but 'with a certain amount of sadness'.

'It surprises me a little,' you answer back, 'that people, the very people who want to stop me putting two words together, can't put them together themselves.'

But Longson keeps blinking into the lights, keeps stuttering into the cameras, blinking and stuttering on and on about acceptance and sadness.

'I feel deeply embarrassed for the chairman,' you tell the same cameras and lights, not blinking and not stuttering. 'And deeply ashamed for Derby County.'

Finally, Jack Kirkland drags the chairman away from the heat of the lights and the gaze of the cameras, drags him back into the board meeting and, as he goes, as Longson goes back into that boardroom, Longson turns and looks into your eyes and spits upon his hand, he spits upon his hand again and winks –

'Right then, Brian, we'll see, shall we?'

And you, you push your way through the press and the television, the pens and the microphones, the cameras and the lights, you push your way back down that corridor towards that boardroom, and those doors they close in your face, slam shut in your face –

In your face, in your face, after all the bloody things you've fucking done for them, they close those doors in your face, slam them shut in your face, and you pick up the jug of water from the table and you're going to throw it through those bloody doors, throw it in all their fucking faces, when Peter takes hold of your arm, Peter takes hold of your arm and lowers the jug back down to the table and says, 'Leave it, Brian. Leave it.'

★ ★ ★

The bad boy of British football doesn't knock. The bad boy of British football just opens the office door and says, 'You wanted to see me?'

'Yes,' I tell him. 'Have a seat, William. Have a fag and a drink too, if you want.'

Bremner takes a seat. Bremner takes a fag. Bremner takes a drink.

'You're going to miss the Man. City match on Saturday,' I tell him. 'Then the Luton game the following Saturday, the League Cup game against Huddersfield, then the league games against Burnley, Sheffield United, Tottenham and Everton, and also the first round of the European Cup. That means your first match back for us will be the return leg of the European Cup game in Zurich.'

'I've read the fixture list,' says Bremner. 'I know what I'm missing.'

'That's another eight games,' I tell him. 'Top of the three you've missed already. Eleven bloody matches all told.'

He takes another one of my cigs. He takes another glass of my whisky.

'I've told you before,' I tell him again, 'if I had to pick any member of the first-team squad here at Leeds to miss games through suspension, the last name on that list – and even then, way behind any other name on that list – would be yours. Clarkey, Giles, Peter Lorimer, Norman Hunter; anybody but you. There's not another bloody player in this whole fucking club we could possibly miss more than you.'

Bremner puts out his cig. Bremner finishes his drink. 'Is that all?'

'Sit down,' I tell him. 'Sit down and listen, will you?'

Bremner sits back down. Bremner stares back across my desk.

'Like I've told you before,' I tell him again, 'I don't want to lose you on the field but, if I must lose you on the field, I don't want to lose you off the field. Now I'm not going to ask you to travel with us to away games, not unless you want to, but what I am going to ask you to consider is coming to the Central League home games, watching the reserves for me, giving me an extra pair of eyes.'

Bremner doesn't speak. Bremner just stares back across my desk.

'So instead of travelling to Maine Road with us this coming Saturday,' I continue, 'you'd be here watching the reserves play Bolton. If nothing else, it'll be good experience for you, especially if, as I hear it, you're thinking of going into management.'

Bremner doesn't speak. Bremner just stares –

Into my eyes. Into the silence.

Then the door opens again. No knock. Just John Giles standing in the doorway –

'Thousand apologies,' he laughs. 'Not interrupting, am I?'

Bremner stands up. Bremner asks, 'Can I go now, sir?'

★ ★ ★

You and Peter push your way out to your club car in the space reserved for the club manager and then you drive through the press and the television, through the pens and the microphones, the cameras and the lights, past the group of night-shift workers from Rolls-Royce who bang on the roof of your grey Mercedes and beg and beg and beg you –

'Please don't bloody go, Brian. Please don't fucking go.'

But you and Peter drive away from the Baseball Ground, drive away to a garage to have the tyres on your club car changed and the tank of your club car filled up on the club account, and then you and Peter drive on to Peter's house –

To the silence in his sitting room. The silence and the cup of tea –

'What will you do now?' you ask him.

'I think I'll catch a bloody plane to Majorca,' he says. 'What about you?'

'I haven't a fucking clue,' you tell him –

It is Tuesday 16 October 1973, and you are out of a job.

Day Thirty-one

Under another bloated grey Yorkshire sky, they are dirty and panting again, dirty and panting in their purple tracksuits with their names on their backs. There are still no smiles. There is still no laughter. Just the stains on their knees, the stains on their arses. I have given up on smiles here. I have given up on laughter now.

Maurice and Sydney stand to one side, heads together, crooked and hunched, whispering and muttering, whispering and muttering, whispering and muttering.

Jimmy stands in the middle, doing a bit of this, doing a bit of that, a joke here and a joke there. But no one is smiling. No one is laughing. No one is even listening –

Except the press and the fans. Behind the fence. Through the wire –

Their eyes are on me now, inspecting and examining, watching and observing me, staring and staring and staring at me –

No more zombies, I'm thinking. *No more fucking zombies, Brian.*

I walk up to Maurice and Sydney. I take the whistle off Sydney. I take the bibs off Maurice and I get some five-a-sides going; me on one side, Clarkey on another.

I know they all want to tackle me, to tackle me hard, to bring me down, down to the ground, back down to earth, to see me fall flat on my face or my arse again –

Bruised and aching, aching and hurting, hurting and smarting . . .

But I read the move and I collect the pass, collect the pass with my back to the goal, back to the goal and I shield the ball from McQueen, shield the ball from McQueen and I hold it, hold it and I turn, turn and I hit it, hit it on the volley, on the volley straight into the top corner, into the top corner and past Stewart's hand, past Stewart's hand as it flails around, as it flails around and the ball hits the back of the net –

The back of the fucking net, the fucking net –

But there's no applause. No adoration. No love here –

No smiles here. No laughter here.

'Two-hundred and fifty-one goals,' I tell them again. 'Beat that!'

But they're already walking off the training pitch, back to the dressing room, taking off their bibs and their tracksuit tops, throwing them to the ground –

Dirty and panting, panting and plotting, plotting and scheming.

The press and the fans. Behind the fence. Through the wire –

Their eyes on me, inspecting and examining me, watching and observing me, staring and staring and staring at me, but only when I look away –

I feel like death. I feel like death. I feel like death.

John Giles walks over to me. John Giles tells me, 'I'll be meeting up with the Eire squad on Sunday and then I'll be going to go see the Spurs.'

'Are you asking me or telling me, Irishman?'

'Telling you, I suppose.'

'Fingers crossed then,' I tell him. 'Fingers crossed.'

'And there was me thinking you weren't a superstitious man,' he laughs.

★ ★ ★

It takes you a moment to remember. To remember why the phone is ringing. To remember why the doorbell is ringing. To remember why the press and the television, the pens and the microphones, the cameras and the lights, are all camped outside your house –

To remember why your three children are hiding in their rooms, under their beds with their fingers in their ears, their eyes closed –

It takes you that moment to remember you are no longer the manager of the Derby County Football Club, that you are out of a job and out of work –

But then you remember you're not out of work. You do still have a job. You still have television. Still have ITV. England vs Poland. The World Cup qualifier –

The match they must win. Tonight. The biggest story since 1966 –

Bigger even than the resignation of Brian bloody Clough.

★ ★ ★

Bones. Muscles. Broken bones. Torn muscles. Flesh and meat. Carcasses and cadavers. The Friday lunchtime press conference; there should be no post-mortems here, only prophecies; no excuses, only optimism; confidence, not doubt; hope and never fear:

'I only wish I had a fit Duncan McKenzie, a fit Paul Madeley, a fit Michael Jones, a fit Eddie Gray and an available Billy Bremner to take on Manchester City.'

'Would you also like an available Hartford?' they ask me; ask because Manchester City's Asa Hartford was involved in an on-off transfer with Leeds back in 1971, a transfer Don pulled out of on medical grounds –

A hole in the heart; Hartford, not Revie.

'He'll be wanting to show off against us,' I tell them. 'Lots of players want to.'

But they don't smile. They don't laugh. They just look down at their notebooks, their spiral-bound notebooks, and they flick and click the tops of their ballpoint pens, flick and click, flick and click –

In and out. In and out. In and out –

Something in their eyes again –

Carcasses, cadavers and death.

★ ★ ★

The day after your resignation from Derby, the England team are out on the pitch, warming up in the Wembley night, waving to their families and friends, posing for the official photographs, steadying their nerves, their stomachs and their bowels.

You walk down from the gantry, across the pitch, that hallowed turf, to the centre circle, to Roy McFarland, to David Nish, to Colin Todd, to Kevin Hector, and you stick out your hand and tell them, 'Don't worry, lads. It'll all work out.'

And they shake your hand four times but look at you in confusion and in despair, doubt and fear, with worry in their wide eyes, worry on their open mouths, for the things they've seen, the things they've heard –

The things they feel but do not understand.

But then you're gone. Back across that pitch, that hallowed turf, up into your gantry to sit and stare down in judgement on them –

On England and on Alf Ramsey.

But tonight as you sit and stare down on Alf Ramsey, you feel regret, regret for all the things you've said, you've said on television, on panels such as this one, all the things you've said that have hurt Alf, hurt him and you know it –

'How is it he can't pick a team from 2,000 players?' you asked on television, on a panel such as this, after England had lost in Italy last year –

These things that have hurt him, hurt him and stripped him and left him bare; bare and raw to the whispers and rumours that say you should be the next manager of England, that say it is only a matter of time, should the unthinkable occur, should England lose, should England draw –

Should England not qualify –

Then would be your time. Then would be your hour, should England lose. England draw. England not qualify for the World Cup finals –

That hope you'd never dare to utter. This hope you'd never dare to say:

'England will walk it,' you assure the whole nation on Independent Television. 'That Polish keeper's a clown, an absolute clown.'

England do dominate the first half, camped in the Polish half of the pitch, but that clown, that absolute clown, makes save after save after save from Madeley, from Hughes, from Bell, from McFarland, from Hunter, from Currie, from Channon, from Chivers, from Clarke and from Peters.

Then, ten minutes into the second half, Poland finally get out of their own half and break upfield. Hunter misses his tackle and Lato is away down the left, away down the left and free to cross the ball to Domarski, who shoots straight under Shilton –

And there is silence, absolute silence. In the stands and on the pitch, silence –

Except for you up in your gantry, on the television, on your panel, your mouth opening and closing. But no one is listening. Not even to you –

Up in the gantry. In judgement on England. In judgement on Alf Ramsey –

Ramsey rocking back and forth on the bench down below.

But ten minutes later England have equalized after Peters was fouled and Clarke coolly converted the most important penalty in the history of English football. But England still need to score again, score again to win, to win and to qualify, and so Alf, rocking back and forth below, Alf brings on Hector. Hector on his début for those final two minutes. Hector whose shot is cleared off the line and then hears the final whistle –

That final, final whistle and the end of an era.

It is the first time that England have failed to qualify for the World Cup since they first entered the competition in 1950. The first time since 1950 that England won't be at the World Cup, won't be in West Germany. Not in 1974. Not after this night –

This night that ends everything. Ends everything. Everything.

From up in the gantry you sit and stare down as Bobby Moore walks across the pitch to put an arm around Norman Hunter, Norman Hunter who blames himself, and you watch as Harold Sheperdson does the same and leads Hunter from the pitch –

'Hunter lost the World Cup! Hunter lost the World Cup!'

And then you see Ramsey and you watch Ramsey, watch him walk away down that long, long tunnel into that long, long night and again you feel regret –

Regret. Regret. Regret –

Regret not only for the things you've said, the things you've said on television, those things you know have hurt him, but also for those things you've thought –

Those things you've thought and dreamed of, dreamed and dared to hope for –

For England to lose. For England to draw. England not to qualify –

For Alf Ramsey to lose his job as England manager –

For you to take his job as England manager.

But now, this night, you feel regret, regret and hate, hate for yourself.

You walk down from the gantry, across the pitch, that hallowed turf, down that tunnel and into the England dressing room.

'For what it's worth,' you tell Alf, 'you must be the unluckiest man in foot-ball, because you could have done that lot six or seven.'

But when Ramsey looks up at you, stares up at you from the dressing-room floor, there is no recognition in his eyes, only hurt –

Hurt and fear.

★ ★ ★

Never learn; never bloody learn. Never did and never fucking will. The piano bar of the Dragonara Hotel, two in the morning, drunk as fuck; drunk as fuck with the gentlemen of the local press; those scum-bags and hacks, Harry, Ron and Mike –

Something in their eyes again . . .

Harry, Ron and Mike were there at training; Harry, Ron and Mike there at lunch; Harry, Ron and Mike still here with me now at two in the morning in the piano bar of the Dragonara Hotel, listening to my stories, laughing at my jokes, and pouring my drinks –

Something in their eyes.

I stand up. I sit down. I stand up again. I point my glass across the bar and shout, 'Don't you have a fucking home to go to?'

But Bert the Pianist just smiles and segues straight into 'It's a Lonesome Old Town'.

'I never knew how much I missed you,' I try to sing but shout –

Harry pulling me back down onto the sofa.

But I get back to my feet and point and shout, 'Play "Hang My Tears Out to Dry"! Play "Hang My Tears Out to Dry"! Play "Hang My Tears Out to Dry" or you're fucking sacked!'

'Sit down,' Ron is saying. 'Come on, Brian lad, sit down . . .'

'So make it one for my baby,' Mike is singing. 'And one more . . .'

'Shut up!' I tell him, tell them all. 'That's the wrong fucking song.'

'Brian,' they're saying. 'Brian, please –'

'I want "I'll Hang My Tears Out to Dry",' I tell the bar, the hotel, the whole of Leeds. 'That's all I want. "Guess I'll Hang My Tears Out to Dry". Fucking wankers, the lot of you!'

But there's no one here. No one in the piano bar –

Harry, Ron and Mike have all gone home –

Bert the Pianist has gone home too –

No one here but bloody me –

Only fucking me now –

Cloughie.

The barman takes my legs, the waiter takes my arms, but no one takes me home.

Day Thirty-two

England have drawn. England are out of the World Cup. The press and the television want Ramsey out. The press and the television want you in. But all you want this morning is company. Not to be on your Jack Jones in a posh London hotel. Not today; Thursday 18 October 1973.

You leave the capital. You drive back to Derby. There is a man on your doorstep. Man you've never met before. He says, 'I want to help you get your job back, Brian.'

His name is John. John writes plays. Plays about the Yom Kippur War.

'Come on in then,' you tell him. 'Have a seat and have a drink.'

You hand him a large scotch and water. The doorbell rings –

'Brian,' whispers your wife. 'It's the police, love.'

You put down your whisky with no water. You go to your front door:

'Hello, George. Are you coming in?' you ask Detective Inspector George Stewart.

'Not today, Brian,' he says. 'I'm afraid I've got to mark your card.'

'And why's that then, George?' you ask him.

George nods at the Mercedes. 'You do know you're not insured, don't you?'

'Like hell I'm not,' you tell him. 'I've just driven back from bloody London!'

'I'm sorry to have to tell you that Mr Kirkland has cancelled your insurance.'

'He's done bloody what?' you ask him. 'The fucking cunt!'

'Aye,' says George. 'And I wouldn't want you to run into one of our lot who doesn't know who you are, or who doesn't give a shit who you are, or who just wants to make a bloody name for themselves, or just plain doesn't like you very fucking much.'

'Point taken, George,' you tell him and shut the door in his face.

'That's bloody outrageous,' says John. 'Fucking diabolical.'

'Fucking inconvenient and all,' you tell him. 'I've got to drive to Birmingham.'

'About a job?' asks John.

'I bloody wish,' you tell him. 'I'm down to play in a charity match tonight.'

'I'll drive you,' says John. 'I'd be happy to.'

'In that case I'll have another drink,' you tell John as your wife leaves the room to pick up the kids —

To make them their tea. To give them their baths. To put them to bed —

To try to lead a normal bloody life.

Later, much later that night, John is driving you back home from Birmingham, from the charity match and the nightclub: the Talk of the Midlands, where you shared a stage with Mike bloody Yarwood and appealed to the people of Derby for their support —

The people of Derby who gave you a standing fucking ovation —

John is driving you back home when he asks, 'Are you going to the game?'

You open your eyes. You ask him, 'Which one?'

'The bloody Derby–Leicester one,' he laughs. 'On Saturday.'

You shake your head. You tell him, 'I daren't.'

'You what?' he says. 'Cloughie scared?'

You nod your head. 'That's right.'

'Listen to me,' he tells you now. 'If you were to walk around that running track on Saturday afternoon, you'd get an ecstatic reception. The television will be there. Be on all the news programmes. Think of the visual impact. The impact on the public.'

'I can't do it,' you tell him. 'They might throw me out.'

'They won't throw you out,' he laughs. 'You created that team. You're a hero.'

'Well, I've not got a bloody ticket either.'

'You leave that to me,' says John. 'You leave everything to me.'

* * *

Saturday comes again, welcome or not, it comes again like it always does, welcome or not, wanted or not, another judgement day —

The chance to be saved, the chance to be damned.

I sit alone at the front of the coach on the motorway to Manchester and I already know today's result before we've even arrived —

No mystery. Not today. Not there. Not at Maine Road.

I've not been to a game yet when I haven't already known the result before my team has got changed, before one whistle has been blown or one ball has been kicked; I know the result, know the answer –

Because I look into their eyes, I look into their hearts –

No mystery. Not today. Not any day. Not there –

Not in their eyes. Not in their hearts –

No mystery there. Just answers –

In the eyes. In the hearts –

Because in our eyes and in our hearts we have already lost, we are already damned.

* * *

It is Saturday lunchtime. You are at the Kedleston Hall Hotel, your new head-quarters, having a long lunch with John, his mate Bill Holmes, your mate Dave Cox and Peter –

Peter who looks like he's died twice in the last two days.

You're all smoking and drinking more than you're eating; knocking back the booze; knocking back the Dutch courage –

Laughing and joking more than you're talking.

Then John looks at his watch. Then John says, 'It's time, Brian.'

You finish your drink. You pat Pete on his knee. You both stand up. You leave the restaurant of the Kedleston Hall Hotel. You go out into the car park. You get into the Rolls-Royce. The front seat of the golden Rolls-Royce. You turn the key. You start the engine and off you set through the streets of Derby. Pete on the back seat, you at the wheel. Through the deserted streets of barricaded hous-es and police reinforcements, deserted but for the police and the demonstrators and their banners. The demonstrators who have boycotted the match, their ban-ners demanding, 'BRING BACK CLOUGHIE!'

Through the deserted, barricaded streets to the Baseball Ground.

It is five minutes to three o'clock when you park the Rolls and the police-man asks, 'How long do you intend staying, Brian?'

'Five minutes, no longer,' you tell him.

'So you're not stopping to watch the match?'

'Believe it or not,' you tell him, 'I'm just nipping in to say cheerio.'

The policeman lets you park the Rolls, lets you leave Pete on the back seat, so you can nip through the demonstrators, through the cameras and the lights, past the bewildered steward and through the turnstiles, into the ground on your borrowed Derby County season ticket, where you then head off towards the players' entrance, but here the commissionaire blocks your way and thwarts your plans to appear on the running track, so you run instead out beneath the main stand and then up, up, up the steps you go and along the row to your borrowed seat, just along from the directors' box –

And there you stand, risen, your arms outstretched –

Immaculate in your new grey suit –

Your arms outstretched –

Immaculate and back.

The players stop their warm-up, the Derby County players and the Leicester City players, as the Derby crowd applaud their hero –

Applaud, adore and love their hero.

Just along from you, Longson now gets to his feet as his fellow directors and the season-ticket holders behind the directors' box applaud him –

But it's too little and too late. Much too late –

The real applause, the real adoration, the real love is for you –

'Cloughie! Cloughie! Cloughie!'

Then the referee blows his whistle and you're gone, gone again, down the stairs. Through the turnstiles. Past the same steward –

Across the deserted street. Into your golden Rolls-Royce and away –

Down to London. To the Parkinson *show. To television –*

No looking back. No turning back –

Saturday 20 October 1973.

THE SIXTH RECKONING

First Division Positions, 1 September 1974

		P	W	D	L	F	A	Pts
1	Liverpool	5	4	1	0	9	2	9
2	Ipswich Town	5	4	0	1	8	3	8
3	Everton	5	3	2	0	8	5	8
4	Man. City	5	4	0	1	9	6	8
5	Carlisle United	5	3	1	1	6	2	7
6	Stoke City	5	2	2	1	7	4	6
7	Middlesbrough	5	2	2	1	6	4	6
8	Wolves	5	2	2	1	7	6	6
9	Sheffield Utd	5	2	2	1	8	7	6
10	Derby County	5	1	3	1	4	4	5
11	Newcastle Utd	5	2	1	2	10	10	5
12	QPR	5	1	3	1	4	4	5
13	Chelsea	5	2	1	2	8	10	5
14	Arsenal	5	2	0	3	6	6	4
15	Leicester City	5	1	2	2	7	8	4
16	Burnley	5	1	1	3	8	9	3
17	Luton Town	5	0	3	2	3	6	3
18	West Ham Utd	5	1	1	3	4	9	3
19	**Leeds United**	**5**	**1**	**1**	**3**	**3**	**7**	**3**
20	Tottenham H.	5	1	0	4	3	5	2
21	Birmingham C.	5	0	2	3	5	10	2
22	Coventry City	5	0	2	3	5	11	2

The last of the Cunning Men is here –
I have the hair from your comb. I have the hair from your drains –
Tonight I will burn it. Tonight I will bury it.
All the beasts of the field here too –
The birds and the badgers. The foxes and the ferrets –
The dogs and the demons. The wolves and the vultures –
Come to devour, to eat you.

Day Thirty-three

The loneliest bloody day of the week, the loneliest fucking place on earth; under the stands, through the doors, round the corners to the bathroom and toilet in the corridor. The bathroom door is locked, the bathroom mirror broken. There is a dirty grey handkerchief wrapped around the knuckle of my right hand and when I look up into that mirror again there are black splintered cracks across my face, terrible black splintered cracks across my face –

Leeds United lost yesterday. 2-bloody-1 to Manchester City at Maine Road; Leeds United have just three points from five games and have scored just three goals. By this stage last year, Leeds United had beaten Everton, Arsenal, Tottenham, Wolves and Birmingham City; this stage last year, Leeds had ten points from five games and had scored fifteen goals with six from Lorimer, four from Bremner, two from Jones and one a piece from Giles, Madeley and Clarke –

This time last year, when Don bloody Revie was the manager of Leeds United and I was the manager of Derby County; when Don was fucking top and I was second; this time last year, when Alf Ramsey was still the manager of England.

I run the taps. I wash my face. I open the bathroom door. I go down the corridor. *His* corridor. Round the corner. *His* corner. Down the tunnel. *His* tunnel. Out into the light and out onto that pitch. *His* pitch. *His* field –

His field of loss. *His* field of blood. *His* field of sacrifice. *His* field of slaughter. *His* field of vengeance. *His* field of victory!

I shouldn't be here. I should be at home with my wife and with my kids, carving the roast and digging the garden, walking the dog and washing the car. Not here. Not in this place –

This hateful, spiteful place –

Flecked in their phlegm.

It starts to spit again. I put out my cig. I finish my drink. I walk off that field, off that pitch. Down that tunnel, down that corridor. Round those corners, through those doors and out of Elland Road.

In the car park of the ground, in the shadow of the stands, there are four young kids in their boots and their jeans, kicking a jam-jar lid about –

'Morning, lads,' I shout.

'Afternoon, Mr Clough,' they shout back.

'How are you today then, lads?'

'All right, ta,' they shout. 'And you?'

'I'm surviving,' I tell them and walk across the car park, across the car park to the huts on their stilts beside the banking that leads up to the training pitch. The huts are all locked so I have to give the lock a right good kick before it gives in –

'What you doing?' the young lads ask me.

'You'll see,' I tell them and force open the door to one of the huts. I go inside and drag out one of those huge string bags that hold all the old match-day balls. I open up the bag and boot one of the balls down the steps from the hut to the lads in the car park –

'There you go,' I tell them. 'Courtesy of Leeds United.'

'Ta very much,' they all shout.

'You're very welcome, lads,' I tell them and walk back down the steps from the hut, down to the car park and across to my car, a little lad waiting by the door –

He asks, 'What happened to your hand, Mr Clough?'

'I got it caught somewhere, didn't I?' I tell him.

'How did you do that then?'

'Stuck it somewhere I bloody shouldn't have, that's how.'

'Least it weren't your fucking nose,' he laughs.

'You might be right there,' I tell him. 'But there's no need for language like that, not on a Sunday, so you bugger off home and get that big mouth of yours washed out.'

Day Thirty-four

The scenes have shifted, the sets changed again. The curtain falls and another one rises. You have taken your final bow at the old Baseball Ground. You have transferred to London. You have been on the Parkinson *show. You have been in the papers, all over the papers, the front and back pages –*

Never out of the papers. Never off the television –

Risen in your new grey suit, arms outstretched –

Cloughie, Immaculate.

Jimmy Gordon, Judas James Gordon, might be in temporary charge of the team, might be the one who picked Saturday's team, but the Derby players, your players, beat Leicester City 2–1. 'For Brian and Peter,' they said. 'For Brian and Peter.'

Not for Jimmy. Not for the bloody board and not for fucking Longson.

But Longson has not been silent. Longson has responded. Longson in the papers. Front and back pages. Longson on the telly and things have got nasty now; very, very nasty now because Longson has made all kinds of allegations about you; allegations about expenses; allegations about transfer deals; allegations about players' salaries and bonuses; allegations about tickets and petty cash; about money, money, money –

Always funny, funny money –

Not allegations made by the whole board. Just by Longson.

You drove back from London yesterday in a rented car. You kissed your wife. You kissed your kids. You had your Sunday lunch. Then you spent the rest of the day on the phone to your friends, your friends who came round, to drink your drinks and hold your hand, your friends who are solicitors, your friends who went through Longson's statement, paragraph by paragraph, line by line, sentence by sentence, word by word, your friends who helped you repudiate that statement, paragraph by paragraph, line by line, sentence by sentence, word by word. Allegation by fucking allegation.

Today your friends who are solicitors will begin a libel action on your behalf.
They will issue a writ. Not just against Longson, but against the whole board –
'It'll turn them against Longson,' said John. 'It'll drive a wedge between them.
Set them at each other's throats, you'll see. At each other's throats, they'll be.'
You get out of bed. You get washed. You get dressed –
You go downstairs. You go into the kitchen –
Risen again in your new grey suit –
Cloughie, Immaculate –
Unemployed.

★ ★ ★

The sun might be shining outside, the sky might be blue, but I'm under the covers of my bed, with the tables and the fixtures in my head; next Saturday, if Leeds beat Luton then Leeds will have five points. Five points could take Leeds up to eleventh or twelfth, if Leicester lose to Wolves, West Ham lose to Sheffield United, QPR lose to Birmingham, Chelsea lose to Middlesbrough, Tottenham lose to Liverpool, and if Arsenal and Burnley draw, Carlisle and Stoke draw, Ipswich and Everton draw. The problem is Derby vs Newcastle. If Derby and Newcastle draw, both teams will have six points and, if Leeds beat Luton, Leeds will only have five points. The best result then would be a defeat for Derby. Then Newcastle will have seven points and both Derby and Leeds will have five points. Then it will come down to goal average. So Leeds will need to beat Luton by three or four goals to make certain that Leeds climb above Derby; beat Luton who were promoted as Second Division runners-up to Middlesbrough last season –

The tables and the fixtures in my head, the doubts and the fears that should Leeds lose to Luton and then Tottenham beat Liverpool, Birmingham beat QPR and Coventry beat Manchester City, then Leeds would be bottom of the First Division –

The wife is frying some bacon, the kids eating their cereal –

Leeds would be bottom of the First Division . . .

I pour a cup of tea, heap in four sugars –

Bottom of the First Division . . .
Four kisses bye-bye –
Bye-bloody-bye.

★ ★ ★

The Derby players, your *players, have written a letter to the board. This is what the Derby players,* your *players, have written in their letter to the board:*

Dear Mr Longson and the directors of Derby County Football Club,

During the events of last week we, the undersigned players, have kept our feelings within the dressing room. However, at this time, we are unanimous in our support and respect for Mr Clough and Mr Taylor and ask that they be reinstated as manager and assistant manager of the club.

It was absolutely vital that we won against Leicester on Saturday for ourselves, as well as for the club and fans. Now that match is out of the way, nobody can say we have acted on the spur of the moment and are just being emotional.

We called the meeting of first-teamers and it was emphasized that nobody was under obligation to attend. But everybody was there. We then decided to write this letter and again nobody was under pressure to sign. But again, everybody did.

Yours sincerely,

Colin Boulton. Ron Webster. David Nish. John O'Hare. Roy McFarland. Colin Todd. John McGovern. Archie Gemmill. Roger Davies. Kevin Hector. Alan Hinton. Steve Powell.

You have tears running down your cheeks at what the Derby players, your *players, have written about you, a big bloody lump in your throat and the phone in your hand:*

'*I am staggered,' you tell the* Daily Mail, *exclusively. 'Whatever happens I will always be grateful to the players,* my *players, for restoring my faith in human nature.'*

★ ★ ★

The cleaning lady is cleaning the office, under the desk and behind the door, not whistling or humming along to her tunes today –

I ask her, 'How are you today then, Joan?'

'I've been better, Brian,' she says. 'I've been better.'

I ask, 'Why's that then, love?'

'State of that bloody bathroom down corridor,' she says. 'That's why.'

'What about it?'

'You should've seen it,' she says. 'Mirror broken. Blood in sink. Piss over floor.'

'No?'

'I tell you, Brian,' she tells me, 'they don't pay us enough to clean up all that.'

My face is red, my hand still bandaged as I say, 'I'm sorry, love.'

'Why?' she asks. 'Not like it's your fault, is it, Brian? Not you that thumped mirror and bled all over sink then pissed on floor just because you lost, was it?'

* * *

You have your faith in human nature back, but you still have no job and no car. You have to take a taxi to meet the Derby players, your players, for lunch at the Kedleston Hall Hotel, your new headquarters. You have to pay for the taxi yourself. The Derby players are confused and waiting, their heads in their hands; the players are depressed and worried, their faces long; the players scared and furious, their eyes wide, on stalks –

'It's a bloody outrage,' says Roy McFarland; Red Roy, as the press call him. 'The way they've treated you, after all you've done for them. I tell you, last week was the worst week of my whole bloody life. Drawing with Poland and losing you as a boss, the worst week of my life. I didn't hang around after the England match, didn't go back to the hotel with the other lads; I just got in me car and drove straight back home to Derby.'

Eyes filling up and drinks going down, tempers rising and voices choking –

'What can we do, Boss?' they all ask you.

'You've done enough,' you tell them. 'That letter was brilliant. Meant a lot.'

'But there must be more we can do?' they all ask. 'There has to be, Boss?'

'I'll tell you what we'll do,' you tell them. 'We'll have a bloody party. Tonight.'

'A party?' they all say. 'What kind of a party?'

'A fucking big one,' you tell them. 'So bugger off home and get your wives and your bairns and your glad rags on and meet us all at the Newton Park Hotel tonight.'

* * *

There should be no training today. There should be no players in today. They should all be at home with their wives and their kids, the girlfriends and their pets. But then Jimmy told me they were all coming in anyway, coming in for their complimentary club cars, their brand-new bloody club cars. But after Saturday, after Maine Road, they don't deserve a club fucking bicycle between them and so I cancelled their days off and told them to report back here at nine o'clock, Monday morning, if they wanted their bloody fucking club cars –

'The bloody chances you lot missed on Saturday,' I tell them. 'They ought to make you all fucking walk to the ground and back every game, never mind giving you a bleeding club car. Only you'd get fucking lost, you're that bloody thick half of you.'

I turn my back on them. I leave them to Jimmy. I walk off the training pitch. Down the banking. Past the huts on their stilts. John Reynolds, the groundsman, and Sydney Owen are stood at the top of the steps to one of the huts. They are staring at a broken lock and an open door –

'Be bloody kids,' I tell them as I pass them.

Sydney says something that sounds like, 'Bloody big mouth again.'

'You what?' I ask him –

'I said, be bloody big ones then,' says Sydney.

Least there's no Maurice today. Maurice is in Switzerland to watch Zurich play Geneva. To spy on Zurich. To compile his dossier. To write his report. There's no John Giles either. The Irishman is down in London with his Eire squad. To meet with Tottenham. His ticket bloody out of here.

This is what those players are thinking about at training today –

Not Stoke City. Not QPR. Not Birmingham or Manchester City –
Not the chances they missed; the chances they must take –
Against Luton. Against Huddersfield and against Zurich –
Johnny fucking Giles, that's what they're thinking about –
Johnny fucking Giles and Vauxhall bloody motors –

'What kind you going to get, Boss?' Jimmy had asked me first thing this morning.

'I'm not off, am I,' I told him.

'Why not?'

'Not been invited, have I.'

'Why not?' he asked me again.

'Maybe they think I won't be around long enough to need a new bloody car.'

'I hope you're fucking joking,' said Jimmy.

'I wish I were,' I told him. 'Wish I were.'

* * *

You leave the Derby players, your players, until tonight. You drive over to see Mike Keeling. Mike Keeling thinks the board have turned against Longson. He thinks there might be a wedge between them now –

'They're at each other's throats,' he says. 'At each other's throats!'

'Bet you wish you'd not been so bloody quick to resign now, don't you?'

'What about you?' he asks you. 'Is that how you feel, Brian? Is it?'

'You know it is,' you tell him. 'You know it bloody is.'

'Well, just this once,' he says, 'we might just be able to turn back the clock.'

'You really think so, Mike? Really?'

'I can't promise,' he says. 'But I really think we have a chance, yes.'

'So what can I do to help you?' you ask him. 'To help you make it happen?'

'An olive branch, Brian,' he says. 'Some kind of olive branch would help.'

'Well, I've been thinking,' you tell him, 'thinking that if they'll take me back, and when I say they, I'm not talking about that bastard Longson, but if the board will take me back, me and Peter, then I'd be willing to jack in all the telly and the papers.'

'Really? You'd give all that up? The television and the papers?'

'Course I bloody would,' you tell him. 'If it meant I could get my real job back.'

★ ★ ★

I finish my drink. I finish my fag. I leave the office. I lock the door. I double check it's locked. I walk down the corridor, round the corner, up the stairs, round another corner, down another corridor towards the doors to the directors' dining room. I can already hear their Yorkshire voices behind the doors, their raised Yorkshire voices –

I can hear my name, hear my name, and only my fucking name . . .

I light another fag and I listen. Then I open the doors to the dining room and their Yorkshire voices suddenly fall. The dining room silent. Their eyes on their plates. Their knives and their forks.

Sam Bolton looks up from his. Sam Bolton has his knife in his hand as he asks me, 'What the bloody hell is going on with John Giles and Tottenham bloody Hotspur?'

'What you all so bothered about?' I ask him, all of them. 'Not two bleeding minutes ago you wanted the bugger gone, didn't you?'

They've still lost their Yorkshire voices, rest of them. Eyes still on their plates. Their knives and their forks.

'So let's get them bloody fingers crossed,' I tell them –

But no one laughs. No one smiles. No one says a fucking word.

I put down my drink. I put out my fag. I turn back towards the doors. The exit –

'One last thing,' says Bolton. 'We don't much care for being third from bottom.'

'Fourth from bottom,' I correct him.

'Nor do we much care for managers who clutch at straws, Clough.'

★ ★ ★

You take your wife and your kids to the Newton Park Hotel near Burton-upon-Trent. You take your wife and your kids to meet the Derby players, your players, and their wives and their kids. Peter and Lillian come too. It is sup-

267

posed to be a farewell dinner, that's how you sold it to your wife and your kids, to Peter and to Lillian –

But no one wants to say farewell. No one wants to say goodbye.

So the champagne flows, all thirty bottles of it, all paid for by you, as the kids run riot and the wives wilt, as the jokes and the stories start, the memories and the tales –

The jokes and the stories, the memories and the tales of the games and the cups; the games and the cups you've won; the memories and the tales no one wants to end.

'If I'm not playing for the Boss,' says someone, 'I don't want to bloody play.'

'Me and all,' says everyone else. 'Me and all.'

'I reckon we should all boycott the fucking club,' says someone –

Then someone else, 'Let's bloody train in the fucking park with the Boss.'

'We should all get on a plane and bugger off to Majorca,' says another, probably you as you open one more bottle and order another, drink one more drink and pour another, put out one more fag and light another –

'Let's bloody do it,' says everyone else. 'Come on, let's fucking do it!'

Every player on his feet now. Every player halfway to Spain –

'Y viva España,' everyone sings. 'We're all off to sunny Spain . . .'

But then the wives get to their feet and sit their husbands back down, calming them down and squeezing their hands, tighter and tighter –

Your own wife squeezing your hand the tightest of all.

★ ★ ★

The press conference is late. The press conference is about the Irishman and Tottenham Hotspur. The press conference is not about the Manchester City game; not about the chances Leeds missed; the position Leeds are in. But Manny Cussins has still come along; to show his support for me; his confidence in me.

But the press don't want to know about Manchester City. The press don't want to know why the League Champions are just one place and point above the relegation zone. The press just want to know about the Irishman and Tottenham Hotspur –

Thank fucking Christ for Johnny fucking Giles.

'As far as I am personally concerned, I think we should all be very sorry to lose him for his playing ability,' says Manny Cussins. 'We all value him for his wonderful service with us but would give fair consideration to anything that concerns his future.'

'Have Leeds United had an enquiry or an offer from Tottenham about Giles?'

'We've had no communication from anyone at Tottenham,' says Cussins, glancing at me. 'I think Mr Clough would have told us, had Giles been approached.'

'Is that right, Brian?' they ask me. 'You've had no contact with Tottenham?'

★ ★ ★

You are stood in the car park of the Newton Park Hotel with the Derby players, your *players, the Derby players and their wives and their kids, your own wife and your own kids –*

No one wants to get into their car. No one wants to go to their home –

No one wants to say goodnight. To say farewell. To say goodbye –

To say, this is the end, and then let go.

★ ★ ★

Round the corner. Down the corridor. There is a pile of letters and a list of phone calls on the desk in the office. I sweep them off the top into the bin and pour myself another large drink. I tilt the chair back on two legs and light another fag; the fortieth of the day –

There are voices. There are voices. There are voices in the corridor –

Don's voice; I swear it sounds like Don's voice in the corridor –

I sit forward. I put down my drink. I open the door –

The voices are gone, but the echo still here –

'Are you there, Brian?'

★ ★ ★

Last thing tonight, with a head full of champagne and a chest full of cigarettes, you pick up the phone and Keeling tells you, 'They tried to get Bobby Robson.'

'Bobby Robson?' you ask him. 'You're fucking joking?'

'Longson and Kirkland approached Ipswich first thing this morning.'

'He'd never take the job,' you tell him. 'Not Bobby.'

'Sounds like you're right.'

'So who's next on their list?' you ask him again. 'Alf Ramsey?'

'I wouldn't be surprised,' laughs Keeling. 'Alf or Pat Saward.'

'Pat who?' you ask Keeling.

'Pat Saward,' laughs Keeling again. 'Brighton sacked him this afternoon.'

'Brighton?' you ask him. 'What fucking division are they in?'

Day Thirty-five

Jimmy picks me up this morning, picks me up in his brand-new Vauxhall Victor 1800, courtesy of Wallace Arnold Sales and Service Limited and Leeds United AFC –

'McQueen and Hunter got Magnums, Bates the Magnum Estate,' Jimmy gushes. 'Reaney, Jones, Stewart and Duncan all got the Victor 2300; that's the one your Irish mate drives. Bremner, Lorimer, Harvey and Joe Jordan already have the VX 4/90s. Trevor Cherry, Terry Cooper, Madeley and Clarkey all went for this one, same as me.'

'That's lovely,' I tell him. 'All one big happy family, eh?'

'Fuck off,' he laughs. 'You'll be getting yours and you bloody know it.'

'Is that right?' I ask him. 'So what did John McGovern and John O'Hare get then?'

Jimmy stops laughing. Jimmy says, 'They weren't there.'

'I told you,' I tell him again. 'They hate us.'

'Who hates you?' asks Jimmy. 'Come on, who hates you?'

'The players, Syd Owen and Lindley, all the other coaches and trainers, the board, the ground staff, the medical staff, the office staff, the cleaners, the cooks; you bloody name them and they fucking hate us, hate and despise us.'

'So how come I got a car, then?' asks Jimmy.

'Must be something about you I don't know and they do.'

'Now you *are* being paranoid,' he says. 'Just being paranoid, Boss.'

* * *

First thing this morning, with a head full of aches and a chest full of pains, you pick up the phone and Keeling tells you, 'They're trying to get Dave Mackay.'

'Dave Mackay?' you repeat. 'You're fucking joking with me?'

271

'I wish I were, Brian. I wish I were.'

'He'll never take the job,' you tell him. 'Not Dave.'

'Well, Longson went all the way to Northampton to see him last night.'

'Northampton?'

'Mackay was there watching the Forest youth team.'

'He'll never take it,' you tell him again. 'Not Dave. Not Derby.'

'It sounds like he's already as good as taken it, Brian.'

'You're fucking joking?' you ask him again. 'Not Dave Mackay.'

'Yes,' says Keeling. 'Dave Mackay.'

* * *

Under the stands, deep under those stands, through the doors, right through those doors, round the corner, right round that corner and down the corridor, down and down and down that corridor, I sit in the office and I open another bottle. I open another bottle and I light another fag. I light another fag and I tilt the chair back on two legs. I tilt the chair back on two legs and I close my eyes. I close my eyes and I tilt the chair back –

Further and further and further . . .

I tilt the chair back and then I feel the legs begin to give. I feel the legs begin to give until they finally go. They finally go and I fall backwards. I fall backwards and I bang my head on the wall behind the desk. I bang my head and I lie on the floor –

Further and further and further . . .

Under the stands and through the doors. Round the corner and down the corridor, I lie on the floor. My brandy spilt and my cigarette out.

* * *

You have gone round to Archie Gemmill's flat. You and Roy McFarland. Archie Gemmill and his wife have given you tea and biscuits. You and Roy McFarland. Now Roy McFarland gets on the phone to Dave Mackay –

'We've all got every respect for you, Dave, and you're our pal,' Roy tells

Dave, 'but please don't come here, please don't come to Derby . . .'

Roy listens. Then Roy says, 'It's not fair on you . . .'

Roy listens again. Then Roy says, 'We want Brian back and we think we can . . .'

Roy listens. Roy holds the phone away from his ear. Roy hangs up –

'What did Dave say?' asks Archie Gemmill. 'What did Dave say?'

'What do you bloody think Dave Mackay said? He told me to fuck off, didn't he? Told me he's already shaken hands with Longson on it, as good as signed it.'

'So what do we now?' asks Gemmill. 'What do we do now?'

'We go see Longson and the board ourselves,' says Roy. 'In person.'

Roy goes to get his coat on, and Archie goes to get his. Then they both stomp out of the flat and down the stairs to pick up the rest of the first team, to take them to the Baseball Ground, to have it out with Longson and the rest of the board. In person.

You have gone round to Archie Gemmill's flat. Now you are sat on your own on the settee in Gemmill's flat, with a cigarette and with a drink, the lights and the fire off, wondering what to do with the rest of the day –

Tuesday 23 October 1973.

★ ★ ★

Under the stands, through the doors and round the corner, I am listening for the feet down the corridor, the voices –

There are voices. There are voices. There are voices outside the door . . .

'Owl thou art and owl thou shall be,' they whisper. 'And all the birds of the earth shall peck at thee, shall peck at thee, peck at thee . . .'

There are voices and there are feet. Feet down the corridor.

Manny Cussins doesn't knock. Many Cussins opens the door to the office and throws a newspaper onto the desk and says, 'I don't care to be made a fool of.'

I look down at the newspaper. The *Yorkshire Post*. The photograph of John Giles.

'Well, go on then,' says Cussins. 'Read it.'

I pick up the paper. The *Yorkshire Post*. The photograph of John Giles:

'Mr Nicholson rang Mr Clough last week. He asked permission for him to speak to me and Mr Clough gave him the go-ahead. Obviously I am interested in the Tottenham job – anyone who wasn't would be crazy. I am very keen to go into management but if nothing comes from this I shall be just as happy going on playing.'

I put down the paper. The *Yorkshire Post*. The photograph of John Giles.

'There are those upstairs in that boardroom,' Manny Cussins says quietly, slowly, 'who didn't want you here. Who said you would be trouble. Too big for your boots, too quick with your mouth. Who said you'd be too eager to try and run the whole damn show. Who said you'd be out of control. Too interested in Number One, too interested in Brian Clough and not Leeds United. Who said you were the wrong man, the last man, for Leeds United. But I was the one who argued against them. Who persuaded them that Brian Clough was the right man, the only man, for Leeds United and, believe me, they took some persuading. But I told them you had the experience, the experience of winning a Championship, of competing in the European Cup; I told them you had the ambition, the ambition to win more Championships, to lift the European Cup; I told them you'd use your experience and your ambition to command the loyalty of your players and of the whole club and that, together, your experience, your ambition and their loyalty, their ability would bring this club the Championships and the cups it deserves and expects –

'And so here you are; not at Brighton; not in the Third Division. Here at Leeds United, in the First Division, in the European Cup –

'And that was me, Brian, me that got you here, me . . .'

I look down at the paper again. The *Yorkshire Post*. The photograph of John Giles.

Manny Cussins doesn't say goodbye. Manny Cussins opens the door to leave and says quietly and slowly, 'You'd do well to remember who your friends are here.'

★ ★ ★

The Derby County board won't see the players. The Derby County board ignore the players' request for a meeting. But the players won't leave. The players stage a sit-in –

The Siege of Derby.

You have driven back to your house. You have locked your door. You have pulled your curtains. Now you sit in your house and you watch your television, watch –

The Siege of Derby –

Alan Hinton parading up and down outside the Baseball Ground. Alan Hinton with a tea urn on his head. Alan Hinton telling the cameras and the microphones –

'This is the only cup we'll ever win from now on.'

You sit in your house. Door locked and curtains pulled. You listen to your radio:

The rumours that the board are at the Midland Hotel. The rumours that they are about to announce the name of the new manager of Derby County –

You switch off your radio. In the dark. You switch on your television –

Colin Boulton and Ron Webster running down the streets outside the Baseball Ground. Colin Boulton and Ron Webster banging on the roof of Jack Kirkland's car –

Bloody Kirkland telling Boulton and Webster, the cameras and the microphones, the whole of fucking Derby, 'You'll have a new manager in the morning.'

You switch off your telly. Door locked, curtains pulled. You sit in your house –

In the dark.

★ ★ ★

Under the stands and through the doors, round the corner and down the corridor, I still haven't left the office, still daren't leave the office; the feet and the voices outside the door, whispering and whispering and whispering, over and over and over, the fists banging and banging and banging upon the door, again and again and again, the phone on the desk ringing and ringing and ringing, over and over and over –

'Are you there, Brian? Are you still there?'

I don't open the door. I don't answer the phone. I just keep my feet up on the desk, with a fag in my gob and a drink in my good hand –

'Are you there, Brian? Are you still there?'

The door opens and in walks Bolton. In walks Bolton and throws another letter onto the desk and he says, 'Don't you ever answer that bloody phone? Upstairs, now.'

★ ★ ★

There have been protest marches through the centre of Derby. There have been rallies in the bingo halls of Derby. Tonight, there is the first meeting of the steering committee of the Derby County Protest Movement. John and his mate Bill Holmes pass the bucket around the room. The bucket brings back £150.53½.

'The Derby County board will have to listen to us now,' declares Bill Holmes. 'The Derby County board cannot ignore the mass transfer request of an entire first team. The Derby board cannot ignore the wrath of 30,000 protesters.'

You sit on the stage and you want to believe Bill Holmes. Desperately. But Bill Holmes is a Nottingham Forest fan, and there are only 300 people here tonight.

But then Mike Keeling arrives. Mike takes you to one side. Mike gives you hope —

'I've spoken with Bill Rudd,' Mike tells you, 'and Bill says he'd consider taking you and Peter back if you were prepared to toe the line. I told him everything you told me, about how you'd be prepared to give up your newspaper columns and your television appearances if they'd have you back, and Bill said that was good enough for him.'

'That's fantastic,' you tell him. 'Bloody fantastic.'

'It gets better,' says Mike. 'Bill thinks that he'll now also be able to persuade Innes, and even Sidney Bradley.'

'Fantastic,' you tell him again. 'Fucking fantastic.'

'Except for Longson and Kirkland,' says Keeling. 'Bill's been trying to get in touch with them all day, to tell them he wants another board meeting —'

'But?'

'But he's not been able to speak to them, not been able to find them,' says Mike. 'They're not at their homes, not at the ground and they're not at the Midland Hotel.'

'So where the fuck are they then?' you ask him. 'Where are they?'

'Nottingham,' says Mike. 'Reckon they're at the Albany Hotel.'

'Has he called them there?' you ask him. 'Has Bill tried?'

'He's tried all right,' Mike says. 'He's just gone over there.'

'And?'

'And we'll just have to hope and pray he's not too late, won't we?'

You bite your lip. You close your eyes. You nod your head –

You don't believe in God, but you do believe in hope.

★ ★ ★

I walk down the corridor. The photographs on the wall. The trophies
in the cabinets. Down the corridor and round the corner. Round the
corner to the foot of the stairs. Then up the stairs until there on the
stairs is Syd; Syd who says something that sounds like, 'Yesterday, upon
the stair, I met a man who wasn't there. He wasn't there again today. I
wish that man would go away.'

'Pardon?' I ask him.

Syd stops at the bottom of the stairs. Syd turns back to look up at
me and Syd says, 'Round here they say if you pass someone on the
stairs, it'll lead to a quarrel or a parting, and that you'll not meet that
person again in heaven.'

'Don't worry,' I tell him. 'Didn't think I'd be seeing you up there
anyway, Syd.'

'And I didn't think you believed in God or a heaven.'

'Having been here thirty-four days,' I tell him, 'I've changed my
mind, Sydney.'

'Why's that then?' he smiles.

'Well, if there's a hell like this place, then there has to be a heaven
somewhere.'

Syd is laughing now. Really laughing. Syd says, 'If you think it's hell
now, you wait until you bloody lose at home to Luton on Saturday,
away at Huddersfield Town, and then go out of the European Cup in
the first fucking round to Zurich.'

'And that'd be heaven to you,' I tell him. 'Wouldn't it, Sydney?'

'No,' he says and turns away, round another corner and down
another corridor.

I walk up the rest of the stairs, down the corridor to the boardroom doors. I can hear their raised Yorkshire voices again, I can hear my name again. I open the door –

There's Bolton. There's Cussins. There's a man I've never met before.

'About bloody time,' says Bolton. 'What you been doing?'

'We were just about to send out a search party,' says Cussins.

'I'm sorry,' I tell them both. 'I was talking to Syd Owen.'

'Well, I want you to meet someone who I'm sure will be much more pleasant to talk to than Syd bloody Owen,' says Bolton. 'This is Martin Hughes.'

'How do you do, Mr Clough?' says Martin Hughes.

'How do you do?' I reply.

'Martin runs Mercedes here in the north,' says Cussins.

'Mercedes?' I repeat.

'We hear that's what you like to drive,' says Bolton. 'A Mercedes?'

'That's what I used to drive at Derby,' I tell them, 'yes.'

'Well, we can't have Leeds United being outdone by Derby County, can we?' laughs Cussins. 'So Martin here is going to take you over to their showroom and get you sorted out, that's if you're not too busy right now?'

I shake my head. I nod my head. I reach for my fags.

'And smile if you want,' says Bolton. 'What did you think you were getting?'

★ ★ ★

You closed your eyes, you nodded your head and for once in your bloody life you did pray; you prayed and prayed and then you prayed some more, but this is what you got, what you got for all your fucking prayers, for all their rallies and for all their marches, for all their sit-ins and for all their strikes –

The Derby board went to Nottingham. The board had a contract for Mackay. Mackay wanted to wait until after the Forest game against Hull. Five minutes after the final whistle, Mackay put his pen to their paper and signed the contract. Now Mackay is the manager of Derby County –

Dave Mackay. Not you.

★ ★ ★

I drive back to Derby in my brand-new blue Mercedes-Benz. I pick up the wife and the kids in my brand-new blue Mercedes-Benz. We go for a drive round Derby in my brand-new blue Mercedes-Benz. We drive past the Baseball Ground and past the Midland Hotel in my brand-new blue Mercedes-Benz. We stop for fish and chips in my brand-new blue Mercedes-Benz. Then we go back home in my brand-new blue Mercedes-Benz.

'Are you there, Brian? Are you still there?'

I help my wife bath the kids and put them to bed. I watch a bit of telly with my wife before she goes up to bed. Then I sit in that old rocking chair with a drink and a smile because I know we'll beat Luton on Saturday at home. I know we'll beat Huddersfield Town in the League Cup. I know we'll beat Zurich in the first round of the European Cup. I know we will move up the table. I know we will progress in the cups.

'Are you there, Brian? Are you still there?'

I close my eyes but I do not sleep. I do not sleep but I dream. I dream of empty cities after the A-bomb. Empty cities in which I am the only man left alive. The only man left alive to walk around and around these cities. To walk around and around until I hear a telephone ringing. I hear a telephone ringing and I search until I find it. I find it and pick it up and listen to the voice asking me, 'Are you there, Brian? Are you still there?'

'Yes,' I tell them. 'I'm still here.'

'Then who's sorry now, Brian?' laughs the voice on the phone. 'Who's sorry now?'

Day Thirty-six

*You are still in your house. Your door locked and your curtains still pulled. In
the dark. You spend half your time in bed, half your time on the settee. Up and
down the stairs. Ignoring the phone, answering the phone. In and out of bed.
The radio on. The radio off. Up and down the stairs again. On and off the settee. The television on. The television off. Because Dave Mackay is the manager of Derby County FC now. Not you –*

Because today is Dave Mackay's first day in the job. Your job –

Wednesday 24 October 1973.

*There were angry scenes in Nottingham last night, the Nottingham Forest
fans accusing Mackay of betrayal, of leaving a job half done. There have been
angry words in the newspapers this morning, the Derby County players saying
they won't play for Dave Mackay, they won't train for Dave Mackay. They
won't work for Dave Mackay –*

The Derby players, your *players, saying they'll go on strike:*

'To Bring Back Cloughie!'

*Now there are angry scenes at the Baseball Ground, angry scenes as Dave
Mackay arrives for his first day in the job,* your *job, greeted by banners and
protesters –*

'B.B.C.! B.B.C.!' they chant. 'Bring back Cloughie! Bring back Cloughie!'

Behind the door, behind the curtains, you turn the television up, the radio up:

'Fuck off, Mackay,' they shout. 'You're not welcome here!'

But Dave Mackay has guts. Dave Mackay has balls –

*'Who was that?' Dave Mackay shouts back. 'Tell him to come in for a trial.
I think we could use him on the wing.'*

*The press and the television lap it up. The cameras and the lights. The fans.
The autograph books and the pens. Even the protesters laugh.*

*'This job is my destiny,' Dave Mackay tells the cameras and the lights, the
banners and the protesters. 'I have a lot to prove, but I'm not afraid. You either*

see the glass as half full or half empty. I see it as half full and I fancy a drink.'

You switch off the television. You switch off the radio –

You sweep the papers off the bed onto the floor –

You pull the covers over your head.

* * *

I am first out of bed this morning, down the stairs and into my brand-new blue Mercedes-Benz. I am first through the doors this morning, round the corner and down the corridor, shouting, 'William! William!'

But Billy Bremner doesn't stop. Billy Bremner doesn't put down his kit bag or turn around.

Down the corridor, I shout again, 'Billy!'

Bremner stops now. Bremner puts down his kit bag and turns around.

I walk down the corridor towards him. I ask him, 'You coming tonight?'

'Where?' asks Bremner.

'Here,' I tell him. 'For the reserve game against Blackburn.'

'Why?' asks Bremner.

'I told you,' I tell him again. 'I'd value your input on the bench.'

'I have to come then?' asks Bremner. 'You're ordering me?'

'Course I'm not ordering you,' I tell him. 'I'm asking you, because I think . . .'

But Bremner is shaking his head, saying, '*Only a Game* tonight.'

'What?'

'On the telly tonight,' says Billy Bremner. '*Only a Game*; Scotland vs Brazil. Having some friends round, a few drinks. You don't expect me to miss that, do you?'

I turn my back on him. I walk round the corner and down the corridor to the office. I pour a drink and I light a fag. I get out my address book. I pick up the phone and I make some calls. Lots of fucking calls. Then I put down the phone. I put away my address book. I put out my fag. I finish my drink and I get changed. I put on my old green Leeds United goalkeeping jersey. I open the desk drawer. I take out a whistle. I lock the office door. I double check it's locked. I go down the corridor. Round the corner. Through reception and out into the car park. I jog through the potholes and the puddles. Past the huts on stilts. Up the banking. Onto the training ground –

Bastards. Bastards. Bastards.

I blow the whistle. I shout, 'Jordan, Madeley, Cooper, Bates, Yorath and young Gray, you'll all be playing in the reserve game tonight. See you there.'

I turn my back on them and there's Syd Owen and Maurice Lindley stood there, stood there waiting, heads together, whispering and muttering, whispering and muttering. Maurice has a large envelope between his fingers. He hands it to me. 'There you go.'

'What the hell's all this?' I ask him.

'The dossier on FC Zurich,' he says. 'The works.'

'Just tell me if they bloody won or not.'

'They did,' he says. '3–0 away.'

'And are they any fucking good?'

'They are,' he says.

'Ta,' I tell him and hand him back his envelope. 'That's all I needed to know.'

I jog off down the banking. Past the huts. Through the potholes and the puddles. Across the car park and into reception. Sam Bolton is stood there, stood there waiting –

'How's your car?' he asks me.

'It's very nice,' I tell him. 'Thank you.'

'That's good,' he says. 'Now get yourself changed and up them stairs.'

* * *

You are still in bed, still under the covers. Downstairs, the telephone is ringing and ringing and ringing. You don't get out of bed. You don't answer it. Your wife does –

'Brian!' she shouts up the stairs. 'It's a Mike Bamber. From Brighton.'

You put your head above the covers. You get out of bed. You go down the stairs. You put the telephone to your ear –

'Mr Clough, my name is Mike Bamber,' says Mike Bamber. 'And I'm the chairman of Brighton and Hove Albion Football Club. I was wondering if we

might have a chat about a vacancy I have here.'

'Brighton?' you ask him. 'They're in the Third Division, aren't they?'

'Unfortunately,' says Mike Bamber. 'But I believe you're the very man who might well be able to do something about that . . .'

'I might consider it,' you tell him. 'And, if I do, I'll be in touch.'

You put down the telephone. You look up at your wife –

'A job's a job,' she says.

'In the Third Division?' you ask her. 'On the south coast?'

'Beggars can't be choosers.'

* * *

Mike Bamber and Brighton and Hove Albion are taking legal action against Leeds United. Mike Bamber and Brighton and Hove Albion have issued writs against me and Leeds United. Mike Bamber and Brighton and Hove Albion are claiming damages against me for breach of contract. Mike Bamber and Brighton and Hove Albion are claiming damages against Leeds United for inducing me to breach my contract. Mike Bamber and Brighton and Hove Albion claim Leeds United promised to pay them £75,000 in compensation for me. Mike Bamber and Brighton and Hove Albion also claim Leeds United promised to play a friendly match against them at their Goldstone Ground. Mike Bamber and Brighton and Hove Albion want their friendly match. Mike Bamber and Brighton and Hove Albion want their money –

'They're getting nowt,' shouts Sam Bolton. 'Bloody nowt. Same as all these other chairmen and directors who have been calling us all morning, asking us about Joe Jordan, asking us about Paul Madeley, asking us about Terry Cooper, asking us about Mick Bates, asking us about Terry Yorath, and asking us about Frankie Gray –

'They're getting nowt,' says Bolton, 'because we're giving them bloody nowt.'

* * *

You meet the Derby players again, your *players again, for lunch at the Midland Hotel. Just you and Peter and the Derby players*, your *players.*

The Derby board still won't meet the players. The players are thunderstruck. The players are bitter. The players are hurt. These players are young. These players are emotional. These players are loyal. You understand this —

'I played centre-forward for Derby County every week,' you tell them —

They understand this. They know this. They tell you, 'We're not going to train. We're not going to play. Not until we get you back, Boss.'

You thank them countless times. You order countless bottles. You tell them, 'Next time we meet, it'll be up at my house to celebrate my reinstatement . . .'

But tonight the Derby players, your *players, have to meet Dave Mackay —*

'That's not going to resolve anything, is it?' says Red Roy McFarland.

'But he's your manager now,' says Pete. 'Not us, Roy. It's Dave.'

You turn to Peter. You look at Taylor. You shout, 'What? You bloody what?'

'Fucking face it, Brian,' he says. 'It's time to move on. It's over.'

'Is it fuck,' you tell him. 'What about the Protest Movement?'

'Brian, Brian, Brian . . .'

'Go on then,' you tell him. 'You fucking quit if you want to, like you always do. But I'm not giving up, not giving up on this lot. Not after all they've bloody done for us, all they've fucking risked for us. Never . . .'

'Exactly,' says Peter. 'And that's why we shouldn't ask them to risk any more. All this talk of not training, not playing. All this talk of sit-ins, of strikes. They'll be in bloody breach of their fucking contracts. They'll be out of the club and out of a job; banned from playing anywhere else. They'll be out of work, just like us.'

'Fuck off,' you tell him. 'You're a coward. You're yellow.'

But Taylor just shrugs his shoulders. Puts out his fag and stands up. Then Peter shakes each player by their hand, each Derby player —

'Thanks for everything,' he says. 'And best of luck on Saturday, I mean it.'

★ ★ ★

There are only fifteen minutes before the start of the Central League fixture against Blackburn and Elland Road is still empty. Empty but for directors, managers and scouts —

Freddie Goodwin from Birmingham City is here. Alan Brown from Forest too. From Leicester. From Everton. From Stoke. From Villa. From Ipswich. From Norwich. From Luton. From Burnley. From Coventry. From Wednesday. From bloody Hull and even Carlisle, they've all come to this shop window; come for this fucking fire sale –

'Take your bloody pick,' I told them all. 'Everything must go!'

Through the doors. Up the stairs. Round the corner and down the corridor, I walk towards the Yorkshire boardroom doors. Towards the Yorkshire boardroom and chaos:

A man is lying on the floor of the corridor, outside the boardroom –

The man is Harry Reynolds, a former chairman of Leeds United –

People are loosening his collar, people loosening his tie –

People calling for a doctor, for an ambulance –

But Harry Reynolds is already dead.

* * *

The taxi drops you back at your house. Roy McFarland and Henry Newton help you to the door. Your wife lies you down on the settee –

'Don't listen to Peter,' you tell Roy and Henry. 'He's just scared. Yellow.'

Your wife waits until Roy and Henry have gone. Until you've had a little sleep. A nice cup of tea. Then your wife tells you Stuart Dryden phoned from Nottingham Forest. Now Stuart Dryden might only be a committee member at Nottingham Forest, says your wife. But Stuart Dryden has a vision. Stuart Dryden has a dream –

That Nottingham Forest can win promotion from Division Two to Division One; that Nottingham Forest can win the First Division Championship; that Nottingham Forest can win the European Cup; not once, not twice, but time and time again –

Stuart Dryden believes you are the man to realize this dream –

'That you're the only man who can make that dream real,' Stuart Dryden tells you in the middle of the night. In a Nottingham office. In secret.

'Are you offering us the job?' you ask Stuart Dryden.

'I'd bloody love to,' he says. 'But I've only been on the committee for a week.'

'Well, I'm interested,' you tell him. 'And so is Peter. But we're not applying.'

'But you've got to do something to help me get you there,' says Dryden.

'Like what?' you ask him.

'Like phoning the club at 11 o'clock tomorrow morning and making a discreet enquiry about the vacancy. I'll make sure I'm there to take the call.'

'I'll not bloody beg,' you tell him. 'I'll not fucking beg.'

'It's not begging,' he says. 'It's a discreet enquiry.'

'But who's to say I won't be back at Derby this time tomorrow?' you ask him.

'But they've already appointed Dave Mackay,' says Stuart Dryden. 'They've already appointed our bloody manager in your place.'

'You never know. They might just un-appoint him,' you tell him. 'Then Derby would get me back and you'd get Mackay back and we'd all be happy.'

'But we don't want Mackay back,' says Stuart Dryden. 'We want you.'

* * *

The reserve game goes ahead and Leeds beat Blackburn Rovers 3–0, but it doesn't matter. Not now. Now Harry Reynolds is dead. Not now Don Revie has arrived, as if by magick:

'Harry Reynolds was the man who gave me my chance,' says Don Revie. 'Without him there would have been nothing. No man could have done more for a football club than Mr Reynolds. Without his intervention, I would probably have gone to Bournemouth all those years ago. I owe a debt to him that I cannot express in words. I am deeply saddened by his loss and anything I have achieved in my managerial career I owe to him. When I think of the dedication and effort he put into his career as chairman in the early years of my management, his trips with me all over the country to sign players and talk promising youngsters into a career at Leeds, I realize that he was unique . . .'

I have locked the office door. The chair up against it. My fingers in my ears, my fingers in my ears, my fingers in my ears –

The other directors, the managers and their scouts have all gone –

But not Don Revie. Don is still out there. Under the stand. Round the corner. Pacing the corridors, knocking on doors –

'Are you there, Brian? Are you still there?'

You are lying in bed next to your wife. The clock by the bed ticking. You close your eyes but you do not sleep. You do not want to be the manager of Nottingham bloody Forest. You do not want to be the manager of Brighton and fucking Hove Albion. You do not even want to be the manager of England –

You want to be the manager of Derby County. That's the job you want –

The Derby job, that's the only job you want. Your old job –

Your old job back, that's what you want, all you want –

All you ever wanted and all you want now –

Now you have no job, now it's too late –

The clock ticking and ticking –

Now you're unemployed –

Unemployed, again.

Day Thirty-seven

I still can't sleep so I open my eyes again; I am still in my modern luxury hotel bed in my modern luxury hotel room, with an old-fashioned hangover and an old-fashioned headache, my modern luxury phone ringing and ringing and ringing –

'Love? Is that you, love?' I ask. 'What time is it?'

'I'm not your wife or your bloody fancy piece,' laughs the voice on the other end. 'And it's time you were at fucking work, you lazy sod. I know I bleeding am –'

Alan Brown, manager of Nottingham Forest. Alan Brown, friend of Peter –

'Alan?' I ask him. 'What can I do you for?'

'Well, I didn't get that much of a chance to speak to you last night,' says Alan. 'Not with your directors dropping like flies, but I liked what I saw on the pitch.'

'Who did you like?'

'Terry Cooper,' says Alan. 'He would do very nicely for us, assuming . . .'

'Assuming bloody what?'

'Assuming his leg's fully mended and the price is right, that's what.'

'Don't you worry about his bloody leg,' I tell him. 'And don't you worry about that fucking price either.'

'Right then,' says Alan. 'I'll be hearing from you later then, will I?'

'I'll talk to the board,' I tell him. 'Then phone you back with the numbers.'

'Look forward to hearing them, Brian,' he says. 'Look forward to hearing them.'

I hang up my modern luxury telephone. I get out of my modern luxury bed. I go into my modern luxury bathroom and I turn on the modern luxury taps of my modern luxury bath just as my modern luxury bloody phone starts ringing and ringing and ringing again.

288

So I wrap one of them modern luxury towels around myself and pad back across the modern luxury carpet to pick up that modern luxury phone again –

'Don't tell us they've fucking sacked you already?'

Freddie Goodwin, manager of Birmingham and fellow struggler –

'Freddie?' I ask him. 'What can I do you for this fine Yorkshire morning?'

'You can sell us Joe Jordan,' he says. 'That's what you can do for me.'

'Consider it done.' I tell him. 'Consider it done.'

I leave that modern luxury phone off the hook and walk back to the modern luxury bathroom to soak in my freezing cold modern luxury fucking bath –

Thirteen days before the first round of the European Cup –

Leeds United fourth from the foot of Division One.

★ ★ ★

You and Peter are watching Derby County play West Ham United. Not from the bench. Not from the dug-out. Not from the directors' box. You and Peter are not even in Upton bloody Park. You and Peter are watching Derby play West Ham from the studios of London Weekend fucking Television.

It's almost half-time and Derby have given a positive performance, have made most of the running against a very fallible-looking West Ham defence. Roger Davies has had a lot of room in which to collect and distribute the ball, and, from one of his headers, a little nod on from a Boulton punt, Hector is away with only Mervyn Day to beat, but the shot's stopped and the ball bobs away past a post and you and Peter are back down in your seats. Back at your desks. Not at Upton Park. Not in the dug-out. Not on the bench.

You look down at the team sheet: Boulton, Webster, Nish, Newton, McFarland, Todd, McGovern, Gemmill, Davies, Hector, Hinton. Sub.: O'Hare. Manager: Mackay –

You're not at Upton Park. You're not in the dug-out. Not on the bench –

You are here in the studios of London Weekend Television.

You loosen your tie. You undo your collar. You still can't breathe. You get up from your desk. You tell them you are off for a pee. You go out of the studio. You

*go down a corridor. Round a corner. Down some stairs. Out through a door to
find a phone box –*

*'Listen, Mike,' you tell Mike Keeling. 'Can you track down Mike Bamber
for us. The Brighton chairman. Not a bloody clue where he is, but I need to
speak to him . . .'*

* * *

Leeds United is in mourning. Their suits dark, their ties black, their
flag at half mast. The board too busy grieving to see me. Their doors
shut, their lips sealed –

But not the Irishman. The Irishman winks. The Irishman asks, 'Did
you miss me?'

'Like a hole in the top of my skull.'

The Irishman smiles. 'I'll take that as a compliment, Mr Clough.'

'Take it as a reference if you want.'

The Irishman laughs. 'I'll be sure to pass it on to the Spurs.'

'They still want you then, do they?'

The Irishman shrugs. 'Early days yet, Mr Clough. Still early days.'

'But you want the fucking job, don't you?'

The Irishman shrugs again. The Irishman asks, 'Who's to say?'

'There's nothing for you here. You know that?'

The Irishman gets to his feet. 'I'll be seeing you, Mr Clough . . .'

* * *

*Mike Keeling tracks down Mike Bamber. Bamber is in the directors' box at
Hereford. He is watching Hereford United beat Brighton and Hove Albion
3–0. Mike Bamber leaves the directors' box. Runs from the box. Bamber takes
the call from Keeling –*

*'Brian told me to tell you to get the team coach to come through London on
your way back to Brighton. Brian says he'll meet you at the Waldorf.'*

*So Mike Bamber and the Brighton team take a twenty-mile detour to the
Waldorf; the Waldorf where you're staying courtesy of LWT –*

'What have you done with the team?' you ask Bamber in the bar.

'They're waiting outside in the coach,' he says. 'So it'll have to be brief.'

'Well, I've decided to consider your offer,' you tell him.

'That's fantastic,' says Mike Bamber. 'Why don't you come down to Brighton, to my own hotel, either right now or first thing tomorrow? We'll have lunch –'

'I can't come to Brighton,' you tell him. 'Not tonight. Not tomorrow.'

'Well then,' says Bamber. 'How about Monday?'

'Not Monday either,' you tell him. 'But why don't you come up to Derby?'

'Fine,' he says. 'Just name the time and the place.'

'Tuesday lunchtime,' you tell him. 'The Midland Hotel, Derby.'

Mike Bamber sticks out his hand. Bamber says, 'See you then.'

* * *

There are just thirteen days before the first round of the European Cup and Leeds United are fourth from the foot of Division One. FC Zurich have got off to a better start; the Swiss Champions are unbeaten; they are not third from the foot of their division –

The press have got their doubts. The press have got their fears:

'You've got injuries, you've got suspensions,' they say –

I tell them, 'I know I've got injuries, I know I've got suspensions.'

'So why are you trying to sell Jordan to Birmingham?' they ask –

I tell them, 'Look, Freddie Goodwin came up to watch the Central League game last night and after the game Freddie asked me if any of the players were available, and he got the same answer I have given everyone else: no one's bloody going yet!'

'Yet? What about Johnny Giles?' they ask –

I tell them, 'Listen, the ball is in Spurs' court. As far as we're concerned, we can only wait for developments. Giles has not applied for the job and so the next move has got to come from Spurs. If they do want him as manager, I presume they will contact me and we'll take it from there. If in fact they really do want him as manager . . .'

'But what about Joe Jordan? What about Terry Cooper and Forest? Terry Yorath and Everton? Will Jordan and Cooper still play on Saturday? Will Yorath?' they ask –

I tell them again, 'We've got injuries and we've got suspensions and the transfer deadline for the European Cup has already passed. There are only thirteen days to go now. So I'm telling you all, everyone will still be here thirteen days from now.'

'Everyone?' they ask. 'You think *you'll* still be here in thirteen days?'

★ ★ ★

Derby ended up drawing 0–0 at West Ham in Dave Mackay's first game as manager of Derby County. Longson was back on the box –

'I could manage this lot,' Longson told Match of the Day.

You are watching him from your bed at the Waldorf Hotel, lying on that bed in your television suit and your television tie, drinking dry your private bar –

But you're not really watching Longson, watching Match of the Day; *you're thinking about the whispers and the rumours, the whispers and the rumours that the FA are going to throw the book at you again, throw the book at you again for all the things you said and wrote, all the things you said and wrote about Leeds United and Don Revie last summer; the whispers and the rumours that the Disciplinary Committee will finish you in football, ban you for life or suspend you for seasons; the whispers and rumours that Forest have been warned away, that no club will touch you now, no club . . .*

Pete puts out his fag. Pete gets up from his chair. Pete switches off the TV –

'I was fucking watching that,' you tell him. 'Switch it back on.'

'After we've had a little chat,' he says.

'Here we go,' you tell him. 'What have I done now, Mother?'

'I want to know if you're serious about the Brighton job.'

'Like the wife says, beggars can't be choosers.'

'We're not beggars,' says Pete. 'Not yet.'

'I will be,' you tell him. 'This disrepute charge could finish me.'

'Have you spoken to Bamber about it?' asks Pete.

You shake your head. You drain your drink. You light another fag.

'You'll have to tell him,' says Pete. 'Tell him soon and all.'

'Why?' you ask. 'So he can run for the bloody hills with the rest of them?'

'Come on, Brian. Not telling him is not right and you know it.'

You pour another drink and finish that. Light another fag and finish that –

'I've got a wife, three kids and no fucking job,' you tell him. 'I'm scared, Pete.'

'And you call me a fucking coward?' laughs Pete. *'You're yellow through and through, and you know what? I've always fucking known it.'*

'It's miles away,' you tell him. *'Bloody Brighton.'*

'Coward.'

'You seen where they bloody are?' you ask him. *'Bottom of the fucking Third.'*

'You're a football manager,' says Pete. *'It's your job to get them out of there.'*

'With average gates of 6,000?' you ask him. *'It can't be done.'*

'So what you going to do then?' asks Pete. *'Drive a taxi? Buy a pub?'*

'Fuck off!'

'All mouth and no trousers,' says Pete. *'That's the real Cloughie!'*

'Fuck off!' you shout and throw a pillow at him –

'All mouth and no fucking trousers,' he laughs. *'No fucking balls!'*

'All right, all right,' you tell him. *'I'll take the fucking job, if it shuts you up.'*

'If they'll bloody have you,' he says. *'If you're not fucking suspended.'*

★ ★ ★

Under the stands, through the doors, round the corner and down the corridor, there are tears in Terry Cooper's eyes; Terry Cooper who has been with Leeds United for fourteen years, who has played for them 300-odd times; Terry Cooper who has won umpteen medals and nineteen caps, umpteen medals and seventeen more caps than me; Terry Cooper who fights back those tears and asks me again, '£75,000?'

I finish my drink. I pour another. I light a fag and I nod.

'That's all you think I'm worth? £75,000?'

I finish that drink. I finish that fag and I nod again.

'What about my testimonial?' asks Terry Cooper. 'What about that?'

'What about it?'

'I've been here fourteen years. I've played 327 times for this club,' says Terry Cooper. 'I scored the winning goal against Arsenal at Wembley, the winning goal that brought the League Cup here in 1968. First thing we'd ever won.'

'That was then,' I tell him. 'This is 1974.'

You can't let go. You can't walk away. Because no one wants to train for him. No one wants to play for him. They've told you that, a hundred times. To your face and down the phone. No one wants to play for him –

They want to play for you. They want to work for you –

Not Dave Mackay. Not Sam Longson –

They want you –

Cloughie.

Today Derby County are travelling up to Roker Park for tonight's League Cup replay against Sunderland. But no one wants to travel with him. No one wants to play for him. They've told you that, a thousand times. –

If Derby lose this game, if Mackay loses this game, then who knows . . .

No one wants to play for him. No one wants to work for him –

They want to play for you. They want to work for you –

Not Dave Mackay. Not Sam Longson –

They want you –

Cloughie.

So if Derby County lose this game, if Mackay loses this game, then who knows? Who knows what tomorrow might bring?

Cloughie, risen and immaculate –

Cloughie, back again?

* * *

I am last out of bed this morning, down the stairs and into that new blue Mercedes-Benz. Last through the doors and to work, round the corner and down that corridor, the training finished but the players still here; the players still here and wanting a word; wanting a word because John Giles has been busy this morning –

The Irishman has told the rest of the team why he wants to go to Tottenham; why he wants to leave Leeds. Joe Jordan has been busy too. The Scotsman has told the rest of the team what he thinks about playing in the reserves; what he thinks about being sold to Birmingham City. Terry Yorath has also been busy. The Welshman has told the rest of the team what he thinks about moving to Everton. But Terry Cooper has been busiest of all. The Englishman has told the lot of them that he's being sold to Forest; told them his testimonial is in doubt. The lot of them worried now. The lot of them scared. The lot of them angry. The lot of them wanting a word –

'Are you there, Brian? Are you still there? Are you in there or what?'

Under the stands, through the doors, round the corner and down the corridor, I have locked that bloody door and put the fucking chair against it –

Doubt and fear. Doubt and fear. Doubt and fear.

I pour a drink. I light another fag. I cancel the Friday lunchtime press conference. I tell Harry, Ron and Mike that I'll speak to them by phone:

'You're eighteen places below first place . . .'

'I know that.'

'You're averaging a goal a game . . .'

'I know that.'

'But you're still playing Jordan and McKenzie in the reserves . . .'

'I know that.'

'Playing O'Hare up front when he's not even eligible for Europe . . .'

'I know that.'

'Twelve days before Europe . . .'

'I know that.'

'Talking of selling Terry Cooper and Joe Jordan, of Giles going to Tottenham, talking of bringing in other ineligible players . . .'

'I know that.'

'So what are you going to do?' they ask. 'What are you going to do, Brian?'

'I'm going to sweat it out,' I tell them.

'What do you think Don Revie would have . . .'

'I try not to think about Don Revie,' I tell them. 'But it'd have been the same.'

'But he wouldn't have bought McKenzie,' they say. 'He wouldn't have bought McGovern or O'Hare. He wouldn't be trying to sell Cooper, Giles and Jordan . . .'

'Don's gone,' I tell them. 'And it's only winning that can change things now.'

'And if you don't win?' they ask. 'What changes then? Who changes?'

'Nothing changes,' I tell them.

'Something must,' they say. 'Somebody must . . .'

'No one changes,' I insist. 'Like I say, I'll sweat it out –'

Out. Out. Out.

* * *

Mike Bamber and Harry Bloom, the Brighton vice-chairman, drive up to Derby. To the Midland Hotel. To meet you and Pete –

But you are not there. Just Pete –

Bill Wainwright, the manager of the Midland, calls you at home, in bed –

'Give them some beer and sandwiches,' you tell him, 'and I'll be right there.'

But you're not. You are still two hours late. In your scruffy blue tracksuit –

Peter is furious. Fucking furious. Bamber and Bloom too –

'You're well out of order,' says Mike Bamber. 'Making us travel all the way up here and then making us wait around for two hours.'

'Something came up,' you tell them –

They are still furious, Bamber and Bloom, but they are also still desperate –

'And I didn't come all the way up here to fall out with you either,' says Bamber. 'So here's the deal . . .'

Mike Bamber offers you and Pete £7,000 each just to sign for Brighton, then offers you and Pete an annual salary which is more than you were earning at Derby –

Pete's already smiling. Peter's already done his sums. Taylor's already agreed.

'But these are First Division wages,' you tell Bamber –

'You're First Division managers,' says Bamber.

'But are you sure you can afford it?'
'Are you sure you're worth it?'
'I'm sure,' you tell him –
'Then so am I,' says Mike Bamber. 'Then so am I.'

★ ★ ★

Under the stands, the weight on my back. Through the doors, the weight on my back. Round the corner, the weight on my back. Up the stairs, the weight on my back. Down the corridor, that weight on my back. That weight on my back as I push open the doors to the club dining room. The soup is oxtail again. The meat lamb. The vegetables soft and the wine cheap. Their suits are dark and their ties still black –

'Of course he doesn't want to bloody go,' states Bolton. 'This is Leeds United!'

'But I need players who are thinking about winning cups and medals,' I tell him. 'He's more bothered about his bloody testimonial than Leeds United.'

'He's played here fourteen years,' says Cussins. 'He deserves his testimonial.'

'I never said he didn't,' I tell him, tell them all. 'I played the game, you didn't; none of you, not one of you. I got injured; you didn't. I was finished, washed up, and we'd have bloody starved without my testimonial money. I'm just saying that half your fucking team are on testimonials this season –'

'That's an exaggeration,' says Woodward. 'It's hardly half the team.'

'Cooper, Giles, Paul Madeley, Paul Reaney, Norman Hunter and Peter Lorimer,' I tell him, tell them all. 'That's six bloody first-team players on fucking testimonials this season and that makes it very, very difficult to sell any of them.'

'So stop trying to bloody sell buggers then!' shouts Bolton. 'They're Champions for Chrissakes, man. League bloody Champions.'

'Not this bloody season, they're not,' I tell him, tell them all. 'They're old men.'

'That's bloody rubbish,' says Woodward. 'Absolute bloody rubbish.'

'Is that right?' I ask him, ask them all. 'You fucking watching them play, are you?'

'Some might say it's not the players,' says Bolton.

'Is that right?' I ask him, ask them all again. 'So who might some say it *is* then?'

'Some might say it's their manager,' states Bolton. 'Some might say it's thee.'

★ ★ ★

You should be letting go. You should be walking away. But you can't let go. You can't walk away. You should be thinking about Brighton, thinking about the future. But you just can't stop thinking about Derby, about the past –

You just can't stop thinking and thinking and thinking about it, about them:

Derby County only drew with Sunderland. Back from a penalty. Back from a goal down. Back to draw 1–1. But 1–1 is not good enough. Not against Sunderland. The Derby players, your players, know that. The fans and the press know that. Longson and the board know that and, most of all, Dave Mackay knows that –

Mackay then lost the bloody toss. The Derby players, your players, are furious, fucking furious about that too. Now Derby must play Sunderland at Roker Park again tomorrow night; the winner of that match will then be at home to Liverpool in the next round of the League Cup. But, but, but . . .

If Derby County lose tomorrow night. If Derby County fail to reach the next round of the League Cup. If Derby County are not at home to Liverpool . . .

If Derby lose this game, if Mackay loses this game, then who knows?

The players don't want to play for him. The players don't want to work for him. They want to play for you, your players. They want to work for you –

Not Dave Mackay. Not Sam Longson –

They want you, your players –

They want Cloughie; risen, immaculate and back.

So there's no way you can let go yet. No way you can walk away now. No way you can stop thinking and thinking and thinking about it, about them. But, but, but . . .

You've done the deal with Brighton. You've shaken hands with Bamber.

Tomorrow morning you'll be flying from East Midlands airport down to Sussex –

But you hate bloody flying. You really hate fucking flying. Now you've found your excuse and got your cold feet; your address book out and your phone in your hands –

You call Phillip Whitehead, your MP. You ask him what you should do –

'Everyone wants you back,' he tells you. 'But it's your career.'

You call Brian Moore. You ask him what you should do –

'Everyone at ITV wants you here full-time,' he tells you. 'The offer's always open and you know that. But, in your heart of hearts, you're a football manager. I know that, you know that. So I can't tell you what to do, Brian, except to follow your heart.'

You call Mike Keeling. You ask him what you should do –

'No one wants you to go,' he tells you. 'But, at the end of day, it's up to you.'

You call John Shaw. You ask him what to bloody do –

'The people of Derby want you to stay,' he tells you. 'The people of Derby, the supporters of Derby County Football Club, they all want you to stay and they'll fight until you are back where you belong, and you know that I and everyone else involved in the Protest Movement will do everything we can to make that happen. Everything we can. But, in the meantime, you've also got a wife and three kids to feed . . .'

You can't let go. You can't walk away. Because you can't stop thinking about it. You just can't stop thinking and thinking and thinking about them –

You put down the phone. You ask your wife what you should do –

'Talk to Peter,' she tells you. 'Tell him your doubts. See what he says.'

You have a drink. Then another. Then you call Peter; Pete busy packing his case, whistling, 'Oh, I do like to be beside the seaside . . .'

'I can't go through with it,' you tell him. 'I just can't, Pete.'

'We've got a great deal,' says Peter. 'A better deal than the one we were on.'

'It's not about the money,' you tell him. 'I just can't go through with it.'

'Then we're finished,' he shouts, he screams, he rants and he raves –

'That's you and me fucking finished!'

Day Thirty-nine

Saturday's come again, with Saturday's stink again; the sweat and the mud, the liniment and the grease; the steam and the soap, the sewer and the shampoo. The doubt and the fear. The doubt and the fear. The doubt and the fear –

'Some might say it's their manager. Some might say it's thee . . .'

I know no one wants to play for me. To pull on a shirt for me. To put on their boots for me. To walk down that tunnel. To walk onto that pitch for me –

'Some might say it's their manager. Some might say it's thee . . .'

Not Harvey or Stewart. Not Reaney or Madeley. Not Cherry or Yorath. Not Hunter or McQueen. Not Jordan or Jones. Not Cooper or Lorimer. Not Bates or the Grays. Not Giles or Bremner. Not Allan Clarke or Duncan McKenzie. Not even John McGovern or John O'Hare. Not these days. This Saturday –

Saturday 7 September 1974.

Under their feet and under their stand, through their doors and round their corners, I stay out of their dressing room, I stay out of their boardroom; down the corridors, I stay locked in my office with my ornamental animals and my pictures of birds, pouring my drinks and lighting my fags, listening for their feet, listening for their voices –

'Some might say it's their manager. Some might say it's thee . . .'

I pour another drink and I light another fag; another drink, another fag; another drink, another fag. More feet and more voices, knocking on the door, rattling at the lock –

'Boss,' calls Jimmy. 'Boss, the players are waiting for you in the dressing room.'

'What the hell for?' I answer. 'To whisper and mutter behind my bloody back? To ignore and fucking mock me? To plot and to . . .'

'They just want to know who's playing,' says Jimmy. 'That's all, Boss.'

'Harvey. Reaney. Cherry. McGovern. McQueen. Hunter. Lorimer. Clarke. O'Hare. Giles and Madeley,' I tell him. 'With Yorath on the bench.'

'You're not coming down then?' he asks. 'Not even for a word?'

'Not today,' I tell him. 'I'll see you out there . . .'

The sound of Jimmy's feet retreat and echo down the corridor and round the corner; retreat and echo and hide among the sound of thousands of other pairs of feet, climbing to their seats, taking their places for the showdown, this final exhibition –

'Are you there, Brian? Are you still there?'

I finish my drink and put out my fag. I unlock the door and open it. I close and lock it again. I walk down the corridor and round the corner, past the dressing room and down the tunnel. The teams already out on the pitch. I walk into the light and the stadium. Into the silence. I make my way along to the dug-out. To that bench. To that seat. In that silence –

'How shall we live, Brian? How shall we live?'

The 26,450 Yorkshire zombies inside Elland Road silent today. The 26,450 Yorkshire zombies silent until some big black fucking dog barks, 'Bugger off, Clough! You're not the bloody Don and you never fucking will be.'

★ ★ ★

Last night Derby County were beaten by Sunderland. Beaten by a Vic Halom hat-trick. Beaten 3–0 and knocked out of the League Cup. Derby did not play particularly badly, Derby did not play particularly well; but the difference between Derby and Sunderland, according to the press, the difference was that Sunderland would do anything their manager asked of them –

Walk on water! Run through fire!

Anything bloody Bob fucking Stokoe asked of them; they hung on his every word, they lived by his every word, just like your team did, just like your boys –

But Derby County would not do what Dave Mackay asked of them. Derby County do not hang on Dave Mackay's every word. They will not listen to Dave Mackay at all –

Now Derby County will not be at home to Liverpool in the next round –
The press are not impressed. The fans are not impressed –

'Bring back Cloughie! Bring back Cloughie! Bring back Cloughie!'

But this morning you are not back in Derby. This morning you and Peter kissed and made up at East Midlands airport. Now you and Peter are down at the Goldstone Ground, Brighton; flown down first thing, met at the airport and driven to the Courtlands Hotel –

The champagne breakfast. The Rolls-Royce to the ground. The red carpet –

Now you are about to become the new manager of Brighton and Hove Albion FC; unveiled and announced. But there is still time, still time –

You loosen your tie. You undo your collar. You make some excuses. You walk down a corridor. Round a corner. You find a phone. You call John Shaw –

'The whole of the bloody nation's sporting fucking press are here,' you tell him. 'Should I sign or not, John? Should I sign or not?'

'It's your career,' he tells you. 'I can't tell you what to do, Brian.'

'But if I can get back,' you tell him. 'If I can get back . . .'

'We're doing our best,' he says. 'Doing our very best to make that happen.'

'I know you are,' you tell him. 'I know you are.'

'And if the team keeps getting results like last night, who knows?'

'You're right,' you tell him. 'Who knows? It could be only a matter of time . . .'

'That's the only problem,' says John Shaw. 'Knowing how long it'll take –'

'Right then,' you tell him. 'I'll sign, but I'll be back for the meeting tonight.'

'See you then, then,' says John. 'See you then.'

You put down the phone. You find a mirror. You straighten your collar and tie; you've got on your World of Sport tie, a smile on your face, and some quotes ready for the cameras and the microphones, for your audience:

'This is the greatest thing ever to happen to Brighton,' Mike Bamber is saying. 'Now we can really go places . . .'

'And let me say this,' you interrupt. 'This chairman and his directors did a better job of selling Brighton to me than I did trying to sell Derby County . . .'

'You've done it before,' the press tell you. 'Are you sure you can do it again?'

'I am anxious to get started,' you tell them. 'Because I understand there is quite a bit of work to do and I know it'll be tougher here than even at Hartlepools; tougher here because they didn't expect anything at Hartlepools. Tougher here than Derby too because they had the tradition. The history. Now

Peter and me have a reputation, now there are expectations, but there are no fairies at the end of Brighton pier . . .'

'What is your opinion of the Brighton squad?' they ask you.

'There are only sixteen professionals here. Only one goalkeeper, only one train-er, only one secretary, only one groundsman; in fact, only one of everything. So that puts Peter and me in the majority for once, for they've got two bloody managers.'

'What kind of staff and players will you be looking to bring in?'

'Cheap ones,' you tell them. 'With some bloody coal on their faces.'

'What's your response to people who say that fetching Clough and Taylor to Brighton is like engaging McAlpine to decorate your roadside café?'

'What's wrong with a roadside café?' you ask them. 'You lot can stuff your Ritz. You can stuff your Savoy. You get your best bloody food in Britain at a roadside café.'

And you're still the best bloody manager in Britain, the cameras and the microphones still bloody know it, the cameras and the microphones still bloody love you, still adore and applaud you as you take your bow, make your exit . . .

Mike Bamber drives you and Peter to meet the Brighton team at a hotel in Lewes. The team are nervous. The team are afraid –

Nervous and afraid of you.

They hide their nerves and their fears behind their jokes and their bravado, their casual jokes, their casual bravado. You hate them. You despise them. Their nerves and their fear, their jokes and their bravado –

You take off your jacket. You stick out your chin –

'Go on, punch it!' you tell them. 'Show me you've got some fucking balls!'

* * *

I am not Don Revie and John McGovern is not Billy Bremner. The crowd are baying for my blood and the crowd are baying for John McGovern's blood –

'Take the bloody lad off,' says Jimmy. 'He's fucking suffered enough.'

'I wouldn't take him off if we were losing 5–1,' I tell him –

But Leeds are not losing 5–1 to Luton. Leeds United are drawing 1–1 with Luton; newly promoted Luton Town; Luton who are two places above Leeds on goal average. But 1–1 is not good enough. Not against Luton Town. The Leeds players, *his* players, know that. The fans and the press know that. Cussins, Bolton and the whole of the Leeds board bloody know that and, most of all, I fucking know that –

The whistle blows. The final whistle. The match ends –

The curtain comes down to the jeers and the boos of 26,450 Yorkshire zombies, drowning out the loudspeaker –

The loudspeaker which is playing 'Who's Sorry Now?'

I get up off that bench. I leave that dug-out. I make my way along to the tunnel, the dressing-room doors, the corridor and the press; the press, press, press, press, press, press, press –

'Who's sorry now, who's sorry now . . .'

'Our performance was just a yard short of a superb performance,' I tell them –

'Whose heart is achin' for breakin' each vow . . .'

'It was a question of confidence and the confidence is down to me –'

'Who's sad and blue, who's cryin' too . . .'

'I instil or destroy it and, as yet, I have not been able to instil it.'

'Just like I cried over you . . .'

'If we'd stayed 1–0 for a time and got another, we would have blossomed.'

'Right to the end, just like a friend . . .'

'I swear to you it was that much away,' I tell them, indicating half an inch with my finger and thumb. 'I swear to you, just that much. I swear . . .'

'I tried to warn you somehow . . .'

'I am not concerned about the overall situation at all.'

'You had your way, now you must pay . . .'

'You are only concerned if you can't see any way it can improve.'

'I'm glad that you're sorry now . . .'

'I am glad I am the manager of Leeds instead of Luton.'

'Right to the end, just like a friend . . .'

'I am glad I am the manager.'

'I tried to warn you somehow . . .'

'I am the manager . . .'

'You had your way, now you must pay . . .'

'Upstairs with you,' bellows Bolton down the corridor. 'Now!'

I'm glad that you're sorry now. I'm glad that you're sorry now. I'm glad . . .'

THE SEVENTH AND FINAL RECKONING

First Division Positions, 8 September 1974

		P	W	D	L	F	A	Pts
1	Liverpool	6	5	1	0	14	4	11
2	Ipswich Town	6	4	1	1	9	3	10
3	Man. City	6	4	1	1	11	8	9
4	Stoke City	6	3	2	1	9	4	8
5	Everton	6	3	2	1	8	6	8
6	Sheffield Utd	6	3	2	1	10	8	8
7	Carlisle United	6	3	1	2	6	4	7
8	Middlesbrough	6	2	3	1	7	5	7
9	Wolves	6	2	3	1	8	7	7
10	Derby County	6	1	4	1	6	6	6
11	Newcastle Utd	6	2	2	2	12	12	6
12	Chelsea	6	2	2	2	9	11	6
13	Burnley	6	2	1	3	9	9	5
14	Leicester City	6	1	3	2	8	9	5
15	QPR	6	1	3	2	4	5	5
16	Arsenal	6	2	0	4	6	7	4
17	Birmingham C.	6	1	2	3	6	10	4
18	Luton Town	6	0	4	2	4	7	4
19	**Leeds United**	**6**	**1**	**2**	**3**	**4**	**8**	**4**
20	Coventry City	6	0	3	3	7	13	3
21	West Ham Utd	6	1	1	4	5	11	3
22	Tottenham H.	6	1	0	5	5	10	2

I was a Yorkshire Man and I was a Cunning Man –
And I cursed you!
First with gift, then with loss –
I cursed you!
Loss and then gift, gift and then loss –
Until you lost. Until you left –
I cursed you, Brian. I damned you, Cloughie.

Day Forty

You're sorry now, you're sorry now, you're so fucking very sorry now –

You thought you'd never get away. You thought Mike Bamber would never let you leave. You thought he'd lock you in your room at the Courtlands Hotel, Brighton. Then you thought Peter would never agree to come back with you. Not back to Derby with you. Not tonight. Then you thought you'd never find a car. Not at that time. Not to go to Derby. Never find a driver. Then the journey took a lifetime. The traffic. The weather. You thought you'd never make it. Thought the meeting would be over by the time you got here. But here you are, back home in Derby. Here for the meeting at the King's Hall, Derby –

The King's Hall packed. Standing room only. The King's Hall expectant –

You climb onto the stage. You raise your hands. You fight the tears –

'We took the job because we were out of work,' *you tell the King's Hall, Derby.* 'We are football men and the position was open.'

You have come to say goodbye. You have come to say thanks –

'Thanks for everything you're doing,' *you tell them.* 'And don't forget to support Roy McFarland . . .'

You start to cry. You cannot stop. You hand the microphone to Pete and Peter says, 'I think we'd better cool it now. But thank you for your support.'

But the Derby County Protest Movement don't agree. The Protest Movement don't agree to cool it. The Protest Movement still want you back –

'This is incredible,' *you tell John Shaw.* 'If I can get back to Derby, I will.'

'But we're not going back,' *Taylor tells you.* 'There can be no going back, Brian. Not now. Not now we've signed for Brighton. We should all get on with the rest of our lives and stop misleading people. The Protest Movement, the players, the people of Derby. It's not fair; not fair on them, not fair on Dave –'

'Fuck Dave Mackay,' *you tell him.* 'Fuck him.'

'You don't mean that,' *he says.* 'You're only hurting him and hurting yourself. Half these folk that are protesting, asking for you back, they're only doing

309

it to get a bit of free publicity for their businesses, jumping on the bandwagon to promote themselves.'

'Fuck off!' you tell him. 'Fuck off!'

'Open your eyes, man,' he tells you. 'Look around you. No one cares about you. No one cares about Derby County. About a little fucking football club.'

'Fuck off!'

'We've resigned, Brian. We've got new jobs,' he says. 'It's time to move on.'

You storm out. You slam the doors. You walk the streets of Derby. You find a taxi. You get a free lift home. You push open your front door. You run up the stairs. You fall down onto your bed and pull the covers over your head –

'What have I done?' you shout and scream. 'What have I fucking done?'

It is Thursday 1 November 1973.

Day Forty-one

I see it from the motorway. Through the windscreen. *Are you there, Brian?* Fallen off the top of Beeston Hill. In a heap up against the railway and the motorway banking. *Are you still there?* The floodlights and the stands, those fingers and fists up from those sticks and those stones, *his* flesh and their bones. *Zombies, bloody zombies.* No kids in the back today. Just Arthur Seaton, Colin Smith, Arthur Machin and Joe Lampton here today –

You let them bastards grind you down, they whisper. *Those zombies . . .*

'Shut your bloody gobs,' I tell them and turn the radio on, on fucking full blast:

'I was wrong in not acting more decisively and more forthrightly . . . It is a burden I shall bear for every day of the life that is left to me . . .'

Nixon. Nixon. Nixon. Radio on:

'Mr Evel Knievel fell in the canyon leap on his sky cycle over Snake River Canyon, but landed without injury thanks to his parachute . . .'

Parachute. Parachute. Parachute. Radio on:

'Meanwhile, in other sporting news, Leeds United, never out of the top four places over the last ten years, find themselves this morning still three places off the bottom and their new manager, Brian Clough, in an increasingly difficult position . . .'

I switch off the radio as I come off the motorway in my new blue Mercedes-Benz. *There is no heaven and there is no hell.* Round the bends and the corners to the junction with Lowfields Road and onto Elland Road. *No heaven and no hell.* Sharp right and through those fucking gates. *No hell. No hell. No hell.* No big black fucking dog today. *Just other people. Other places. Other times.* The writing on the wall –

CLOUGH OUT!

Brighton and Hove Albion, autumn and winter 1973. Hotels and nightclubs, the Courtlands and the Fiesta Club, the best of everything, the very best –

'Oh, you don't like to be beside the seaside . . .'

Champagne and oysters, smoked salmon and caviar –

'You don't like to be beside the sea . . .'

Nights on the town; Dora Bryan, Bruce Forsyth and Les Dawson –

'You don't like to stroll along the prom, prom, prom . . .'

But it's not the life for you, a table by the window, a bloody table for one –

'Where the brass bands play . . .'

You miss your wife. You miss your kids. You miss your Derby –

'Tiddley-om-pom-pom!'

★ ★ ★

The sun is shining, the rain falling. The sky black and blue, purple and yellow. No rainbows here, only training. It should be a day off, a day of rest for the players. Except we drew against Luton Town on Saturday, at home. Except we are fourth from the bottom of Division One, with four points and four goals from six games. Except we play Huddersfield Town tomorrow night in the second round of the League Cup, away. There are no days off, no days of rest now, under these bloated Yorkshire skies –

'Enough pissing about,' I tell them. 'Let's get into two teams, now!'

In their purple tracksuits with their names on their backs, they pull on their bibs and wait for the whistle and then off we go, go, go –

For hours and hours I run and I shout and no one speaks and no one passes, but I can read their game, I can read their moves, so when the Irishman picks up the ball in his own half and shapes to pass, I move in towards him, to close him down, and the Irishman is forced to turn, to pass back to Hunter, a short, bad pass back, and I'm after it, this short, bad and deliberately stray pass, Hunter and Giles coming, Hunter and Giles coming, my eye on the ball, my mind on the ball, and Hunter is here, Giles is here and –

Cruuuuuuuuuuuuuuuuuuuuuuuuuuuuuuuuuuuuuuuuuuuuuuuuuuuuuuuuuunch . . .

Black and blue, purple and yellow; the silence and the lights out –

'Get up, Clough! He's fucking codding is Clough . . .'

I am on the ground, in the mud, my eyes wide and the ball gone. I see their faces standing over me, looking down at me. They are dirty moons. They are panting moons –

'How shall we live, Brian? How shall we live?'

'We call that the suicide ball, Mr Clough.'

★ ★ ★

It is the dead of night, November 1973. The dead of a Derby night. You have driven through this night. From Brighton. Back to Derby. You park outside the Barry McGuinness Health Club in London Road. You take the carrier bag off the passenger seat. You lock the car door. You walk into that health club –

The Derby players look up. John Shaw and Barry McGuinness look up –

'I'll burn down this restaurant, Barry, and kidnap your kids, John,' you tell them, 'if you bloody damage these players' fucking careers.'

John and Barry blanch. John and Barry nod.

'And I want you lot bloody home,' you tell the players. 'In your beds now, go!'

The players nod, your players, and they get to their feet. They start to leave, slowly. David Nish the last. Always the bloody last. David Nish dawdling –

'Go on with you, David,' you shout after him. 'Dragging them bloody feet would have cost you ten fucking quid a few weeks ago.'

You open the carrier bag. You take out three bottles of ale and three glasses –

'I've brought my own beer and one each for you two,' you tell John and Barry. 'Now then, gentlemen, what are you two going to do for me?'

'You've just bloody blown it,' mumbles John. 'The players had come here to tell us they were all ready to come out on fucking strike for you.'

You pour your brown ale. You drink it down in one. You wipe your mouth –

'Go to the Baseball Ground,' you tell John and Barry. 'Find Tommy Mason. He's in the second team. Nice lad. Never make it. Tell him to get the bloody reserves out on strike. Then the fucking first team will follow.'

★ ★ ★

I am alone in the shower, I am alone in the bath, I am alone in the dressing room, sat on that bench, beneath those pegs, my towel around my waist and over my legs, my legs bruised but not broken, not broken but hurting, *Keep on fighting* above the door, the exit.

* * *

You don't like driving so you get Bill from the Midland, your old mate Colin or John Shaw to drive you back and forth, Brighton to Derby, back and forth, Derby to Brighton. Today, it's Bill with his foot down as you change into your tracksuit on the back seat –

Bamber has a meeting with you in your office at the Goldstone Ground –

But you are late, late again, and he's waiting, waiting again –

Him in his suit and tie, you in your tracksuit and boots –

You put them boots up on your desk, your hands behind your head and tell him, 'Mr Chairman, I've shot it. I've been off for three weeks and training's whacked me.'

'You're a bloody liar, Brian,' laughs Bamber. 'It's been pouring with rain here all morning and your bloody boots are as clean as a fucking whistle.'

'Well done!' you tell him. 'You've caught me out already!'

* * *

Under the stands, through the doors, round the corners and down the corridors, here come the feet, here come the voices and here come the knocks –

'Boss?' say John McGovern and John O'Hare. 'You wanted to see us?'

'Yes,' I tell them. 'Sit yourselves down. Drink? Fag?'

John McGovern shakes his head. John O'Hare shakes his head.

'Right, listen,' I tell them both. 'There's no bloody way I can play you two, because you don't fucking deserve to take all this off them. I've got to leave you both out. You understand why, don't you? You understand my position?'

John McGovern nods. John O'Hare nods.

I light another cig. I pour another drink –

I offer them the open packet, the bottle –

They shake their heads again. They get up. They go.

★ ★ ★

Back to square one; John Shaw went round to Tommy Mason's digs; John drank cups of tea with Tommy's landlady; John heard Tommy coming down the street, back from training; Tommy saw John; Tommy couldn't believe his luck; Tommy thought you wanted him down at Brighton; John broke the bad news, then John broke the good news; Tommy agreed to bring the second team out on strike. But Webby heard the rumours of plots, the rumours of strikes; so then Webby issued threats, threats of writs; so the rumours of plots, the rumours of strikes rescinded –

Back to square one; back to Plan B; Operation Snowball –

You are sat alone in Mike Keeling's flat. Mike Keeling and John Shaw are across the road with Archie Gemmill and Colin Todd in Gemmill's flat.

'When you hear the word "snowball",' Shaw and Keeling are telling Gemmill and Todd, 'you and the rest of the team are to come out on strike.'

'Did the Boss tell you to tell me that?' asks Gemmill.

'No,' says Keeling. 'He's the manager of Brighton now. This is me telling you.'

'Will you do it?' asks John Shaw.

'Only if the Boss tells me.'

Mike Keeling and John Shaw come back across the road to where you are sat alone waiting in Keeling's flat. Keeling and Shaw tell you what Gemmill said –

'Send the wee lad over here,' you tell them.

John Shaw goes back across the road. John Shaw returns with Gemmill –

'Would you go on strike to get me back?' you ask him.

'I would, Boss,' says Gemmill.

'Would you do it without my asking?'

'No,' he says. 'I'd only strike if you told me to.'

And so that is the end of Plan B; the end of Operation Snowball.

But that very night, you meet your Derby players and their wives again; you meet them at the Midland Hotel, then invite them back to yours –

To finally admit defeat. To finally say goodbye. But the players won't admit defeat. The players won't say goodbye –

They'll never admit defeat. Never say goodbye –

The Derby players, your *players, draft a letter to Dave Mackay:*

We, the undersigned players, refuse to report to Derby County
Football Club until 1.00 p.m. on Saturday 24 November, for the
following reasons:
a) Dissatisfaction with the present management and
b) The refusal to reinstate Mr Brian Clough and Mr Peter Taylor.

*Your wife then marches the wives down to a meeting of the Protest Movement,
while you open another crate of champagne and light another cigar –
No one is admitting defeat. Never. No one is saying goodbye. Ever –
The results are going against Mackay. The results going your way –
Only John O'Hare will report for training tomorrow morning.*

★ ★ ★

Down the corridors and round the corners. Up the stairs and down
another corridor. In the Yorkshire boardroom, the Yorkshire curtains
drawn, I am drinking French brandy, tasting Yorkshire carpet.

'You're not selling Cooper and you're not buying Todd,' states Bolton
again. 'You're not selling Harvey and you're not buying Shilton.'

'I bloody am.'

'You're bloody not,' shouts Bolton. 'Not Harvey. Not Cooper. Not
for £75,000. Not for £175,000. Not when all you've bloody got is
four bloody points out of twelve. Not when we're bloody fourth from
the fucking bottom.'

'Is that what you all think?' I ask them. 'The whole bloody lot of you?'

The Yorkshire board stare back at me. The Yorkshire board nod.

'What about Bob Roberts?' I ask. 'Where's Bob Roberts?'

'Bob's on holiday,' smiles Bolton. 'Bob can't help you now.'

On that Yorkshire carpet, behind those Yorkshire curtains, in that
Yorkshire boardroom, this is when I see it, see it clearly in his eyes, in
his eyes and all their eyes –

This is when the penny finally drop, drop, drops.

★ ★ ★

Dave Mackay has had enough; had enough of the rumours; had enough of the threats. He has lost to QPR. He has lost to Ipswich Town. He has lost to Sheffield United. Dave Mackay has yet to win and now he faces Leeds United, Arsenal and then Newcastle –

Dave Mackay has had enough; had enough of the results; had enough of the B.B.C. campaign; had enough of the Derby players, your players –

Dave Mackay has finally hit the roof. Dave Mackay has taken off his gloves now. Read them the bloody riot act. In no uncertain fucking terms:

'Clough's not bloody coming back,' he tells them. 'If it isn't me here, it'll be someone else, but it won't be Brian fucking Clough. Now if you don't want to play for me, then you can put in your transfer request and fuck off. If that means the lot of you, so be it; I'll play the bloody reserves. The choice is yours – stay or fucking go.'

Dave Mackay then takes them to one side, one by one, player by player, and one by one, player by player, they make their peace with Dave Mackay. Last of them all, Roy McFarland makes his peace and he shakes Dave's hand in front of the dressing room. Then Roy calls for the Derby County Protest Movement to end its activities.

But you still hope, hope against hope, that something will happen today because today Dave Mackay and Derby County are at home to Don Revie and Leeds United –

It is Saturday 24 November 1973.

Today Brighton are at home to Walton & Hersham, an amateur side, in the FA Cup. But you're not thinking about the cup, not thinking about Walton & Hersham. Today you are distracted. Today you are diverted. Today you're only thinking about Derby County, thinking about Leeds United. You know this is the big test, the big test for Dave Mackay. You know he is only one defeat away from the sack; the sack that could bring you back. Distracted and diverted, your thoughts at the Baseball Ground while here at the Goldstone Ground Brighton are losing –

Losing 1–0, losing 2–0, 3–0 and then 4–0 –

Brighton have lost 4–0 at home to an amateur side in the FA Cup.

You stand in that beaten dressing room. You stare at that beaten team; your beaten Brighton team who dare not even look you in the eye –

Who cannot pull on their shirts, who cannot lace up their boots –

Cannot pull on their bloody shirts or lace up their fucking boots without you –
That beaten bloody Brighton team who are scared fucking shitless of you –
Tears down their cheeks. Tears down their shirts. Tears down yours –
Derby County have drawn 0–0 with Leeds United.

★ ★ ★

The sharp knife and loaded gun. The long rope. The post-mortem. The press conference:

'All we've got to do is get out there and bloody win on the field,' I tell them. 'That solves everything, a win on the bloody field.'

But there is something in their eyes . . .

'There was no question of me being carpeted. The board wanted to be informed of everything that goes on within the club, and rightly so. I informed them of everything. It has always been my policy to work with the chairman of a club, and the board, and everyone connected with a club, and this will continue to be my policy.'

No questions today, just something in their eyes . . .

'The bid from Forest wasn't high enough. I feel Terry is worth more. We think he can do Leeds more good. Forest's bid didn't meet with our valuation of him. The price we have on Terry Cooper.'

The way they look at me, the way they stare, but only when I look away . . .

'I have never been so convinced of anything in my life as that I am getting the full support of the players. That the players back me.'

Like I'm sick, like I've got cancer and I'm dying but no one dare tell me . . .

'The situation is beautiful and clear.'

★ ★ ★

Just when you think things could get no worse, things get bloody worse, much, much fucking worse; Brighton and Hove Albion lose 8–2 at home to Bristol Rovers; this is the single worst defeat of your career, as a player or as a manager.

You put your youngest lad in the car and drive to London. You sit your youngest lad on your knee in the studios of LWT. In front of the TV cameras. This is your defence. This boy is your defence. This boy is your protection –

'The Brighton players are a disgrace,' you tell Brian Moore and his cameras.
'They do not know their trade and they shirk all moral responsibilities –
'All moral responsibilities.'

★ ★ ★

I put out my cig. I finish my drink. I lock up the office. I double check
the door. I walk down that corridor. Past those trophies. Past those
photographs. Through those doors and out into the car park. To my
brand-new blue Mercedes-Benz –

There are two young lads stood beside the car, in their boots and in
their jeans, their scarves round their necks, their scarves round their
wrists, hands in their pockets –

'How are you this evening, lads?' I ask them.

They nod their heads and blink. They nudge each other with their
elbows.

'Were you here on Saturday, were you?' I ask them.

They nod their heads again. They sway from side to side.

'What did you think then?' I ask them.

'Rubbish,' says one of them, and the other one giggles.

'Why do you think that was then?' I ask them.

'Because of that John McGovern,' says the one that speaks. 'He's
rubbish, he is.'

'He won the Championship at Derby,' I tell them. 'Just give him
time, will you?'

The quieter lad asks, 'But are you going to bring all the Derby players here?'

'Don't believe all that crap in the papers, lads,' I tell them. 'And don't
worry, it'll all come right in the end. You'll see.'

They nod their heads again and blink.

I take out my car keys. I open the car door.

'Where are you going?' they ask me.

'Home,' I tell them. 'Now don't you get too pissed tonight, eh, lads?'

They smile. They laugh. They wave –

'Cheerio then,' I tell them. 'Cheerio, lads.'

Day Forty-two

Derby County draw with Arsenal. Derby County beat Newcastle. Derby County beat Tottenham. Dave Mackay has started winning. Dave Mackay keeps winning. Leeds United keep winning too. Don Revie keeps winning. But Brian Clough keeps losing.

The only good result you get is from the FA Disciplinary Committee; the FA find you not guilty of bringing the game into disrepute for all the things you said and wrote about Leeds United, for all the things you said and wrote about Don Revie –

The things you said and wrote, over and over, again and again.

This result will open doors, you think; open better doors. Because another good result comes in another defeat for England under Alf Ramsey, England losing 1–0 to Italy; the pressure mounting now on Alf Ramsey and the FA –

These results will open other doors, you think. These will open better doors.

* * *

Things are never the way they say they are. Things are never the way you want them to be. Things just get worse and worse, day by day, hour by hour. Then things fall apart. Things just collapse –

I get out of bed. In silence. I eat breakfast. In silence. I leave the house. In silence. I drive to work. In silence. I park. In silence. I walk across the car park. In silence. Up the banking. In silence. To the training ground. In silence –

No smiles. No laughter. No banter. No jokes. No conversations. No chat. Not here.

I stand at the edge of the training ground and watch them practise and practise. Jimmy comes over. Jimmy says, 'Thought we'd knock it on the head now, Boss?'

'Fine,' I tell him and then I ask, 'What were they practising just then?'

Jimmy smiles. Jimmy says, 'Dummies, Boss.'

'They could have used me for once then,' I tell him and then I traipse back down the banking. Past Syd and Maurice. In silence. Past the huts and across the car park. The puddles and the potholes. In silence. Into reception –

'Players' lounge,' says Bolton. 'Ten minutes.'

★ ★ ★

You put down the phone. You know it's over now. No chance of going back –

Derby County Football Club have held their Annual General Meeting for 1973. Mike Keeling presented a petition of 7,000 signatures demanding your reinstatement. The board presented a counterpetition of 22,000 signatures.

There were still chants against Jack Kirkland. Still chants against Sam Longson; the meeting dissolving into catcalls and chaos as Longson held a microphone to his ear and stared into space, the stewards picking up Keeling and throwing him down the stairs.

But it's over now and you know it. No going back. Not now.

★ ★ ★

The players' lounge, Elland Road. Deep in the West Stand, off the main corridor. Two doors locked and an empty bar. Low ceiling and sticky carpet. Mirrors, mirrors on the walls. Fresh from their baths in their black mourning suits, the players file in; the players and directors heading straight to the funeral of Harry Reynolds, straight after this; this players' court, this charade, this first funeral, *mine* –

'I say, I say, I say,' Manny Cussins begins. 'We held a board meeting last night because we feel there is some unrest in the camp, that things aren't quite right . . .'

'Never mind that crap,' says Bolton. 'We want to know what's going on here.'

Heads low, their fingers and their nails between their lips and their teeth, there is silence from the players.

I turn my chair around and sit down. I rest my arms on its back and ask them, 'Listen, lads, how about we start all over again and try to improve things?'

Heads low, their fingers and their nails between their lips and their teeth, there is still only silence.

'Perhaps if Mr Clough were to step outside,' says John Giles, 'then perhaps we would all feel a little more like speaking our minds.'

I look at the Irishman. The Irishman smiles. The Irishman winks –

Bastard. Bastard. Bastard. Fucking bastards. The bloody lot of them . . .

I don't wait. I stand up. I turn my back. I leave –

'We're not happy with the handling of the team . . .'

I leave them to it. Under the stand, through the doors and round the corners, I walk –

'We never see him and when we do he tells us nothing . . .'

I walk back down that corridor to the office. Back to find Jimmy by that door –

'We're not allowed to mention Mr Revie's name . . .'

'That's it,' I tell Jimmy. 'There's no way I can continue to manage this club.'

'What I want to know is why, after all the things he'd said about us, did you appoint him in the first place, Mr Cussins?'

'What you going to do, Boss?' asks Jimmy.

'It wasn't just me who appointed him, boys . . .'

'I'm resigning,' I tell him. 'But I'll make sure your job's safe.'

'So what are you saying, lads?'

'I'm not bloody staying here without you,' says Jimmy. 'No fucking way.'

'What the lads are trying to say, Mr Bolton, is that he's just not good enough . . .'

'Right then,' I tell him. 'I want you to go home tonight and work out how much bloody brass you're going to need . . .'

'Not good enough for Leeds United.'

'. . . because I know that's what I'm going to fucking do.'

***

You are not at work. You are up in the air. Thirty thousand feet up in the air. On your way to New York City. On your way to see Ali–Frazier II at Madison Square Garden. All expenses paid. Thanks to the Daily Mail; *the* Daily Mail *who will introduce you to Ali:*

  Ali vs Clough – the Meeting of the Mouths – Ego vs Ego.

You don't care. Thirty thousand feet up in the air. On your way to New York City. On a charter flight in the company of the Victoria Sporting Club. The Victoria Sporting Club who sweep every miniature from the drinks trolley and then toss them over to you –

  'Help yourself to whatever you bloody like, Brian,' they shout. 'You just take as many as you fucking like, old son.'

  Up in the air, drunk and scared. You pull out the paper, the Daily Mail:

'Clay and I want each other bad,' says Frazier. 'I still call him Clay; his mother named him Clay. If you've been around this guy long enough, you can have a lot of hate in your heart when the bell rings, but otherwise you kind of look at him and you laugh. There's something wrong with the guy. I'm aware now that the guy's got a couple of loose screws someplace.'

  Up in the air, drunk and scared, this is how 1974 begins for Cloughie – Drunk and scared, up in the air, nineteen hundred and seventy-four.

***

I watch them climb down the steps and off the team bus still in their black suits and their black ties, with their paperback books and their packs of cards, but I don't bother to count the hearts, not this night –

  This night has 30,000 eyes but no hearts. Thirty thousand eyes plus two: Don in the crowd. Don in the stands. Don in his black suit. His black tie. His funeral suit. His mourning suit. Here for my final game, same as my first game:

  Huddersfield Town vs Leeds United –

This time it's no friendly. This time it's the Football League Cup, second round.

Huddersfield Town in their royal blue and white vertical-striped shirts, white shorts and white stockings: Poole. Hutt. Garner. Pugh. Saunders. Dolan. Hoy. McGinley. Gowling. Chapman and Smith –

Versus –

Leeds United in their yellow shirts, yellow shorts and yellow stockings: Harvey. Reaney. Cherry. Bates. McQueen. Hunter. Lorimer. Clarke. Jordan. Giles and Madeley. No McKenzie. No McGovern. No O'Hare –

They are Leeds United, the Champions of England. But they are not my team. Not mine. They win a penalty and Lorimer scores. The referee demands it be retaken and Lorimer misses. They go a goal behind with only eleven minutes left, a goal behind to a Third Division team, a goal behind before Lorimer crashes a volley into the back of the net with only one minute left. There will have to be a replay now at Elland Road in two weeks' time. But I will not be there. I will not be their manager –

Because they are not my team. Not mine. Not this team, and they never will be –

In their dirty yellow shirts, dirty yellow shorts and dirty yellow stockings . . .

They are his team. *His Leeds.* His dirty, fucking Leeds and they always will be –

In his black suit. His black tie. In his funeral suit. His mourning suit . . .

Not my team. Never. Not mine. Never. Not this team. Never –

They are not Derby County and I am not Donald Revie.

* * *

Derby keep winning. Leeds keep winning. Brighton keep losing. But you are never there; Sunday through Thursday, you're never, never there –

You are shaking hands with Muhammad Ali, shaking hands with Frank Sinatra. You are not on the back pages of the papers, you're on the front.

You're also back on the streets of Derby, on the stump for Phillip Whitehead; Phillip Whitehead, the Labour MP for Derby North; Phillip

Whitehead who stood by you at Derby; Phillip Whitehead, your friend, who
you want to help, and help full-time:

'But how can you do that when you're the manager at Brighton?'

'No bloody problem,' you tell him. 'I only go there on Fridays and then I'm
back home here in Derby by Saturday night . . .'

In the sleet and in the drizzle. On the estates and on the streets. On the stump:

'I'm Brian Clough,' you tell the voters of Derby, shout through your loud-
hailer. 'And I think you should all come out and vote for the Labour Party.'

In the sleet. In the drizzle. On the estates. On the streets. You are a Pied Piper:

'I'm Brian Clough,' you tell them. 'And I want you all to get down to the
polling station now and vote for Phillip Whitehead, your Labour candidate.'

In the sleet and in the drizzle, on the estates and on the streets, you love all
this; the canvassing on the doorsteps, the speeches to the packed halls –

'A slice of bloody cake for all!' you tell them. 'That's what Brian Clough says.'

'When you coming back to Derby, Cloughie?' shouts someone during one
of the question times as the whole hall applauds and stamps its feet –

'Let's get Phillip elected first,' you tell the hall. 'Then let's see what happens.'

In the February 1974 General Election, Phillip Whitehead retains his seat
with a majority of twelve hundred, against all the predictions. All the odds –

That's what happens in Derby. In February 1974. Just that.

★ ★ ★

The five-mile coach journey from Leeds Road, Huddersfield, back to
Elland Road, Leeds, is a long one; the longest bloody one of my whole
fucking life. No paperback books tonight. No packs of cards. No
bloody hearts tonight. No one laughs. No one jokes. No one speaks at
all. Not one single word until Manny Cussins says –

'Can I have a word with you, Brian?'

'A word?'

'Yes,' he mumbles. 'A word and a drink? Back at my flat.'

★ ★ ★

You are up in the air again. You are up in the air and on your way to Iran at

the personal invitation of the Shah; the Shah of Iran who wants you to man-
age his national team –

You and Bill and Vince from the Sunday Mirror. *First Class all the way.*

The Shah offers you £500 a week to manage the Iranian team, twice your
Brighton salary, with a palatial apartment and your own private swimming
pool, luxury cars and chauffeurs at your beck and call, with flights back home
at your every whim and fancy, the American School for your three children –

You feed apples and oranges to the Shah's horses and shake your head; it's
not for you, not this country, not this national team.

But the phone keeps ringing and ringing, and the offers keep coming and
coming. Aston Villa. Queen's Park Rangers. But not England. Not for you.
Not England. Not yet.

The trips keep coming too, the concerts and the photo opportunities –

The variety and the television shows, the newspaper columns –

But it's not enough; not, not nearly bloody enough –

Derby keep winning. Leeds keep winning –

But not Brighton. Not you. Not yet.

★ ★ ★

Manny Cussins pours the drinks. Manny Cussins lights the cigars –

Manny Cussins says those five words, 'It's not working, is it?'

'What's not working?' I ask him. 'I haven't been here five fucking
minutes, so how can anything be bloody working yet?'

'The players are unhappy with you,' he says. 'The players and the fans.'

'So what do you want to do about it?'

'If it's not working,' he mumbles, 'then we'll have to part company.'

★ ★ ★

This time last year you were trying to reach the final of the European Cup. Now
you're trying to keep Brighton in the Third Division; trying and failing –

'We've bloody shot it,' says Taylor.

'No,' you tell him. 'You have.'

'Fuck off!'

'You're never here,' you tell him. 'You're always away watching so-and-so.'

'I'm never fucking here? What about you?' asks Taylor.

'What about me?'

'The players never fucking see you —'

'They see me on Fridays and Saturdays —'

'Aye,' says Taylor. 'When you dash down from the fucking television studios just in time to frighten them out of their bloody wits and then dash straight back to those studios to have a bloody go at them in public on the fucking box.'

'Fridays and Saturdays,' you tell him.

'It's not enough, Brian,' says Taylor. 'It's not enough.'

'You're right,' you tell him. 'It's not enough; not enough to be struggling down here at the bottom of the Third Division, not after what we've tasted —'

'It's gone, Brian,' whispers Taylor. 'It's gone and you've got to let it go. We've got to start again, start again here. That's how we'll get back, that's the only way. But first you've got to let go of the past, Brian. You've got to let it go, Bri.'

'I can't,' you tell him. 'I just can't, Pete.'

Day Forty-three

I wake up in that modern luxury hotel bed in that modern luxury hotel room and the first bloody thing I hear is the sound of my own fucking voice:

'*It is ridiculous to suggest that I would deliberately go out of my way to destroy a team . . . I am no destroyer . . . No man in the country wants Leeds United to continue to be successful more than I do . . . It was the kind of thing I believe they call a "clear the air" meeting. I had a few words, the chairman spoke and then the lads had their say . . . The chairman asked if I had any objection to him having a word and obviously I am in favour of anything that might help to restore confidence . . . It was agreed the best thing for the club would be for everyone to give their utmost so that we could win a couple of matches. That is what we need most of all. That is how we can regain confidence and then there will be no need for meetings like these . . .*'

I switch off that modern luxury radio and then I smash that modern luxury hotel room into a million fucking pieces and check out, a message waiting for me at reception.

* * *

You've been in this wilderness too long; this drunken, lonely seven-day week where the only sound is the sound of your own name repeated endlessly: Cloughie, Cloughie, Cloughie . . .

Now it's someone else's turn. Now it's Ramsey's turn.

In February 1974 the FA set up a sub-committee to 'consider our future policy in respect to the promotion of international football' under the leadership of Sir Harold Thompson, Bert Millichip, Brian Mears, Dr Andrew Stephen and Len Shipman –

On 3 April 1974 England draw 0–0 with Portugal in Lisbon –

'I've had a very long journey and I'm tired,' says Alf. 'No autopsies.'

On 18 April 1974 Ramsey announces his summer squad for the upcoming Home Internationals and the tour of eastern Europe –

'If you ask a stupid question,' he says, 'you'll get a stupid answer.'

On 19 April 1974 Ramsey is summoned to Lancaster Gate to hear the Thompson Committee make its report, to hear 'a unanimous recommendation that Sir Alf Ramsey should be replaced as England team manager'.

Ramsey is given £8,000 and a meagre pension. Ramsey goes on holiday –

'I still believe in England,' he says. 'And Englishmen and English football.'

On 1 May 1974 the FA make an official statement terminating Ramsey's position as manager of the England football team and, pending the appointment of a successor, appoint Joe Mercer as temporary caretaker of the national side –

Down beside the seaside, you wait for the phone to ring, for the call to come –

But the phone never rings, the call never comes and another season ends.

Brighton have played thirty-two games under us. Brighton have won twelve, drawn eight and lost twelve for us. Brighton have scored thirty-nine goals and conceded forty-two for us. That got Brighton thirty-two of their forty-three points. That left Brighton and us nineteenth in the Third Division –

It is your lowest ever league finish as a manager, lower even than your first season at Hartlepools United, lower than your first season at Derby County –

Derby County and Mackay have finished third in Division One –

Revie and Leeds are the Champions of Division One –

You are still in this wilderness, this drunken, dark and lonely place where the only sound is the sound of your own name repeated endlessly: Cloughie, Cloughie, Cloughie.

★ ★ ★

In the centre of Leeds. In a multi-storey car park. His headlights flash twice. He is in his sunglasses. In his hat. His collar up –

'They say you're going,' whispers Sniffer.

'Who says?'

'The players, the papers,' says Sniffer. 'The whole of Leeds.'

'It's what they all bloody want, isn't it?'

'Not everyone.'

'You could have fucking fooled me.'

'That meeting yesterday,' says Sniffer. 'That was wrong.'

'You tell them that, did you?'

'I was too bloody angry to speak,' says Sniffer. 'Them folk with their knives out, folk revelling in it. I might have said something I regretted. But it's left a nasty taste in my mouth. I can't get it out of my mind. It was wrong.'

'Thank you.'

'Not just me feels that way,' says Sniffer. 'Joe Jordan and Gordon McQueen. Terry Yorath and Frankie Gray. McGovern, O'Hare and Duncan McKenzie, of course. But Paul Reaney too. Trevor Cherry and all. None of them said a bad word about you.'

'None of them said a good word though, did they?'

'How could they?' asks Sniffer. 'They're young or new or . . .'

'Don't worry about it,' I tell him.

'But I do,' he says. 'And I just wanted to let you know that you have my full support and I'm sure you have the full support of them other lads too.'

'Thank you,' I tell him again. 'But it's too late. I'm off to see Cussins today.'

'Well then,' says Sniffer, 'I want to come with you.'

'In disguise?' I ask him. 'You sure about that?'

Sniffer takes off his sunglasses and his hat and says, 'I'm sure, Boss.'

★ ★ ★

On 4 July 1974 Don Revie is appointed as the new manager of England –

'I made the first move, not them,' says Don Revie. 'I made the call, not them. Because I fancied being the manager of England . . .'

There was a shortlist and there were interviews; Ron Greenwood (West Ham), Jimmy Adamson (Burnley), Jimmy Bloomfield (Leicester City), Gordon Jago (QPR), Bobby Robson (Ipswich) and Don Revie of Leeds –

You were not on the shortlist and not at the interviews, not even on the long list.

'You should have called them,' says your wife.

'I'll not beg,' you tell her.

'That's what Revie did,' she says.

'I'll not bloody beg,' you tell her again. 'I'll never fucking beg.'

'I shall be very sorry to be leaving Leeds,' says Revie. 'And the first result I will look for every Saturday will be Leeds United's. But, when you are ambitious, you want to get to the top, and the England team manager's job must be the ultimate ambition of every top-class manager . . . every manager's dream.'

'Sod it,' you tell your wife. 'Let's go on holiday.'

★ ★ ★

I turn off Elland Road. Sharp right and through the gates. Into the ground. The West Stand car park. Past the big black dog. The writing on the wall. The space reserved for the manager of Leeds United. The press waiting. The cameras and the lights. The fans. The autograph books and the pens. I turn off the engine. I open the door. I do up the cuffs of my shirt. I get my jacket out of the back. I put it on. I lock the car –

The hills behind me. The churches and the graveyards . . .

I look at the press. The cameras and the lights. The fans. Their autograph books and their pens. The rain in our hair. In all our faces –

'Fuck off, Cloughie!' they shout out. 'You're not good enough for us!'

Up their steps. Through their doors. Into their foyer. Their silence –

No one says, 'Good morning, Mr Clough.' No one says, 'Hello, Boss' . . .

Round their corners and down their corridors, past the photographs on their walls and the trophies in their cabinets, the ghosts of Elland Road, Syd Owen and Maurice Lindley turning on their heels –

'The peacocks screaming and screaming and screaming . . .'

'Morning, Sydney,' I shout. 'Morning, Maurice.'

Down their corridor. Past more photographs. Past more trophies. More ghosts. More feet and more voices. Down their corridor to the office. Jimmy outside the door. Jimmy waiting. Jimmy smiling. Jimmy saying, '£3,500.'

'You talk to the wife?' I ask him. 'You tell her what's happening?'

'She knows.'

I open the door. I sit him down. I pour us both a drink. I ask him, 'And?'

'And she thinks it's for the best.'

'Even if you can't get another job? Even if you end up on the dole?'

'I'll do anything,' says Jimmy. 'As long as I don't end up back down a mine.'

'It couldn't be worse than this,' I tell him. 'It couldn't be.'

'Well, it's never lonely,' laughs Jimmy. 'I'll say that for the pit.'

We smile. We raise our glasses. We touch them –

'Down in one,' I tell him. 'Then let's go find that bloody axe again.'

* * *

You are face down on a beach in Spain: Majorca, Cala Millor –

A man in a suit is walking along the beach. A man with his trouser legs rolled up. His socks and his shoes in his hands.

This man in a suit stands over you. This man you've never met before. His shadow cold. He takes out his handkerchief. He wipes his brow. His neck –

'You're a hard man to find, Mr Clough,' he says.

You don't turn over. You just lie there. Face down and ask, 'Why me?'

'They saw what went on when you left Derby,' he says. 'They want the kind of manager whose players are prepared to go on strike for him. Walk on water, run through fire. They want the kind of manager who can command that degree of loyalty.'

Now you turn over. Now you tell him, 'There's no answer to that.'

'So now what?' he asks. 'Job's yours if you want it . . .'

You blink into the sun. Sand in your mouth, sand . . .

'On a plate,' he says. 'So do you want it?'

* * *

In their Yorkshire boardroom, behind their Yorkshire curtains. No Samuel Bolton today. No Percy Woodward. No Roberts. No Simon. Just Manny Cussins, Sniffer and me –

'You have to give him more time,' Sniffer begs Cussins.

'There isn't any more time,' says Cussins.

'That's ridiculous,' says Sniffer. 'Bloke's only been here five minutes.'

'The players don't want him.'

'That's rubbish,' says Sniffer.

'There was more than just him speaking yesterday.'

'That was all wrong,' says Sniffer. 'To go behind the manager's back like that.'

'It was the only way to find out how they felt,' says Cussins.

'But players have always got axes to grind; be the same at any club in the land. And the minute the directors do that, the manager's got no chance. No chance.'

'You should have been a lawyer, not a footballer,' smiles Cussins.

'I'd like to be a manager one day,' says Sniffer. 'But I tell you this, if a board of directors ever treated me the way you lot have treated Mr Clough, I'd tell you where to stick your bloody job.'

'I understand what you're saying,' says Manny Cussins. 'I even agree with it. But the board have made a decision and Leeds United is a democratic institution –'

'What?' asks Sniffer. 'You've employed the best man in the business and before he's even had five minutes you're bloody sacking him?'

'There's nothing more I can do,' says Cussins.

'Back him and let him get on with the job.'

'It's too late,' says Cussins. 'It's too late.'

Sniffer looks over at me. Sniffer raises his palms –

I smile and I wink. I shake his hand and I thank him. He asks me if I fancy a farewell drink. Not tonight, I tell him. Not tonight . . .

Tonight I walk out of that Yorkshire boardroom and down that long, long corridor. There is a clock ticking somewhere, laughter from another room, behind another door –

I open that door on a meeting of the Norman Hunter Testimonial Fund. I look around that room, at the men in that room, and I point at Norman Hunter. 'You lot who are looking after this lad,' I tell them, 'you work as hard as you bloody can to earn as much money as you can for him, because there is no one in this fucking club who deserves it more than he does.'

★ ★ ★

You put down the phone. You walk back out onto the balcony —

White concrete and sand, blue sky and the sea —

Your boys with a ball on the beach below.

You come up behind your wife. Your beautiful, beautiful wife. You put your hands on her shoulders. She tilts the ice in her glass. She has caught the sun —

'You've never?' she says.

'I have.'

'What will Peter think?'

'He'll think what I tell him.'

She shakes her head. She says, 'Why, Brian? After all the things you've said.'

'Because of all the things I've said.'

'But you hate them. You hate him,' she says. 'And they hate you.'

'All water under the bridge now.'

'But it's such a hateful place,' she says. 'Such a spiteful place.'

'Back in the First Division? The European Cup?'

'Silly bugger,' she smiles. 'You'll regret it.'

'I might,' you tell her. 'But I know I would if I turned them down.'

'Can't win then, can you?'

'I hope I can,' you tell her. 'I bloody hope I can.'

★ ★ ★

Tonight I go straight back home. Tonight I make my plans. Tonight I make my calls. To my mate at the Inland Revenue. To my accountant. To my solicitor. I make my calls and I make my plans —

For tomorrow's Big Match.

Then I get a taxi into Derby. To the Midland Hotel. To meet John Shaw and Bill Holmes and the rest of the Derby County Protest Movement. *These people still want me back.* These people who have not watched Derby County play in the year since I resigned. *These people still want me back.* These people who have not watched Derby play since the day I left —

These people still want me.

Day Forty-four

It is Sunday 21 July 1974, and your plane is late, your luggage lost. A silver Mercedes is waiting in the rain. A small man under a big umbrella. A small man with white hair and dark glasses. A small man with a cashmere coat and a Cuban cigar –

'Mr Clough?' says Manny Cussins, the chairman of Leeds United AFC Limited. 'How do you do?'

You shake his hand. You ask him, 'They brought back rationing yet?'

'Not in Yorkshire,' he says.

You follow the Leeds United chairman into the back seat of his silver Mercedes. You accept his cigars. You accept his brandy.

'Of course,' says Cussins, 'your chairman is still playing silly beggars.'

You smile and raise your glass. 'As is his right.'

'Expects us both in Brighton tonight. To buy him his dinner at his own hotel.'

'He's disappointed,' you tell him. 'He's losing me, isn't he?'

'Not just you either,' says Cussins. 'Peter Taylor too.'

You glance at your watch and you finish your brandy.

'I told him, it's both of you or neither of you.'

You look at your watch again. You hold out your glass.

* * *

'Not a penny more,' I tell them. 'And not a penny less.'

'£25,000 for forty-four days' work?' shouts Bolton. 'That's daylight bloody robbery.'

'That's not all,' I tell him. 'I also want an agreement that Leeds United will pay my income tax for the next three years.'

'What?'

'Plus the Mercedes.'

'Bugger off!' shouts Bolton. 'Who the bloody hell do you think you are?'

'Brian Clough,' I tell him. 'Brian Howard Clough.'

* * *

Beside the seaside. You are in the toilets of the Courtlands Hotel, Hove. The directors of two football clubs are waiting for you in the bar. Slim Whitman singing 'Happy Anniversary'. You have your partner. Your only friend. Your right hand. Your shadow. You have him by his throat in the toilets of the Courtlands Hotel, Hove –

'It's not getting older, just much better . . .'

'We'll be fine,' he is trying to say. 'Let's stay put. Give it another year.'

'You bring me so much happiness each day . . .'

'It's the Third Division, Pete. We only fucking won twelve games last season.'

'Everything you are, keeps me so in love . . .'

'But don't forget who it was who came in for us when we were out of bloody work, when you could have been fucking suspended. Who it was while everyone else was hedging, not returning your calls. Who it is who's backed us all the way. No interference. Full support. Cash for transfers –'

'I thank the heavens that you came my way . . .'

'Aye, and the players you're saddling me with down here can't fucking play –'

'Let us stop and count our many blessings . . .'

'Give it time, Brian. Give it –'

'Because a love like ours doesn't happen every day . . .'

'You never see them bloody play –'

'And year after year we'll keep remembering . . .'

'Best hotels. New Mercedes coach for team travel. What more do you want?'

'Our anniversary in our special way . . .'

'The First Division, Europe; I want another crack at the European Cup.'

'So, darling, happy anniversary . . .'

'Another season,' he says. 'Just one more.'

'Another year of love has gone by . . .'

'The offer's here,' you tell him. 'Let's go to Leeds.'

'Thank you for each day you've given to me . . .'

He closes his eyes. He shakes his head. He opens his mouth –

'My darling, happy anniversary . . .'

'Not this time, Brian,' says Peter. 'This time you're on your own.'

★ ★ ★

They love me for what I'm not. They hate me for what I am. They love me. They hate me. In the shadow of the stands. On the steps of Elland Road. In the lights of the cameras and the spits of the rain, Manny Cussins is searching for the words, trying to find the words –

'Mr Brian Clough and Leeds United have come to a mutually agreeable arrangement to terminate his employment effective as from tonight . . . What has been done is for the good of Leeds United. The club and the happiness of the players come first. Nothing can be successful unless the staff is happy . . . The majority of the players found it difficult to work with the new manager. They seemed to criticize the tactics, the training and so forth of Mr Clough . . . And there had been a little bit of discontent . . . But I feel we are big enough to say we can be wrong . . . Mr Clough has received a reasonably substantial golden handshake but both Leeds United and Mr Clough have agreed not to reveal the actual figure . . . It was a moral agreement which we have decided to honour . . . And we hope to announce the name of the new manager tomorrow.'

'But why is he going?' ask the press. 'There is no answer to our question.'

'Perhaps because we have been spoilt by Don Revie . . . For a new manager to come in after thirteen or fourteen years of success . . . It's a very difficult act to follow . . .'

'And how do you feel, Brian?' they ask. 'About Leeds United and Mr Cussins?'

In the shadow of the stands, on the steps of Elland Road. I love them, I hate them. In the spits of their rain and the lights of their cameras, I find the words to tell them –

'We are all parting on the best of terms and so I am feeling very friendly towards Mr Cussins. Everything is fine but I think it is a very sad day for Leeds and also a slightly sad day for football. So everything is a little bit sad at the moment . . . I do not think there was any trouble with the players. It is very important for them to get on with the job. It is important for them to win the league, the European Cup and the FA Cup. If they can do this it will be good for football . . . But, whatever happens in the next few weeks, Mr Cussins has been absolutely superb in my dealings with him . . . I have only been here seven weeks, but it seems like seven years . . . And I hope the guy who takes my position finds it much smoother . . . Two or three players have been to see me in my office today and they expressed 100 per cent support. I was not fired by the players . . . I feel terrible about being fired by Leeds United. But the accumulation of every single thing has caused it: injuries, suspensions, bad results, the board of directors, a couple of players and so on . . . But anyone who took over from Don Revie would have met resentment from the players. If they are the best team in the country, they have fallen down on this . . . But I still believe they got the best man to replace Revie . . .'

How shall we live, Brian? How shall we live?'

'And I hope to be back in football in four or five days' time.'

'But have you got all you really wanted, Brian?' they ask me.

★ ★ ★

Talks back and forth. Fuck him. Extra time. The spanner in the bloody works. Judas. Break for dinner. You loosen your collar. Undo your tie. You make an excuse. You take your chance. You get to the phone. You make your calls. You spike their guns. Fuck him. Fuck them all. This is one bloody chance that's not going to get away. No fucking chance. Not this time. Past midnight. Six hours back and forth. No result. Adjourn to the bar. Out of the basement. Up to the lounge. Cussins and Bob Roberts walking up the stairs ahead of you, wringing their hands and shaking their heads, whispering to each other about unexpected complications, muttering about how they wanted both Clough and Taylor, and now they're not so sure; Revie on the radio, Revie on the telly, calling Clough a daft bloody choice, calling for protest groups and petitions, calling for the appointment of Johnny fucking Giles instead of you. You push past Cussins and Roberts, past Bamber and Taylor. You take the stairs two at a time.

Into the lounge. The press and TV waiting. Tipped off. Their cameras flash, their microphones on –

'Gentlemen,' you tell them, 'I've just been appointed manager of Leeds United.'

* * *

John and Bill drive me to the studios of Yorkshire TV. Of *Calendar*. For their special, *Goodbye, Mr Clough*, with Austin Mitchell, Brian Clough and tonight's special guest, back by popular demand and as bold as the brass on the buttons of his blazer, the Don –

'When you walked in, when you walked in, when you walked in,' says Revie, 'did you have a meeting on the first day with them?'

'No.'

'Why?'

'Because I didn't think it was necessary to have a meeting the very first day.'

'So you were taking over as manager of a new club . . .'

'Yes.'

'And you didn't call all your players and all your coaching staff and all your office staff together . . .'

'No.'

'And introduce yourself and meet them and tell them exactly what you feel and what you want to try and do?'

'Go on!' I tell him. 'The first day I walked in I came back from my holiday and I did two hours' training with them.'

Don Revie shakes his head. Don fiddles with them buttons on his blazer. He says, 'But there was a lot of nervousness and apprehension among the players and the staff, and there have obviously been meetings and discussions among the players and the directors, and there must have been a very good reason to do that. I don't condone players doing that in any club; it is totally wrong and the directors are wrong to listen to it . . . But I think Brian is a fool to himself. He has criticized so many people whose records stand to be seen, and I think it is totally wrong for the game of professional football.'

'But listen, Don,' I tell him. 'When you've taken over the job of a man that's been there for ten or fifteen years . . .'

'Thirteen,' says Don.

'Thirteen years, thank you, and who's been regarded as the King Pin, as the Father Figure, as the Man Who Made Everything Tick, then within seven weeks it is impossible – utterly impossible – to replace that type of thing . . .'

'But why try to replace it, Brian? You talked to them about winning the Championship better or differently, but our record is there to be seen for eleven years . . .'

'Yeah,' I tell him. 'Yeah . . .'

'Right, the first four or five years, and I've always said this, we played for results. But the last four or five years, we've been the most entertaining side by crowd entertainment, and topping charts with national newspapers and television . . .'

'Also, Don, the disciplinary chart. You topped that.'

'We topped that once.'

'Well, you topped it for the last two or three years.'

'No, no, no. That's not true. It wasn't 100 per cent right, I'll agree. It wasn't quite right. Discipline on the field. And last year we straightened it out.'

'It was,' I tell him. 'You were the top.'

'But yeah, yeah, when you, you see, you, Brian, when you talk about coming to the Leeds job and you had all these things, these worries about stepping into my shoes and one thing and another . . .'

'Which I had . . .'

'Yes, you had. But why, why did you come from Brighton to Leeds to take it over when you had criticized them so much and said we should be in the Second Division for this and we should do this and we shouldn't do that? Why? Why did you take the job?'

'Well, because I thought it was the best job in the country.'

'Of course it was the best job in the country.'

'I was taking over the League Champions.'

'Yeah, you were taking over the League Champions. You were taking over the best bunch of players you had ever seen.'

'Well, I didn't know about the players, Don.'

'You didn't know?'

'I didn't know them intimate like you do. But I knew you were the League Champions and I was taking over the League Champions. And I wanted to have a crack at the European Cup this year. I think it was near and dear to your heart also. I wanted to win it. I wanted to do something you hadn't done. Now when I said, I think I said it to Trevor Cherry actually or most of the other players, he said to me, what can you do that the Boss hasn't done? You're the Boss, Don, he's referring to you. I said I want to win the league, but I want to win it better. Now there is no other reply to that question because you had won the league.'

'Yeah,' says Don. 'But there's no way you could win it better.'

'Why not?'

'No, no, no . . .'

'But that's the only hope I've got . . .'

'But we'd only lost four matches.'

'Well, I can only lose three.'

'No, no, no . . .'

'I couldn't give any other answer and I wanted to win the European Cup. Now I believe it was just a fraction, just a fraction, Don – I don't know this because I haven't spoken to you – but I believe it was just a fraction whether you took the England job or had another shot at the European Cup.'

'That is totally true,' says Don. 'Because I was so involved with the players and everyone at Elland Road . . .'

'Good lad,' I tell him. 'Now I wanted to do that and I wanted to do it better than you. You can understand that, can't you?'

'Yes. But –'

'Thank you,' I tell him. 'Thank you, Don.'

The credits roll, the music plays; *I can see clearly now.*

* * *

Down the motorway, their fingers and fists, their sticks and their stones, getting smaller and smaller; John at the wheel of my new blue Mercedes, Bill opening another bottle of champagne. But the sun is not shining, rain only falling; the blue sky is black, the yellows all purple, and I'm in the back with my two feet up and their cheque for £25,000 in my hands –

I don't believe in God. I don't believe in luck. I believe in football –

'I've just come up on the pools,' I shout. 'The bloody pools!'

I believe in family and I believe in me; Brian Howard Clough –

It is Thursday 12 September 1974, and I wish you were here.

The Argument II, cont.

In May 1979
Margaret Hilda Thatcher and the Conservative Party won
the General Election,
and Brian Howard Clough and Nottingham Forest won
the European Cup –
No Milton. No Blake. No Orwell –
D.U.F.C.

Sources and Acknowledgements

This novel is another fiction, based on another fact. That fact was found in the following sources:

A Kind of Loving by Stan Barstow (1960).
Biting Talk by Norman Hunter (2004).
Bremner! by Bernard Bale (1998).
Champions Again: Derby County 1967/75 by Gerald Mortimer (1975).
Christie Malry's Own Double-Entry by B. S. Johnson (1973).
Clough: A Biography by Tony Francis (1987).
Clough: The Autobiography by Brian Clough (1994).
Cloughie: Walking on Water by Brian Clough (2002, 2003).
Derby County: The Clough Years by Michael Cockayne (2003).
Don Revie: Portrait of a Footballing Enigma by Andrew Mourant (1990).
Hard Man, Hard Knocks by Terry Yorath (2004).
His Way: The Brian Clough Story by Patrick Murphy (1993).
In a League of their Own by Jeremy Novick (1995).
Leeds United Match Day Magazine and Programmes, 1974–75.
Marching on Together by Eddie Gray (2002).
Only a Game? by Eamon Dunphy (1976).
Peter Lorimer: Leeds and Scotland Hero by Peter Lorimer and Phil Rostron (2002).
Psycho Mike and the Phantom Ice Rink by Don Watson.
Room at the Top by John Braine (1957).
Saturday Night and Sunday Morning by Alan Sillitoe (1958).
Selected Poems by Tony Harrison (1984).
Sniffer: The Life and Times of Allan Clarke by David Saffer (2001).
The Elland Road Encyclopaedia by Paul Harrison (1994).
The Football Managers by Johnny Rogan (1989).

The Glory Game by Hunter Davies (2001 edition).

The Goalkeeper's Revenge by Bill Naughton (1961).

The Ice Age by Margaret Drabble (1977).

The Leeds United Story by Martin Jarred and Malcolm Macdonald (2002).

The Loneliness of the Long Distance Runner by Alan Sillitoe (1959).

The Official FA Year Books, 1966–76.

The Real Mackay by Dave Mackay and Martin Knight (2004).

The Unforgiven: Don Revie's Leeds United by Rob Bagchi and Paul Rogerson (2002).

The *Yorkshire Post,* July–September 1974.

There Was Some Football Too . . . 100 Years of Derby County by Tony Francis (1984).

This Sporting Life by David Storey (1960).

Welcome to Elland Road: LUFC in Pictures by John and Andrew Varley (1999).

Winning Isn't Everything: A Biography of Sir Alf Ramsey by Dave Bower (1998).

With Clough by Peter Taylor (1980).

I would like to thank the following people for their assistance and their support: Mrs Scriven and the staff of the Balne Lane Library, Wakefield; Andrew Vine and David Clay at the *Yorkshire Post*; Sarn Warbis and Richard Hall; François Guérif, Agnès Guery, Daniel Lemoine and all the staff of Payot & Rivages, Paris; Luca Formenton, Marco Tropea, Cristina Ricotti and all the staff of il Saggiatore, Milan; Shunichiro Nagashima; Kester Aspden, Andy Beckett, Gordon Burn, Giuseppe Genna, Peter Hobbs, Eoin McNamee, David Mitchell, Justin Quirk, Ian Rankin, Cathi Unsworth, Martyn Waites, and Tony White; William Miller, Junzo Sawa, Hamish Macaskill, Peter Thompson and all the staff of the English Agency Japan; Stephen Page, Lee Roy Brackstone, Angus Derby Cargill, Anna Pallai, Ian Bahrami and Kate Ward and all the staff of Faber and Faber Limited. Finally, I would like to thank my family and friends, in Britain and Japan, and particularly my father, Basil Peace.

ff

Faber and Faber – a home for writers

Faber and Faber is one of the great independent publishing houses in London. We were established in 1929 by Geoffrey Faber and our first editor was T. S. Eliot. We are proud to publish prize-winning fiction and non-fiction, as well as an unrivalled list of modern poets and playwrights. Among our list of writers we have five Booker Prize winners and eleven Nobel Laureates, and we continue to seek out the most exciting and innovative writers at work today.

www.faber.co.uk – a home for readers

The Faber website is a place where you will find all the latest news on our writers and events. You can listen to podcasts, preview new books, read specially commissioned articles and access reading guides, as well as entering competitions and enjoying a whole range of offers and exclusives. You can also browse the list of Faber Finds, an exciting new project where reader recommendations are helping to bring a wealth of lost classics back into print using the latest on-demand technology.